Patricia Burns was bo[...] decided to train as a te[...] novels.

She is now happily single and lives in Essex with her three children, a cat and a deliquent tortoise. *Keep Safe for Me* is Patricia Burns's third novel. Her previous two, *Trinidad Street* and *Cinnamon Alley* are also available in Arrow paperback.

# KEEP SAFE FOR ME

## Patricia Burns

ARROW

Published by Arrow Books in 1996

1 3 5 7 9 10 8 6 4 2

© Patricia Burns 1995

The right of Patricia Burns to be identified as the author
of this work has been asserted by her in accordance
with the Copyright, Designs and Patents Act, 1988

First published in the United Kingdom by

Century
Random House UK Limited
20 Vauxhall Bridge Road, London SW1V 2SA

Random House Australia (Pty) Limited
20 Alfred Street, Milsons Point, Sydney,
New South Wales 2061, Australia

Random House New Zealand Limited
18 Poland Road, Glenfield
Auckland 10, New Zealand

Random House South Africa (Pty) Limited
PO Box 337, Bergvlei, South Africa

Random House UK Limited Reg. No. 954009

A CIP catalogue record for this book
is available from the British Library

Papers used by Random House UK Limited
are natural, recyclable products made from wood grown in
sustainable forests. The manufacturing processes conform to
the environmental regulations of the country of origin.

ISBN 0 09 938541 4

Printed and bound in Germany by
Elsnerdruck, Berlin

To the Novel Group –
a source of inspiration

# 1

1941

It was always the same thought that dominated their minds as they got near to the corner of Trinidad Street – will it still be there?

Rita Johnson hitched up her bundle of bedding and held on tighter to the handbag containing all the precious papers, the special photos and her one lipstick. She was not quite sure how she would feel if she found her home reduced to rubble. It was not as if she was happy there. Around her, the family were talking loudly, all of them trying to cover up their anxiety.

'Like the Ritz down the shelter now they got them bunks fixed up, ain't it?'

'I bet they don't have lice down the bleeding Ritz.'

'I wonder what it's been like down at Dagenham last night,' Rita said. Her children were there, with her sister Joan at their brother George's place.

'Let's hope they had a nice quiet one in their own beds,' her mother said.

Her mother-in-law fetched a great sigh.

'I wish I could have a night in my own bed.'

'Perhaps I'll fetch them back here again soon. It ain't as bad as it was, is it? Not like what it was back in the autumn,' Rita said. She knew it was an empty thought. She couldn't risk her children's lives here on the Isle of Dogs, and she did not want to drag them down the Underground every night.

'We're always going to get it bad here, ain't we?' her husband Ron said. 'Stands to reason, with the docks and all. I don't know why you don't just take 'em back to the country again. You was safe there. Bleeding stupid, coming back here again.'

He was right, in a way. It was safe in the country. But Rita knew very well that wasn't the reason why he kept on about her

1

evacuating with the children again. He just wanted them all out of his way.

'I'm not letting flaming Hitler drive me out of my home,' she said.

'That's right, ducky,' her mother agreed. 'He thought we was all going to run away, but we ain't.'

They were a scruffy little group, returning from their night in the Underground. They had all slept in their clothes and were crumpled and unwashed. They carried their bedding and bags of personal possessions and their gas-mask boxes dangled from their shoulders. Rita had fared the best since she had taken to wearing trousers, which suited her tall, slim figure. She had combed and pinned her fair hair into a fashionable style and pulled her beret on at a jaunty angle, but nothing could diguise the heavy eyes and pale face brought on by months of broken sleep. The two older women were a study in contrasts. Rita's mother Florrie was small and thin, her back straight and her mouth set in a line from refusing to give way to the many worries that beset her. Her mother-in-law Maisie lumbered along, her swollen feet in slippers, her shapeless body wobbling as she walked. Ron slouched in the rear of the party, hands in pockets. With his shoulders slumped, he was slightly shorter than Rita. Stubble sprouted from his cheeks and the difficulties with the water supply made the ideal excuse for him not to wash for days at a time.

'I wish I knew where our Lily's got to,' Florrie said for the hundredth time.

Rita sighed.

'Don't worry, Mum. She'll be safe somewhere. There's shelters near the dance hall, and that Jack Wilkinson sounds like a nice bloke.'

'All her boyfriends sound like nice blokes till she goes and gives them the elbow. I just don't like her out when the raids are on. I like to know where everyone is.'

'I know, Mum. But you can't expect a young girl like her to stay in every night.'

It was a family argument that went on and on. Rita took her sister's side, but envied her. How lucky Lily was to be young and

2

free, bouncing from one boyfriend to another. At her age, Rita was already married.

They made a detour round a huge crater in the West Ferry Road. Three shops had been reduced to rubble, unsafe buildings all around were roped off and a cloud of brick dust still hung in the air with the smell of gas and drains and burning. They were so used to it now that they were no longer shocked by the devastation. They asked after the people who had lived there. A whole family killed, they were told. Refused to go down the shelter. The three women shook their heads in sympathy. Ron just shrugged.

'Bleeding stupid, then, weren't they? Asking for it.'

Rita rounded on him.

'It's you that's stupid. Nobody asks to be bombed, do they? We didn't start this war. We're just getting it all.'

But inside her a small guilty thought had taken root. This was just round the corner from Trinidad Street. If a bomb had dropped here, perhaps they would be all right.

'I ain't got time to stand round here arguing. I got to get to work,' Ron said.

'You ain't the only one,' Rita told him.

Ron threw her a venomous look. He hated her being out at work. With her own money, Rita had escaped from his total control.

On the dirty brick wall of the corner building the street sign remained, Trinidad Street. Home. Now for it. Rita looked at her mum's tense face and repeated the prayer that always rose in her heart at this moment. *Please God, don't let it be Dad or the shop. You can take my place, God, but keep Dad safe for Mum.* She held her mum's arm as they turned the corner.

They all stopped dead. There was glass and roofing slates all over the road and thick black smoke drifting in the cold wind. A crowd had gathered to assess the damage. Rita's eyes strained to see the far end of the street, where her parents' corner shop stood. At first she could not make it out, then the smoke drifted and there it was, still intact. Her heart calmed a little. Behind her, Maisie let out a wail.

'My house! What's happened to my house?'

It was only then that Rita realised that the section of terrace that she and Ron shared with his mother was wrecked. It was still standing, but the front door sagged open on one hinge, the tattered remains of the blackout curtains flapped at the broken windows and bits of china and furniture lay scattered about the street. With a cry, Maisie started forward, rolling as she trotted towards her home. Rita and Florrie swooped one either side of her, took her arms, tried to reassure her.

'It's still there, dearie. It ain't a hole in the ground.'

'It mightn't be as bad as it looks. We can soon clean it up. Everyone'll help.'

A figure detached itself from the crowd in the street and came towards them, a thin man in an ARP uniform, covered in dirt.

'Dad!'

'Jim – oh thank God!'

Jim Croft gave his wife a brief hug. His face was grey with fatigue, the lines on it etched in grime.

'It's all right, me old girl, I'm still in one piece.'

'My house,' Maisie sobbed. Fat tears ran down her cheeks. She made to break away from Rita and Florrie.

Jim laid a restraining hand on her arm.

'I'm sorry, Maisie, but you can't go in. It ain't safe. The gas has gone and it might fall down at any minute.'

'But it's my home! Me and my Will moved in there just before the last war. My Ron was born there –'

'It's for your own safety, Maisie. There's a flaming great bomb landed just over the back and there's big hole where your privy used to be. The whole back wall might fall into it.'

'But my things – all my things are in there –'

'They're only things, Maisie. Them Bateses was under the stairs. They're digging them out now.'

Rita stared in the direction of the house at the back of theirs. The neighbours there swore by their little den, retreating there every night while others made the trek to the Underground or the public shelters. It was fine when other places went down, but it couldn't have protected them from a direct hit.

'Dad's right,' she said. 'We're all still alive, ain't we?'

But Maisie seemed not to hear.

4

Gazing over her mother-in-law's shaking shoulders to the house in which she had spent all of her married life, Rita expected to be feeling shock or loss or anger. She had seen enough people return to their bombed-out homes to know how most of them reacted. But for her there was only relief. At last, something had happened that might change things between her and Ron. That was what she had hoped at the beginning of the war. She had been evacuated with the children in the first rush, on top of the world at leaving him behind in London, but then the bombs had not come and her mother had missed her terribly so she came back, only to find that her marriage was still as phoney as the war seemed to be. Then she had got a job in a factory making parts for submarines and loved that, despite the long hours and the grinding boredom. The money gave her economic freedom for the first time in five years, but Ron resented that and took it out on her. Now they were living with almost nightly bomb raids and at least down the public shelter Ron couldn't touch her, but that made him even more bad tempered, so still things went on the same between them. But now – now they no longer had a home. Now something had to change.

'What am I going to do?' Maisie was sobbing. 'Where am I going to go?'

The other families who had been made homeless commiserated with her, but pointed out that at least they were still here to tell the tale, unlike the Bateses. The neighbours were gathering round with offers of help, while the kids that still remained at home capered about smashing the glass into still smaller pieces and looking for shrapnel. All the people whom Maisie had grown up with – the Turners, the Johnsons, the Crofts and the O'Donoghues – were there with sympathy and practical suggestions.

'You better come and stop with us, Maisie. We still got room.'

'Come and have breakfast with us, love. Make you feel more the thing. Can't do you anything cooked, but we got bread and a bit of ham.'

'I got some clothes might do for you. They ain't what you might call fashionable but they'll serve you a turn.'

Someone even managed to conjure up a cup of sweet tea.

'They still got the gas on down my daughter's street. She done me a thermos.'

One of Maisie's daughters-in-law appeared.

'I just heard the news. Ain't it a terrible sight? Breaks your heart, don't it? Now, you come and stop with me and Bert, Mum. Best thing to do. What with the kids away and all, we got a spare room. Make you comfy as anything.' She stopped and looked at Rita and Ron, indecision creasing her face. 'You're welcome to come and all,' she said, rather less convincingly. 'We got a put-u-up in the front, if you don't mind that.'

'Thanks,' Rita said, equally half-hearted. A put-u-up in a relative's house could only be a change for the worse.

'They'll come to us,' Florrie said, in a voice that stood for no argument.

It was no less than Rita expected, but still she was relieved. She turned to Ron.

'Of course, if you want to go and stay at Bert's with your mum –' she said hopefully.

But it was no use. Ron disliked his big brother, who regarded him as the spoilt baby of the family and was always on at him to be a man and join up. Even staying with Rita's family was preferable to that.

People were beginning to disperse, taking the newly homeless with them, beginning to cope with the problems of the new day.

'Where's the nearest standpipe, Jim? There's all this bleeding mess to clear up.'

'I got some full buckets in my kitchen, dearie, I'll bring 'em along your place.'

'God, I'd kill for a cuppa.'

'Mobile canteen's turned up over the back. They got tea and cheese rolls.'

'I got to go and see if them poor Bateses is out yet. They might of made it, you never know.'

'How long till we know when we can go back in the house, Jim? It don't look too bad. There's all sorts of things I want to get out.'

The full meaning of the situation suddenly came home to Rita. Until she could find out if anything could be salvaged, all she had left in the world was a bedroll, a handbag and what she stood up in.

'My soap!' she cried. 'I got a whole new bar of Gardenia soap in there. I'm filthy and I stink and I can't get my soap.'

'Bleeding hell, if you're going to start snivelling I'm off. I'll get something at the mobile canteen,' Ron said, and sloped off up the street, hands in pockets.

'Huh. Going without a wash never did bother him,' Rita said.

'Come on, dear,' Florrie said. 'I've got some soap and some water, and I'm sure our Lil will lend you something to change into – oh!' She stopped and clapped a hand to her face. 'Lily! I only went and forgot about her with all this going on. Jim – has our Lily come home yet?'

Jim patted her on the shoulder.

'Now then, old girl. She'll be back, right as ninepence, don't you worry.'

Florrie shook her head.

'I don't know – I don't think I'll ever get used to it. There's Joan and all the kiddies down at Dagenham and Lily out I don't know where and you on ARP duty in the middle of it all. I can stand the bombs and the shelters and all, but I do like to know where we all are. If we're going to go, we ought to all go together. If it weren't for Rita here, I don't know what I'd do.'

Rita gave her a hug.

'Well, there you are. Mum, I'm coming back to live with you proper now.'

She looked down the little street she had lived in all her life, except for the brief evacuation. It had never been much of a place, Trinidad Street. Just two rows of two-up, two-down houses letting straight on to the pavement, with a break two-thirds down where Cinnamon Alley led to some warehouses. It had been an ugly enough place before the war, built of yellow brick that had blackened over the years and overhung with the filth and fumes of the myriad factories, foundries and processing works around it. Now it looked far worse. The first terrifying night of the Blitz had brought down half the houses on the north side. Four whole familes whom Jim had not been able to persuade to take shelter had been killed. Over the months since then, many more homes had, like Rita's, become uninhabitable and Cinnamon Alley obliterated. Even so, the street had been lucky compared with others on the Isle of Dogs. Whole terraces had been bombed flat or gutted by fire. And yet the people were still there. Of those who had not been killed or injured, some had taken flight and gone to seek safety elsewhere. Many more had dispatched their children back to the country again. But in Trinidad Street, nearly half the original inhabitants remained, defying the bombs and getting on with their daily lives as best they could.

Beside Rita, her mother was also surveying the destruction.

'Blimey, if I was a man I'd join the RAF and go and give it back to that Hitler.'

There was such venom in her voice that it made Rita uneasy. She tried to turn it into a joke.

'If you got in one of them bombers, Mum, he'd run for his life.'

'I mean it and all,' her mother insisted. 'If he thinks he's softening us up, he's got another think coming, 'cause we ain't soft. And if he thinks he's going to come up the flaming Thames and invade London, well, just let him try, that's what I say, 'cause I'd like to have a go at him, killing people like this and smashing up their homes.'

She said it with such total conviction that Rita knew it was true. Her mother, a thin middle-aged woman, worn from childbirth and constant work, would stand up and defend her loved ones with her own bare hands.

'He won't beat us, Mum. Not any of us,' she said. 'Come on, I got to get to work. I'm late already.'

They were just turning away when there was a call from the far end of the street.

'Coo-ee! Mum! I'm back!'

'Lily –' Florrie pressed a hand to her heart. 'Lily – thank God – she's back.'

But Rita hardly noticed her sister as she came tripping through the rubble in her high-heeled dancing shoes. Her eyes were fastened on the man whose arm Lily clung to, a tall young man in an RAF bomber jacket. She was suddenly very conscious of her appearance, creased and dirty and still in her shelter outfit.

Lily hurried forward and gave her mother a hug and a kiss. Her eyes were bright and her face glowing.

8

'Oh Mum – now don't you be cross, because I couldn't of got back, honest I couldn't. Oh – it was dreadful over Poplar, weren't it, Jack? Oh, by the way, this is Jack Wilkinson. He's a navigator on the bombers.' This was said with palpable pride. RAF men were very sought after as boyfriends, and those who actually flew even more so. Lily had caught herself a real prize.

# 2

Rita and Lily looked at their mother. Florrie was normally deeply suspicious of all Lily's boyfriends as a matter of course, and this one had been out all night with her, even though there was the good excuse that there had been a raid on.

'Morning,' she said pointedly, looking the newcomer up and down.

Jack Wilkinson was not intimidated.

'Pleased to meet you, Mrs Croft.'

Rita was surprised. From his voice, it was obvious that he was a local man, yet she had to look up to study his face as he spoke to her mother. It was not often that she met a man who was nearly a head taller than she was, not round this area. There was something faintly foreign, too, about his dark colouring and the set of his features. And he had a charming smile, which he now had trained on Florrie.

'I hope you won't be too hard on Lily, Mrs Croft. I didn't think you'd want me to try to take her home through the raid.'

Florrie held out against him.

'Yeah, well, time was when me and her dad said she had to be back home by half-past ten. That was before the war, of course. Decent girls was in by half-past ten then, and no argument.'

'Things was different then,' Jack Wilkinson pointed out.

Florrie pursed her lips.

'No reason for standards to slip. But I suppose if there was a raid on you didn't have no choice. Mind you, when the raids first started I said she had to stay with us every night and not go gallivanting out.'

'We was in a public shelter with a couple of hundred other people,' Jack said, with a persuasive smile.

'Yeah well –' To everyone's amazement, Florrie suddenly gave way. 'I suppose you're only young once.'

Rita heard Lily's suppressed gasp. Being allowed out was the biggest battle in her life, causing endless family arguments, yet here was her mother actually seeing it her way.

Jack Wilkinson, unaware of the great concession that had just been made, was making a joke about it being war work, entertaining men like him on leave. Florrie took it seriously.

'I don't mind so much if she's with someone like you. You look like you'd look after her proper. And you're on the bombers and all.'

She suddenly held out her hand, which Jack clasped.

'It's a pleasure to meet someone what's giving it back to them, Jack. That's what keeps us all going, knowing what they're going through and all. How about coming back for a cuppa? I'll send one of them kids round the canteen for some.'

'That'd be lovely, Mrs Croft. Thanks.'

Lily glowed with triumph. At this rate, she was going to be allowed out with her new conquest as often as she wanted.

Jack turned to Rita.

'And you must be Lily's sister.'

From being a bystander in the conversation, Rita suddenly found herself at its centre. She looked up to find the brown eyes focused on her, and was horribly conscious of her scruffy, unwashed state.

'That's Rita,' she heard Lily explain.

'Pleased to meet you, Rita.'

She found that she was shaking his hand, that his clasp was strong and warm. She tried to smile naturally, to say something bright and clever, but instead found herself grinning like an idiot and nothing at all coming out of her dry throat. After what felt like an age, she managed to croak, 'Me too.' Somewhere far away, she could vaguely hear her mother saying something about her having been bombed out.

'That's terrible for you,' Jack said. He sounded genuinely sympathetic. Lily was babbling away, saying how awful it was and how sorry she felt, but Jack was not listening to her. His attention was entirely on Rita. 'Is there anything I can do?'

With absolute certainty, she knew that if anyone could do anything, then he could. She thought of poor Maisie. She was not

11

over-fond of her mother-in-law, but Maisie had been devastated by the loss of her home.

'There must still be some things that can be rescued, but my dad says it's not safe to go in,' she explained.

'Where is it?' Jack asked.

Rita nodded towards her house.

'That one.'

'Don't look too bad to me. Let's have a recce.'

'Oh no!' Fear made her lay her hand on his arm. 'You mustn't. It's dangerous. They're only things, after all. We're still alive, that's the main thing.'

Lily chimed in, holding tight to his other arm, begging him not to be silly, but Jack just laughed.

'Get away with you! Anyone'd think there was a machine-gun nest inside there. If I don't go in, someone else will, and there'll be nothing left to rescue then.'

'There ain't no looters in our street,' Florrie declared.

'Maybe not, Mrs Croft, but there's plenty ready to come in from elsewhere. They sniff out a likely place and they're in before you know it. It's happened in my mum and dad's street. I'll have a look round now, before they have time to arrive.'

'I'll come too,' Rita said.

This sparked off a new round of argument, but Rita insisted.

'It's my home, and I'm going in,' she said.

They crunched their way over the glass and debris to where the front door hung drunkenly off its hinges. Through the gap the parlour could be seen, grey with fallen plaster. The door through to the kitchen was also open, and unaccustomed light laden with dirt and dust came in through the great gap in the back wall. In the middle of the floor lay a blue china vase, intact.

'There you are,' Jack said, 'prize number one. Come on.'

While Florrie and Lily stayed by the front door, urging them to be careful, Jack and Rita stepped inside. There was a smell of wet plaster, dirt, gas and drains. The parlour was bad enough, but the kitchen was much worse. The sink had been ripped off and was lying in the middle of the floor, surrounded by bricks and rubble. Water from the fractured pipes had soaked everywhere. It was hardly recognisable as the place where Maisie had sat by the fire drinking tea and complaining about how tired she was while Rita set about washing the sheets or scrubbing the floor. Just clues remained to tell whose property this had been – the rag rug, full of glass splinters, fragments of the blue and white striped plates, the postcard of Clacton still stuck to the wall, souvenir of her Aunt Ellen's last holiday that hot summer of 1939. Rita found one of Maisie's floral overalls that had miraculously escaped without a hole, and they piled in everything that was usable. It was precious little, for there had not been much to start with, but Rita knew that Maisie would be delighted to see her kettle, only slightly dented, and her fancy tea tin.

'You're very brave. It must be heartbreaking to see your home ruined like this,' Jack said, picking up two cups without handles.

'Not really –' Rita straightened up and looked around her, thinking it through. 'It ain't heartbreaking, because my heart was never in it. It was never really my home, y'see, it was my mother-in-law's.'

'Ah well – that must make a difference.'

He must think her very hard, she thought. But it was no more than the truth. It was not like having your own place wrecked. Her sister Joan had been devastated when she heard that her house had been hit, even though she was in the country at the time. For Joan it had been the place where she had lived with the man she loved; her little kingdom. It had never been like that for Rita. She looked at Jack Wilkinson as he sifted through the wreckage, retrieving bent pieces of cutlery. The warmth had gone out of his expression, and there was a severe set to his features. She wanted desperately to explain, to tell him that hers had not been a love match, that she had had to marry Ron. But what was it to Jack Wilkinson, after all? He was Lily's boyfriend. She was just the older sister, the married sister, someone to keep the right side of so that he could take Lily out as often and as late as they both wanted. As if to confirm this, Lily's voice floated in from outside.

'Are you all right?'

'Yeah, fine,' Jack called back.

'I don't think we're going to find much more in here,' Rita said.

13

'Do you want to try upstairs?'

Rita looked up. The ceiling was bare in places where the plaster had come down. The whole top floor could be ready to fall.

'Why not?' she said. 'No point in stopping now.'

The stairs creaked as they went up, but neither of them worried about that. It was well known that stairs were the strongest part of a house. The little front bedroom was not in too bad a state. The plaster had come down from the ceiling, but most of the glass had fallen outwards. The room was almost completely filled by the two single beds. Rita looked at the nearest one, stripped and bare now. This was the bed her two children had shared. For the first time a lump came to her throat.

'I'm glad the boys ain't here,' she said, and the words came out as a croak.

'You sent them away?'

She thought she heard disapproval in his voice. Sent them away. As if they were a couple of unwanted parcels. Not only did she not care about her home being destroyed, but she got rid of her kids as well. Rita rounded on him.

'Well, I couldn't keep 'em here, could I? Not with things like what they are. I know some people do, but I think that's wicked. I couldn't risk their lives like that.'

'All right, all right. Keep your hair on. I only asked.'

He raised his hands in mock submission. He was grinning at her, a teasing light in his eyes.

Rita felt foolish. She had over-reacted. All the same, she had to defend herself.

'You got no right to judge,' she told him.

'I'm sorry.' He was serious now. 'You're right. Where are your kids? In the country somewhere?'

'They're with my sister down Dagenham.'

'But they get raids there, don't they?'

'Yeah, but not like here, and they got their own Anderson. It ain't like dragging 'em down the Underground every night. And with my sister they're still with their own family, see. If I sent them to the country they'd be with strangers. There's people round here sent their kids off to the country and when they go to

14

see them the little horrors don't want to know. They got used to living in posh families and they got all the manners and that. Just imagine! Having your own kid turn round and tell you you're not talking proper English! Enough to break your heart. But it's not like that with my lot – they can't wait to see me again.' She stopped, a new thought striking her. 'I suppose I'll have to tell them about this. Oh hell. What am I going to say? But maybe they won't take it too bad – they're both little still and it's eighteen months now since they actually lived here. I hope so.'

'Anything of their's here we can get?'

'No, I've taken it all down Dagenham. There's just some baby stuff –'

Rita stepped forward carefully and pulled a cardboard box out from under the bed. She opened the flaps and peeped inside. There was the yellowing shawl, the tiny mittens and bonnets, the little gowns. She picked up a pair of bootees and held them to her cheek. It was all she had here of the boys except for the one precious photo that she kept in her handbag. She took a deep breath and stood up.

'I'm glad I got these, anyway. We better get Maisie's things, and all the bedclothes. She'll be wanting them.'

At last there was only the back bedroom. Rita did not want to go in there, but Jack carefully pushed the door open. There, exposed to the world by the gaping hole in the wall and covered with dirt and glass, was the bed she shared with Ron. Rita flushed with embarrassment, then was cross with herself. He knew she was married, didn't he? But still she did not want to rub it in.

'I'll get the bedclothes,' she said, without looking at Jack.

She pulled off the top blanket and shook it, then groaned with disappointment. The shards of glass had ripped into it, making a lacework of holes. When she turned to her clothes, hung on pegs behind the door, they were almost as bad.

'Oh no –' she cried, holding out tattered fabric. 'Look at this. My favourite dress. I can't mend that, it's had it. All this lot's good for is salvage.'

She looked towards the chest of drawers in the alcove next to where the window used to be. That was still standing

15

miraculously intact, so at least her underwear must still be all right. She started towards it. The floorboards creaked and showers of dirt and plaster fell from the ceiling.

'Come back,' Jack said. 'It ain't safe.'

But the chest of drawers held all that was left of her clothes.

'It's all right,' she insisted.

She stepped carefully. There was only about a foot of floor between her and the hole where the wall used to be. A thin rain was falling; it wet her face and chilled her skin. She was just one step away when an ominous shudder went through the house.

'Stand still!' Jack said.

Rita stood, her heart thudding in her throat. Two bricks fell from the edge of the gap.

'Come back, very slowly.'

Rita lifted a foot, and the floor groaned beneath her. She looked back at Jack, who was edging his way round the walls towards her. He reached the chimney breast.

'Come on –' he held out his hand across the corner of the bed. 'Slowly . . .'

She stretched out and grasped his hand, and as she did so there was a tremendous crack, and a sliding, rumbling roar as the back of the house collapsed. Rita screamed as the floor gave way and she felt herself falling. There was a wrenching jerk on her arm and she hung, suspended. She yelped with pain as the foot of the bed thudded into her stomach and scraped down her shins. She was choking, her mouth and throat full of grit. Then she was being dragged back up. Her flailing feet found something firm to stand on, and at last she was being held by two strong arms. She clung on, coughing up the suffocating dust as the whole world seemed to fall around her. In the middle of the noise and dirt and fear she felt Jack's firm body and his arms around her, his hand cradling her head against his shoulder.

'Hold on – it's all right,' his voice reassured her.

For what seemed like an age they stood, a still island in a landslide nightmare, until the roar died away, the monsoon of debris died to a shower, the remains of the house settled. Jack carefully released his tight hold. Rita slowly opened her eyes and looked up at him. She gave a shaky laugh.

16

'You should see yourself! You got dust in your *eyebrows* –'

'You don't look a fashion plate yourself,' he retorted.

Voices could be heard from outside, shrill with fear.

'Rita, you there? You all right, Rita?'

'Jack, Jack – answer me, Jack!'

Jack drew breath to reply, choked on the dust and tried desperately not to succumb to a fit of coughing. Rita called out for both of them.

'Yeah – we're all right, we're safe.'

'Don't come in,' Jack managed to wheeze.

'Don't come in,' Rita repeated. 'Stay there. We're coming out.'

She looked around at what was left of her bedroom. The floor had almost completely collapsed into the kitchen below, and the back wall of the house was gone. As the dust settled a little, she could see just the ends of splintered joists sticking out from the walls.

'How?' she said to Jack. 'How we going to get out?'

'Very carefully,' he told her.

Rita looked down. The bed lay twisted in a heap of rubble and jutting timber. If she had fallen down there . . . She found she was shaking.

'You saved my life,' she whispered.

'We got to get out yet,' Jack said.

He shifted a foot on to the nearest joist, testing it to see if it would hold.

'Right. Follow me. Hold my hand.'

Their backs to the wall, they edged along the chimney breast, across the gap where the alcove used to be, along the back wall. Twice they had to stop as the house seemed to shudder again. Once a timber gave way just as Rita put her foot on it.

'Bloody disgrace, the way these places was built. A kid could push 'em down,' Jack said.

They reached the door. There were the stairs, still firm and steady. As she went down them, Rita's legs began to shake, until she had to cling to the rail to stop herself from falling down. She staggered out into the street.

'Rita!'

17

Her mum flung her arms round her.

'Rita, don't you never do that again. You nearly give me a heart attack.'

Rita was shaking all over now. She fought to hold back tears.

'I won't, Mum. I promise – Look – I'm all in one piece. Jack saved me –'

She looked round to speak to him, and saw that Lily had claimed him. Her sister was clinging on to him, gazing up with adoring eyes. Jack was smiling down at her. Rita felt totally rejected. Just minutes ago, she had been clasped in his arms, snatched from mortal danger. Now she was forgotten. Jack belonged to Lily.

# 3

Sometimes it felt like she spent half her life in the Underground. A mole, that was what she was turning into. A mole, living in tunnels. But today it wasn't so bad, because instead of being on the platform trying to sleep she was on the train travelling down to Dagenham. What was more, she even had a seat. Luxury. But somehow she couldn't settle her mind, not even when she thought about her children. Rita opened her handbag and took out the precious photograph. It had been taken by her Uncle Harry just two weeks before the war started, and showed her boys standing in the back garden of Uncle Harry and Auntie Ellen's house in Tilbury. Peter was glaring rebelliously into the camera while little Mikey wore a happy grin. In the background was the newly turned hump of earth over the Anderson shelter. Rita gazed at the boys' faces, but even they could not hold her attention. The picture blurred before her eyes, and once more she heard the crack and rumble of falling masonry, felt Jack Wilkinson's arms about her. She felt almost sick with the painful stir of emotions.

'Lily's,' she said out loud. 'He's Lily's.'

'What's that, love?' the fat woman next to her asked.

'Oh – nothing . . .'

'You look a bit peaky, dear. You not been well?'

'I'm all right. Working blooming long hours, that's all.'

She did not want to admit to being bombed out. There was too much she had to keep to herself.

'They your kiddies, dear?'

'Yeah, I'm going to see them.'

'Ah, that's nice, ain't it? Hard when you have to send 'em away. Bleeding Hitler. I ain't seen my grandchildren since the summer. Five, I got, and I ain't seen hide nor hair of 'em. Here – I got a picture. I'll show you –'

Normally, Rita would have been glad to have someone to talk

19

to. Today she found it intensely irritating. There never seemed to be any time to sit quietly by herself. At the factory it was noisy and dirty, and even when people weren't shouting things at her, the work was so repetitive that she found her mind going round and round on the same small thought in time with the process of fitting components together. At home, her old home, there was always Maisie going on and on even when Ron wasn't there making demands. Back at her parents' the place was full of people, with the ceaseless jangle of the bell as customers came and went. And at night-time she slept in the middle bunk of a tier of three surrounded by hundreds of other shelterers. She had been looking forward to this journey down to Dagenham, but had reckoned without the new matiness that had got into everyone. Instead of ignoring each other, people struck up conversations with complete strangers.

'Your hubby away, dear?' the woman was asking.

'No, not yet.'

More's the pity.

'Oh – why's that, then?' Faint disapproval coloured the woman's voice. 'Both my boys have gone, and my old man's in the ARP.'

'God knows – his papers just ain't come yet, that's all.'

Plenty of men round her way had gone and joined up almost straight away. It was work, and that was scarce. The pay in the Forces was terrible, but at least it was regular, unlike work on the docks. Ron thought they were stupid.

'I'm not going till they make me,' he said. And by some quirk of luck, the call-up seemed to pass him by.

Rita looked at posters and listened to broadcasts urging women to join the Forces, and longed to go. To see new places, meet new people, learn new skills seemed like an opportunity sent from heaven. To get away from the restrictions of north Millwall, most of all to get away from Ron, would be sheer bliss. She thought about it through the long hours trying to sleep in the Underground, but always the same thing stopped her. If she joined up, she could be posted anywhere, and she would only see the children once every three months. She couldn't bear that.

'All right for some,' her travelling companion commented.

Rita was caught off guard.

'Ha. I can't wait for him to go,' she said.

The woman tut-tutted.

'Never say that, dear. You don't know what they're going to be sent to. My older boy's gone off to North Africa. Dunno where, exactly, but I suppose he's frying in some tank in the middle of the bleeding desert.'

'I'm sorry,' Rita said.

Of course, when Ron finally did get called up, he'd probably be found to have flat feet and end up with some cushy number in a kitchen somewhere. Ron was like that.

'You dunno how much you're going to miss 'em until they go, dearie. Mine went off to the last do. Missed him something terrible, I did. Still, at least he did come back. Plenty didn't.'

'Yeah,' Rita said vaguely. She knew she would miss Ron like a hole in the head.

One mistake, one silly slip, and she had found herself bound for life. It had been at her sister Joan's wedding. It was one of those hot June days and after the ceremony everyone was thirsty and ready for a good knees-up. Off they all went to the Rum Puncheon on the corner the moment the doors opened, all their own relations – the Turners, the Johnsons, the Crofts – plus all Ted's lot and most of the street as well. Rita had been going out with her cousin Ron for just three weeks, and was already getting a bit fed up with him, but what with the excitement of the wedding and the thrill of having a new dress to wear and all the fun of the party, she was just in the mood for a really good time. Drinks got passed out of the pub and Rita found herself swigging port-and-lemons like water, mixing them with the occasional half-pint of mild. She was only seventeen and not usually allowed to drink. Someone brought a gramophone out to the street and everyone started dancing. Ron held her close as they swayed over the cobblestones together, and she found a strange irresistible excitement boiling up inside her. When Ron suggested they go for a walk down to the river, it did not even occur to her to refuse.

Under the towering walls of a warehouse, he began kissing her. Rita's head was spinning. Ron's hands were everywhere and she seemed to be unable to stop him. She could do nothing but giggle, and gasp as her body reacted to his urgent explorations. Before she knew what was happening, they were lying down and Ron was dragging her knickers off. She made a token protest then, but it was far too feeble and too late. She was swept drunkenly along on the tide of events. Just like the tide, it was much too strong to swim against. She cried out at the sudden pain, and almost immediately Ron cried out in triumph. And then it was over, and Rita burst into tears.

Three months later, when she could no longer close her eyes to what was happening to her, she confessed to her mother. Florrie was shocked and horrified. Girls in their family were expected to behave themselves. Rita wept and assured her that she had never let a boy do more than kiss her before, that she had been drunk and that she hadn't meant to do it. But none of it undid the fact that she was expecting a baby. There was only one thing to be done. Ron was summoned, there were acrimonious family meetings and a wedding was hastily arranged. The young couple started their life together in an atmosphere of mutal resentment. Neither of them wanted to be married, both of them felt trapped, and each blamed the other.

'You'll shake down,' Florrie had said. 'You'll have to. You ain't got no choice.'

In a way, they had. Once Peter, and then Mikey, arrived, Rita put all her depth of emotion into loving them. She ignored Ron as much as she could, and when that was impossible, gave back his sniping as good as she got. When it came to verbal abuse, she could run rings round him. It was only when he came home drunk and resorted to physical violence that she came off worse. Even then she did not give in. Often Ron had to go into work of a Monday with a black eye while Rita nursed her bruises at home. The war had brought a welcome chance to go back to work. Ron had not liked that. He enjoyed having a hold over her, having her come to him for money. Now she had cash of her own, and could get her hair done and paint her nails and wear trousers, each a little victory. So she had managed, keeping her end up, not expecting anything different. Until yesterday.

Yesterday, Jack Wilkinson had come along and she was forced to face up to the fact that here was a gap in her life as ugly and gaping as the one left in the terrace where her home used to be. She took a long shuddering breath and let it out in a sigh.

The women next to her patted her hand.

'Never mind, dearie. You got them kids. They're what counts, ain't they?'

'Yeah,' Rita agreed, 'Yeah, I got them.'

The train was running above ground now, through West Ham. After the devastion of the East End, it looked almost peaceful, with cabbages and chickens in the back yards and men digging for victory on the railway cuttings. Back in Trinidad Street, everything was upside down. Everyone was dead tired, working long hours and sleeping down the Underground, there were bomb sites everywhere you turned, the water was off more than it was on, and now her home had been hit. No wonder she felt strange. It would be all right once she saw Peter and Mikey. Everything would be normal again.

Joan, waiting on the platform at Dagenham Heathway, could hardly contain the excitement of the two boys. The moment their mum stepped down from the train, they flung themselves at her and clung on, like a pair of monkeys.

'Hello, darlings – how are you? Oh, it's so lovely to see you again!'

Rita looked even more strained than usual, Joan thought, as her sister hugged the boys' round little bodies to her and kissed their eager faces.

'Mum, Mum, we got a new teacher, she's ever so old, she don't even know our names yet –'

'Mum, I can run more faster than Bobby *and* I can jump more higher –'

Joan stood holding the hands of her own quiet pair as Rita listened and exclaimed and drank in the presence of the boys. At last she put them down, and was free to look up. Something in her face disturbed Joan: a tension, a feverish brightness.

'Hello, Joan love.'

Joan gave her a hug and a kiss.

'Lovely to see you, sis. Everything all right?'

'Yeah, yeah, we're all fine, considering –'

23

'Mum and Dad OK?'

'They're coping. It's amazing, really.'

A great wave of relief flooded over Joan. That was the worst question out of the way. She asked after Ron, but more diffidently, knowing that her sister's marriage was not like her own.

'Oh well –' Rita glanced down at the two boys, obviously moderating what she would have liked to say. 'He's the same as ever.'

There was something, Joan was sure.

'And Lily? Lily's all right, is she?'

'You know Lily, out every night having a whale of a time. She's got a new boyfriend.'

Joan could have sworn there was an odd note in her sister's voice.

'Mum, Mum, come on –' Peter was tugging at Rita's hand.

'Mum, carry –' Mikey begged.

'What, carry a big boy like you?' Rita exclaimed, but she bent down all the same and gathered him up on to her hip.

'Me too!' Peter demanded.

'Oh no, I can't carry two of you. You're much too heavy, Peter.'

'Not fair!'

Sorting the squabble out took them to the station exit. They set off up the road with Peter and Michael scrapping round Rita's legs as she walked, until she suddenly snapped.

'Pack it in, the pair of you! I don't know how your Auntie Joan puts up with you all the time, really I don't.'

'They're all right,' Joan hastened to assure her. 'They're just over-excited, that's all.'

She did not add that even when they weren't all worked up, Peter and Michael were far more of a handful than her own docile Bobby and Doreen. But at least she was with her children all the time. She could not have borne being away from them, not with Ted away. Ted – the worm of fear, never quite still, twisted inside of her. It was bad enough having him away in the wilds of Scotland. At least she knew he was safe there. How was she going to cope when he was sent abroad, as surely he must be? It hardly bore thinking about.

'It's ever so brave of you, staying up there with Mum and Dad,' she said. 'I don't know how you do it, working all day and down the tube all night and coping with everything.'

'Well, we agreed, didn't we, that one of us had to stay? One to keep an eye on Mum and Dad, and one to look after the kids. That's what we decided.'

'Yeah, I know, but – if only Mum would agree to shut up the shop and move out.'

Rita gave a short laugh.

'You know Mum! She loves that shop. And now more than ever she won't leave. It's like that's her personal fight with Hitler, keeping open whatever. And you wouldn't move Dad neither, so you wouldn't move her even if the shop got a direct hit, God forbid.'

Joan knew it, really. Her mum and dad were like her and Ted, they had something special. She only wished it was the same for Rita. She drew breath to say as much, then stopped. All the children were still clinging about them. Instead she asked after her father.

'What? Oh – Dad. Well, he's dead tired, of course. When he comes off duty, he looks all in. But he does a smashing job as a warden, you know. Everyone says so. When you think how he was before the war. He never liked working in the shop, not really. Not after being on the docks.'

Joan knew just what Rita meant. Their dad had been forced to give up stevedoring when he injured his back, and serving in the shop was not what he considered a real man's job.

'It's so dangerous, though,' she said.

'But he's being useful. It's not just the rescuing and things. People look to him to organise things. He's a really important person in the neighbourhood.' Rita swung the boys' arms as they walked along. 'Ain't he, your grandad? A really important person.'

'When can we see Granny and Grandad again?' Peter asked.

'When I can make them take a day off.'

Bobby and Doreen were trotting on ahead, stopping every now and again to peer through a gate or call to a friend. Soon Peter, and then Mikey, joined them. Joan looked at her sister as

25

she followed the boys with her eyes. There was still that tight look about her. She put an arm round her shoulders and Rita jumped.

'Now then,' she said. 'What's up? What's really happened?'

'Oh –' A tell-tale flush flooded Rita's cheeks. 'Does it show that much?'

'Blimey, girl, it stands out a mile. I can read your face like a book. If it's not Mum, or Dad, or Lily, then what is it? Is it the shop?'

'No, no –'

'Then it must be your place – oh Rita, is that it? You been hit?'

There was an odd hesitation, then Rita gave a joyless laugh.

'Can't hide nothing from you, can I? Yeah – night before last. It looked all right at first – the windows was blown but but that's always happening – but the yard was a big hole and the back wall was partly gone, and when we went in to get what we could out of it, it nearly fell in round our ears –'

She shuddered, and Joan held her tighter, feeling for her. It all came back to her, the way she had felt when her home had been hit. As if everything permanent in the world had been blown away, leaving her drifting and rootless.

'You poor love, how awful. I know how you feel, I really do. No wonder you look so poorly.'

Rita gave her a hug back, then drew away.

'It's all right,' she said. 'Really. I'm all in one piece, that's the main thing. It's just that all my clothes was ruined. Lil lent me this dress to come here today.'

'You always was braver than me,' Joan said. But she was sure Rita was just putting a good face on it. That was Rita all over, never one to admit that things were bad. Joan turned over what she had said.

'You said you was in it when it went down?'

'Yeah, me and this Jack Wilkinson –'

'Who?'

'He's Lily's latest, he's in the RAF, a navigator on the bombers.'

Joan made noises of approval.

'She's a one, is our Lil. What's he like? Is he nice?'

'Yeah,' Rita said. 'Smashing looking – tall, dark, almost foreign. You know – lovely dark eyes.'

26

Joan could just picture him with her little sister. A lovely couple they'd make, the dark handsome man in his RAF uniform and the pretty fair-haired girl. Once Joan had been jealous of the fact that Rita and Lily had been blessed with the looks in the family while she was the ordinary one, small and mousy with no figure to speak of. But now that she had her Ted she no longer worried about it. Except sometimes, with him away so much, when she wondered what the local girls were like up there in Scotland, and what Ted might be leaving out of the brief and stilted letters he sent her. But she mustn't think that way. Ted was all right, he would no more think of looking at someone else than she would. She pulled her thoughts away from it, concentrating on Lily's latest romance.

'Trust Lily. Posh, is he?'

'No – no, not at all. He's from round our way somewhere. Not the Island, I don't think, but somewhere in the East End. He talked about houses in his mum and dad's road being looted.'

That sounded all right.

'So what's he like, then?' she asked.

Rita hesitated. She drew breath as if to speak, then stopped. Finally she said, 'He's good in a tight corner. If he hadn't caught hold of me, I would of gone down when the bedroom collapsed, and God knows what sort of a state I'd of been in. Could of been killed, easy.'

Joan went cold and hugged Rita again, just to make sure she was really there.

'You didn't ought to go taking risks like that, Reet. It ain't worth it. Blimey, thank God he was there to save you.'

Rita said nothing. She seemed to be off in some daydream. Or maybe a nightmare. Joan hastened to pull her out of it.

'How long's he home for, this Jack what's-his-name?'

'Oh, I don't know –'

'Won't be for long,' Joan thought out loud. 'That's for the best, really. If he's as nice as what you say, Lily'd only get hurt. Those RAF boys get shot down all the time, God help them.'

At least her Ted was not with that lot. The RAF was more glamorous than the army, but she gladly traded glamour for the knowledge that Ted slept safe in his bed each night. For the time being.

She looked at Rita again, and it struck her as it had done many times before that her sister was in more danger than Ted was. In fact, it seemed that all of her family was doing more for the war effort than she was. Mum was keeping the shop going, Dad was a warden, Rita and Lily had taken over men's jobs and her brother George was making army vehicles at Ford's. Her war work seemed to consist of keeping the four children out of her sister-in-law Queenie's way and waiting in queues.

They had reached the gate of George and Queenie's home, with its neat privet hedge, its spotless concrete path, its front garden planted with cabbages and broccoli. A sigh escaped from Joan before she could stop it.

Rita looked at her.

'Bad as ever, is she?'

'Worse. She's decided that as George is tired when he comes in, the kids have all got to be silent at teatime. Silent! And when one of ours says something, she gets that look on her face. You know.'

They looked at each other, gave wry smiles, then laughed.

'Stuck-up cow. I wouldn't mind so much if she had something to be stuck-up about, but she ain't. You're worth a hundred of her, girl, and don't you forget it,' Rita said.

'I won't,' Joan promised. It was always better when Rita was here. Even if Queenie was even worse after she left, it was worth it. 'Oh Rita, you're a tonic, honest you are. I dunno what I'd do without you coming down here every week and cheering me up. I really look forward to it.'

Her sister gave a laugh that sounded suspiciously forced.

'Nice to know someone's glad to see me.'

Something about the way she said it started prickles of worry in the pit of Joan's stomach.

# 4

'Look at all these blooming coupons. How on earth am I going to get them all sorted and counted?'

Florrie looked despairingly at the heap of little squares of paper, while outside the shop, the queue of women coming home from the factories was steadily building up.

'I'll do 'em,' Rita volunteered.

'Oh, but you only just got in from work, lovey. You must be dead beat.'

Rita was tired, but then wasn't everyone these days?

'I'm OK,' she said. She nodded at the waiting women. 'And if you didn't stay open so long, you'd have a bit of time to put your feet up and all.'

'If I shut when the big shops do, how would they get to feed their families, eh? Poor things, they get out in the dinner hour, but it's all queues then and all. They don't never have time to shop proper. Beats me how they manage at all, it does.'

Rita knew that this was so. She was lucky, for Maisie had always done the shopping when they were living there, though she usually had to cook whatever Maisie had found, for buying the food was enough exertion for her mother-in-law for one day. Back here at her parents' house they at least had the basic groceries to hand, and her mum generally found time in the afternoon to go out and get vegetables, and meat when they had enough coupons. Some of her workmates had a terrible time of it: up at the crack of dawn to take children to minders, in to the factory by eight, working all morning standing up at the repetitive task of riveting small pieces of metal together, out in the dinner hour to try to find something for tea, work until six or even later, then home via the minder's again followed by cooking, housework and more often than not a night down the shelter. Her life seemed easy by comparison. She looked at the haggard faces in the queue.

'I'll help you serve this lot, then we'll sit and sort coupons after tea.'

Anything to help get her mind off Jack. Try as she might not to think about him, he had filled her imagination all the long day. Serving meant she had to concentrate at least part of her mind on what people wanted and what they were saying.

Lily came bounding in, her face glowing and her eyes shining as if she had just been for a healthy country walk. Rita could guess why.

'Lily can help and all, can't you Lily?' she said.

'What? Oh, sorry, but I'm going out with Jack tonight.'

Rita succombed to a sickening lurch of jealousy, then immediately felt remorseful. Lily was young and free, and entitled to go out with whoever she chose.

'Well, you can blooming well put the spuds on. Mum and me are are busy here,' she snapped.

Lily pouted.

'Mum –' she appealed. 'Have I got to? I got to have a wash and everything before he comes. Look at me! My hair's a mess and I've run out of lipstick. They said they had some in down Bootses and I queued all dinner time and when I got there it'd all gone.'

Rita measured out two ounces of tea and a pound of flour for a customer and clipped the coupons. The next woman took her place, asking for dried egg.

'You can have a use of mine,' she offered, rubbing in her own pain in order to punish herself. After all, Jack was on the bombers. He might not come home from his next op. He deserved to go out with a pretty girl and have a good time. As for herself, she was a married woman, a mum, she shouldn't be thinking of men like this.

Lily flung her arms round her and kissed her noisily.

'Oh Rita, you're a brick! I'll love you for ever.'

'Put them spuds on and I'll draw the lines up your legs,' Rita said, taking money, giving change. Nobody seemed to notice the gruffness in her voice from the ache in her throat. She would have given anything to change places with her sister at that moment.

With two of them working, it took half an hour to serve the

queue, and at last Rita was able to pin the 'Closed' sign to the boarded-up door.

Ron arrived back just as they were about to sit down to tea. He flung his coat over a chair back and dropped into his place at the table, his face thunderous. Regular employment did not suit him; he much preferred the casual system of the docks where he had worked before the war.

'What's for tea?' he demanded. 'If it's bleeding Woolton pie again I'm going out.'

'Bangers and mash and be grateful for it,' Rita told him. 'We're still cooking on the fire. Even Dad can't find out when the gas is going to be back on.'

'We should of kept the old range,' Florrie said, for the umpteenth time.

Ron did not care about the difficulties of getting a meal on the table. He wanted food like it used to be.

'Bangers! If they're bangers I'm a bleeding Chinaman. Why can't they call 'em bread and gristle rolls and be done with it?'

'They was the last ones in the butcher's,' Florrie said. 'There was plenty behind me would of been happy to get them, I can tell you.'

Ron speared the offending object and shoved a piece in his mouth.

'Wouldn't be quite so bad if we had some brown sauce to put on 'em. You sure you ain't got none tucked away nowhere? What's the point of having a shop if you can't get no perks?'

'I couldn't rest easy if there was people with kiddies going without while we had extras,' Florrie said. 'And anyhow, you know as well as I do that I can only get what the wholesaler lets me have. Rations is rations, and that's that.'

'That's right,' Jim said. 'They're a blooming nuisance, but they're fair. Not like last time. End of the last war, we was near to starving down here while the nobs up the West End got everything that was going. You go up West now and they're queueing with the ration books same as what we are. Eating the same sausages and all.'

'If you don't like these, they got vegetables rissoles, eightpence a pound,' Florrie added.

'Vegetable rissoles? What sort of grub is that? Rabbit food,' Ron grumbled. But he knew that he was outnumbered here in Rita's family, and shovelled the mash silently into his mouth. At least there was plenty of it. Potatoes were unrationed.

Lily bolted down her tea and took the kettle of water that was warming precariously over the fire of salvaged house timbers in the grate. Soon the sound of splashing and singing could be heard from the scullery. Florrie squeezed the last cup of tea out of the pot and sat back savouring the pleasure of an unhurried drink before the trek to the tube.

'Ah, just listen to her. Young love. Nice to hear someone happy, ain't it?'

Rita nodded, unable to speak.

Ron snorted.

'Only after one thing, them Raff blokes.'

Rita rounded on him, her eyes stinging.

'You have to go and spoil it, don't you? Why can't you keep your dirty thoughts to yourself?'

She was shaking. One more remark from Ron and she knew she would lose control and really scream at him.

There was the sound of knocking at the shop door. Rita jumped up, grateful for the excuse to get away.

She felt her way through the familiar semi-darkness of the shop and drew back the bolts. On the doorstep was a tall figure in an RAF greatcoat. Jack Wilkinson. She tried to stifle a gasp.

'Oh –'

'Hello, Rita. What's the matter, expecting someone else?'

'Oh – no, of course not –'

'I'm a bit early, I know. Can I come in?'

Rita flushed, furious at herself for acting like a kid of fourteen. She stood back, holding the door open for him.

'Of course.'

His coat brushed her as he stepped past. Trying to keep her voice steady, she fumbled for the light switch.

'Hang on, and I'll put the light on. We got the electric back, anyway.'

A dim glow from the forty-watt bulb illuminated the shop with its sparse shelves and worn counter. Rita's eyes sought Jack's face. There he was, just as she remembered him, only a good deal cleaner. Unable to help herself, she stared, taking in every detail. She thought he looked pale beneath the olive skin.

'How are you?' he asked. 'Got over our adventure in the house?'

'Oh, yeah – I'm fine, thanks.'

But he wasn't. She was sure of it now.

'Did you get to see your nippers yesterday?' he asked.

Pure pleasure flooded through her. He had remembered that detail of her life.

'Yeah, bless 'em. Full of beans, they are. I told them about the house but they didn't seem to be too bothered. Peter was angry at first and Mikey was a bit upset, but they soon got over it. They got all their toys and stuff down at Dagenham. I think they look on that as home now.'

'Kids can adapt a lot better than what grown-ups can,' he said.

They were at the door through to the back room now. She wanted desperately to keep him here to herself in the fragile privacy of the shop. There was so much she wanted to say, to ask. She knew nothing about him. When Joan had asked, there was hardly anything concrete she could tell her. She knew that once they went into the other room, her mum and dad would claim the right to talk to him. Worse still, Ron might make one of his stupid remarks. And then Lily would come in all done up to the nines and slide an arm through his in that seductively possessive way of hers and that would be it.

'You sound like you know about children,' she said, pausing with her hand on the doorhandle. 'Have you got younger brothers and sisters?'

'No, I'm the only one, but I got cousins with families.'

Rita treasured up one more fact gleaned about him. Through the door her mother's voice wafted.

'Who is it, Rita love?'

Reluctantly Rita opened the door and let him through.

Her parents welcomed Jack, making him sit down, offering tea and cigarettes. Ron sat eyeing him balefully. Rita was sure he was going to say something embarrassing any minute.

'You home for long?' Jim asked.

'Not sure. I got a Board on Friday.'

'A Board?' Florrie echoed. 'What's that when it's at home?'

'Medical Board.'

'You been injured?' Rita cried.

Ron's head snapped round, and he glared at her, but Rita ignored him. Suddenly it all clicked into place. She was the reason for Jack's pallor this evening. She was still bruised and aching from the jolt to her arm and shoulder as he saved her from falling through to the kitchen, and she was fit and healthy. Whatever had it done to him, taking her full weight like that and hauling her back up when he had recently been wounded?

Jack played it down.

'Bit of a bumpy ride home from Berlin. I'm on the mend now, though. I expect they'll pass me fit on Friday.'

And then he would go back to his unit, back to flying through the hostile skies. Next time, the ride might be more than bumpy. He might be shot down. The thought of it made Rita feel sick.

'They didn't ought to let you go back till you're really fit,' Florrie said, echoing Rita's thoughts. 'It's dangerous on them bombers.'

'Dead cushy, though, being in the Raff, ain't it?' Ron said. 'Moment the girls see that uniform they come running.'

Jack's eye ran briefly over Ron, noting his lack of uniform, RAF or otherwise.

'It ain't all cushy, no,' he said. 'Not all of it.'

Ron took a drag of his cigarette.

'Yeah, but you can get any bit of skirt you like, can't you? Must be like putty in your hands.'

'Ron!' Rita was shaking again. Her fingers itched to strangle the smutty breath out of him.

There was a clatter of heels on the staircase and Lily appeared, made up, smiling and dressed to kill.

'Jack! I never heard you come in. I didn't keep you waiting, did I?'

'You're worth any wait, you are,' Jack responded.

Any man would be proud to be seen out with her, Rita realised. From her shining fair hair to her tiny waist to her slender ankles, Lily was a picture.

'Where you going tonight?' she asked, trying to sound nothing more than the interested older sister.

'The pictures,' Lily said, as if she had been invited to a ball at Buckingham Palace.

'They got *Rebecca* on at the Toledo, or there's a western at the Coliseum,' Jack said.

'Oh – *Rebecca*,' Lily breathed.

'I thought you seen that last week,' Ron said.

'But I want to see it again. It's the most wonderfullest film in the world.'

Jim broke in, addressing Jack.

'She's to be back by half-past ten, remember, if there ain't no raid on.'

Lily protested. Jack nodded and said, 'Right you are.'

Rita looked at her father and realised that Ron's words had done their work. Jack was no longer Wounded Hero in her father's eyes, not fully anyway. He was now tainted with Rapacious Serviceman, ready to take advantage of his sweet innocent little daughter.

The small room was silent and claustrophobic after Jack and Lily had gone. Rita looked at Ron, still hunched over the table, smoking, and felt almost choked with loathing. He dirtied everything he touched with his insinuations. And now she had to spend the long night down the tube in his company. She didn't know how she was going to bear it.

She started to gather up the used dishes and take them through to the scullery. Florrie made a move to help her, but Rita shook her head.

'It's all right, Mum, I'll do them.'

Anything to stop herself from having a go at Ron, because she knew that once she started it would get really vicious, and she didn't want that to happen in front of her parents. Her head throbbed with the effort of keeping it all inside. If only there was some way of getting away from him.

And then it came to her, blindingly obvious: she would volunteer for the night shift at work. Her mum wouldn't like it, she would worry terribly if she wasn't down the tube with the rest of them, but it would definitely be for the best. That way, she would hardly see anything of Ron at all. The prospect gave her the courage to deal with the night ahead.

# 5

Out in the shop, Rita's mum was talking to someone. Rita only took any notice when she heard her own name mentioned.

'. . . you're welcome to stay, if you like. Rita's out the back. She'll make you a cuppa.'

Rita groaned out loud, and considered doing a bunk upstairs. Whoever it was that her mother was directing through, she did not want to talk to them. She had only been on night work for two nights, and her body had not yet adjusted. They had not even had any breaks for raids, as the bombers had left London for once and gone to wreak havoc on Bristol and Plymouth instead. All she wanted to do was catch up on her sleep. She got up and plodded towards the stairs, but her reactions were so slow that she did not get there before the shop door opened.

'Hello, Rita –'

Jack. Rita's hand went to her hair. Why did he always turn up when she was looking her worst? She turned to him, forcing a smile.

'Wotcha, Jack. Didn't expect to see you this time of day. Lily's still at work, you know.'

'Yeah, I guessed she would be, but I thought I'd just drop in anyway. Is it all right? Your mum said to come through.'

Rita wasn't at all sure that it was all right, but she certainly didn't want him to go away again.

'Of course,' she said. 'Sit yourself down. I'll put the kettle on.'

She wanted to apologise for Ron's behaviour the other evening, but felt too embarrassed to start, so instead they talked about the street, and the fate of her old house, which the heavy demolition men had now flattened. It was only as the water was boiling that she suddenly remembered what day it was, and its significance.

'Of course! You had your Medical Board today, didn't you? How did it go?' She sent up a quick prayer that he had not been passed as fit.

'Oh – fine. I'm A1 again, they say. I'll be going back on Monday.'

'I see.'

The future suddenly seemed bleak and empty. Rita fiddled around with the tea things.

Jack gave a crooked smile.

'The truth is, I came here rather than go home and face my mum. She was hoping they'd give me a bit more time. I think she'd shoot me in the foot if she could.'

Rita had every sympathy with her.

'All mums feel like that. No woman wants her kid going off into danger, even if he's as big as what you are. My mum worries something terrible. Always did, even when there weren't no war on.'

'Yeah, I'm sure you're right. It's just that I'm the only one. If my mum had daughters and grandchildren around, it'd take the pressure off a bit, sort of.'

'You'll have to get going on producing a few grandchildren for her then,' Rita said, and immediately regretted it. It was a pretty stupid stab at a joke.

Jack smiled, but took it seriously.

'Not such a good idea at the moment. Not if they wanted to have a dad there to see them grow up.'

Rita poured the tea and pushed Jack's cup towards him. Her hand shook, slopping some into the saucer.

'Is – is it really as dangerous as they say?'

Jack shrugged.

'I think I'm just as likely to get run over in the blooming blackout.'

He was lying, of course.

'But you're up there for hours at a time, aren't you, with ack-ack and fighters and that coming at you?'

'Yeah –' Jack frowned into his teacup. Rita thought he looked a lot older than the man who called to take Lily out. She wished she hadn't asked now. He didn't want to be reminded of all that, not while he was still on leave. That was why he liked going out with Lily. She never had a serious thought in her head. All she cared about was dancing and film stars and having a good time.

That was what made her so popular; that and her looks, of course. That was what men on leave wanted, not to sit talking about how dangerous it was going to be when they went back. She opened her mouth to change the subject, but Jack spoke first.

'The thing is, up there you're really doing something. You're getting back at the bastards. That's what I wanted. That's why I joined up and why I went in the RAF. You get up there and you knock out a factory or a railway yard or a harbour and you think, "That'll stop the sods for a bit." And God knows, somebody's got to stop them. They're evil bastards, those Nazis.'

Rita nodded.

'Oh yeah,' she agreed.

'I'm not just saying it. I know. I come from Whitechapel. My dad's got a furniture factory, just a small place, used to have four men working for him. But most of the families in my street are Jewish. I grew up with them, they're my mates. I used to go in of a Sabbath and light fires and that for the stricter ones. Some of them have got relations living with them now, refugees from Austria and Poland and Czechoslovakia, and you should hear what they got to say. The way the Nazis are treating the Jews, it makes you sick to the guts. Some of them only had enough money to send their children out, so they put them on a train right across Europe with a packet of food and a suitcase and hoped they would get to safety. Some of them kids, they've written home but they've never got no reply. They don't know whether their parents are alive or dead.'

Rita shivered, trying to imagine putting her two on a train all by themselves to travel hundreds of miles to a foreign country. It was bad enough having them living only a short way away with her own sister and seeing them once a week. To wave them off maybe never to see them again was almost too horrible to think about.

'You got to be desperate to do that,' she whispered.

'Yes.'

'You're not Jewish, are you?' she asked. That would account for his dark colouring.

'Does it make a difference?' he said, a sharp edge to his voice.

'No – no, not at all. It's just that you look sort of foreign, that's all.'

'My grandfather, my mum's dad, was from Crete. He was a sailor. Right character, he was. Only died a couple of years ago. If the Cretans are all as tough as he was, the Germans'll have a hard time of it if they try to invade there.'

'What an interesting family you got,' Rita said. 'We're all very ordinary.'

Jack shook his head.

'No, that's where you're wrong. Nobody's ordinary. None of us knows what we can do till we got to. Look at your dad, organising his ARP area. What was he before the war?'

'He was on the docks till he had his accident.'

'There you are, then. An ordinary bloke, a docker. Yet now he's responsible for the safety of all them people. I bet nobody thought of making him a foreman, but he can do it, and do it well and all. That's something I learnt, you see –' he leaned forward, his face alight. 'You get all sorts on a bomber. As long as you can do the job, it's yours. Don't matter where you come from or what rank you are. My last crew, we had a bloke from Strathclyde, from the shipyards, with such a strong accent you couldn't hardly understand what he was saying, then we had an insurance clerk from Wolverhampton, a young chap straight out of Cambridge university with a degree in philosophy, and two of us from London. Me from Whitechapel and Reggie from north Harrow. And you know who the skipper was? Jimmy Livermore from Wolverhampton. Never even driven a car till he joined up. Bloody wonderful pilot, he was. Lucky Live More, we used to call him. Got us home when nobody else could of.'

Rita noticed he used the word 'was', but did not question it.

'You must get to be very good mates when you're all together like that, depending on each other.'

'You're telling me. You got to be able to rely on each other, or you're for it. Now Tim, he was the Cambridge bloke, he used to come down the pub and get Brahms and Liszt and sing his head off with the rest of us, but you get him discussing stuff, and he was amazing. Whatever you said, he'd make you justify it. I tell you, it was the first time in my life I ever really used my head. They never wanted you to do that at school, did they? Learn stuff, yes, but not question it, not really think about it. I mean, I was luckier than most round here, I went to the Central and stayed on till I was sixteen. So when it came to learning about navigation, I was all right, I could do that, and it was very interesting and all. But actually thinking, that's another thing. He was all right, was Tim. He's given me some of his books, but it's not the same as sitting there jawing with him.'

Rita had to say it then.

'Were they all killed, then, on your last run?'

'All except me and Reggie. Reggie managed to fly us home. Just got us over the North Sea and put her down in a field outside Great Yarmouth. I'm going to go and visit him in hospital on the way back.' His fingers were white round the cooling mug of tea.

Sorry seemed too weak a word. She had said it a lot these last few months, to people who had lost loved ones under tons of rubble. What else could you say? You were sorry, truly sorry, but saying it never brought them back. At least now she knew a bit about how people reacted. She reached out and put her hands on his.

'You mustn't feel guilty about them being dead when you're still alive. That's just the way it happens.'

He looked into her eyes, genuinely surprised.

'How did you know – ?'

'It's natural. They're gone and you think, why them and not me? But that's the way it is, nowadays. Ain't no justice to it. P'raps your mate knew the answer.'

'Tim? No – he never gave no answers. That was it, you see, he just asked questions –'

He broke off, his head bowed. Carefully, Rita got up and went round to his side of the table, and put an arm round his shoulders.

'It weren't your fault,' she said. 'You got to remember that.'

He was tight and resisting beneath her touch. Rita cursed herself. She had done the wrong thing, offering comfort when he did not want to admit to needing it. She was about to take her arm away again when he put his hand up to cover hers, and leaned against her.

'I know,' he said. 'I know that really.'

'It's just the way it happens,' Rita repeated.

'Yeah.'

For a few brief moments, he rested his head against her breast. She looked down at the dark curling hair and longed to kiss it, but knew that to do so would spoil the fragile bridge she had built.

Jack drew a shaking breath and sat up. Rita went back to her chair again. But their hands remained clasped, lying on the table between them.

'Tell me what it's like up there,' she said.

'Bloody terrifying. And the best time I ever had –'

Rita listened as he described it. As he talked, she felt the tension of the crew beneath the crude jokes, heard the roar of the engines and shuddering of the wheels on the rough concrete, felt the relief as the heavily laden plane lumbered into the air just before it ran out of runway. She saw the North Sea glittering in the moonlight and the searchlights ahead on the Dutch coast, saw Jack's charts vibrating as he drew lines and made calculations. She heard the scream of fighter engines, the rattle of guns, the shouts of the crew. She felt the cold creeping up her arms and legs and into her body, heard the numbing drone of the engines, on and on towards the target, the endless waiting, the worry of straying off course. Then the sudden deafening uproar of attack, flashes of tracer, splintering glass, cries – ignoring it, keeping eyes and brain tuned to the charts, the instruments, keeping the plane on target, till there it was beneath them, laid out like a toy: a railway yard, a munitions factory. The bombs falling away, down, down, down, into the dark, the flash of explosion and the fierce triumph, then the long journey home, back again for more hours, through more barrage, with the engines' drone uneven and the fuel running low. Limping over the sea now, till at last the dark line of the coast and home, and a shaky landing, the deafening quiet, the exhilaration of survival and the ambulance men taking the wounded gunner out of his shattered tower . . .

Rita felt elated and drained, at the same time.

'How do you go on doing it, time after time?' she asked.

Jack shrugged, and gave a sudden smile.

'Oh well, we have a few laughs, you know. And the girls all love us.'

42

Ron's remarks of the other evening lay between them, souring the atmosphere of trust.

'I shouldn't of asked,' Rita said.

Jack became serious again. He held her hand in both of his.

'I'm glad you did. Truly, I'm grateful. It's funny, but I never told no one how it is, not like that. We don't never talk about it between ourselves, the crew, I mean. We just want to forget it in between ops. Go out and get pissed and find ourselves a girl. And I could never tell my parents, it'd worry them sick. But I'm sorry I bent your ear with it.'

Rita was dizzy. Of all people, he had told her.

'I was pleased to listen, really.'

He stood up, leaned across the table, kissed her forehead.

'You're a smasher, Rita. Thanks.'

She sat there looking at him, tingling where his lips had touched.

Just as his hand reached for the door through to the shop, Florrie came in.

'Oh – you're not going, are you? Lily'll be in in twenty minutes.'

'I got to get home, Mrs C. I'll be back for Lily this evening. And thanks again, Rita.'

'Don't mention it.'

A bang of the door, and he was gone. Florrie looked at Rita, mystified.

'What was all that about?' she demanded.

'Nothing,' Rita told her. 'We was just talking.'

# 6

The postgirl was coming up what was left of the street just as Rita got home from the night shift.

'Still here, then?' she said, nodding at the shop.

'Yeah, still standing. Got anything for us?' Like Ron's call-up papers, for instance.

'One for Miss L. Croft. That's your sister, ain't it?' The girl was quite new to the job, busy learning everyone on her round. She squinted at the blurred postmark. 'Whittingley. Where's that?'

'Lincolnshire.'

Rita wanted to snatch it from her hand. Whittingley. RAF Whittingley.

'She's got a boyfriend in the RAF, then? What's he do? Is he nice?'

'He's a navigator.'

'Oo – lovely. Lucky old her.' The girl turned it over to see if it had SWALK written on the back. It hadn't.

Rita held her hand out.

'I'll give it to her.'

The letter from Jack burned in her fingers as she let herself into the shop. The family weren't back from the Underground yet; there must have been some hold-up somewhere. She stood in the back room, turning the letter over and over, smoothing it with her fingers as if she might guess the contents that way. Was he well? When was he next coming back on leave? Did he mention her at all? The thought flitted into her mind that she could steam it open. She blushed, ashamed of herself, and put it down on the table, then went to make a cup of tea. At least the gas and water were on. That was something to be grateful for. She tried to keep her mind on everyday things, cutting the brownish National bread thick and putting it under the grill. Should she have jam on it, or treat herself to a slice of the precious bacon ration? But the

44

problem could not keep her from glancing at the letter. She did not really want to read it, she told herself. She would not like what it had inside. It was a love letter to Lily.

The shop door rattled. Voices sounded – her mother's, Lily's, Ron's – and then there they all were, filling the little room, asking after her night, demanding tea, telling of what had happened at the shelter. They were like a big family now, on their platform. There had been a talent contest and Lily had got second place for her take-off of Marlene Dietrich, and the woman who had slept in the next set of bunks was now in hospital with her new baby.

'A boy,' Florrie said. 'Lovely, her mum says. They're calling him Winston.'

There was a squeal as Lily noticed the letter. She snatched it and disappeared up the stairs. The smell of frying bacon suddenly made Rita feel queasy.

'D'you want mine?' she said to Ron.

Up in her bedroom, Lily flopped down on the bed and ripped open the envelope. Her eyes slid over the contents, hungry for the only words that mattered. *My darling . . . I love you . . . I miss you* . . . As always, there was a faint sinking feeling of anti-climax. What she wanted was a long love letter steaming with passion. What she got was a brief account of what he had been doing, with just a bit of romance in the closing sentences. But this time there was something to really get excited about. He was coming back on a forty-eight-hour pass next week. Swallowing down her disappointment at his less than red-hot words, she hid the letter in the shoebox underneath the floorboards and bounced downstairs. She didn't want them to think it was anything other than perfect. Especially not Revolting Ron.

Her mum looked up and smiled as she came back into the living room.

'All right, lovey?'

'Yeah, wonderful.'

Ron leered at her.

'Got you all worked up, has he?'

Lily ignored him. He was disgusting. She did not know how Rita put up with him. She spoke to her mother.

'He's got a forty-eight-hour pass next week.'

From the kitchen, there was a sharp intake of breath from Rita.

'What's the matter, dear?' Florrie called out.

'Nearly burnt myself,' Rita said.

'You be more careful. You're tired. I'll come and see to that.'

'No, no – I'm all right.'

'It's a long way to come, down here to London, just for forty-eight hours. He could spend half of that travelling, the way the trains are,' Florrie pondered.

Lily preened.

'He's coming, all the same.'

He must love her, to do that. He was just not the sort of man who put things down in letters, that was all. He'd been passionate enough on that last night before he left for Whittingley. She sat at the table, chin in hand, reliving it. They'd said goodbye on the platform with all the steam and smoke wafting around them . . .

'Wake up, Love's Young Dream. Bacon and egg.'

Her sister plonked a plate in front of her. A thick slab of fried bread stared back at her, topped with a thin slice of streaky and a quarter of a one-egg omelette. Hunger got the better of Lily and she attacked it with vigour.

Across the table, Rita was sitting down with a slice of toast and a cup of tea.

'Ain't you hungry, lovey?' their mother was saying.

'You ain't in the club, are you?' Ron asked, with horror.

'No, of course not. I just can't get used to eating breakfast after work instead of before, that's all.'

Lily distracted herself from the unsatisfactory parts of her letter by considering her sister. Rita wasn't looking too bright. Once upon a time, she'd been a pretty girl, like Lily was now. Marriage to Ron and the war and all this night work had put paid to that. Of one thing Lily was certain: she wasn't going to throw away her chances like Rita had. Rita had been stupid. She could have done much better for herself. Lily could remember the boys who used to come calling for her. Nice-looking boys who would have treated her well and been decent husbands if she had played her cards right. But no, she had let Ron go all the way and

46

landed up marrying him. Lily was not going to let that happen to her. She knew what the score was. A girl had to use what she had. Lily was adept at going just far enough to get a man under her power. She laughed and flirted and fluttered her eyelashes and showed off her magnificent figure, but if any man tried to get a hand up her skirt, he was out of luck. She was saving that for the one she really wanted. And how glad she was that she had, for now she had met Jack and she knew that he was one she had been saving it for. But even Jack hadn't been allowed more than a taste so far. Lily wanted nothing less than a ring on her finger and the prospect of a husband in Air Force blue before she was giving anything away.

Reluctantly, she went to get ready for work, then cheered up as she realised that she had something to boast about to the other girls. They were already dead jealous of her. Having Jack rushing home just to see her was going to make them really sick.

Rita watched her go out into the kitchen to wash, saw Ron's eyes following her. He would just love to make an excuse to go out there and catch her half dressed, but he did not dare with all the family around.

'You ought to get to sleep. You look all in,' her mum said.

'Yeah, in a minute. I'll just wait for Dad to come in,' Rita said.

Every bone in her body ached with tiredness. She longed for her bed, but sat on. Wanting to see her father in was only half the truth. In fact, she was waiting for Ron to go. If she went up now, Ron was sure to follow. He didn't care if he was late for work. All the factories were so desperate for workers that nobody was scared of getting the sack any more, and if he got money docked off his pay he didn't care. After all, he had Rita bringing in a fortune from the night shift. Rita comforted herself with the thought of the savings she was salting away. Every week, she paid into the accounts, some for each of the boys and some for herself. It gave her a feeling of power. She had never had money to fall back on before. When she was single, she spent whatever was left over from paying her keep. Once she was married and had the boys to keep on Ron's erratic earnings, there was seldom enough to go round, let alone save. Now it was different, and when she was feeling particularly low she would get out the savings books and look at the slowly accumulating totals. She didn't know what it was for exactly, but she knew that with a bit of money you had more choices. There had been very few choices in her life since the day she realised she was pregnant.

She certainly needed something to hold on to in the next few days. Lily drove them all mad with her anticipation of Jack's return.

'What am I going to wear?' she wailed, changing into each of her outfits in turn and parading them in front of Rita and Florrie.

'That looks nice,' Florrie said to each one.

'Where are you going to go – dancing, pictures, what?' Rita asked, making a great effort to be helpful.

'I don't know, he never said. Oh, I can't wear none of these, they're all horrible. I'll have to go up West and see if I can get something nice. There ain't nothing round here. Even the shops what ain't been bombed ain't got nothing decent in them.'

'How you going to do that? You'll never get there before the shops shut,' Rita pointed out.

Lily's pretty mouth hardened into an obstinate line.

'I'll go sick. I'll say I got the runs. Everyone does it.'

To Rita's surprise, Florrie did not veto this.

'Just this once, mind,' she said. Then she turned to Rita. 'Do you good to do a bit of shopping and all. Get you out of yourself a bit. You been looking really peaky lately.'

Rita thought of her depleted wardrobe. She had hardly bothered to replace everything that she had lost. It hadn't seemed very important. After all, where was she going to go? Only to work and to visit the children. She didn't need to dress up for them.

'I got enough really,' she said.

But Florrie insisted.

'It's April now, be summer soon. Why don't you go and try and find y'self a nice cotton frock?'

Rita protested that she didn't have the time to go traipsing round the West End and queueing, but her mother said she could go first thing in the morning, and sleep after that. Lily backed her.

'Be nice to have someone to come with me.'

48

In the end she agreed, and to her surprise she actually enjoyed it. Just as she had predicted, there were long queues, especially outside the shoe shops. The Oxford Street stores had taken a pounding, but just like everyone else, they took pride in staying open whatever the circumstances. Lily's enthusiasm was hard to resist, carrying them both through all the frustrations. After a lot of tramping about and waiting, they both managed to find something that they liked, could afford and which fitted. Rita began to get back some of her old spark. It was nice to have something new to wear. The dress she found was skimpily cut, in line with all the new regulations to save material, but it was a smart blue and white spotted cotton and the rather severe style suited her.

'What that needs is a hat,' Lily said.

'A hat! What do I want one of them for?'

''Cause it'd look smashing, that's why. A little navy straw, on the side of your head.'

The hat department at Dickins and Jones was completely empty.

'It's for my brother's wedding. He's getting married on Saturday, then he's being sent off to the desert,' Lily lied.

'Oh well, I'll just go and see what I can find,' the shop assistant said.

Rita could hardly contain herself until she had gone.

'Lily!' she squealed. 'You little devil! How can you stand there and say things like that?'

Her sister shrugged and grinned.

'So what? Everyone does it. And I bet you she has got something hidden away at the back. You'll see, a good sob story works every time.'

She was right.

'Now you owe me one. You can buy me some knickers,' Lily said.

Laughing, Rita agreed. They joined a long queue in the ladies underwear department. Rita's feet and legs were throbbing after the waiting and the walking on top of a night's work, but she had got into the swing of the shopping expedition, and exchanged tips with other women in the queue as to where precious shoes or

49

children's wear might be found. When they got to the head of the line she found that they actually had bras in, and bought one. Lily leaned confidentially over the counter.

'You got any really *nice* knickers?' she asked. 'You know – rayon, with lace and that sort of thing? It's for a wedding present for a friend. Her fiancé's only got a forty-eight-hour pass for the wedding, so she wants to – you know – make the best of it.'

The young assistant blushed and giggled, and produced a beautiful pair of pink French kickers, shiny and slippery. They didn't have lace, but they did have a pretty scalloped edging to the legs. Lily sighed with pleasure.

'I'll have them. My sister'll pay.'

Rita obligingly opened her purse. There would be nothing left for savings this week.

'Come on,' she said. 'That's it, I'm skint. I just about got the bus fare home. You are awful, you and your lies. Wedding present, indeed!'

Lily gave an arch smile.

'Might not be so far from the truth. I'll save them for my wedding. I'd love to have them taken off of me – by the right man.'

Rita's happy mood evaporated.

'It's got that serious then, has it?' she asked, carefully controlling her voice.

'Oh yes –' Lily was airily confident.

They stood waiting for the bus, along with a dozen other women clutching precious purchases. It was easy to see what people had bought, what with the shops being forbidden to wrap up their goods. Anything too big to go in a shopping bag simply had to be carried unwrapped. Past them flowed the stream of shoppers, a high proportion of them in uniforms of some sort, women as well as men. Rita noticed none of them. So Lily was thinking of marrying Jack. The prospect weighed on her heart like a black stone. She tried to tell herself that it was only to be expected. Jack was a good catch, Lily was a pretty, lively girl. She knew it perfectly well, knew too that she was a married woman with responsibilities – and yet she wished that it could be anyone but Jack. Lily was welcome to get married. Rita would be happy to see her settled with a nice man. She loved her sister and wished her well. But not with Jack

'Oh Rita, he's just so wonderful,' Lily was saying, her face alight, her eyes dreamy. 'He's so handsome, and he knows all the best places to go, and dance – you should see him, Rita, he's a lovely dancer. Real Fred Astaire. Glides round the floor and steers you so smooth you never bump into no one –'

'Is that all you ask of a man?' Rita said. 'Looks and being good on the dance floor?'

'No, of course not.' Lily was indignant. 'He's got to be nice as well. And rich.'

'Jack's not rich.'

'No, but he's a sergeant, ain't he? And his family's got a furniture factory. He ain't a nobody, that's for sure.'

It was true. He was a brave and capable man, as she had found out that very first time she met him. And he cared about things, had a depth to him. But did Lily appreciate this? Rita rather thought not.

'No, he ain't a nobody,' she agreed.

The bus arrived, its windows criss-crossed with brown tape, a conductress standing on the platform. Rita sank thankfully into a seat, and tried not to listen to Lily chattering on about Jack. She had to learn to live with it, she told herself. After all, there never had been anything between them. It was all her own imagination.

## 7

From the roof of the factory, the devastated streets of Poplar could been seen laid out clear and sharp in the moonlight. Bombers' moon, everyone said, looking up at it sailing bright and malevolent in the black sky, lighting the shreds of cloud. But at least Jack would not be up tonight, on his way to Germany. He was on a train somewhere, coming to London. Coming to Lily. Maybe he was here in the city now, dancing the night away with her. She had been expecting him from late afternoon onwards, and had gone to meet him at Kings' Cross, but they had not returned by the time Rita went off to work.

Rita tried to put it to the back of her mind. She concentrated on her present task. She checked her equipment – sand, buckets, stirrup pump. If her mum knew she was up here, firewatching, she would have kittens. Her mum thought that when the alert went all the people in the factory scuttled down to the cellars, safe below the building. Rita did not dare tell her the truth: that if everyone did a bunk every time a siren sounded they would spend half their time underground and cut production so much that it wouldn't be worth having a night shift. So instead there was a spotter up on the roof. When the aircraft actually came into sight, then the factory bell was rung and the machines stopped. Only the firewatchers stayed up top then, perched high on the roof ready to put out incendiaries before they took hold. Tonight it was Rita's turn.

It was strangely beautiful up here right now. Buildings showed up in silvery detail, with dense black shadows in between. The worst of the destruction was hidden, leaving a monochrome world purged of its daytime tawdriness. Rita looked to the south, towards her home. The Isle of Dogs crouched in the glinting arm of the Thames, such a glaring target that it was a wonder it had not been totally obliterated. For eight months now the bombers had been coming, night after night with only the odd respite. Many had been killed and injured, many more had lost everything, plenty had fled to safer areas, but still the heart of the city beat on. Those who had stayed on were used to it now. It was almost routine. They had either staked their places in shelters, like Rita's family, or simply slept in their own beds each night, claiming that if a bomb had their name on it, it would get them wherever they were, and if it hadn't, they were all right. But how much longer was it all going to go on, Rita wondered. How long would it take to flatten all of London? More than months, that was for sure. It could take years. Surely Hitler must see soon that they were not going to give in and beg for mercy? But then it was no use expecting him to think like a normal person. Perhaps he would just keep throwing stuff at them for years.

She tried to drag her mind away from that, too. No use thinking that way. Best not to think at all. She started to sing to herself, silly, cheerful songs to keep her spirits up. At least it was better up here than slaving over her riveting machine. She had calluses on her fingers from handling the same tiny components time and time again. She shivered in the April chill.

All around the east and south of the city the searchlights stabbed the sky, white fingers reaching up thousands of feet and ending in an area of mist, sometimes lighting up the barrage balloons, silver whales tethered in the air. Far away, over Bromley or Orpington, the first shells could be seen bursting like Bonfire Night sparklers. Rita rubbed her arms, getting the circulation going. This was it, they were coming. More search-lights, nearer, and now she could hear the ack-ack pounding.

'Get them,' she said out loud. 'Get them, for God's sake.'

Get them before they could drop death on the city.

Then there it was, the unmistakable throb of aircraft engines. At that moment a searchlight caught one in its glare and the silver shells streaked upwards, seeking the target. Rita was so taken up with the drama that she forgot to run for the alarm bell. The first parachute flares fell, drifting slowly down, lighting earth and sky with a greenish glare so bright it hurt her eyes. They were going for the East End again.

'Jesus!'

53

Rita leapt up, propelled by fear. She grabbed the lever and set the warning going. Down below her, the bell clanged, and the machines shut down.

'Hurry, hurry!' Rita cried. What if they did not get to the cellars in time? What if the factory was hit and they were all killed and it was her fault?

The ack-ack on the Mudchute, just south of her home, was crackling now. There was a sound like sheets ripping, one after another, as the bombs began to fall, followed by the thud and blast of explosions. And then it was all around her, the swish and rush of the high-explosive bombs, the sharp spatter of incendiaries. Dogs howled, burglar alarms rang, fire engines clanged, shells screamed and the splinters rained down, hot and needle sharp. Rita cowered, pressed down against the dirty brick parapet in mind-numbing terror. There was light everywhere, red from the greedy crackling fires, green from the incendiaries; it seemed to pick her out, expose her to the bomb that was seeking her out, coming to get her.

There was a tremendous crash and the roar of walls collapsing filled Rita's ears. The whole building shuddered. She moaned, covering her head. She had not even heard that bomb falling, it had been so close. Then a harsh clatter sounded, right next to her, it seemed. Gasping, she looked up. An incendiary, just feet away; beyond it another, and another – sinister little black objects the shape of wine bottles. The terror fell away in the face of the need for immediate action. Rita leapt up.

Two buckets of sand – plonk – first one covered, step right over it, scramble on, douse the second, back to get more sand, slipping and staggering in her haste, get the third one as well.

She stood still, the breath rasping in her lungs, looking about the flat roof. Around her it sounded as if the whole world was being ripped apart, each crump and whistle and roar so close that it blended into a continuous barrage of sound. But Rita had got beyond fear now that she had something to do. Just down the street a building was blazing, the heat of it penetrating her winter coat and siren suit, making her run with sweat. They were not going to set her factory alight. She would stop the bastards before they took hold.

'All right, girl?'

Rita jumped and spun round. One of the foremen was at her shoulder, behind him three other men. She had not heard them arrive.

'Yeah,' she yelled above the din. 'So far. Put out three of 'em.'

'Well done. Thought you might need a hand. Bit busy tonight.'

'Yeah, sort of.'

Together, they chanced a look over the rooftops.

'Bloody hell, look at that!'

One of the men pointed. Rita looked. There, floating down to the west of them, was a group of parachutes, and dangling beneath each one a huge black cylinder, big as a pillar box.

'Land-mines. They're going for the City.'

Smoke was drifting across from the fire, making their eyes water, and with it a choking acrid smell.

'Must of got the chemist's. Bleeding awful, ain't it?'

Rita nodded.

'Wish I'd of brought my gas mask.'

Again that heart-stopping rattle, and they all leapt into action. But this time it was difficult to see. The small black incendiaries were hidden in the billowing smoke. Rita blundered about with her buckets of sand, her eyes streaming, feeling with her feet. She stumbled right over one, dropping a bucket, but managed to smother it with the other load. Then there was a hiss somewhere to her right and a blinding greenish-white glare. One of them had gone off. Disorientated, she looked about. Where was her store of equipment? She spotted the chimney vents, got her bearings, ran for the stirrup pump.

The spitting white flames were shooting along the roof. From somewhere in the smoke cloud, the foreman materialised.

'That's it, girl, I got it in the water – get working!'

Rita put her foot in the stirrup and grasped the handle. She heaved. Nothing came out.

'Come on, come on!' she wailed.

Up, down – and then a thin squirt of water. Faster, her back and arms protesting, and a steady stream emerged, hissing and sizzling on the flames. Frantically she kept at it until every muscle screamed in protest, and she was standing in an ever-widening pool. And then, miraculously, the flames died back, became smaller, fizzled out.

'You done it, you done it! Good girl!'

Rita's heart was pounding, her body trembling. But the danger was over, for the moment. She began to laugh. She was alive, when all around her reigned death and destruction.

'Yeah, I done it,' she said. She felt an immense sense of satisfaction. She had cheated them. They had not got her.

There was little time for congratulation. Burning debris was floating on to the roof now. They dashed about, stamping on the smaller pieces, putting sand on the larger ones.

The raid seemed to go on for ever. Rita's head was bursting with the noise, her lungs sooted up with smoke, her body heavy with fatigue. There were fires all around them. It was some time before she realised that the planes had gone and the bombs had stopped falling, for still the world was ringing with fire bells and roaring with flames and the sound of buildings collapsing. The foreman had rung the bell to get the factory back to work and she had not even noticed, she had been so busy stopping flames catching hold.

Dawn spread across the sky. All but the worst fires died to smouldering heaps. The air was heavy with the stench of the aftermath – fallen masonry, wet ashes, coal gas, dirt and the acrid prickle of high explosive. Rita sat slumped against the parapet, filthy, weary but strangely elated. She had won. She had defended her territory. All over the roof there were scorch marks, but none had turned into real fires. The foreman appeared again, his teeth and eyes white in a blackened face.

'Come on, girl, tea up. Reckon you deserve it.'

She had never been more ready for a cuppa in her life.

Down in the warmth and familiar racket of the factory, she found she was the heroine of the hour. A steaming mug was thrust into her sooty hands, together with a sugary bun. She gulped both down, ravenous. People asked what it had been like. She talked and talked, repeating herself, until her raw throat could take no more. Someone slipped her a nearly new bar of soap, and she was sent off to have a clean-up in the cloakroom.

The basin of hot water was heaven. She was trembling now, but still high on the effects of the night. Looking at her fever-bright, red-rimmed eyes in the mirror, a phrase of Jack's slipped into her mind. 'Bloody terrifying, and the most exciting thing I've ever done.' Now she had some idea of what it was like for him.

The day shift began to straggle in, telling tales of loss and fire and miraculous escape. A bomb had landed in the north transept of St Paul's, but the great dome was undamaged. People grinned, relieved. The cathedral had become a symbol of the city's ability to survive. Hundreds of people's houses had not been so lucky: whole streets were blocked off as unsafe. The night shift left, knowing only too well what they would see as they went outside, uncertain whether their own homes would be there when they managed to get back.

The effect of Rita's triumph was beginning to wear off. Her limbs felt leaden now, her skin shrivelled, her lungs seared and clogged. Bruises she had not noticed before were starting to hurt, making movement difficult.

'You all right, Reet?' one of her workmates asked.

'Yeah, yeah. Just dead on my feet, that's all.'

Someone fetched her coat. A group of fellow Islanders appeared. 'Come on, we'll see you home.'

She hoped she would get back before the family, but they had to make so many diversions that she did not succeed. Her mother was horrified at the sight of her.

'I'm all right, Mum, honest,' she insisted. 'I just want a sleep, that's all.'

Florrie fussed about, heating water for her to wash her hair, lecturing her about having a care for her life for her children's sake, if not for her own. Rita had no energy left to even reply. The warm water was left unused. She dragged off her siren suit, fell into bed in her jumper and underwear, and went to sleep without even being conscious of her filthy head touching the pillow.

It was late afternoon when she woke suddenly from a dream filled with fire and falling bombs. Confused, she lay shaking as her beating heart steadied. Then the familiar sights and sounds of home seeped in, reassuring her. Voices in the shop below, someone – her father, presumably – tuning the wireless, the background clatter and rumble of industry. She got up, groaning as all the bruises ached, and went to face the prospect of another night.

Half an hour later, she was feeling much better. Washed and dressed in clean clothes, she sat winding her wet hair into curlers and drinking tea while her father told her what had happened in his area during last night's raid.

Her mother came in and out between customers, filling in what she had heard. Several hospitals had been hit, and a lot of churches. Maples' furniture store had gone up like a torch, part of Selfridges had been set on fire.

'Selfridges!' Rita exclaimed, remembering the fun of the shopping expedition.

'And one of them land-mines landed on the Charing Cross railway bridge,' her father said. 'The navy disarmed it right there, on the spot.'

They were all silent for a moment, awed by such bravery.

But through all the tales, one question nagged at Rita. At last she managed to voice it.

'Jack got here all right, did he?'

'Oh yeah. Him and Lily called in just after you left for work. Went off to see his mum and dad and sheltered with them last night. We saw them this morning but they been out ever since,' Florrie said.

'Oh,' was all Rita could say.

Relief was mixed painfully with an irrepressible envy. He was safe and well, but he was with her sister. Her fingers shook as she wound the last locks of hair round the metal curlers. Jack was out with Lily and soon Ron would be home from work. And tonight she had to face another endless shift with her mind stuck in the groove of thought, just wishing and wishing that things were different. She almost wished she could be on firewatch again. At least then she would not have time to think. She knelt before the fire, cooking her damp head and wondering what was going to happen to them all. Whatever it was, Lily had all the advantages and she, Rita, could only try to carry on.

A waft of draught, a banging of doors, and suddenly there was Lily, as if summoned by Rita's thoughts.

'Hello, hello, here we are! Blimey, you should see it out there – nearly as bad as what it was at the end of December.'

Rita glanced up, and found herself looking straight into Jack's eyes. He smiled. Her hand flew to her head. Her curlers! What must she look like? She always looked dreadful whenever he saw her.

'So you was out on the roof all last night?' he said.

Rita got painfully to her feet. Her face felt flushed, but at least he would put that down to her sitting by the fire.

'That's right. Doing my bit.'

Everyone was talking. Lily was trying to claim back his attention, Florrie was going on at length about it not being right, girls doing that sort of thing. Rita heard none of it. Jack was still looking at her, with admiration in his eyes.

'Christ,' he said softly. 'Who needs the RAF when there's people like you?'

# 8

The row erupted over the tea table.

'No!' Lily shouted. 'I won't go down the Underground with you! I'm going to the station with Jack.'

'You'll do as you're flaming well told, my girl,' Jim told her.

'No I won't. I'm seventeen and I'll do what I want!'

'I don't care how old you are, you're my daughter and you're living under my roof, and I say you're going down the shelter with your mum.'

'That's right. You do what your dad says. If they come back tonight like what they did last night, I'll be a bag of nerves, worrying about you,' Florrie put in.

'That's right, think of yourself –'

'She's not thinking of herself, she's thinking of you, and don't talk to your mum like that,' Jim thundered.

Ron sat back grinning, enjoying the spectacle of his wife's family at each other's throats.

'That's right, you tell her, Pop,' he said.

Lily rounded on him.

'And you can shut your flaming mouth and all. Going down the Underground each night all safe and sound when there's real men out there fighting.'

Ron flushed.

'I can go and fight any time I choose. I just got more sense, that's all.'

'Sense! Just want to keep your head down, more like. Why don't you get off of your bleeding arse and join up?'

'Lily, language,' Florrie gasped.

Rita sat tongue-tied. She agreed wholeheartedly with her sister, but could not say so out loud. She felt ashamed of them all, shouting at each other like this in front of Jack. She stole a look at him. He was sitting stony faced, his dark eyes moving from one person to another as the row revolved. Then he spoke, and his voice cut through the anger with quiet decision.

'Your dad's right, Lily. You must go down the tube as usual.'

Lily gaped at him.

'But – but –' she stammered.

'I don't want you risking your life. It's stupid, just for the sake of another hour.'

The high colour drained from Lily's face and she slumped back in her chair.

'All right, if you say so,' she submitted.

Jim and Florrie bust out with speeches agreeing with Jack. Seeing that the fun was over, Ron stood up.

'I'll see you later on tonight. I got to go out.'

Rita did not bother to ask where. She really did not care. It took a big enough effort just to say goodbye as he went out of the door. Florrie, having won her battle for the safety of one of her chicks, turned her attention to Rita.

'You ought to give yourself a night off and come with us and all,' she said.

'I told you, Mum, I'm all right. I done my stint on the roof. I'll be down in the cellars when the raid starts.'

'It's still dangerous on the streets up Poplar,' Jim said. 'UXBs all over the shop, and there was so much damage last night the heavy squad ain't got round it all to make it safe.'

'I'll be all right,' Rita said.

'If you like, I could go with Rita as far as her factory, then go on to the station,' Jack offered, speaking to Florrie.

Rita could hardly believe her ears. She held her breath, wanting to jump in and accept with alacrity, but very conscious of her sister sitting opposite her, stiff with outrage.

'Oh, that'd be lovely. It'd take a great weight off of my mind,' Florrie said. Between them, they settled it. Rita was handed round like a parcel, but a very willing one. Lily sat visibly fuming.

Ten minutes later, Lily and Jack went outside to say goodbye. Lily came back in with her lipstick smudged, crying, and grabbed her bedroll and bag. Still sobbing, she set off with Florrie to call for friends up the street before trekking off to the family pitch on the platform. Jim put on his tin hat and went off to his wardens' post. Jack and Rita were left outside the boarded-up front of the shop. He shouldered his kitbag.

'Ready, then?'

'Yeah. Let's go.'

They passed odd remarks on things they saw, wondered about the night to come: the shallow chat of acquaintances, as if neither of them quite knew where they stood. It was not until they were on the bus, jammed together against the cab by the number of standing passengers pushing on, that they began to talk properly.

'You don't mind me coming along with you like this, do you? I should of asked you in the first place, but –'

'But Lily wouldn't of been very pleased,' Rita finished for him, forcing a smile, making a joke of it.

'No.'

'I don't mind at all. Far from it. I'm very grateful. It ain't very nice going through the streets of an evening when there's been a raid.'

'That's all right, then. I didn't want to force myself on you, like.'

The bus braked and they were thrown together. Through the layers of clothing, she was acutely conscious of his body. He took hold of her arm to steady her. His fingers seemed to burn into her flesh.

'All right?'

'Yeah – fine.' If she could just carry on like this for ever, step out of life and all its complications, just be beside him in this smelly bus, how easy everything would be then. She gave herself a mental shake. She was being stupid. He was on his way back to his squadron. This might be her last chance to talk to him.

'How are your mum and dad bearing up?'

He told her about his family, then about his new crew. The rear gunner was an Ulster lad, an amateur musician. He played the accordion and was much in demand for singsongs, but drove them all mad by whistling all the time he was firing, the same snatch of tune over and over again.

The journey took far longer than usual. It was almost as if Rita's wish had been granted, and they were destined to stay for ever in a rumbling limbo as the bus diverted round backstreets and was held up in blocked roads.

They missed the connection for the next bus and the one after failed to arrive. Rita's clocking-on time came and went before one turned up. This time, they got seats. They sat with shoulders and elbows and thighs touching as they bumped over rubble-strewn roads. Evening darkened imperceptibly into night.

Outside, the siren started up, its chilling wail rising and falling, penetrating the soul. There was a stirring of unease, but the bus carried on. Once, back at the start of the Blitz, it would have pulled over and the passengers would have made a dash for the nearest shelter, expecting any moment to be blasted to kingdom come. Now they were hardened to it. They all had places to go, and a mere alert was not going to stop them. By the time Rita got to her stop, the ack-ack could be clearly heard.

'You don't have to come with me to the door,' she said. 'It's only a short way from here. You could stay on.'

'I said I'd see you there, and I will,' Jack insisted.

She did not even want to argue with that.

As they got down from the bus, the drone of aircraft could be heard.

'This way,' Rita said, hurrying forward.

But she had forgotten about the changes wrought by last night's raid. The quickest route to the factory was cordoned off. Faintly by the light of the moon they could make out the notice – DANGER. UNEXPLODED BOMB.

'We'll have to go round the block,' Rita said.

They turned the corner, and suddenly the whole street was as light as day, hurting their eyes with a brilliant amber glow as a parachute flare drifted down overhead. An air-raid warden appeared at the run, blowing his whistle.

'Oi! You two! Take cover – can't you see the bleeders are back again?'

'I'm taking her to work, mate. She'll be safe enough there,' Jack shouted back. And to Rita, 'How far is it?'

'Only a hundred yards or so.'

'Right – come on!'

They began to run, but not fast enough. The raid caught up

with them, battering their ears with its cacophony, urging them on. A noise like nails on a blackboard set their teeth on edge, then there was a tremendous crash. The earth juddered under their feet. Rita gasped and instinctively reached out, to find Jack's hand already seeking hers. It was as if reality had fallen apart. The air was disintegrating around her quite soundlessly. She was lying in the road, swept by waves, clinging, clinging for dear life as if to rocks in a stormy sea. She scrabbled for a hand-hold, convinced that she was about to slip, to fall down, down, that she had to save herself from dropping into an abyss. There was nothing in the world but the gritty surface of the road, and the need to hang on . . . Then an age later, from far away through the ringing in her ears there was Jack's voice, calling her name, but she could not answer, was unable to make a sound.

'Rita – Rita, are you all right? Answer me, Rita!'

The falling sensation lessened, and drained away. She became aware of what she had really known all along: that she was lying face down in the road.

'Rita –' his voice sounded normal now, close, and sharp with anxiety.

Slowly she turned her head, to find that he was crouched beside her, his head just inches away from hers.

'Jack?'

Her mouth was full of dirt. She coughed and spat.

'Oh thank God, you're all right. Can you move? It was the blast – the blast caught us.'

'Yes – I think so –'

She made a few experimental moves. Everything seemed to be working.

'Come on, there's a basement over there. It's been hit but it's still intact. We can shelter.'

She realised then that the raid was still going on around them. Any minute now they might get caught by another blast, or by a bomb itself. She let herself be helped across to where cracked area steps and a broken door led to a basement beneath a shattered building, and found herself in the remains of someone's home.

'We'll be all right here, it's had its bomb,' she said, happy to believe the current superstition.

Before the words had left her mouth there was another ear-shattering crash, and plaster and brickdust fell around them.

'Get down!'

Jack pulled her to the floor, curving his body over hers, cradling her head in his arms. In the midst of the destruction, she was swept with a sweet wave of delight. She reached up to hold him, to cling to him with all her strength. He responded by drawing her nearer, turning protection into something far closer. They lay wrapped round each other, a small oasis of security in a world gone mad. Around them the ground shook and the scream and crash and roar of the bombardment filled their ears. The building above them trembled and shifted. It seemed as if the entire force of the *Luftwaffe* was concentrated on their one tiny patch of London. But just as last night Rita had forgotten fear in the need to defend the factory, now she was surrounded by a shell of pure happiness. The danger was nothing. She had Jack here with her, his breath on her neck, his scent in her nose, the feel of him around her. She turned her head until her lips met his, firm and warm, and as eager as her own. She lost all sense of the outside world then, as they kissed with the depth and passion of two people hungry for each other. There was only his lips, his tongue, the intoxicating weight of his body. He paused briefly, his breath hot on her face.

'Rita, Rita – I've wanted to do this for so long –'

She could hardly believe it, though she wanted to so much.

'But I thought –'

She could not quite get Lily's name out.

'There was only ever you.'

They kissed again, and he ran his hands over her, his touch burning through the layers of her clothing. She pressed closer to him, twining her legs with his, giving herself up to the pleasure of enjoying what she had ached for. Every bit of her felt alive and filled with an urgent need to be part of him.

When he spoke again, she realised that she could hear him without his having to shout. Dizzy with the effect of his lips, she looked up at him. His face was lit by a flickering orange glow. On the edge of her consciousness, she became aware of a fire nearby. His dark eyes shone in its partial light.

'I love you, Rita. You're the most amazing girl I've ever met.'

'Oh Jack –' She touched his face with tender fingers. 'I've thought of you so much. I knew I didn't ought to, but I couldn't help it. I've thought of nothing but you ever since that first morning. You know – when we went into my house?'

'I've never forgotten it. I wanted to kiss you then.'

'Me and all.'

It was so wonderful, she could hardly believe it was happening. And yet it was true. He was here, with her, telling her he loved her.

'I shouldn't of come back, I suppose, but – it's no use thinking ahead, you see. No use making any plans. I just wanted to see you again, that's all. I never meant to say anything.'

'I'm so glad you did. I dreamed this would happen, but I thought it was only that – a dream.'

They kissed again, happy in the knowledge of each other's love. They undid their coats, the heat of their bodies burning up the cold of the night. Rita's fingers explored the texture of his hair, slid inside his jacket to feel the play of muscles across his back. She moaned with pleasure as he caressed her buttocks and cupped her heavy breasts. She wanted nothing but for it to go on like this for ever, just the two of them together, but some last vestige of loyalty impelled her to speak.

'What about Lily?'

Jack sighed. He drew back and lay looking at the lopsided ceiling. Rita wished she had never spoken.

'She's a smashing kid, your sister, I like her a lot. I thought – I thought there weren't no harm carrying on going out with her, 'cause there weren't a hope in hell that you – but it's all different now.'

'Yes . . .'

It was all different now. What had been a secret longing had been brought out into the open. The dream had come true. The trouble was, life wasn't like dreams. They couldn't just walk off hand in hand into the sunset. Not with Ron and Lily standing between them. The livid light from the burning building glinted on the wedding ring on her finger and she knew that all she had just been given was about to be snatched away.

Jack was watching the changes of expression on her face.

'I didn't ought to of done it, did I?'

'What?' she said, though she knew what he meant.

'Everything – carried on going out with Lily when all I wanted was to see you, for a start. Most of all I didn't ought to have come with you this evening, and say all those things.'

A sudden fear gripped her.

'You did mean it, didn't you?'

'Yeah, I meant it all right.'

She reached out to pull him close to her again.

'I'm still glad you did. You can't imagine – it makes such a difference to me, knowing, but –'

But she was a married woman with two children to think of. He was going out with her sister. It was impossible. She swallowed.

'It can't go on,' she said.

He kissed her again, fiercely.

'They needn't know,' he said.

'They'd know. And even if they didn't –'

Even if they didn't, they would still be there between them, a silent presence, ruining everything.

'Yeah, you're right,' Jack admitted. 'I suppose I wouldn't love you so much if you was the sort that didn't give a damn about these things. But it's hard . . .'

'It's hard for me and all. Don't think it ain't. I wish – I wish things was different.'

The sounds of the raid were growing less as the wave of bombers passed over. They could hear the crackle of the flames in the nearby building now. Jack sat up, putting an end to the impossible conversation.

'I got to go.'

They emerged into a street swarming with firemen. There was a crater in the road and a whole terrace of houses alight. They turned to look at each other.

'Is this it, then?' Jack asked.

Rita nodded.

'You go. You got to get back.'

For a long moment they gazed at each other, then fell into each other's arms for one last passionate kiss.

'Goodbye, my lovely Rita.'

Then he was gone, leaving her shaking and incomplete, as if a part of her had been torn away. She stood on the pavement, tears running unheeded down her face as she watched him march round the crater, over the snaking hoses, to be swallowed up in the confusion of men and leaping shadows.

'Keep safe,' she whispered. 'Keep safe for me.'

# 9

'I suppose we got the pleasure of your sister's company again today,' Joan's sister-in-law Queenie said heavily.

Joan tried to keep from snapping back at her.

'That's right. You know we have. She always comes down of a Sunday.'

Queenie sniffed.

'It's like running a boarding-house round here, it is. Can't never get a moment's peace. Always someone visiting.'

Joan knew just what she was on about. Ted had been back on leave the week before, so the sleeping arrangements had to be changed.

'You know me and Ted would of gone to our own home if we could of. Only it ain't there no more,' she said.

Her throat ached at the thought of it. If she still had a home of her own she might well go back to it, bombs or no bombs. It was horrible being here when Queenie made it so clear she resented them.

Rita's two boys came chasing into the room. Michael tripped over the mat and fell against the table, hitting his head. He began to howl. Joan at once went over to comfort him, rubbing his bump. Queenie sniffed.

'Place is a madhouse with them two in it. Proper pair of hooligans. That's what happens when a mother goes off and leaves her responsibilities with others.'

From behind his Sunday papers, George's voice came in mild reproof.

'They are family, Queenie. And there is a war on.'

'Don't I know it?' his wife retorted. 'Can't even get enough polish to put right the scratches them two are always making.'

Joan sighed. She had only just finished clearing away the breakfast things and Rita's train wasn't due in for ages, but it seemed tactful to get the children out of the house. When

69

Queenie was in this mood, and it seemed to be happening more and more often, she didn't even like them playing in the street outside. It was best to get them right out of the way.

'Come on, Mikey,' she said. 'Get your coat on, we're going for a walk. And you, Peter. Where are Bobby and Doreen?'

'In the garden,' Peter told her.

'They better not be mucking about with that spinach. I need that for dinner,' Queenie said.

Joan ignored this. Her two knew better than to touch anything in the garden. They knew the consequences only too well.

'Want me to take yours and all?' she asked.

The offer was refused. Queenie's well-trained children were needed to get on with the weeding and planting. George was an enthusiastic digger for victory. Joan suspected it was mostly because it got him out from under his wife's eye.

Out in the street, Joan felt a bit better. It was a nice spring day. White clouds were scudding across a blue sky. The trees were in blossom. Birds were flying about with twigs and straw in their beaks. Even the dull sameness of the estate with its endless rows of identical houses had a certain cheerfulness about it. The long freezing winter was over. The country had been through Dunkirk, the Battle of Britain and eight months of Blitz and they were still on their feet and Hitler was still on the other side of the Channel. Maybe the dreaded invasion wouldn't come. Maybe the tide of the war had turned. Maybe Ted would not have to go abroad and fight. Joan wished she understood what was going on. It was the rule in the house that there had to be absolute silence for the BBC news each evening. They all gathered round, solemnly listening to the rounded vowels of Alvar Lidell or John Snagge. But though Joan heard it all, she could never quite make out whether things were going well or not. What she liked best was listening to Mr Churchill speaking. When he made one of his speeches, she was always left convinced that everything was going to be all right in the end.

The four children ran on ahead, glad as she was to be out of the repressive atmosphere of the house. She wondered for the thousandth time whether it would be better to take lodgings somewhere else, maybe somewhere really in the country, away from any danger of bombing. But the same old arguments swayed her. It would be more expensive. Doreen and Peter had settled well into their school. It would be much more difficult for Rita to come and visit. Most potent of all, family was family. When danger threatened, families needed to stick together.

' 'Morning, Joan. Lovely day!' A friend called to her from her front step, where she was taking in the milk.

'Lovely! You all right?'

After all, she did have friends here now. They were a nice neighbourly lot. If she could just know what lay ahead for Ted . . . It had been so sweet, seeing him again. She missed him so much when he was away. The trouble was, his leaves were never quite as idyllic as she hoped. She longed and longed for them, but when they came, Queenie was always more sharp than usual and the kids got difficult. She had got into the habit of letting them come into bed with her, so they didn't like it when their dad came back and they were turfed out. Once Ted had had to lock the door, and Doreen had sat outside and screamed. Joan had not known which way to turn.

They went the roundabout way to the station. Joan hesitated outside the newsagent's, wondering whether to part with some precious sweet coupons and buy some chocolate. In the end she decided against it. Best to save them till after Rita had gone again, when Mikey and Peter needed comforting.

The moment Rita got down from the train, Joan sensed that something had happened to her. Fear gripped her. There had been two nights of very bad raids in the last week. Had Rita been waiting to see her face to face before breaking the news?

They kissed and hugged as usual, but had to wait for the children to leave them alone before they could talk. Michael seemed to hang about his mum even longer than usual, clutching her arm and demanding attention.

'Shall we go for a walk round before we go back to George and Queenie's?' she suggested. 'It's nice day. We could go up the park.'

Rita agreed. She had no wish to face Queenie yet. She knew she wasn't welcome in her sister-in-law's house, but chose to ignore the pointed remarks for the sake of family unity. She bent down to give Michael another hug. It was good to hold his chubby little body again.

The swings finally induced Michael away from her. When all four children were happily competing to see who could get the highest, she found her sister taking her by the arm.

'Come on then,' Joan said. 'Out with it. What's up?'

The need to tell somebody was irresistible. It had been building up from the moment Jack left her standing in the street. It was impossible to tell her mother, of course, for she would have been shocked and disappointed. No use confiding in anyone at work either. They were such a lot of gossips there, there was no knowing how far the story would spread. It could even get back to Lily, since friends of hers worked there. But keeping it all to herself was so hard. She felt as if she might blow up and burst if she didn't say something.

'Oh Joanie, I'm in love!' she declared.

The moment she said it, she knew she shouldn't have. Joan was stony-faced with disapproval.

'What do you mean, in love?' she asked.

Rita sighed. She had hoped her sister might understand.

'Nothing. Look – forget it, will you? I didn't say nothing.'

'But I can't forget it, Rita. Are you carrying on with some bloke? Is that what you mean?'

'No – no I'm not. Nothing like that. I'm sorry I spoke. Let's leave it.'

Joan couldn't leave it. Her brow creased with anxiety.

'You can't say "I'm in love," then leave it. If you're not carrying on with someone, then what it is? Who is it, more like?'

'Look – it's over, all right? Over before it begun –' Now that she had started, she couldn't stop. It all came tumbling out. 'I liked him from the very moment I saw him. Well, more than that, fancied him and all. He's . . . he's everything Ron ain't, Joanie. He's brave and kind and nice to talk to – like – interesting, you know? And – well – when he looks at me . . .'

'In the forces, is he?' Joan asked.

'Yeah, the RAF –' she stopped short, but the words could not be wiped out.

Joan's mouth set in a hard line.

'It's Lily's bloke, ain't it? That Jack?'

Rita could only admit the truth.

'But it's over, Joanie, I swear it –'

'Shouldn't never have started. What do you think you're playing at? You got two kids. And your own sister's boyfriend! Don't you know there's a war on?'

Rita almost laughed.

'What's that got to do with it?'

'It's – it's – standards, that's what. You got to keep up standards, or it all falls apart. You're a married woman, Rita, and a mum. I know your Ron's got his faults, and I know you had to marry him, but you are married to him now, and that's that. You can't go playing around. It ain't right.'

Rita had never felt more miserable.

She did not know how she got through the rest of the day. On the train going home, she could not even remember anything of what happened after the conversation in the park. In the past, whatever had happened to her, Joan had always been there. She had never realised till now just how much she loved her sister and relied on her quiet support. When she had had to get married to Ron, when she was up all night with sick babies, when Ron came home drunk and hit her, when money was short and Maisie was at her infuriating worst, and most recently, when the bombing forced difficult decisions on them and she parted with the children, Joan had always been ready with understanding and common-sense answers. But not this time. She felt totally rejected.

On the train home, it came to her that she was alone. She lived in a city that was forced to be awake day and night, she worked in a busy factory, her home was overflowing with four other adults in it, she was married. She was never by herself. Even now, due to the disruptions on the line, the trains were few and very overcrowded. But despite all this, she felt alone.

People jostled and pushed around her, complaining or making the best of it, striking up conversations with whoever was next to them as if they were long-lost friends.

'Cheer up, sweetheart! It might never happen,' more than one person said to her.

'It already has,' Rita said, and repelled any further attempts to lure her into a chat.

She wished fervently that she could be truly alone, by herself: up a mountain maybe, or on a desert island. Perhaps then she could get things sorted out in her head. She stood hanging on to the strap, bumping and lurching with the uneven progress of the train, resenting every one of the people around her.

The shift at work was nightmarish. There were no raids to speak of, so she was at it for the full stretch. Her concentration was all to pieces, she ruined part of a consignment, had a row with the foreman and caught the full resentment of the rest of the line, whose wages would now be less because of her mistakes. The journey home seemed to take for ever, as the buses were still as rare as gold dust, so when she finally got there she just wanted to crawl into bed and die quietly. Instead she found herself pitched into a scene of high emotional drama.

Her mother was clearing away the breakfast things. She looked even more worn than usual. When Rita came in, a look of relief came to her face.

'Oh Rita, there you are. P'raps you can talk to her. She won't listen to me.'

'Who?' Rita asked, confused. Then she heard the sound of sobbing and wailing coming from upstairs, and went cold with fear. Her whole body seemed to go numb. She could not move, or speak. This was it, what she had been dreading ever since that very first morning. Jack had been shot down. She was not sure that she could bear it. To know that he loved her, and then to have him snatched away.

With a huge effort, she managed to say his name. It came out as a croak.

Florrie nodded.

'Yeah. You could of knocked me down with a feather. I thought they was all lovey-dovey. Well, she is, poor little soul, but it seems he's not. Given her the push, he has. There was a letter this morning waiting for her when we come back from the shelter. I ain't never seen her so upset. Went rushing upstairs and locked her door and I can't get her to let me in. She's been crying and crying like that ever since.'

The relief was so overwhelming that Rita had to sit down. It was all right. He wasn't dead, he wasn't a prisoner, he hadn't been shot down at all. He was all right. If she had had the energy, she would have laughed out loud. What did anything matter, just so long as he was still alive?

'. . . Rita, could you?'

She became aware that her mother was still talking, was asking something of her.

'What?'

'She might listen to you. She thinks I don't understand, though God knows, I do. But you're nearer her age, she might think you know what she's going through. You go and talk to her – would you, lovey? I can't bear it.'

'Right,' Rita said automatically. She was seized with such a complex rush of emotions that she could not possibly cope with refusing and having to argue about it. She pulled herself up the narrow stairs, hardly knowing what she was doing. Relief, guilt, hope, more guilt, a streak of perverse happiness and even stronger guilt churned within her as the thought took hold and would not go – *had he done this because of her?*

She had arrived at Lily's bedroom door, but had no idea what she was going to say. She knocked.

'Lily? It's me – Rita.'

The sounds of misery inside rose to a hiccuping sob.

'Go away.'

'Come on, love – let us in. Please –'

It took some persuading. Rita did not know how the words kept on coming out of her mouth. She was so tired she couldn't speak properly. She was slurring like a drunk. She was just about to give up when there was a thump and then the door opened.

Lily looked dreadful. Her eyes were red, her pretty face blotched and ugly, her hair on end. Rita reached for her, sympathy swamping everything else she felt.

'Oh, you poor darling,' she said.

Lily gave a great howl and fell into her arms.

'Oh Rita, I love him so much. I just want to die.'

'I know, pet, I do. It's just terrible –'

Tears gathered in her own eyes, and fell unchecked. They sat on the bed together, weeping, hugging each other, while Lily sobbed out all the things she loved about Jack and how she couldn't live without him.

'I know,' Rita kept assuring her. 'I know just how you feel. I really do.'

'He said he done it for m-me,' Lily wailed.

'Done what, love?

'F-finished it. Because there weren't no f-future in it. S-said it weren't fair on me when he might get killed any day.'

Rita wasn't sure how to take this. It sounded plausible enough, but she could not suppress the hope that it was just an excuse, a way to let Lily down gently.

'He meant well, Lily.'

'But I don't want him to. Don't you see? I just want it to go on as long as possible.'

'I know, lovey.'

They finally fell asleep, exhausted, their arms still round each other. Rita's last thought was to pray that Lily would never find out just how true it was that she knew what it was like to lose Jack Wilkinson.

# 10

It seemed as if the bombing was going to go on forever. There was a particularly heavy one on the night of the tenth of May. Five hundred planes flew over London in a raid that left nearly a third of the streets in central London impassable and hit the House of Commons, Westminster Abbey, all the mainline stations and fifteen hospitals along with countless other buildings. The casualty toll was the highest ever for one night. Londoners waited for the planes to return the next night, but to everyone's amazement, they did not. Nor did they the night after, or the one after that. For the first time in what seemed like eternity, Londoners managed to get more than two nights' consecutive unbroken sleep. Nobody could believe it would last, but as the nights went by and the skies remained empty but for the barrage balloons, it looked as if the city was to be treated to a respite.

Then, just as people began to think that life might just get back to something like normal, clothes rationing was imposed. Compared with the threat of being killed by a high-explosive bomb, it was a minor inconvenience, but to weary women with growing children, worn down by eight months of Blitz, it was the last straw. Pessimists ventured the opinion that it was to take people's minds off the possibility of imminent invasion, now that summer was here. The pessimists were proved wrong. Hitler did not invade Britain. Instead he looked east, and turned upon the Russians. There was precious time to gather strength.

Rita plodded on with her life, working long hours, seeing the children each Sunday. She watched as Lily devised her own way of coping with a broken heart. After three weeks of extravagant grief, she took to going out with as many different boys as possible, a new one every night if she could manage it.

Florrie was very worried, thinking that her youngest daughter was just making herself cheap. Rita reassured her.

'She's got her head screwed on, Mum. Besides, they're all so young. Kids, the lot of 'em. Younger than her, some of 'em. Much too young to do her any harm. She can't bear the sight of a man in uniform right now, specially the RAF.'

She wished she could find some way of easing the ache in her own heart. Not that she wanted to go out with a lot of young boys; or with anyone, for that matter. It was just that there was nothing to distract her from the dreary routine of work and sleep and making the coupons go round. The only time she really managed to escape was at the pictures. She took to going to matinée performances, watching anything that was on. The trouble was, however successfully she lost herself in the film, there was always reality waiting for her when she got out.

Then one morning in November, a buff envelope arrived for Ron. Rita, back before he was up, stared at it. A small knot of something close to excitement formed inside her. Could it? Could it really be that they had caught up with him at last? She turned it over carefully, trying not to build too much on it. It could be anything official.

A heavy tread sounded on the stairs, along with Ron's smoker's cough. Rita put down the letter as if it burnt her and bolted into the kitchen to put the kettle on.

' 'Morning,' she called, trying to sound normal. 'Want a cuppa?'

'Yeah.'

There was the scrape of a match as he lit his first cigarette of the day, then a grunt of surprise. Rita supposed he had seen the letter. Trepidation warred with hope as she heard the envelope being ripped open. If it was what she thought, he was not going to like it, to put it mildly.

'Bleeding hell! The bastards!'

The door through to the kitchen flew open, revealing Ron in pyjama bottoms and pullover, a printed letter in his hand.

'Why didn't you tell me about this?'

'What?' Rita said, to gain time.

'This, you stupid cow – my bleeding call-up papers –' He brandished then in front of her face.

'Oh – is that what it is? Oh dear –'

78

'Oh bloody dear! Is that all you can say? Why didn't you tell me?'

'I only just got in myself. And you was upstairs –'

'Jesus! I get my call-up papers and you just go and make bleeding tea. What sort of a wife is that, for Christ's sake?'

Rita knew very well that since he was going away she could afford to be patient, but it had been a long night at work as usual and she had had more than enough of him.

'What do you expect me to do? Call up the flaming War Office and tell them not to take you?'

'Yeah, why not? Why ain't you upset? You ought to be upset.'

'You're upset enough for both of us.'

Ron took a threatening step nearer, his fists clenched. He drew breath to hurl insults at her. Rita did not hear the footsteps coming through the shop.

'What's up?'

Jim appeared in the kitchen doorway.

'Ron's had his call-up papers,' Rita explained, carefully bland. She did not look at either of them.

'Hard luck, mate.' Her father was cheerfully sympathetic.

Ron grunted.

'More than hard bleeding luck, if you ask me.'

'Well, comes to everyone in the end, don't it? You got away with it longer than most.'

'Huh. I don't see why I got to go. Plenty of others.'

Rita looked up then. There was her father, knocking on sixty and with his bad back, who had been working night and day for the people in his area, rescuing them, digging out bodies, collecting possessions, directing them to shelters, helping and protecting them in a hundred ways, and here was Ron, twenty-six, fit and tucked up down the shelter every night that danger threatened, and he was moaning about being called up. She saw her father's mouth tighten as precisely the same thoughts went through his mind. But Jim had never been one to lose his temper. Instead he looked at his son-in-law with contempt in his eyes.

'Don't you know there's a war on?' he asked.

Then he stepped past Ron, ignoring him, and asked Rita for a cup of tea. Ron was totally outmanoeuvred.

If he had been hoping for sympathy elsewhere, Ron was out of luck. While not very many had rushed off in a fit of patriotism to join up, everyone knew that they all had to do their bit. Men in reserved occupations were regarded as lucky bastards, though even they had to watch it now that more and more women were taking over men's jobs. When your papers came, that was it. Your mates took you down the pub and got you drunk – if the beer didn't run out – and off you went. As men of Jim's generation pointed out, it wasn't like going to the trenches.

Rita tried very hard not to examine her feelings during the days that followed. She kept it all firmly shut down, and attempted to think only of immediate practical problems. But it was like trying to keep the lid on a boiling kettle. The hard, almost painful knot of excitement would not go away, and whenever she let herself admit that it was there, she felt guilty. She ought not to be feeling like this. She should be worried, unhappy. She remembered how Joan had been when Ted had got his papers. She had been brave, for Ted's sake, the children's sake, not wanting to add to the burdens, but under it all she was inconsolable at the prospect of her man leaving her. But then Joan and Ted loved each other.

Ron was so obviously hating the thought of the army beckoning him that in the end Rita found she did actually feel a bit sorry for him. He really was going to loathe it, being bawled at, square-bashing, bull. That and the guilt drove her to try to be nice to him.

'What's got into you?' Ron demanded, when she presented him with twenty Players she had got at black-market prices at work.

She shrugged.

'Just thought you'd like them, that's all. You can't never get enough.'

He stared at her, his eyes narrow with suspicion.

'What's this for, then?'

'Like I said, I thought you'd like them.'

'Why now? Why ain't you never given me fags before?'

'Someone was flogging them at work.'

He took a couple of steps nearer, thrusting his face into hers.

'You're enjoying this, ain't you? You just can't wait to see me go, can you, you bitch?'

She bit back the reply he was expecting. She was ashamed to admit to it.

' 'Course I ain't.'

'Like hell. Why all this making up to me, eh? What's got into you? What's it all about?'

She couldn't have explained, even if he had been willing to listen.

'It's only a packet of fags, for God's sake,' she snapped. 'I'll give 'em to someone else if you don't want 'em.'

But he snatched them up and walked out.

When it got out at work that her husband was being called up, the foreman actually told her to take a night off.

'Got to send the old man off with something to remember, eh?' he said, giving her an obscene wink. Rita felt sick.

When she told Ron she was not going into work on his last evening at home, he was unmoved.

'Oh. Well, me and the boys are going up the pub.'

'Suit y'self,' Rita said, covering up her relief. With a bit of luck he might get so drunk he'd be incapable.

She spent the evening with Florrie, sitting listening to the wireless and knitting a jumper for Michael. It was nice not to be slaving over a noisy machine, nice to chat to her mum in the comfortable familiarity of her childhood home, but she could not enjoy it. Her eyes kept going to the clock, and every time she looked, the hands had crept nearer to half-past ten. Soon, he would be home again. Soon, she would have to go to bed with him. She prayed that his mates would bring him back paralytic.

At ten, Florrie made cocoa and started fussing about when Lily might arrive.

'There's warm water here for you,' she said.

Rita accepted the inevitable and went to wash. Perhaps if she got to bed first, he would just fall in and pass out.

She had just got in between the worn sheets when she heard singing in the street outside. There was a lot of stumbling about and swearing and raucous laughter, then a rattle and a series of thuds as Ron tripped in through the door of the shop and blundered about finding his way through to the back. More banging of doors and unsteady footsteps on the stairs and then he was there, in the bedroom, bringing with him a reek of beer and cigarette smoke. Rita pretended to be asleep.

The light snapped on.

'I'm back.'

He sat down heavily on the bed.

'I said, I'm back. You ready for me?'

Rita said nothing. Ron reached over and thumped her on the backside.

'Oi, wake up.'

'Oh – hallo,' she said, pretending drowsiness. 'Had a nice time?'

He leaned over, leering at her.

'Going to have a nice time now, ain't we? Very nice.'

Clumsily, he pulled off clothing till he was down to his vest and socks, made a lurch at the light switch, then stumbled back across the room and into bed. Rita shrank inside as his hands groped for her breasts.

Soon he was muttering and sweating with frustration.

'Bloody hell, got the bloody woman in bed at last and now I got the bloody droop. Come on, you bugger –'

His best efforts had no effect. He grabbed Rita's hand and thrust it at his crotch.

'Come on, do something about it, you bitch.'

Rita's half-hearted attempt did nothing but anger him. He reared up on his knees above her and slapped her face.

'Don't just lie there like a bleeding warm corpse, do something.'

He put his hand over hers and made her work faster.

'You hate it, don't you?' he taunted her. 'You really hate it, you cold bitch, and you're going to do it, because you got to.'

Anger stiffened him. She could feel it emanating from him, anger at her, at the army, at the great grey-faced array of Them, whom he resented as getting at him personally. He could not vent his fury on Them, or the army, but her he had at his mercy. He tore at her pyjama trousers.

'Get them bleeding things off –'

82

She knew better than to resist when he was like this. At this stage of drunkenness, he was much stronger than her and only needed goading to start enjoying hurting her. He rolled on top of her and thrust into her, grunting his triumph at subduing her. Rita detached her mind from her body, as she had done so many times before, and just lay there, letting him get on with it.

'Move, come on, move – ' there was a desperate note to his voice. Sweat was running off him and dripping all over her. She could feel him softening inside her. He caught hold of a breast and gripped hard. Rita flinched and cried out in pain. That did it. He rammed into her with renewed anger and finally shouted and collapsed. Within half a minute he was asleep, snoring, a dead weight on top of her.

The next day, she went with him to see him off at the station. King's Cross was crowded with men in uniform coming on or off leave, with their wives and girlfriends and mothers and children. Rita found herself amongst a group of women on the platform, seeing off their menfolk on the same train. As the whistle went and the wheels squealed and moved they waved, blew kisses, shouted frantic messages, held up babies, wept. Rita stood, an automaton, a smile pasted to her face, her hand raised. In the midst of all the emotion, she could feel only relief.

# 11

1942

Ted was a regular correspondent. Every Thursday evening, so
long as he wasn't on duty, he sat down and wrote to Joan, so she
always had something to look forward to on a Monday morning.
The fact that there was rarely anything interesting in the letters
never really bothered her. She knew he wasn't much of a one for
writing things down. All she needed to know was that he was all
right and still thinking of her.

So when a letter arrived on a Wednesday, she was immediately worried. She stood in the cramped hallway of
Queenie's house, turning it over in her hands, and wondering
what had made him break out of the usual routine.

Her sister-in-law appeared at the kitchen door.

'Post arrived?' she asked, meaning had anything come for her.

'Yeah. It's from Ted.'

Joan went upstairs to the chilly little back room she shared
with the children, shut the door and tore open the envelope.
There was just a brief note inside. He was coming home
tomorrow, for a fortnight. She sat down suddenly on the nearest
bed. A fortnight, out of the blue like this, could only mean one
thing. Embarkation leave.

She tried to keep cheerful, for the children's sake. Daddy was
coming home for two weeks, she told them. Wasn't that lovely?
Queenie sighed and said she supposed that meant she would
have to put camp-beds in the dining room again and she didn't
know how she was going to manage. That brought Joan face to
face with the practical problems. How were she and Ted going to
manage to stand a fortnight in February in a house that wasn't
their own? It wasn't like being in your own place, where you
could come and go when you liked, and eat when you wanted and
have the fire lit or not as you decided and all those other

84

important little everyday things. They would have no real time alone together. Whatever they did, whatever they said, Queenie would be lurking about, watching and listening with that sharp look on her face. Joan longed for her own little home in Trinidad Street. It hadn't been much, it had been dark and damp and always seemed to make dirt, but it had been hers, her own place where she was in charge, and now it was just a flattened pile of bricks.

She put on a cheerful face to go and meet Ted at King's Cross, and by the time she got to the station, she did not have to act any more. Her body ached with the prospect of holding him again. She stared at her reflection in the mirror of the Ladies. Would he think she had aged? She brushed her hair and applied some lipstick and powder and wished she had been blessed with looks like Rita and Lily.

The train was late, of course. She hung about for over two hours while a dull day turned into a bleak evening and then a damp night. The station buffet was packed out, so she paced round the crowded concourse, shivering with cold, unable to concentrate on anything but her need to see Ted again. Then at last the train was there, steaming into the platform, and she was part of a knot of women waiting at the gate, craning her neck, straining her eyes to see through the gloom. Doors swung open, people got down. So many in uniform, so many in khaki, it was hard to make out individuals. Then she saw him, one head amongst the many, his kitbag on his shoulder. Her Ted. Her man. She jumped up and down and yelled and waved, then elbowed her way to the front with a ferocity that would have surprised her had she stopped to think about it. She flung herself at Ted and held on to him with all her strength. He swayed with the impact and gave an uncertain laugh.

'Steady on, girl – what's all the fuss about?'

But he put down his kit and held her close, then kissed her, right there in the middle of all the people, and she knew that it didn't matter that she wasn't pretty like her sisters, and that he felt the same way as she did.

She said nothing about why he was there, not wanting to break the spell. She kept it up all the journey back to Dagenham. But that night, when they lay locked together and satisfied in the single bed in the tiniest bedroom, she found the courage to face up to the truth.

'It's embarkation leave, ain't it, love?'

He hesitated, then agreed. Fear twisted inside her.

'Where – where is it?'

'Blimey girl, you don't expect me to know that, do you? The army don't tell you nothing. You just go where they send you.'

He was lying, she could tell. He never had been any good at it.

'Come on, you do know something,' she insisted. Now that she had started, she wanted to know the worst.

But Ted ran a hand over her thin body, lingering on her breast.

'Come on, love, let's give that cow Queenie something to really look po-faced about in the morning.'

So she found herself sidetracked, in the nicest possible way.

But not for long. The next morning, she unpacked his kit for him and folded it neatly away in a chest of drawers. Ted came in and found her staring at a flappy pair of khaki shorts.

'Oh –' He sat down on the bed.

'Why didn't you tell me?' she said.

'I didn't want to worry you, love.'

'But I am worried, I can't help it. And anyway, I just want to know. Is it the desert?'

Her Ted, a desert rat.

'I don't know, love, honest I don't. There's rumours, but you know what rumours are. Could be anywhere hot.'

With that she had to be satisfied. It made her wish all the more for some real time together. Every hour was precious.

They both went down to meet Rita on Sunday morning.

'Ted!' Rita gave him a hug and a sisterly peck on the cheek. 'What a nice surprise. Joan never said you was going to be home.'

'I never knew till the day before he come.'

When she learnt the reason for the leave, Rita came straight to the point.

'You can't be staying the whole time with George and that cow Queenie, surely?'

Joan glanced at Ted. They had been through all this. Space was short in both their families, and army pay was dreadful.

'Well, we're coming up to stay with Ted's mum for a couple of days. And we'd like to get away, even if it's just for a night –'

'One night! Blimey, we must be able to think of something more than that –'

Rita frowned at the pavement as she walked, ignoring the demands of her boys.

'I know. You must both come and stay with Mum and Dad.'

'But the kiddies –' Joan protested. 'There ain't half enough room for all of us at Mum's, and Queenie won't look after them.'

'Too right,' Rita agreed. 'Bring them with you, mine and all. Lily and me'll find somewhere to kip down for a few days. Someone'll take us in. Then you and Ted and your lot'll fit in at Mum and Dad's. And I'll take time off. They owe me some. I can take the kids off of your hands a bit and you two can have a second honeymoon.'

'But –' It all sounded wonderful. Too good to be true. 'We can't do that. Not turn you and Lily out of your home.'

'Rubbish. It's not for long. And it's in a good cause. Lily won't mind, and I don't.'

Still Joan hesitated. All those people being put out because of her.

'I don't know,' she said. She looked at Ted.

'Sounds like a good idea to me,' he said.

'Of course it's a good idea. You must. It means I'll have a bit of a holiday with the boys. It'll be lovely.'

'But – the bombs –'

'Oh, there ain't hardly none now. Nothing to speak of, anyway. Not like what it was last year. Come on, you know I'm right. Ain't I, Ted? You'd like to come back up to the Smoke, wouldn't you? See all your family.'

'Bossy cow,' said Joan, giving in.

Ted clapped his sister-in-law on the back.

'Blimey, Reet, you ought to be in the services. Make a good officer, you would. Better than a lot of the clots we got.'

So it was decided. Rita went back that night to tell her parents of the plan and sort out where she and her children and Lily were going to go, and Ted and Joan were left with the pleasurable task of packing up and telling Queenie that they wouldn't be getting in her way for a while.

It was the start of a lovely ten days. Jim and Florrie were delighted to see their daughter and grandchildren, and they always had approved of Ted and got on well with him. Joan did sometimes feel guilty at Rita and the boys having to camp out at their Auntie Daisy's, and Lily at a friend's down the street, but most of the time she was too happy just being with Ted again to feel too bad about it. The fact that he was going away gave each moment a poignant brightness. Joan tried not to think about it, but it was there at the back of her mind all the time, lending an intensity to everything they did. Just simple things like walking in the park or going to the pictures or eating fish and chips were imbued with a deep significance. She tried to store it all up, to remember it all for when Ted was no longer there. She knew she was going to need memories to take out and look at in the months to come.

Rita organised it all as she had promised, getting time off work to be with her boys and take Ted and Joan's two off their hands when they wanted her to. It made her happy to see the two of them together and enjoying themselves because of what she had arranged, though she often had to suppress a twinge of envy. If only she had a marriage like that.

But when the short days passed and the time came for Ted to rejoin his unit, she realised that there were two sides to everything. Not for Joan a sense of relief at her husband's leaving. She didn't say much, but Rita knew that her sister was dreading the moment of parting.

She was there when Joan came back from seeing Ted off at Waterloo. He was bound for Southampton and had made a lot of jokes about going on a cruise in the *Queen Mary*, which everyone went along with except Joan, who had forced a smile and said nothing. Rita's heart was wrung at the sight of Joan's anguished face when she came into the shop alone.

'Come upstairs,' she said, leaving Florrie to distract the children.

They went into the room they had shared as girls. Joan dropped on to the bed and covered her face with her hands.

'Oh Rita, I can't bear it – if anything was to happen to him . . .'

Rita put her arms round her and rocked her as she sobbed. She had never seen Joan so distressed. Joan had always been the calm one, a source of gentle strength in the family, like their mother. It shocked Rita to see her so openly unhappy. She held her for a long time, until her weeping quietened into spasms of racking sobs.

'Oh Rita, I'm sorry – I didn't mean –'

'It's all right. It's only natural. You just cry as much as you like.'

'Only I love him so much –'

'I know. And he loves you and all.'

'Yes. Yes, he does . . .'

That thought seemed to calm her a little. She began to talk, haltingly, of things Ted had said and done, signs that he did love her. Rita encouraged her, adding observations of her own.

'Oh but it's so horrible, thinking of him going all that way, and all them submarines and things and then the heat and the tanks and Rommel –'

'I didn't think he was in a tank regiment.'

'No, but – I don't know. I just want him to be safe, that's all.'

'Of course you do. He'll come back to you, Joanie. I know he will.'

Florrie tapped at the door, and came in carrying three cups of tea.

'Drink it up, dearie, it's got two sugars in it,' she said, as if that alone would make matters better.

Joan took a shuddering breath and took a sip.

'You got to be brave, and believe he'll come back. That's what I done when your dad went,' Florrie said. 'And that's what I've had to do when he's been out in all them raids and all.'

'Oh Mum, how do you bear it? I just worry and worry so much.'

'Me and all, dear. But you just got to. You ain't got much choice. You got them kiddies to see to.'

It was a subdued little party that travelled back to Dagenham. Joan was too depressed to say much and the children were

89

scratchy and irritable. Rita felt quite worried leaving her to Queenie's mercy.

'Look,' she said, as they drew nearer their stop. 'You don't have to go back there, you know. You could come back to Trinidad Street. We'd work something out.'

Joan shook her head.

'No, not while there's still bombing raids. You never know when they might start doing it every night again. I couldn't do that to the children, put them in danger, like.'

Rita did not argue further. The children's safety had to come first.

Going back to London alone was even worse. It had been wonderful to have the boys with her day and night and now she felt bereft. It was for their own good, she knew, but still she missed their cheerful company and small wriggly bodies. She thought about Joan and Ted and what they had between them, and compared their marriage with her own. She found herself wondering if it was all her fault. Perhaps if she were to make an effort when Ron came home, try to be more like what he wanted, maybe things would be better. She ought to try to make the marriage work, for the boys' sake. They deserved to have a mum and dad who weren't at each other's throats all the time. She must stop thinking about Jack, stop reading and listening to everything even remotely connected with Bomber Command, and concentrate on her marriage. With Ted and Joan's example still sharp in her mind, she sat down directly she got back and wrote Ron a long letter, telling him all about what she and the children had been doing in their time together and even ending up by saying that she was looking forward to seeing him when he came on leave. She put it in the post and felt better. She had made the first move; now all she had to do was to keep it up.

There was no reply in the next few days, but then she didn't expect one. Ron hated writing, and rarely did more than send her a postcard when he was due home. But still she kept her new resolution in mind.

Then one morning she came out of work, weary and aching, and was about to set off for the bus stop when a figure detached itself from the shadows and approached the group she was with.

A man in an RAF greatcoat, some lucky girl's boyfriend here to meet her. Despite herself, her heart turned over. She nudged the girl next to her.

'Who's – ?' she started to say.

Her voice dried in her throat. As he came nearer, she could see clearly who it was. It was not some other lucky girl's boyfriend. It was Jack.

# 12

'I thought I'd come and see if you was all right.' he said.

Rita was so overcome she could hardly get a word out.

'Oh – yeah – well –'

All those months since that night he left, since his letter to Lily, and never a word. Often she had wondered whether he was dead. Once or twice she had tentatively opened the subject with Lily, to see if she knew anything, if she had maybe gone to visit his parents. But Lily's face had frozen at the mention of his name.

'I don't want to talk about it,' was all she would say.

And now here he was, large and solid and real. Rita tried to pull herself together, conscious of the stream of people flowing past her, looking curiously. Gossip was the blood of life on the shop floor. They needed something to get them through the long hours.

'I didn't know if you was still here. I hoped you was.'

'Oh yeah, still here . . .'

Women pushed past them, laughing.

' 'Bye Reet. See you tomorrow.'

'If you can't be good, be careful.'

This was awful. It would be all over the place by tonight.

'I can't stay. I got to get home,' she said. She even made to move away, but he put a hand out and touched her arm.

'Rita –'

She looked up at his face, lit by the feeble light from the open factory doors. He was thinner than she remembered. His cheekbones were sharper, giving him a drawn look, his eyes shadows. She couldn't leave.

'How long have you got?' she asked.

'I've had a week. I'm going back tomorrow.'

A week. He'd been in London a week, only streets away, and she hadn't known it.

'Why – ?'

There was so many questions she wanted to ask him. All better unanswered, she knew very well.

'I just wanted to see you again. Going off like that, last April, it was – messy. All loose ends, you know? All left hanging.'

'I know.'

She had gone over and over that intense episode in the basement, reliving it, making it end in different ways.

'I thought – look, it's cold here, and you're tired I know. Let's go somewhere and talk for a bit. Please.'

Her thumb found the hard metal of her wedding ring, moved it. It was loose on her finger, for she had lost weight. She knew what she should say, what she should do. She should just walk away. But she hungered to be with him, just to look at him, to be near him, if only for a while. She bit her lip, caught in an agony of uncertainty.

'I shouldn't of come. I'm sorry, it was stupid of me.'

Jack shoved his hands into his pockets and turned away.

'No!'

Rita was compelled into acting without thinking. She caught his sleeve.

'Don't go. There's a café round the corner. We could go there.'

It was dark now; the factory doors were closed, the last of the night shift were on their way. His face was only a pale shape in the shadows but she could hear the smile in his voice.

'Thanks, Rita.'

The decision made, she felt light with happiness. She threaded her arm through his and he closed his hand over hers. They walked in step together.

'I went to find that place – you know – where we sheltered, but it had gone,' he said.

'It got hit again two days after. The heavy squad demolished it.'

She had been back as well, many times, even though it was nothing but a heap of bricks. Just looking at it brought it all back, made her weak with need of him. She had thought she would never see him again, had told herself that it was all over, what little there was between them. But always, despite herself, there had been hope. And now, here he was. She could hardly believe it. She could hardly believe what she was doing, either, yet here she was, a married woman, arm in arm with him.

The café enveloped them with a steamy heat. It smelt of wet dishcloths and frying and was packed with night-workers coming off shift and day-workers having breakfast before starting. The only table free was right at the back by the kitchen entrance.

'What would you like?' Jack asked.

She didn't think she wanted anything, didn't want to eat at all, but the sight of eggs on other people's plates was too much for her. Real eggs, not powdered rubbish, each with a frill of crispy brown round the white. She hadn't had one to herself for a fortnight.

'Oo –' she said longingly. 'A fried egg.'

Jack laughed and ordered. Thick white cups of strong tea were plonked down in front of them. Rita shovelled in two luxurious spoons of sugar. They looked at each other across the greasy table. She felt suddenly shy.

'Well,' she said, her voice bright and forced, 'and what have you been doing all this time?'

He answered in the same tone.

'Oh, the usual old things. Eating, drinking, sleeping. You?'

'Me and all. Working. Surviving. You know.'

'How's your family?'

She gave him a rundown, asked after his parents. There was a difficult pause. There seemed to be an invisible barrier between them. Or was she just imagining all that happened before? Was it just that they really were only passing acquaintances?

Two chipped white plates were thumped on the table, the eggs and fried slices sizzling fresh from the pan. Thankfully, Rita set to.

'This is better than the NAAFI,' Jack said.

Rita took a breath. 'What's it been like?' she asked.

'Oh – wonderful. Couldn't be better.'

She wanted to kick him. He had come to meet her, for God's sake, and now he was closing up on her.

'No, I mean really.' She looked at his thin face, at the lines round his eyes. 'You been ill, ain't you? What happened? Was you shot down?'

94

He didn't answer.

'Was you?' Rita persisted, though she knew the answer already.

'Yeah,' he admitted. 'Over the North Sea.'

'Oh my God.'

Rita put down her knife and fork. She felt cold all over.

'What happened?'

He shrugged.

'Usual old thing. Limping home with two engines and a bloody Messerschmitt got us. Sitting duck, really.'

'And you went down in the water? When was this?'

'September.'

The North Sea, at night. She had been swimming in the sea off Southend in summer, and that had been chilly enough. In spite of the fug in the café, she felt the killing cold of the black water gnawing at her bones.

'Oh my God.'

'We was lucky. The navy picked us up. Destroyer saw us go down and sent a lifeboat for us.'

As long as she lived, she would be grateful to the navy.

'But you could of caught your death, in the water like that. You could of got pneumonia.'

'Yeah, well –'

'You did, didn't you? You got pneumonia?'

'A touch.'

'A touch! You don't get a *touch* of that, you get ill. I knew you was.'

'Dear Rita.'

He closed a hand over hers. Her throat felt tight. His face blurred before her eyes.

'Oh Jack, I worried so much about you. I was afraid you was dead, and I wouldn't even know.'

'I been worrying about you and all. You're in just as much danger. You ought to go somewhere safe.'

A glow started deep inside her, and spread slowly through her body. He had been worrying about her.

'Really?' she said.

'Really. When I'm on my own, when I was in hospital, I

thought about you all the time. When I was in the water – I kept myself going by talking to you. You have to keep awake, you see. Once you lose consciousness, you've had it.'

'Oh – I never believed . . .'

She had never dared believe he might feel the same way as she did. Not for all this time. It wasn't the same for him, he was free, he could go out with any girl he chose. Every day of the week he met girls who were as free and available as she was tied. On top of that, he was in constant danger. She expected him to fall for someone else. Sometimes, when she was feeling strong, she even hoped he would, because it would be better for him if he did.

'You must of gone with girls up in Lincoln?'

'Yes,' he admitted.

Jealousy surged through her, a painful sickness.

'But they weren't you. None of them was you.'

'Oh –' Maybe it would be better for him to fall for one of them, but she was so glad he hadn't. Recklessly, she made her own confessions. 'I told myself I ought to forget about you, but I couldn't. When *Target for Tonight* was on, I went to see it eight times. I cried every time they got back safe. I thought, if they can get back safe, then you could.'

Jack smiled.

'Well, you don't have to worry about that now, I did my tour. I'm training other poor blighters now, or until the powers that be decide I got to go back and plug up the gaps.'

Relief flooded through her,

'Oh thank God. You're safe, then. Or as safe as any of us are. Oh, I wish I'd known that. I wouldn't of worried so much.'

'I nearly wrote, lots of times, but then I thought it'd only cause trouble, and anyway you might not want to know.'

'Yeah,' Rita sighed. 'It would of caused trouble. Lots. Ain't no secrets in our house. We all knew when you wrote to Lily. It was me what had to mop the tears up.'

'I'm sorry, I truly am. I didn't want to hurt her. I like her, but I couldn't carry on going out with her. Not . . . not with things as they were. It wouldn't of been fair.'

'No. No, you're quite right.'

'Was she upset?'

'Yeah. Very.'

And if she ever got to know about their meeting here today, like this, she would be even more upset. The whole thing was impossible.

'Look, Rita –' Jack took hold of her hands across the table. 'I know I'm asking a lot. Hell, I don't even know what I am asking. A chance, I suppose. A chance to see you again.'

Put like that, it didn't seem too dreadful. Especially as she wanted so much to see him as well. Meeting like this, in a café, surrounded by people, couldn't add up to cheating anyone, surely?

'I don't know,' she said.

She couldn't bear to look at his face. If she did, she would give in. Her eyes dropped to his uniform, the grey-blue fabric and the badges. He might not be on ops any more, but there was still a danger of his aerodrome being bombed. She would never even know what had happened to him. As if reading her mind, Jack reached into his pocket and produced a diary and a pencil. He began to write.

'This is where I live –'

'I know,' Rita interrupted. She had read the postmark enough times on his letters to Lily. 'RAF Whittingley.'

'I'm not there any more, but anyway I mean my home, my parents' place. I could be posted somewhere else. Abroad, even. But my mum and dad will know where I am. If you want to contact me or anything, you can go there.'

He tore out the page and handed it to her.

Rita looked at it: Prittlestone Road, Whitechapel. She knew roughly where it was. She folded it up and tucked it into her bag. Now she had something of his to keep.

'Next time I'm back, I could get them to forward a letter on to you to let you know. Nobody in your family would suspect anything if you just got a local letter, would they? Then I wouldn't have to wait for you by the factory.'

She wanted to say yes so badly that she couldn't stay sitting there any longer. 'I got to go home,' she said pulling on her coat and gathering up her things.

Jack paid for the meal and came with her.

'I'll walk you to the bus stop.'

It was almost light. A thin drizzle was falling, turning the already drab landscape to shades of grey. Rita shivered. Jack put an arm round her shoulders. She leaned against him, feeling him move as they walked. She had to say goodbye this time. It was no good making promises or saying she would write. She ought to give that address back. She opened her mouth to tell him that he wasn't to contact her, that she wasn't going to see him again, but somehow the words wouldn't come.

The bus came round the corner almost as soon as they reached the stop. Not the familiar red, but a chocolate brown one drafted in from some provincial town. Now, now she must tell him.

Jack pulled her into his arms and kissed her, his mouth urgent and demanding on hers. All thought dissolved. She kissed him back every bit as greedily, desperate for love and comfort.

'Now forget me if you can, Rita Johnson,' Jack said, and she knew she never would.

The bus drew up beside them with a squeal of brakes and a fog of exhaust fumes. Rita broke free and jumped aboard. She stood on the platform, hanging on to the rail as the bus moved off.

'I love you,' Jack shouted, his hand raised in farewell.

'I love you too,' Rita called back, then stumbled to the nearest seat and wept.

## 13

'I don't believe a word of it!' Lily shrilled. She was so shocked, she didn't even know whether that was a lie or not. It was just her instinctive answer.

The other girl shrugged. She and Lily had known each other practically all their lives. They had been to school together.

'Suit y'self. I know what I saw with my own two eyes.'

'You always did like stirring it up, didn't you, Peg?' Lily said accusingly.

Peggy put on an aggrieved expression.

'I thought we was friends. I'm doing you a favour. I don't like seeing people being cheated on.'

'Friends! You call y'self a friend when you go and say things like that all over the place, I'll shut your mouth for you, so help me!'

Peggy grinned.

'I'd like to see you try, Lily Croft. Anyway, I know I'm speaking the truth, and there's plenty as'd back me up and all. Why don't you ask that sister of yours? See what she says?'

Lily glared at the taunting face, then whisked around, giving a contemptuous toss of the head.

'I wouldn't sink that low,' she said, and made off down the street.

Anger boiled inside her. It couldn't be true. It couldn't. But she could not suppress the treacherous niggle of doubt. For Rita had been late getting back that morning: she still hadn't got home when Lily left. By the time she reached the shop on the corner, the niggle had grown to a horrible suspicion.

A queue stretched out of the door and five houses down the street. Women stood patiently, with mixed expressions on their faces. They hoped they would be lucky and get whatever item it was that had just come in, but were resigned to the hard fact that everything nice was in short supply and it might well be them that lost out.

Lily marched past the line and in at the shop door. Despite her parting shot at Peggy, she wanted to have it out with Rita straight away. She almost choked with frustration when she found that her sister was helping behind the counter. A box of tinned pineapple had pride of place, and Rita was dealing with the points while Florrie took the money. A woman was just leaving, clutching her prize.

'I want a word with you,' Lily said, ignoring her mother's greeting.

She thought Rita went a bit pale, but when she spoke she sounded normal enough.

'When I've helped Mum clear this lot. There's only a dozen or so left.'

Florrie's glance flicked to the waiting women, all listening avidly to the exchange, then rested on Lily with clear warning. *Not here. Not in front of everyone.*

'There's tea in the pot in the kitchen. It only wants hot water on it.'

Very reluctantly, Lily obeyed the silent orders.

She sat at the table in the back room, sipping tea. It was horrible, not only stewed but weak as well, but she knew better than to make a fresh pot. Tea was her mother's lifeline, and wasting it was a major sin. Pain and suspicion were now churning round inside her with the anger. Peggy must know something. She was a cow, but she didn't make things up, not something like that. If she'd said she'd seen Rita with anyone else, she would either have just laughed, or shrugged, wishing her sister the pleasure of it. That Ron was a bastard. But Rita and Jack . . . ? The more she allowed herself to imagine it, the more she felt as if she had been kicked in the stomach. She had loved Jack from the moment she met him, and loved him still. He was so tall, and handsome, and such a wonderful dancer, and when he looked at her with those lovely dark eyes, she just went weak inside. Nobody else even started to measure up to him. She had accepted his Dear John letter at face value, believing it because she wanted to. He didn't want to go on with her because of the danger of what he was doing. She could live with that, just. But this –

She lit a cigarette and dragged on it as if her life depended on it. She wanted answers. She wanted to be told it wasn't true.

Rita came through from the shop.

'That's that lot seen to. There'll be a lot of happy families this teatime, with pineapple on the table. That tea worth drinking?'

Lily could have strangled her. How could she talk like that, sounding so bright and cheerful?

'I been talking to Peggy Marshall,' she stated.

There was no missing the wary look that flew into Rita's face.

'Oh? What's that nosy cow got to say?'

'She said she saw you outside the factory with someone this morning.'

She watched Rita carefully. Her sister avoided her eyes, fiddling around with cups and saucers.

'She'd say anything.'

'So it ain't true then?'

'What ain't?'

'That you met Jack outside the factory and went off with him.'

Rita hesitated. Only for a moment, but in that moment Lily knew that it was true.

'You did!' she yelled. Her voice cracked on the rising tears. She swallowed them back, consumed with a need to hurt Rita as much as she was hurting. She launched herself at her sister, slapping her face, grabbing a handful of hair.

'You cow, you bitch! How could you? How could you take my boyfriend? Mine? I hate you. I'll hate you for ever!'

'Stop it! I never!' Rita tried to catch her hands, to twist out of her grasp.

'Pack it in, you two.'

Her father appeared from the back yard. He caught hold of Lily's wrists. Almost simultaneously, her mother came bursting in from the shop. She stood with her fists on her hips and glared at Lily as she tried to fight against the hand that held her. Lily stared back in defiance.

'What's all this about? Fighting when there's customers in the shop. I won't have it, d'you hear?'

Behind her, her father said, 'Disgusting.'

Enraged, Lily indicated Rita with a jerk of the head.

101

'It's her what's disgusting. She's been seeing my boyfriend. My Jack! And her a married woman.'

Rita said nothing. Florrie looked from one of her daughters to the other. Then she spoke to Jim: 'Go and see to the shop, would you, love? I'll sort this out.'

Only too glad to be out of it, Jim complied. Lily rubbed her wrists. She took a step towards Rita. She wanted to draw blood, mark her face. Her fingers curled in anticipation.

'Sit down!'

Eighteen years of training could not be overcome. When her mum spoke in that tone, you obeyed. Lily sat.

'And you.'

Rita lowered herself cautiously into the chair opposite. Her face was white and closed, her mouth clamped shut. She folded her arms defensively across her chest. Florrie looked at her first.

'Well?'

'I don't know what she's talking about.'

'She does!' Lily cried, her voice cracking. 'She met him after work this morning. Peg Marshall saw them.'

'And you believe what Peg Marshall said? She'd say anything, that one.'

'But –' Lily was suddenly stumped. She wanted to think it was all a lie, but she couldn't. 'Why would she say that? About Jack?'

'God knows. Jealous, I suppose. They're a plain bunch, them Marshalls, and she's the plainest of the lot. Not got strings of boyfriends like what you got.'

It made sense. But still the murderous pain had her in its grip. Lily tried to make Rita look at her, but she avoided her eyes.

'You tell me it's not true,' she demanded.

'It's not true,' Rita repeated, as if it was some instruction.

'Then where was you this morning? Why was you late in?'

'The – the buses was up the creek again.'

'There.' Florrie turned to face Lily. 'Your sister says it ain't true. I'm ashamed of you, Lily Croft, for even listening to such a story, and from that Peg Marshall and all. Everyone knows she likes spreading lies. And that's what it is, a filthy lie. Ain't it, Rita?'

Rita jumped.

'Yeah,' she whispered.

Lily watched her. She was lying, she knew it.

'What did she see, then? Who was you meeting if it weren't Jack? Who do you know what's in the RAF?'

'No one. She's making it up.'

'Of course she is,' Florrie agreed. 'And to think that someone in my family would believe such a thing. I'm ashamed of you, Lily. Rita wouldn't be meeting some man after work. She's a married woman, and a mother. She don't go carrying on. We're not like that in our family. Are we?'

Neither sister replied.

'Are we, Rita?' she insisted.

'No,' Rita said.

'Lily?'

Lily looked at her mother. It was all wrong. If Rita really was the little white innocent, then she would have said so. She would have fought back, too, and called Lily names for suspecting her. What was more, their mum knew that. She was covering up. Lily kept obstinately silent. She was not going to play along with this game.

But Florrie was not going to be defied.

'No one in this family goes sneaking around seeing people on the quiet. And no one says they do and gets away with it neither. So if you hear that Peg Marshall or anyone else saying things like that, you tell them to keep their filthy traps shut and stop spreading lies. That clear? I don't want no stories spreading around about my family. We always been respectable, we have. Not like some I could mention. We got our pride. So I don't want to hear nothing about this ever again. That clear? Rita?'

'Yeah.'

'Lily?'

Lily held her mother's hard gaze for several seconds. It was no use. Whatever she said, her mother was never going to let on.

'Well?'

'Yeah.' It hurt to say it.

'Good.' Florrie brushed her hands, as if dusting away the problem. In a forced bright voice, she told Rita to put on the kettle. Lily escaped upstairs. She did not want to talk to either of them for as long as she lived.

She managed not to see Rita again by refusing to come down to tea and staying in her room until she heard her leave for work. Then she got ready and went out for the evening. She did not make any effort to talk or listen to the boy who had begged her to go out with him. Nor did she see much of the film they went to. She sat there staring at the screen and ignoring her escort except to brush his hands away, but she took in hardly anything of the story. Instead, her mind played over and over the conversations with Peg and with Rita and her mother. Rita was guilty, and all her mum cared about was not giving the neighbours something to gossip about. Out in the cold night air and the dark of the blackout, she asked to be taken straight home. Humiliated, the boy did not even try anything on when they got to her door; he knew he would get nowhere. Lily hardly answered his mumbled goodnights.

She lay in bed, wide awake in the darkness, planning unlikely forms of revenge. Then suddenly, it came to her, clear and plain and simple. The perfect answer. Her mother would be horrified and Rita would be sick with jealousy. She would do it tomorrow. Content after a fashion, she fell asleep.

Having made the decision, she went about it carefully. They must not suspect anything until she had done it. She heard Rita come in. Normal time. So she hadn't been anywhere this morning after work. She went down and ate her breakfast, not bothering to talk to anybody, but watching them all the while, thinking about what they were going to say when she made her announcement. It gave her a hard, malicious pleasure.

She went out at the usual time, wearing her working clothes. But instead of going to work, she took the bus to Poplar. It was far too early when she arrived, so she walked around a bit, looking in the windows of the few shops with glass left in them, keeping her resolve up by imagining Rita's reaction when she heard what she had done. When the office opened, she was the first one in.

By the time she got home, she already felt as if she had entered a new world. She was exhilarated, frightened and queasily proud. She walked down Trinidad Street with a swagger. Peg Marshall was deep in conversation with a couple of older women. Lily regarded her with loathing. She wasn't going to let that bitch think she was doing this because of anything she had said.

'Evening, Peg,' she called out. 'What's the latest lie, then? Your mum gone off with Hitler?'

She did not wait to hear a reply. As she approached home, apprehension gnawed at her. She took a deep breath. She was going to show them!

It was teatime before she could spring it on them. She nearly died with the effort of keeping her mouth shut, but knew that she had to wait until they were all together. And at last, there they were: her dad sitting at the table, Rita setting out the knives and forks, her mum mashing potatoes. Lily could contain herself no longer.

'D'you know what I done today?' she asked, her voice loud and defiant. 'I went and joined up. I'm going to be a WAAF.'

# 14

'I wonder what Lily's doing now, the poor little thing,' Florrie said, for the thousandth time.

Rita clamped her mouth shut and tried not to listen.

'Look at it out there – it's raining cats and dogs. She'll be out on the parade ground or whatever, marching in them heavy boots. It's not right, for a young girl. Women shouldn't be in the forces. It ain't natural. That's men's work, fighting.'

Rita could stand it no longer.

'For God's sake, Mum, she ain't going to be riding a tank across the desert. She ain't even in the army, she's in the Air Force, and she ain't going to be rear gunner on a bomber –'

'That ain't the point. She's in uniform, ain't she? I know what they was like in the last war. The army's groundsheet, that's what they called them WAACs.'

'Mum! She's in the WAAFs. And anyway, it ain't like that now. All us women are doing men's jobs now. I'm doing a man's job at my place.'

'That's different. You're not living with them. I don't know who she's having to share with. What sort of ideas is she going to get hold of, living with a whole lot of strangers?'

'Better ideas, p'raps,' Rita said, unwisely.

'Oh yes, you would say that. You always did think y'self a cut above Dog Island, didn't you? Ever since you got that job in the West End when you was sixteen. What's the matter, ain't we good enough for you?'

Guilt helped Rita to keep her temper. It was because of her that Lily had joined up. She would never have done it if she hadn't found out about Jack coming to see her. Her mum was only going on like this because she was eaten up with worry, and the last thing she wanted was to cause her mum anxiety. That had been the reason for staying on in London without the children, so that Mum had as many of her family about her as possible. She had felt it when George married Queenie and went off to live in Dagenham. Rita, Joan and Lily had not minded. The moment he began courting Queenie he started changing from the big brother they had once known, ready to stick up for them and fight their battles, into a critical young man concerned with appearances, until they were quite glad to see the back of him. Not so Florrie. She hated having her chicks out of her reach, and now, with Joan out at George's and Lily away, there was only Rita left at home of the four children. She tried to change the subject.

'That's daft, Mum, and you know it. Now, what are we going to give Joan and the kids to eat when they come up on Sunday? You got enough coupons? Joan said she'd bring something along with her.'

Florrie sighed.

'Lily would of loved to of seen them kiddies again. Loves them, she does. And they love her and all. They'll be so upset when she ain't here to play with them. It won't be the same. God knows when we'll all be together again. P'raps never.'

It was all her fault, that was the beginning and end of it. Her fault that Lily had gone, her fault that Jack had come back, her fault that her mum was in a state. When her family was all around her, her mum was a rock, taking on any number of problems and coping with them with ease. Without them, she dwindled. Rita felt blame pressing in on her, squeezing her as if between two stones. If she had been a good wife to Ron, and given Jack his marching orders good and proper that night of the raid, then none of this would have happened. In a fit of remorse, she took the scrap of paper with Jack's address written on it out of her handbag, and threw it on to the fire before she had time for second thoughts.

'What was that?' Florrie asked.

'Nothing,' she lied, and went off to get ready for work.

When Joan arrived on Sunday morning, she felt the atmosphere straight away. Her mum made the usual fuss over the children, hugging them and exclaiming over how they had grown, but Joan could see the lines of strain about her face.

'How are you, Mum?' she asked. 'You don't look too good.'

Florrie's mouth tightened into a hard line.

'It's a wonder I ain't a nervous wreck, what with everything what's been going on in this family. My little Lily in the Forces! I don't know what the world's coming to.'

'She'll be all right, Mum. For a start, she's safer where she is than here in London. And it might do her a lot of good. She'll get to see a bit of the country. We none of us been further than Margate, have we?'

The letter she had at last received from Ted was still in her handbag. She carried it everywhere with her. Compared with what he might be going to, all this fuss about Lily seemed a bit silly. But her mum did not see it like that.

Florrie sniffed.

'Ain't nothing wrong in that. Never saw the point of travel, myself. If you got a decent home, why leave it?'

She hauled Bobby on to her knee and drew Doreen close to her.

'Poor little mites. They ain't got no home at all. It's wicked, the way this war's breaking up families.'

'They're happy enough up Dagenham, Mum. There's more space for them there, and the air's cleaner. You should see their school – lovely big windows what you can actually see out of, and a big bit of playing field. Not like what we had. It was like a prison at Dock Street, all dark, and them horrible brown tiles and nothing but a yard for us to play in.'

Florrie was not convinced.

'Families should be together.' She reached out and put a hand on Joan's knee. 'But at least you're acting like what a proper mum should. That's something. That's a big comfort to me. At least you know the right way to behave. Not like some.' She threw a dark look towards the kitchen, where Rita was making tea, hindered by her two sons.

'Rita loves them boys, Mum. You know she does. It hurts her something cruel to be away from them, but she done it for their own good. You know that,' Joan said, deliberately misunderstanding.

'That ain't what I mean, and you know it. She's a married

woman and a mother. She didn't ought to go seeing –' she dropped her voice to a dramatic whisper – 'other men.'

Joan agreed, but tried to find something to say in defence of her sister.

'It was only the one, and it's not like she's carrying on with him, Mum. Ain't nothing like that.'

'Rubbish. I don't know where I went wrong with you kids. I thought I brought you all up to behave proper, and now there's Lily gone off and joined the WAAFs and Rita seeing her sister's boyfriend and you saying it don't matter. This war's got a lot to answer for, that's all I can say.'

The two children wriggled about and clamoured for attention. Florrie talked to them, asking about what they had been doing and who their friends were out in the wilds of Dagenham. Rita came in with the tea, carrying the tray with difficulty as Peter and Michael dodged around her feet, pushing each other in an effort to have the most of her. In the chaos of people trying to find space in the small room, Florrie leaned over to speak in Joan's ear.

'I wish you'd have a word with her, love. She might listen to you. What I say don't seem to count no more.'

Joan thought of the bad feeling there had been between her and Rita that time when Rita had first confessed to loving Jack. She didn't really want to rake all that up again. But her mum's fingers were digging into her arm, and her eyes were dark with worry.

'All right,' she agreed. 'I'll do my best.'

It wasn't easy to get to see anyone by themselves. It was a rainy day and everyone stayed in. With four adults and four children indoors, the little house was full to the seams. At dinner time the table was extended to its full size and practically filled the room. Rita and Florrie brought in two large meat and potato pies with roast potatoes and carrots and a big jug of floury gravy. Joan could see the children's faces falling at the sight of the carrots, and fixed them each in turn with a warning stare.

'That looks lovely, don't it?' she said.

Her own two heeded the signals, but not Peter.

'I don't like carrots. We have broccoli. Uncle George grows lots of broccoli. We have it with cheese sauce.'

'It's all right for them with gardens,' his grandmother said.

'That was a nice bag of veg what Joanie brought from George, weren't it, Mum?' Rita put in.

'Very nice,' Florrie admitted.

'There was an onion in there and all. Must of been one of his last, weren't it, Joanie?'

Joan took up the subject with energy.

'Yeah, you should of seen Queenie's face. She didn't want to send it at all, but she was so glad to get rid of all us lot for the day, she let him put it in.'

'Be lovely to have an onion. We can make a real nice stew now, can't we, Mum?'

'I was thinking of keeping rabbits. I got mates with allotments down the Mudchute. They said they'd give me all the outer leaves and other stuff they can't eat in exchange for a carcass every so often,' Jim said.

'That's a good idea, Dad. Nice bit of rabbit pie, eh, Mum?'

Between them, they managed to keep the conversation on food shortages going all the way through the first course. With the pudding, a solid roly-poly with a bit of jam in it, it looked as if Lily's name was about to be raised again, but Joan started on clothing coupons.

'I dunno how I'm going to get Doreen a couple of frocks for the summer. I spent nearly all the coupons getting them all new shoes when they had 'em in down the shops. I was dead lucky. I was just there when the shop opened and I got all of 'em kitted out. You should of seen the queue by the time we come out! Right down the street it was. Word got about that quick. The ones at the back had no chance. I got some dirty looks, I can tell you, coming out with four pairs, but they all really needed them.'

'I got a skirt you can cut up for her, if you like,' Rita volunteered. 'You know, that one with the orange flowers. It's not the fashion now, that full shape, but I ain't got time to alter it. Look nice as a little dress, that would.'

'I won't be needing no summer frocks, all I need is some more socks. You just knit me a couple of pairs, girl, and you can have some of my coupons,' Jim said.

Discussing ways and means of dressing the children took them right through to the cup of tea that ended the meal.

'Rita and me'll clear away, won't we, Reet?' Joan said.

Florrie objected, but was overruled, and asked to mind the children. Joan shut the door on the rest of them and put water on to heat for the washing up. Rita scraped the dishes vigorously.

'I hope you ain't going to go on at me,' she said.

Joan sighed. This wasn't going to be easy.

'What makes you think that?' she asked, to gain time.

'Come off it. I saw Mum talking to you. And I tell you, Joanie, I heard it all from her already. I know I'm a disgrace. I don't need to be told no more.'

'Oh Rita – what made you go and do it, eh? You said it was all over before it hardly started. Why did you have to go and see him again?'

'It was him what come to see me. I come out of work and there he was, waiting. All I done, Joanie, was go and have breakfast with him in a caff and talk. That's all. Nothing else. I know I didn't ought to have, but there he was and I didn't have the heart to say no. But the way Mum's going on, you'd think I was carrying his kid or something.'

'Rita!'

'Well, I'm sorry, but if it hadn't have been for that nosey bitch Peg Marshall, no one would of known. And it really was the last time, Joan. I won't never see him again. I probably won't even get the choice, if he goes back on ops.'

She sounded so bleak that Joan could hold out no longer. She put her arms round her sister.

'Oh Rita. I know just how you feel. It's the same with me. I don't know how I'm going to bear it.'

Rita held her tight.

'What is it, Joanie? You heard from Ted?'

Joan couldn't speak. She had held it back all day, but now she could be brave no longer. Tears formed in her eyes and spilled over.

'What is it? He'll all right, ain't he? He's not – ?'

'No, no –' Joan wiped her eyes on her sleeve and tried to control herself. 'He's all right so far, or at least he was when he wrote. But oh Rita, he ain't going to North Africa, he's on his way to the Far East. I don't know when I'll see him again. It was bad enough when he was in Scotland and I only got to see him once a month. What am I going to do now? It's so far. I looked it up on the atlas at the school and it's halfway round the world. I think of him on a troopship going across all that ocean and –'

It was such a relief to be able to sob on Rita's shoulder. In front of the children she had to put on a brave face, and it was no use expecting any sympathy from George or Queenie. But Rita understood.

'That's right, you have a good cry.' Rita rocked her and patted her shoulders. 'P'raps it won't be so long. We got the Yanks in the war now. That must be a good thing. They're fighting out in the Far East, ain't they?'

Joan made a squeak of agreement, ready to grasp any hope.

'And you got the kids, just remember that. You got them to look after for when he comes back.'

'I know . . .'

It was some while before she was able to stop. Rita gave her a clean handkerchief. She felt an empty calm, as if all the emotion had drained out of her.

'Better now?'

'Yeah. Thanks, Rita. I'm sorry.'

'Don't be so daft. Done you good, I expect. Here –' Rita handed her a flannel. 'Give your face a wash. You look a sight, you do. If Ted could see you now he'd run a mile.'

Joan managed to raise a feeble smile. She did feel a lot better. It didn't bring Ted back, but it helped. She felt a pressing need to impart her other piece of news. She hadn't meant to say anything yet, but now she wanted to share it with her sister.

'You know something? He's going to have another kiddie to come home to.'

Rita's face lit up.

'You're not? Oh Joanie, I am pleased. That's the best thing for you. Born mum, you are. Here, we got to tell Mum, she'll be beside herself.'

'No – no, not yet. I ain't been to the doctor's yet. I mean, I'm almost certain, but I don't want to say nothing yet.'

112

Rita gave her another hug.

'Just as you want, sis. It's your baby. Oh, ain't it nice to hear something cheerful for once? That's really made me feel better, that has.'

Joan felt lighter, as if someone had taken a real physical weight off her shoulders. She looked at Rita, and pitied her. It was hell having Ted away and not knowing what might happen to him, but it was better than being in Rita's situation.

'Look, I'm sorry I bit your head off that time – you know. It's easy for me to talk, because me and Ted are happy together.'

She stopped, trying to think out what she wanted to say.

'I hate to see you like this. Unhappy. Can't you . . . ain't there a way to make things better with you and Ron? I mean – I know he ain't that wonderful, but who is? There's worse husbands. And now he's in the army, can't you make a bit of an effort, like, when he comes home on leave? It wouldn't be for long, after all, and p'raps if you, like, was a bit nice to him, he'd come round a bit.'

Rita sighed.

'I expect you're right, Joanie. Well – I know you are, really. I'll try. But I tell you, it won't be easy.'

Joan squeezed her shoulders.

'It'd be worth it, Rita, I'm sure it would.'

Her sister deserved to be happy.

113

## 15

It was easier said than done. Ron was due home in just a week, and Rita was trying not to think about it. When she did, it was with something nearer to dread than pleasure. Since he had gone, she had felt as if a stifling blanket had been lifted from over her head. But there was no avoiding it, he was returning on a weekend leave. She decided to try to take Joan's advice. She must put Jack out of her head and her heart.

Once she had made the decision, she put all she had into it.

'Can't we get a bit of proper meat this Sunday, Mum?' she asked. 'A nice roast or something?'

'A roast? It'd take up half a week's coupons,' Florrie objected.

'I know, but, well, Ron does hate all this carrot and potato stuff, and they eat better in the army than what we do. He's used to that now.'

Her mother brightened up no end at this encouraging sign.

'Oh well, I'll see what we can do. I managed to get us some sausages for today and if you get us fish and chips tomorrow, perhaps there'll be enough coupons left for a hand of pork or something. I could make that last for three or four days after, with a bit of stretching. That sound all right?'

'That'd be lovely, Mum.'

Florrie nodded.

'Could make a treacle pud and all, if you like.'

At least she was back in her mother's good books again.

Next was the problem of what to wear. She had taken no trouble over clothes for ages. The navy dress she had bought that day she went shopping with Lily still hung unworn, but it was far too cold to get that out. It did not take long to realise that she had nothing smart at all. There was only one thing to be done – she raided Lily's wardrobe.

As she squeezed into a green skirt and flowery blouse that Lily had left behind, she remembered her sister bouncing downstairs wearing the very same outfit before going out on a date with Jack. She had twirled round in front of them, anxiously asking if she looked all right. They had all told her that she looked beautiful, but still she had nearly gone back upstairs to find something different. She had looked so happy that evening, getting ready to meet the man she loved. Rita tried to swallow down the guilt. It was not as if she had gone out to take Lily's man from her. She had never flirted with him, and she had always looked at her worst when she met him, in her work clothes and tired, with her hair all anyhow and her face bare of make-up. She thought of her Roman Catholic friends, doing penance for their sins. Perhaps dressing up for Ron and trying to make a go of their marriage would count as penance for the unhappiness she had caused.

Rita looked at herself in the mirror. She was slightly taller and bigger round the bust than her sister, so the skirt was a bit short and the blouse straining at the buttons. But Ron would like that. He was always staring at women's breasts. Inside her head, she could hear his voice: 'Look at that – you don't get many of them to the pound.'

She wanted to reach for her ugly work overalls. Instead she picked up her hairbrush.

By the time she finished, she knew she looked good. Her fair hair was caught up on either side of her head with combs, and turned smoothly under at the back, she had on her one decent pair of stockings, and Lily's clothes suited her. The only problem was her face. Attractive enough, adorned with powder and lipstick and carefully applied eyebrow pencil, but strained. None of the glow of expectation that Lily had worn that evening she had paraded the same blouse and skirt. Rita pulled her mouth into a smile. It lifted her features, but did not reach her eyes. She had another go.

'Hello, Ron,' she said out loud, trying to sound like a welcoming wife. 'Hello, darling, how wonderful to see you.'

She sounded like an actress in a B picture.

Of course, the train was late getting into Euston. Other trains came and went, and still she hung about, buffeted by the milling crowds and choked by billowing smoke, with the cold creeping up through her aching feet. She tried to get a cup of tea, but there was a huge queue in the buffet and the WRVS stand was for service personnel only. She walked up and down, hands thrust into her pockets, shoulders hunched against the cold, tension locking the base of her skull and throbbing through her head. The hands of the station clock jerked round with agonising slowness.

And then at last it was steaming in: Ron's train.

Doors swung open, men with kitbags stepped down, women waved and called. Rita stood in the middle of it all, straining to see through the smoke and the gloom. All the men seemed to look alike, clad in khaki and carrying their kit. She began to wonder if she had got it wrong, or if he had caught an earlier or later train. Perhaps – her spirits lifted a little –perhaps he wasn't coming at all. Then she saw him, not five yards away. He had a cigarette hanging from the corner of his mouth as he talked to the man next to him. Both of them broke into the sort of laughter that suggested the sharing of a smutty joke. She took a breath and stepped forward, acting a smile.

'Hello, Ron – ' the voice was no more convincing than when she had practised at home.

'Christ!'

Ron was genuinely astonished.

'Rita. What the hell are you doing here?'

'What do you think I'm doing? I'm meeting you.'

The other man was gaping at her.

'Blimey, Ron, who's this? Your bit on the side?'

'Nah – no such luck. It's the old woman, come to check up on us.'

'She's your wife?' He looked Rita up and down with open admiration. 'Blimey, Ron, you lucky bugger. I never knew you had it in you.'

Immediately Ron's attitude changed. His back straightened. He flung a possessive arm round Rita's shoulders.

'Yeah well, some of us have got it when it comes to women – ain't we, darling?'

He fastened an open-mouthed kiss on her. He tasted of old cigarette smoke and his teeth clashed with hers.

His friend stared at them with open envy.

'You won't be coming out on the booze tonight, then?'

'Why – ? No, no,' Ron said, correcting himself just in time. 'No – I got better things to do. Be hell to pay if I don't give her a good seeing to. Won't there, darling?'

Rita smiled and nodded, not trusting herself to speak.

The soldier gave Rita a leering grin.

'Well – best be letting you two lovebirds get on with it, then. Nice meeting you, missus. See you, mate – enjoy y'self.'

'I will,' Ron assured him.

He stood with his arm still firmly round Rita till his friend disappeared into the crowd. Then he let go of her.

'So why are you here, then, all tarted up?'

This was the Ron she remembered only too well. She shrugged.

'Why shouldn't I come and meet you? We're married, ain't we?'

'Don't you forget it, sweetheart. Come on, I'm dying for a beer.'

They made their way across London via a series of pubs. Ron managed to cadge drinks by stating loudly to anyone within hearing distance that he was on the last day of his embarkation leave. Rita could only wish it was true. They finally got home after closing time, stumbling through the blackout. The shop and the house were in darkness.

'Want a cup of cocoa?' Rita asked, trying to put off the moment of getting into bed.

'Nah. Come on upstairs.'

'I – I got to clean my teeth. And take my make-up off. I won't be a minute.'

Ron grabbed hold of her and clamped a hand over a breast. She could feel a new strength in him. Army life had made him fitter and harder.

'Stop pissing about and come upstairs.'

'I got to go out to the lav, Ron. Honest. There weren't no Ladies in that last pub. I'm busting.'

Reluctantly, he let go.

'But hurry up. I'll be waiting for you.'

She stayed in the freezing outside lavatory for as long as she could, hoping that he would fall asleep once he lay down. But she was not to be let off so lightly. When she finally went into the bedroom, the light was on and Ron was sitting up in bed in his army vest, smoking.

'About bleeding time, too. Now get undressed.'

She wished then that she had been quicker. She knew what he wanted. He wanted a slow, seductive unveiling. A small voice at the back of her mind told her that if she really wanted to be a good wife, that was what she should do. But she couldn't. Not for him. And neither was she going to let him know how much she hated having him sitting there with that expression of anticipation on his face, watching her. He knew he was unlikely to get the strip act, but he was willing to settle for enjoying her discomfort and embarrassment. So she fixed him with a defiant stare and took off her clothes in as businesslike a manner as she could manage, briskly unbuttoning the blouse and stepping out of the skirt and hanging them up neatly. She switched off the light, ignoring Ron's protests, and wriggled rapidly out of her underclothes. She knew her way about the room perfectly well in the dark. It was not difficult to snatch her warm nightie from under the pillow and slip into it before Ron knew what she was up to. Then she got into bed.

'Cold bitch.'

Ron took a last long drag at his cigarette and stubbed it out.

'If you think you're going to put me off, you got another think coming.'

Rita said nothing. They were married. She had to put up with this. Her body shrank from the feel of his hands on her flesh, but she did what women have done down the generations, and distanced her mind, her real self, from what was going on. All Ron wanted was to get inside her as soon as possible. She let him do it, and lay there while he heaved and thrust, waiting for it to be over. After what seemed like hours, he groaned and collapsed, and almost immediately fell asleep. Carefully, she eased out from under him. He grunted and mumbled, but did not wake. While he sprawled right in the middle of the bed she lay straight and still on the very edge, wide awake, not letting any part of her body touch his.

It would not be like this with Jack.

The moment she let him back into her thoughts, her body, which had stayed dead and unmoved all the while Ron had been working on it, was flooded with desire. She ached with the need to feel his arms around her, his skin touching hers. She wanted his lips, his touch, his naked flesh. She wanted not to just lie and be made love to, but to explore and enjoy him. She wrapped her arms round herself, shivering with need, hot and hollow and empty, while beside her, her husband snored.

She hated him, lying there drunk and sated. He was the ball and chain holding her down, keeping her from a love that she knew could be good and wonderful. She put her fist to her mouth to stop herself from groaning aloud, and bit hard at the knuckle of her thumb, trying to distract herself with the pain. But it did not work. She gave in, and turned over, and made love to Jack, riding the swift hot waves to the glorious release and a sweet deep sleep.

The weekend did not improve as it went on. Ron woke late and bad-tempered on Saturday morning, and was not happy to learn that he was expected to go and see his sons. Reluctantly, he went out to Dagenham with Rita to be received very frostily by Queenie. The boys had almost forgotten what he looked like, and Michael was wary of him at first, which annoyed him.

'They're turning him into a right little nancy boy,' he complained.

He put George's back up by going on about its being a real man's life in the army, and when was George going to stop hiding inside his reserved occupation shelter and join up? Rita had to grit her teeth to stop herself from reminding him that he had not gone until he was forced to. It did not help that Joan kept giving her encouraging smiles and murmuring that she was doing fine. It was a relief when Ron said he could not stay to tea as he had to get back to see some mates.

It was even more of a relief when Rita realised that she was definitely not wanted on the evening's booze-up. She stayed home and helped her mother count up the coupons, and went to bed early. This time when Ron came in he was too drunk to undress himself. Rita guided him on to the bed and pulled off his boots. By the time she had got the covers over him, he had passed out.

The joint that Florrie had bought was brought to the table Sunday dinner time, but Ron was not there to eat it. He got up late with a hangover and went round to see his mother and the rest of his family. Florrie was not pleased.

'You might of told me,' she said to Rita. 'All that fuss about a nice bit of meat, and now he's not here.'

'I didn't know what he was going to do. He don't tell me nothing,' Rita said.

'Ted wouldn't of just gone off like that, letting a good dinner go to waste.'

Rita looked at the hunk of pork, glistening with fat, and felt sick. It wasn't as if her mother liked Ron; she just wanted the pair of them to be like every other married couple. She sighed. Her good intentions for the weekend had all been for nothing.

'Look Mum, I'm sorry. I wish we was like Ted and Joanie, but we ain't. We're different people.'

'It's this war. It's changing us all,' her father said.

'Ron ain't changed. He's just the same as he always was. It's just that he's away most of the time now,' Rita said.

Suddenly she felt better. Soon he would be off again. She had tried, maybe not hard enough, but she had tried, and she had only found out what she knew all along – that she and Ron were two people who disliked each other and were tied together because of their children. But thanks to the war, she did not have to be with him day after day.

That thought carried her through the rest of the day. She packed up Ron's things for him and went along to Euston to wave him off.

'You're bleeding cheerful, ain't you? Glad to see the back of me?' Ron asked, with devastating accuracy.

'You wouldn't like it if I was crying all over the place. You hate crying women,' Rita pointed out.

'Dunno why you have to come to the station. Checking up on me all the time.'

'You wouldn't like it if I didn't come, would you? Your mate'd think we'd had a row,' Rita said.

She was doing the best for everyone – keeping up appearances for her mum, making sure the boys saw their dad, reassuring her sister that she wasn't stealing Lily's boyfriend, boosting Ron's standing in the eyes of his mates. It was only when the train had gone, and she saw the tears on the faces of the other women, that she wished there was something for herself.

# 16

Lily got off the bus at the West Ferry Road. To her amazement, everything looked just the same, except that there was a bit more bomb damage. Same boarded-up shops, same queues, same tired-looking people wearing the same drab clothes. After all the new experiences she had encountered, the places, the people, the things she had to do, she had somehow expected home would be as different as she felt. But no, the only change was that it seemed smaller, dirtier, duller than she remembered it.

She hitched up her haversack and adjusted her cap at a jaunty angle. Her air-force blue uniform now fitted her beautifully. It had taken hours of patient work to transform a too-long skirt and baggy jacket into something fit to be worn, but it had been worth the effort. If only they were allowed to wear pretty shoes . . . the clumpy lace-ups were hideous. But apart from them, she looked good enough to eat, and she knew it.

What was more, she was doing an important job. She was part of the fighting Forces. Maybe she was only a kitchen assistant, but everyone knew that an army marched on its stomach. The men couldn't fly the bombers if they weren't fed. She lifted her chin and stared with disdain at the civilians. Poor things. They didn't know what it was all about.

She turned the corner into Trinidad Street and there, to her delight, was a group of her old friends. Amongst them was Peggy Marshall. It brought it all back, seeing her there: the pain, the jealousy, the sense of betrayal. But only for a moment. The cow was going to be made to believe that she had done her a favour. Lily waved and went over to join them.

'Still here, you lot? God, you look browned off. I don't know how you stick it round here, I really don't.'

'Lily!'

'How you doing?'

'Just look at her –'

Lily struck a film-star pose.

'Good, ain't it? Men really go for a woman in uniform. You should see 'em! Blimey, the men at my station, they're just queueing up. I mean, there's nothing left round here worth having, is there? All the best ones went ages ago.'

Peggy Marshall sniffed.

'That's just the sort of thing you would say, Lily Croft.'

Lily gave a smile.

'The last dance I went to round this way, you was doing the slow quickstep with that fat girl from the baker's. When you wasn't being a wallflower, that is.'

She turned to the others.

'You should see the dances we go to! Every Saturday, there's a dance somewhere. If there ain't one on the station, then there's buses laid on to take us into town. Must be three men to every girl, and all. Even the ugly girls get them fighting for the last waltz. Even you'd be all right, Peggy.'

She could see they were trying very hard not to show their envy.

'You wouldn't catch me putting on army boots and being shouted at by some old battleaxe,' one of them said. 'Marching and that? No thank you.'

'Oh, it ain't like that at all,' Lily said, conveniently forgetting the horrors of square-bashing and being bawled out for getting out of step. 'Not for us girls. We got more important things to do than all that saluting and stuff.'

'Yeah, but ain't you got to be in at ten and that? And got to stand by your bed for inspection?'

'Oh, that's nothing. All you got to keep clean is yourself and your stuff and the bit round your bed. I mean, it ain't the same as housework, is it? And getting in and out's easy. Nothing like having your mum and dad breathing down your neck all the time. I mean, nobody goes on at you about who you're seeing and what's he like and when are you going to bring him home and what were you doing out to that time of night and what will the neighbours say, they'll think you're cheap?'

She put on a nagging voice, and the others laughed, except for Peggy. They all suffered from suspicious parents.

'You can go out with someone different every night, if you want. They're all there waiting to give a girl a really good time. Me, I don't go out with nobody under a sergeant. Wouldn't waste my time. I had to turn down four of them this weekend. There's this big dance on at the place down the road and they got the Squadronnaires playing. Then there's this lovely flight lieutenant wanted to take me to Buxton for the weekend, wherever that might be. He said it was nice, anyway. But I said, "What do you take me for? I don't go on dirty weekends, not to Buxton or Brighton or anywhere. I'm going home to see my mum and dad." He was dead disappointed.'

They couldn't hide it now. It was written plain on every face. Envy. Lily knew what their lives were like – working all hours at factories, expected to help their mothers at home, not enough coupons to buy decent clothes and not enough unattached men of the right age to go round. What was more, they knew that she knew.

But Peggy Marshall had one last weapon.

'Pay's not good though, is it?'

Lily shrugged.

'Who needs money? We get fed, we get our clothes, we got a roof over our heads. And if we want to go out, there's always a man to pay. Nothing to spend it on, really. Only magazines and lipstick and chocolate and that.'

They were defeated. Lily flashed a bright smile.

'Well, I can't stand here gossiping all day. My mum's expecting me. If I know her, she'll be in a right state. T.T.F.N.'

She bounced on up the street, leaving a disgruntled group of girls in her wake. That had told them. Now for Rita.

Her mother was behind the counter as always, serving a queue of customers in the gloom of the boarded-up shop. The place seemed even more cramped and the shelves even emptier than she remembered.

'Lily, lovey! You're back!'

'Yeah, large as life and twice as natural.'

She lifted the flap in the counter and gave her mother a hug, amidst approving noises from the customers. They didn't mind an extra wait while the family reunion went on. A child returning on leave was a big event; a daughter even more so. They smiled benevolently and shifted their weight from one foot to the other like patient workhorses.

Florrie held Lily at arm's length and studied her.

'You're looking well,' she had to admit.

'Oh, I'm fine, Mum. Never better. We get three hot meals every day and lots of exercise, and in bed every night by ten. Like being at some posh boarding-school. The girl in the next bed to me, she went to one. Ever so posh, she is. Talks with a real plum in her mouth. She says she wakes up every morning thinking she's got to go and do lessons.'

Her mum looked flabbergasted.

'Really? You got people like that with you?'

Yes, and a right bitch she was as well, but Lily knew just what to keep quiet about. Like the ones that smelt and the one who had fits and the one that got carted off with VD.

'Oh yeah, we got all sorts. Smashing, it is. And the corporal's like a second mum to us all. Clucks round like a hen she does, making sure we're all right and behaving ourselves.'

The women all nodded and muttered amongst themselves. Soon it would be all up and down the street that Lily Croft was being watched over proper and had not turned into a scrubber when she put on a uniform. That would please her mum.

Her dad came through from the back and gave her a hug and a kiss.

'Lovely to see you back, girl.' He turned to Florrie. 'I'll take over here. You go and have a cuppa with Lil.'

'But you been on night duty, Jim, you only just got up,' Florrie protested.

Jim overruled her and chased the pair of them out of the shop. Lily went into the back room and looked about. Rita did not appear to be up yet.

Florrie folded her in her arms again.

'Oh, my poor baby. How is it really? You can tell your old mum.'

'Honest, Mum, it's lovely. I love all of it.' Except the medical examinations and the discipline and the bull. 'It's like one big family. They look after you real good. And I'm really getting to

125

do my bit, you know? Releasing a man to go and fight and all that.'

'I don't know –' Florrie scanned her face anxiously. 'You're looking well on it, I got to say, but I still don't think it's right for a young girl, being in the forces –'

'Oh mum – I'm not running around with a gun, you know. I'm in the kitchens.'

'That's what your sister says. But she don't know nothing. She ain't there.'

'She's right, though.'

It went against the grain to agree with anything Rita might have said, but she did not have any option this time.

'Where is Rita, anyway? It's gone twelve. I been travelling since eight o'clock this morning. Trains are blooming awful, as usual.'

'My poor little pet. What would you like to eat? I'll put the kettle on. Rita'll be down any minute, and then we'll have some tea. We got faggots, I thought you'd like them. You want something now to keep you going?'

Lily gaped at her.

'Something to eat before a meal? Blimey, Mum, you feeling all right?'

'Well – it ain't every day my little girl comes home.'

Lily sat back and basked in the fuss and attention. She was on her second cup of tea when Rita came down. She looked haggard and tired. For a moment Lily could almost feel sorry for her. She was working nights in that awful place, stuck with that pig Ron and still living here with Mum and Dad. But then she remembered how Rita had pretended to be so sweet and kind when Jack wrote that letter, when all along she knew why he'd really given her the elbow, and how she had gone on seeing him behind everyone's backs, how she would still be doing it now if they hadn't been seen. She could never forgive Rita for that, never. For an awkward moment they just looked at each other. Then Lily got up.

'Rita! You not well? You look awful.'

'Thanks a million. You look wonderful.'

'Oh – it suits me, service life. Best thing I ever done, joining up. I wouldn't be still living here for all the tea in China.'

All though the meal, she entertained them with accounts of life in the WAAFs. Whenever the shop bell went, she jumped up and insisted on going to serve, saying that it made a nice change. Everyone who came into the shop asked how she was doing and wished her well.

'Good on you, girl. We need more like you to keep them planes flying.'

After dinner, Jim went out to see to his rabbits and Florrie returned to the shop, leaving the two girls to wash up.

'Bit of a busman's holiday, this, ain't it?' Rita said. 'You must see enough of dirty plates.'

'Oh, I don't hardly notice 'em, we have such a laugh,' Lily told her. She launched into another long tale of just how wonderful it was in the Air Force.

'. . . and the people you meet! From all over – Scotland, Wales, Ireland – and all sorts and all. We got an actress, a school-teacher, a girl whose dad's got a handle to his name, a vicar's daughter, all in our billet, as well as all us lot from shops and factories and things. Real eye-opener, it is. You learn all about what their lives are like. Talk about different! I didn't know there really was people what lived like that. Maids and cooks and that. And schooling! Do you know, two of them girls stayed at school till they was eighteen. Eighteen! And then went to college. Didn't get out till they was twenty-one. Just think, most of us down here on Dog Island, we've left school, got a job, got married and had kids by the time we're twenty-one. Makes you think, don't it?'

Rita nodded.

'Yeah.' She did not even try to disguise the longing in her voice.

Relentless, Lily drove the point home.

'You'd love it, Reet, honest you would. I mean, a clever-clogs like you'd get a better job even than working in the kitchens. Not that I don't like the kitchens, mind. It beats an outside job on a cold day. And you get around and all. Might be posted anywhere.'

She had been terrified, standing on the station with her stiff new kit and her first travel warrant and instructions to get to deepest Hampshire by six o'clock that evening. She had never done anything like that by herself before. The first train she had got on had turned out to be going the wrong way. She went fifty miles up the line before she realised her mistake. But then a bunch of infantrymen had taken her under their wing and sorted her out. Normally, she would not have looked at 'brown jobs', as the girls scathingly dismissed anything that wasn't dressed in either navy or air-force blue, but then she had been only too grateful for their help. She had finally arrived at the aerodrome at ten o'clock at night, to be put on a charge for lateness.

'Mind you, I really like it where I am, but if they post me somewhere else, well, that'll be nice and all. You know what they say, travel broadens the mind.'

'Yeah.'

'It's really pretty in Hampshire. You'd like it, Reet. All fields and cows and that, and nice little village pubs with beams holding the ceilings up. I mean, I'd be bored stiff living in the real country, but it's like the best of both worlds, 'cause we got lots of life going on at the station. The fun we have! And now the Yanks are supposed to be moving in ten miles up the road, so we're really going to see some good times.'

'Sounds lovely.'

'Oh, it is. I tell you, it's a laugh a minute. Always some fun going on, you know, like just between people, and then there's the dances and the concert parties and all that sort of thing. I don't know how I stood life in civvy street, same boring old thing day after day.'

'Some of us got to keep the supplies going, you know. Stuff I make goes into submarines.'

'Yeah, I know, but it ain't much fun, is it? Now, the other day –'

It wasn't too difficult, talking Rita into submission. The trouble was, it didn't really make her feel good. Not as good as she had anticipated, anyway. She had really been looking forward to rubbing her sister's face in the fact that she was doing all the things Rita had always wanted to do – get away from Dog Island and meet lots of different people. But coming home again had brought her face to face with the reason she

128

had gone. Much as she was genuinely enjoying her new life, she would give it all up right this minute if it meant getting Jack back.

Not that she would have admitted that for the world. She kept up the show through all the rest of Saturday and Sunday morning. Straight after Sunday dinner she had to make a start back to the aerodrome, for she only had a forty-eight-hour pass. Rita had gone to Dagenham as usual to see the children, but both her parents came to see her off at Waterloo.

'Now, you take care, Lily. Don't do nothing you wouldn't do at home,' Florrie said. There were tears in her eyes.

'Don't you worry, Mum. I'm a good girl, I am,' Lily told her, and thought of the date she had that very evening.

'I know you are, pet.'

Her mother kissed her cheek.

'Keep smiling, girl,' Jim said, embarrassed at all the emotion.

'I will, Dad. Take care of Mum for me.'

She waved out of the window at them as the train pulled away, tears catching at her throat as she saw how worn and old they looked, standing together on the platform. Then she sat back in the seat she had managed to bag and heaved a great sigh. She had shown them all what for this weekend. That Peg Marshall had had her nose put out of joint good and proper, and Rita had looked really sick at all her stories of service life.

There was a group of sailors sitting opposite her. They grinned and offered cigarettes. Automatically, she started to flirt, playing one off against the other, watching them compete for her attention. It was easy, and fun, and she never tired of doing it, but however hard she tried, however men she had after her, none of them ever measured up to Jack.

## 17

'I don't never listen to the news nowadays. Ain't nothing good on it at all. Nothing but defeats and retreats,' one of Rita's workmates said.

'There's been them thousand-bomber raids on Germany,' Rita said. She hoped Jack was not on them, on ops again.

'Yeah, but where's that got us? Ain't done nothing to stop the sods, has it? And now we even got our sweets rationed. Eight ounces a month! I ask you. That's two ounces a week. What use is that? I go to bed dreaming of chocolate.'

'I dream of my Billy,' one of the younger women said.

'I tell you, girl, sweets are better. They can't give you a baby, for a start, and the pleasure lasts longer.'

There was a howl of laughter, and the women argued the relative joys of men and chocolate.

'What d'you think, Reet? You ain't said nothing,' someone said.

'Oh – I don't get neither. I give my sweet ration to my kids and my old man's away. Not that he's much use when he's here.'

There were cries of mock sympathy. Someone mimed playing a violin.

'You poor old thing. Not much in your life, is there?'

'Get away. She's got a secret boyfriend. RAF bloke.'

'You ain't! Tell us.'

' 'Course I ain't. What d'you take me for? That was my sister's boyfriend that time, come to ask me to patch up a row.'

Rita was saved from further interrogation by the end of the tea break. Grumbling, the women dispersed to their various machines. It was one in the morning and there was a long time to go before the end of the shift. There wasn't even much of a chance of an air raid to break the monotony. London had been left alone lately in favour of the smaller and prettier historic cities. Not that Rita wished for the bombs to come back, but at least they did interrupt the deadly routine of the shift. She perched on her stool and picked up the first component. She had been promoted to a more skilled operation, which required careful setting and accurate fixing, but when it came down to it, she was still doing the same process time after time. In fact, in many ways it was worse than the unskilled work, as it was just as boring but needed far more concentration.

The words of her workmate echoed in her head as she assembled the various fiddly pieces: 'Not much in your life, is there?'

There was plenty in her life. She might hate this job, but it was bringing in good money and she was doing her bit. She had her trips to the pictures to look forward to, and most of all she had her children. A lot of her spare time was spent searching for something to buy them for Christmas. It was three months away yet, but she had started looking now because toys seemed to have vanished from the shops. It wasn't so bad for girls. Dolls could be made out of scraps of wool and fabric. But what she dearly wanted was a tricycle for Peter and Michael. Just one would do, and they could share it, even if it would mean squabbles. If they had something like that from her, to play with every day, they wouldn't forget her. She wanted to get something nice for Joan's children too. Joan would appreciate that far more than something for herself, and Joan deserved a treat. She had only heard twice from Ted since he reached Burma, and worried constantly about him. It was always the nice ones who got sent into danger. Ron had got himself a cushy number in an anti-aircraft unit in Sunderland.

Ron. At least he was a good long way away. With the trains as bad as they were, he did not bother coming home on his forty-eight-hour passes. But he had been back on a week's leave recently, and it had been the usual routine, but with one new angle: he was no longer happy to have her lie torpid in bed, he expected her to react to him, to do things to him.

'You're not a proper woman at all, you're like a bloody dummy,' he complained. 'Other women like to give a man a bit of fun, they know what they're doing. You – you're enough to freeze the balls off of me.'

'So what do you know about other women?' Rita challenged.

'Plenty, darling. Them ATS girls, they're all hot for it. Quiet night out at the ack-ack post, and they're all at it. Can't wait for it, they can't.'

If he meant to make her jealous, he failed.

'Why don't you stay up there with them, then?' Rita asked.

'What, and leave you to do what you bleeding well like? Oh no. You're married to me, darling, and you got to be a proper wife.'

What with him coming home and expecting her to be exciting in bed, and Lily turning up with her tales of fun and freedom and companionship in the WAAFs, she was learning to dread visits from her family. She knew that Lily was also trying to make her jealous. The difference was that Lily succeeded. Rita would have given almost anything to follow her into the Forces. Anything but her weekly visits to the children. So here she was, still putting together bits of metal night after night. There seemed to be no end to it all.

There was a flurry of movement about her. Then she realised that the alarm bells were ringing. It took a moment or two for it to sink in.

'Come on,' the woman next to her on the bench said. 'It's a raid.'

Rita deliberately finished the bit she was doing, then reached for her bag and gas-mask case and joined the crush of people heading for the basement.

'Thought them bleeders was leaving us alone for a bit,' someone in front of her said.

'That's what they want us to think, mate. Then they can catch us napping.'

'London's too important to leave alone. Specially after what we been doing to them German cities.'

'God, I wish I had a fag. Anyone got a fag? I can't face that flaming basement without one.'

'Here –' Rita said, taking one out of her bag. She had been saving a packet for her father, but this seemed a more pressing need. She wondered if he was all right. He was on duty tonight, and her mother would be alone in the house. She had given up going to the tube each night since the worst of the raids had ceased. Perhaps she ought to give up this job and go back to day work now that she didn't have to face Ron every night.

Down in the basement, people were settling into the usual routine. The gramophone was wound up and Vera Lynn put on the turntable. Card schools started up; knitting came out. Everyone tried to mask the underlying tension.

'Here, what's this?' someone asked Rita, seeing the matinée jacket she was knitting. 'Little stranger on the way?'

'Not mine, my sister's. She's due next month,' Rita explained.

She tried to concentrate on the stitches, an intricate lacy pattern. She wanted this to be really pretty for Joan's baby. Beneath her, the ground shook. The bombs were getting near. The basement was not like being down in the Underground: you could still feel and hear the raid going on. She looked up at the ceiling. Above them were hundreds of tons of metal machinery The woman next to her read her thoughts.

'Don't worry, mate. If it ain't got our name on it, we're all right.'

The words were hardly out of her mouth when there was a tremendous crash and all the lights went out. Gasps and screams came from thick darkness. Dirt showered down from the ceiling. Rita felt for her knitting bag and put the little jacket away. She wasn't going to let all that careful work and precious wool get spoilt.

'It's all right, it ain't us,' she said loudly. She almost wished she was up on the roof. At least out there she would be doing something, not just sitting here hoping.

The whole world was rent with a deafening explosion. The floor shuddered and the building above them shifted on its foundations. For a long moment, everyone held their breath. Rita felt a hand groping for hers and held on to it with feverish strength. Then came the sound they had been dreading: the unmistakable roar of a collapsing building. Instinctively, Rita curled up and clasped her arms round her head. Her scream was choked by falling dust as the ceiling splintered and cracked. The sound went on and on, falling bricks, splitting timber, sliding machinery. Her head was filled with it and her mouth and throat and lungs were filled with dirt. There was nothing but noise and dark and suffocation.

Slowly, she became aware that it had ceased. She was confused. It was totally black around her: she hardly knew whether her eyes were open or closed, whether she was sighted or blind. Her face was pressed against the concrete floor. Every time she tried to breathe, she took in more dirt. Coughing only made it worse. For a long time she just concentrated on getting air inside her. As the ringing in her ears subsided, she started to tune into the noises around her. Coughing, moaning, groans. So other people were still alive. She tried out her voice. At first nothing came out, then she managed a croak, then a word, the name of the woman next to her who had asked about the knitting. A long time ago now, it seemed. A different life. There was no answer.

'Marge?' she said again, a bit louder.

'Who's that?'

The reply came from somewhere behind her. It was not Marge, but never in her life had she been so glad to hear a human voice.

'Oh thank God. It's Rita. Who are you?'

'May. You hurt?'

'I don't know.'

She tried moving her fingers and toes. They all seemed to be working. She was bruised and shaken, but not in any unbearable pain. With a sense of wonder, she realised that she might well have been lucky. Sudden tears came to her eyes and ran down her face. She was still in one piece.

'What's up?' came May's voice.

'Nothing. I'm all right. I can't believe it. You?'

'I can't move my legs. Can't even feel them.'

'Oh God.'

Rita stretched slowly out, feeling around her. Less than an arm's length in front of her was a piece of metal. By the complicated surface of it, she guessed it was one of the machines. Then her fingers met flesh. A hand. Marge's hand? It was warm, but totally lifeless. With a gasp of revulsion that set her off coughing, she recoiled from it.

'What is it?' May asked.

'Nothing.'

134

She tried feeling upwards. About a foot above her was a thick wooden beam. Behind her was empty space. She attempted to turn over, but moving only brought more showers of dirt down on her. May was coughing and rasping. She fought down a sense of panic.

'They'll get us out,' she said. 'The heavy mob. They'll be here soon. We just got to hang on.'

'Yeah,' May whispered.

Rita lost all sense of time. It seemed that there was nothing but this small precarious cell of safety beneath the hundreds of tons of timber, masonry and machines. She did not dare move. Her body became cold and cramped as dust-filled air grew stale. Her breath came in shallow pants. May stopped speaking to her. She was all alone.

Then there was movement around her. Bricks slipped and fell. One hit her head and she howled with fear and pain. This was it, she was going to be buried. She thought of Peter and Michael, of their bright faces and soft bodies and the feel of their strong little arms around her.

A rush of air hit her face, cold and damp and smelling of outside. More bricks fell, dust mixed with the air, and there were voices somewhere above her, voices shouting out: 'Is there anyone there? Call out if you can.'

Rescue. She could hardly believe it. She tried to call back, but at first nothing would come out. Then she managed a thin cry.

'Yes, yes. Here. I'm down here.'

She sobbed with relief.

'Hold on, love. We're coming to get you.'

She lay listening to the voices.

'Careful, that's about to go.'

'Can't get through here.'

'Over here, quick, help me with this –'

'Ready? Heave!'

Rita covered her head with her arms again. Rubble was tumbling down now. She could feel the weight of it on her shoulders, her legs. Far from getting her out, they seemed to be burying her.

'No, no –' she cried, but they took no notice.

A torch pierced the darkness, blinding her with its light.

'Here, she's here!' someone shouted.

Hands reached down, pulling the rubble away, reaching out to her. She was dragged from under the beam, eased up through the jagged hole.

'That's it, girl. We got you.'

'Put your arm round my neck. That's it. Can you walk? Over here.'

Dazed, she let herself be taken over. A blanket was wrapped round her, she was sat down in a lighted room and a mug of hot sweet tea was put into her hands. She was alive. Alive, and free from the suffocating dark.

'There'll be another ambulance along in a minute, dear. They just taken the last lot to the Royal London.'

Outside, there were sharp shouts of warning.

'Get back, get back, it's going to go!'

That unmistakable roar again. Rita screamed and dropped her tea. What was still standing of the factory collapsed, burying Marge and May and most of the others under it. But Rita had escaped.

## 18

It was no use staying in bed, so Rita got up and came downstairs. Her mother was in the kitchen stirring the porridge. She took one look at Rita's pale face and hurried to pour her a cup of tea.

'How did you sleep, lovey?'

'Oh – not too bad,' Rita lied. 'I think I'll go down the labour exchange this morning and see what's going.'

Florrie looked worried.

'Why don't you take a few days off, lovey? You could do with a break. You was buried under a building, after all.'

'I'm all right, Mum, honest. I'm alive, ain't I?'

Not dead beneath the ruins, cold and crushed. There would be no more joking and gossiping for most of her workmates, no more moaning about the foreman or skiving off for a quick fag in the lavs. Rita could not bear to think of their husbands and parents and kids, of their grief, of the gaps left in their lives. It was too painful, when here she was, with nothing but cuts and bruises to show for her miraculous escape. There was so much loss; if you let it into your head, it could overwhelm you.

'I don't want to hang about, I want to get back to work. One thing with this war, you know there's plenty of jobs going,' she said.

The moment she was inactive it all came back to her, the dark and the fear and feeling that at any minute she was going to be crushed or suffocated to death. Her dreams were haunted with it. She needed to keep busy so that it did not swallow up her days.

It was going to have to be another factory job. There were lots of women from posh offices in factories now, doing their bit for production, so someone like her wasn't going to get anything different. But she did wish she could get something a bit more interesting, not just fixing the same things together a few hundred times a day, every day. Before she married Ron, she had started to learn the stock control and ordering side of the store she worked in. The manager had said she was the quickest trainee he had ever worked with, and she had enjoyed the challenge and the responsibility. She had not had to do anything since that needed the use of her brain like that, and she did miss it. She was sure that she could take on something similar now, but had nothing to actually prove she could do it.

The labour exchange gave her two addresses, both in the East End. She decided to go to the nearest one first, and got off the bus in Whitechapel. A passer-by gave her directions, but she had only gone fifty yards when the name on a side street caught her eye: Prittlestone Road. Her heart turned over. She had burnt the piece of paper, but the words stayed clear and sharp in her mind. 53 Prittlestone Road, Whitechapel. Jack's home. Her feet took her down it of their own accord.

It was a street of mixed houses and workshops, and like nearly every other street in the East End, it had had its share of bombs. As she noted the numbers, Rita's heart beat faster and her mouth went dry. She looked ahead, working out which one Jack's family must live in, and realised with a jolt that it must be where there was recent damage. Just about halfway down the street there was a gap where buildings had been demolished, then a small factory with wooden buttresses against the walls to shore it up and tarpaulin over the roof. Outside, a bent old man was adding to a great heap of broken pieces of furniture and a woman was leaning on a broom, talking to a man up a ladder who was tying down the tarpaulin. Leaning against the wall was the remains of a sign: *Wilkinsons, Manufacturers of Fine* – the missing word could only be *Furniture*. That was it. Those must be his parents. With her stomach tying itself in excruciating knots, Rita crossed the street.

'Hello,' she said to the woman, 'got caught in the last lot, did you?'

Mrs Wilkinson glared at the sad heap of splintered chairs, tables and sideboards. She was a tall woman with a strong-featured face, still handsome despite the effects of time. Rita could see where Jack had got his looks. 'Those Germans – they occupied my father's homeland and now they've got us. We thought we'd got away with it. Went all through last winter with only a few slates off the roof and the windows gone, and now this.'

Rita nodded.

'We all thought they'd gone off to give it to someone else, didn't we? I was caught in it and all. Place where I worked came down on top of us. There was thirty-two killed, and a lot more injured.'

Despite herself, she found her voice shaking. She fought to control it.

'I heard about that –' Mrs Wilkinson was staring at her. 'I know you, don't I? – no it ain't. She was younger. It's funny, you look just like a girl my son was going out with a while back.'

Rita swallowed. She was caught now. No point in denying it. She tried to sound normal.

'That must of been my sister, Lily.'

'Lily! That's it. Lily Croft. Pretty little thing.'

There was a slight reservation in her voice.

'Well I never. Small world, ain't it? So you're Lily's sister? And your factory was in that raid as well. You wasn't in it when it went down, was you?'

The rushing noise of the collapsing building roared in her ears. It was all around her, on top of her, burying her. From a long way away, it seemed, a concerned voice was speaking, but it was totally unconnected with what was going on.

'You all right, dear? What's the matter? Here, Wally, bring a chair, quick –' A heavy weight bore down on her shoulders.

And then she was sitting down, and the noise reduced, and the voice made sense.

'There, that better? More yourself now?'

Rita found herself on a chair on the pavement, with Mr Wilkinson peering anxiously at her. The weight on her shoulders was not a falling beam, but Mrs Wilkinson's arm. She felt acutely embarrassed.

'Oh, I'm sorry – I don't know what came over me. I'm not usually like this.'

'That's all right, dear. It's shock. It gets different people in different ways.'

Mr Wilkinson nodded gravely.

'Nasty business. It was only the night before last and all, weren't it? Takes a bit to get over something like that.'

'But I was one of the lucky ones. A lot of my mates never made it,' Rita said.

She found herself telling the Wilkinsons all about it. They listened and made sympathetic noises and let her talk herself out. Finally, Mrs Wilkinson squeezed her shoulder.

'Must of been terrifying. Me, I really dread that, I do, being trapped. I think I'd go mad if that happened to me. The noise is bad enough. We was down at the street shelter when this went. The bang! I said to Bill – that's my husband, Bill – I said, "That's our place gone, I'm sure it is." He said it weren't, and I suppose he was right, 'cause it was next door's, but it's bad enough.'

Rita found she was almost herself again, able to hold something like a normal conversation.

'Can you carry on?' she asked, looking up at the building. It was in a fairly bad state, but she had seen plenty worse.

'Carry on? Of course we'll carry on. We'll be getting back to work this afternoon, mending the stuff what can be mended. This business has been in Bill's family for three generations. We're not going to give in now. We had to fight to stop the government from closing us down. "Non-essential," that's what they said we was. Non-essential, when there's people bombed out of their homes with not a stick of furniture, crying out for anything they can get! But we kept going when others was closed down, so we're not giving in now. Mind you, it's difficult. We used to have four skilled cabinetmakers and half a dozen apprentices working here. Now there's just my Billy and Wally –' she nodded at the old man, who was bringing out another mangled chair. 'All been called up, you see, or redirected into firms what They think are essential. And the paperwork! I can't make head nor tail of it. Poor Bill here, he struggles with it, all them regulations, and it takes all the time he ought to be making stuff. Now my son, he's the one with the brains, he'd make short work of it, but he's in the RAF –'

Rita caught her breath.

'Yeah, I –' she began, but Mr Wilkinson chimed in, his face glowing with pride.

'Yeah, he's a clever lad, our Jack. He'd find his way through all this blooming red tape we got these days. Seems like you have to fill in a dozen forms to buy a plank of wood, let alone get hold of a new blade for a spokeshave. But there, he's training new navigators, he is. That's a very responsible job.'

'Oh, it is,' Rita agreed.

Mr Wilkinson looked at his wife.

'What about a cuppa tea, girl? I reckon the young lady could do with one and all.'

'Oh no, I couldn't –' Rita protested. 'I gone and taken up too much of your time.'

'We was going to have one anyway,' Mrs Wilkinson assured her. 'Come on in. It's nice to talk to someone what knows our Jack. Did you see a lot of him?'

She just could not refuse an offer like that. Five minutes later she was sitting at a salvaged table in a corner of the factory, drinking tea and listening to Mrs Wilkinson's fond reminiscences of her son. She felt she had never met such welcoming and friendly people; it was as if she had found a second home. It was a shock when she realised the tea break was over and the Wilkinsons and Wally were about to get back to their task of clearing up.

'Look, you've been so kind. You must let me help you,' she declared.

The Wilkinsons both protested, but Rita insisted.

'After all, I am a sort of friend of the family. Your Jack was the nicest bloke my sister ever went out with. I was really sorry when they broke up.'

It all came out quite glibly. She could hardly believe she was saying it, but desperation aided her. She had to stay here, in his home, just a little longer.

'Well –' Mr Wilkinson said.

'You done me a real favour. You got to let me pay you back.' She turned to Mrs Wilkinson. 'If you could give me a lend of a headscarf and an apron. I'm a really good clearer-upper. And I'd enjoy it, honest I would. It'd . . . help me take my mind off of things.'

At this hint that they could be helping her by letting her stay, they gave in. While Mr Wilkinson and Wally sorted the furniture into what could be repaired, what could be cannibalised and what was beyond hope, Rita and Mrs Wilkinson swept, cleaned and put everything to rights. By dinner time, it was looking quite orderly.

'I reckon you could start on the repair work this afternoon,' Mrs Wilkinson said.

Her husband looked gloomily towards the little partitioned-off corner that served as an office.

'There's all them papers and stuff to see to yet.'

Rita took a deep breath.

'I could do that for you. I like doing that sort of thing.'

'Oh no, you done more than enough already,' Mrs Wilkinson said.

'I couldn't put all that on you,' Mr Wilkinson told her, but without much conviction. It did not take too much persuasion to get him to at least let her have a try.

'If you're staying, then you better have dinner with us. And before you say no, don't worry, it ain't much, in fact it's just sandwiches, so you come along and share them with us,' Mrs Wilkinson insisted.

Rita willingly gave in.

After a cheerful dinner of spam sandwiches, she settled herself in the office cubbyhole. Mr Wilkinson showed her the various books and papers, and left her to look through them.

'It's all a bit of a muddle, I'm afraid. The blast caught it and there was stuff all over the place, all mixed up with the timber and whatnot. I sorted some of it yesterday, but it needs putting to rights. Just see what you can do.'

He left her to it with a palpable air of relief. While she blew dust off receipts, invoices, dockets and pattern books and put them into piles, she could hear him chatting away to Wally, who seemed to be a man of few words. Mr Wilkinson was an optimist, predicting that they would soon get the firm back on its feet again, but Wally's answer to nearly everything was, 'I doubt it.' Every now and again, Mr Wilkinson would call over to her: 'All right there?'

Each time she assured him that she was fine, then took the

opportunity to ask about some mysterious piece of paper. Often, it seemed, it was totally irrelevant or out of date. She rapidly came to the conclusion that the office had been gathering waste paper ever since Jack left.

By six o'clock, her head was throbbing.

'How've you done?' Mr Wilkinson asked.

'I think I'm getting to grips with it,' Rita said, with a massive stretching of the truth. 'It's looking a lot tidier in here, anyhow.'

'You're right there, girl. Wouldn't hardly of known the place. Can't tell you how grateful I am.'

Mrs Wilkinson, who had come in to see how things were going, looked at the neat piles of paper with admiration.

'You'd almost think Jack was back again.'

Rita took a steadying breath. A dizzying opportunity might just be within reach. Without stopping to consider the consequences, she tried to grasp it.

'I could take over your office work. I'm out of a job.'

'Really?'

'I thought you said you was doing factory work, dear?' Mrs Wilkinson said.

'Oh, everyone's doing factory work these days, ain't they? I know what it's like dealing with government bumph, I do all the forms and things for my mum's shop.'

This wasn't strictly true, since Florrie jealously guarded everything to do with her kingdom, but Rita was familiar with it all. She went on to exaggerate her West End job. By the time she had finished, it sounded as if she was a fully experienced secretary and bookkeeper.

'Well, you done a first-rate job in here this afternoon, and I could certainly do with someone like you. But you'd no sooner get to know the ropes than They'd be sending you off somewhere, surely? Munitions or the women's forces or something,' Mr Wilkinson said.

'No – I'm married and got two little kids. I'm non-directable. I'm working 'cause I need the money and I want to do my bit. My other sister looks after the children.'

'Well – it'd be a godsend. I hate all that side of the business. I'm no pen-pusher. Cabinet-making is what I'm good at. Feeling the timber shaping in my hands. Our Jack was doing all the business side until the war started.'

'Why not give me a month's trial?' Rita suggested.

Mr Wilkinson tried to hold out.

'I can't pay you as much as what you'd of been getting piece rate on night shift.'

'It'll be worth it to see the daylight again,' Rita assured him.

He capitulated.

'You're on. Welcome to the firm.' He held out his hand, and they shook on it. 'Eight o'clock tomorrow, then, bright and early?'

'Eight o'clock it is,' Rita agreed.

As she walked home, her feet hardly seemed to touch the ground.

## 19

Lily sat on her bed and stared at the letters. So it was true. She had known it all along, really. What with Rita being so close about it all, and Mum reacting like she did, it had been obvious. But she had been forced into pretending it was all just gossip. If she was honest, it had not just been because of Mum and her need to keep up a respectable front in the street. Her own pride had demanded it as well. She needed to show that Peg Marshall that she wasn't even touched by her words, and she needed to keep at bay the thought that Jack – wonderful, handsome Jack – should prefer her over-the-hill sister to herself. He had ditched her because he might get shot down at any time. If he had gone to meet Rita – and sometimes she had to admit the possibility that he might just have done – then it was just to ask after her, because he still loved her. That she could live with.

But now this. Rita's usual weekly report on all the little family doings had not come last week, which had worried Lily vaguely when she had time to think about it. So she had been pleased when this belated one had arrived this morning. The lapse was explained. Rita had been bombed. Lily shivered. She might hate her sister at times, but family ties were too strong to overcome. The thought that Rita had come close to death shook her. Then, almost as an afterthought, the mention of her new job. At Wilkinson's.

All around her there was the flurry of girls getting ready for the dance.

'These horrible stockings. If only we were allowed to wear silk –'

'It ain't fair. The Wrens are allowed to wear their own clothes off-duty.'

'Anyone got my lipstick?'

'My hair looks awful, it's all sticking out.'

Lily hardly noticed. She was too preoccupied with her own thoughts and feelings.

Someone stopped by her bed.

'Come on, Lil, buck up. It's half-past already.'

It was Betty, her best friend, a solid girl with freckles, the youngest of six children of a farm labouring family in Somerset.

'All right, all right,' Lily said, but still she did not move.

Betty plumped down beside her.

'You're not still upset about that, are you?'

'Betty, she's my sister, for God's sake! What does she think she's doing, working for his dad? It must be so as she can meet him when he comes home on leave. He was my boyfriend, mine! I loved him. I still do . . .' a wave of longing rose up to choke her. If she could just see him again.

'What's in the other letter?' Betty asked.

Lily glanced at it and shrugged. It was from her mother.

'I dunno, I ain't opened it. It'll only say the same.'

'Go on, open it now.'

With a sigh of impatience, Lily did so. To her surprise, it did not say anything about Rita or the Wilkinsons. It was a short note to tell her that Joan had had her baby. A boy, seven pounds two ounces, named Edward for his absent father. Mother and child were both doing well.

'Oh – en't that nice?' Betty's gentle West Country voice was soft with pleasure. She loved babies. When she got married, she wanted at least four, she said.

Lily supposed it was nice. She was pleased for Joan, it was what she wanted, but somehow the news could not touch her. She never could see what all the fuss was about babies. And it was all so distant, somehow. What mattered was Rita, going every day to Jack's place, getting in with his parents.

'Look, it's no good sitting here like this,' Betty said. 'Won't do you no good at all. There's a dance on this evening. That nice bloke of yours'll be there. You better start doing yourself up. You en't going to let her get the better of you, are you?'

No, she wasn't. That was why she had joined up: to get back at Rita. The murderous rage she had felt then flared up anew, burning any other emotions in its path. She would find some way to get even with Rita if it killed her. In the mean time she was

146

going to the dance and she was going to have a good time. Better than Rita was having, for a start.

'Too right, mate,' she said, and set off for the bathroom.

The place she was billeted at would knock Rita's eyes out. She had written home about it at length. No more Nissen huts. This was a stately home. The room she shared with eleven others had been the blue drawing room. The furniture and carpets had been taken away and replaced by two rows of iron bedsteads and cheap wooden lockers, but the walls were still covered with blue watered silk, the fireplace was still marble and when the girls lay in bed and thought about their boyfriends they could gaze up at a wonderful ceiling of painted moulded plaster. As Betty said, it was grander than the Odeon.

Lily washed swiftly in lukewarm water, changed into a freshly ironed shirt and newly brushed skirt and turned her attention to her face and hair. In less than thirty minutes she looked better than most of the girls who had been titivating for two hours or more. Betty looked at her with undisguised envy.

'You look smashing.'

'So do you,' Lily responded. It was true enough. Betty had a wholesome appeal and a dimpled smile. But Lily's blonde shapeliness put her in the shade.

From downstairs came the sounds of a three-piece band tuning up. The dance was right here in the ballroom of the house. Lily felt the familiar bubbles of excitement gathering in her stomach. She adored dancing. It was absolutely her favourite thing. And to think that she, Lily Croft from the Isle of Dogs, was living in a house giving its own dance in its own ballroom. A year ago she would never have believed it.

Nobody wanted to be down first. There was a lot of hanging about and last-minute preparations, while the noise level grew higher and higher with the excitement. The little Welsh girl went to hang over the banisters and find out what was going on. She came haring back.

'The lorries have arrived from the camp. They're all coming in,' she shrieked.

The milling about stopped. They all set off in a group, down the wide oak staircase with its shallow steps, across the panelled hall where contingents of servicemen coming in were eyed up and assessed, through the gracious red drawing room to where the double doors were thrown open to the ballroom.

Lily caught her breath. It was only another wartime hop, with one barrel of watered-down beer, an indifferent combo of piano, drums and sax, scarcely any heat coming from the fire and everyone dressed in grey-blue or khaki. But what a setting! The cream and gold room looked like something out of a fairytale, and though there were no balloons or ribbons or fresh flowers, the armfuls of greenery that the girls had brought in from the grounds during the day looked wonderful under the sparkling light from the chandelier. The anger and bitterness began to dissolve. Lily was going to enjoy herself.

It was the usual early evening set-up. A few established couples were dancing a quickstep, but most of the men were gathered round the beer at one end of the room, while the woman stood in small knots or sat on chairs round the edges. Both camps sized each other up and made remarks to their pals.

Lily took a swift look round. Her current boyfriend, Joe, a flight sergeant, was not here yet. She did not want him to find her waiting around for him when he arrived. She stationed herself and Betty where they could be clearly seen and chatted animately while affecting not to even know that there were potential partners in the room. She knew it wouldn't take long. Men always noticed her. Her confidence was justified. By the time the next number started, a presentable fitter was asking for the pleasure, and what was more, he had dragged a friend along for Betty. It worked like a dream. Once they were on the floor, they were marked out as girls worth dancing with, and both of them had another partner lined up the moment the tune was over. Lily was foxtrotting round the room with great enjoyment when Joe appeared. She pretended she had not seen him for a couple of circuits, then gave him a casual flutter of the fingers over her partner's shoulder. He looked satisfyingly put out.

'Having fun?' he asked, as the foxtrot finished.

Lily sparkled at him.

'Yes thanks. Smashing dance, ain't it?'

'I dunno yet.'

148

'I just love this place. It's like I'm Cinderella or something. Bit of a change from a canteen or a village hall, ain't it?'

He had to admit that it was.

'Just fancy coming to a do here before the war. All ball gowns and that. Must of been lovely. I fancy ice blue and silver. Satin. All clingy, like.'

Joe looked at her with undisguised lust as this picture took hold of his imagination.

'You'd look a knock-out like that. You look smashing now.'

Lily smiled and patted her shining hair.

'We girls do make an effort for you flying heroes, you know.'

'Glad to hear it. D'you want to dance?'

Lily shrugged.

'Might as well.'

It was a waltz. Joe was a good dancer, leading firmly and steering her past other couples with ease. As they glided round the floor in perfect unison, Lily knew they made a striking pair, with her blonde prettiness and his dark good looks. If he was just a couple of inches taller, and broader across the shoulders, she could almost imagine she was with Jack . . . She tried to push the thought away. Joe was here and Jack was not. Joe was crazy about her.

Her first partner was hanging about waiting for her.

'Sorry, mate, she's spoken for,' Joe said.

Lily feigned indignation as the disappointed fitter walked off.

'Who says I'm spoken for?'

'Me.'

'Huh. I'm not your property, y'know.'

Joe took her in a close dance hold.

'We'll see about that,' he said.

The evening was beginning to warm up, both in temperature and in atmosphere. With the room packed with young people intent on forgetting the war and having a good time while they could, the dance could not fail. There were more men than women, so the plainest girl was sure of a string of partners, and even the out-of-tune piano and inept sax player did not matter, so long as they played everyone's favourites. Lily sang happily along with the words.

149

'Not much cop, are they?' Joe said, jerking his head at the trio.

'They're not the Powers Girls, that's for sure,' Lily agreed. 'Did I ever tell you Poppy Powers come from down our street?'

'Lots of times. But you can tell me again,' Joe said.

'It ain't everyone has a famous dance-band leader used to live down their street, you know. Not that you can see where she used to live now. Her gran's old place went on the first night of the Blitz.'

'Shame.'

They quickstepped and foxtrotted and tangoed till both of them were red-faced and sweating. The floor was packed now and the cheerful noise increased by the minute.

'I'm parched. Fancy a drink?' Joe asked.

'Please.'

The beer was being sold as lemonade shandies, to make it go further. The men complained, but accepted it. They were lucky to get even that. Some dances were tea and biscuits only, but were still worth going to just for the chance of a night out.

Lily drank a lemonade and thanked her lucky stars she was not on duty. Instead of being out here dancing, she could have been sweating away behind the scenes washing glasses. She spotted Betty tangoing with a skinny aircraftsman. Her friend had a happy smile on her round face and was putting her all into the passionate dance. Lily was pleased for her. She was all right, was Betty. She had shown her the ropes when she first arrived and stuck up for her against one or two of the cattier ones. It was nice to have a real pal.

Joe drained his glass.

'Fancy a breath of fresh air?'

In other words, a snog in the dark. Lily wasn't ready for that yet.

'No thanks.'

'Oh come on, Lily. Give a bloke a chance.'

'No, I don't want to.'

'Just for a bit. Just five minutes.'

'Oh yeah, I know what that means.'

A prolonged squabble got Joe nowhere.

'I come here to dance,' Lily said and just to really annoy him, went off with someone else. She could see Joe glowering as she quickstepped round the floor.

The evening went on its predictable course. After half-time it got steadily rowdier, with a Paul Jones and then a burst of 'Knees up Mother Brown', then as the pairs sorted themselves out, the more romantic numbers were played and couples danced closer and closer. Lily allowed Joe to make it up with her, and a few numbers before the end, finally agreed to slip out.

'No need to go right outside. It's too blooming cold,' she said. 'There's loads of places in this house.'

Plenty of other people had the same idea. Most of the rooms were locked, upstairs was out of bounds and practically every corner of the winding passageways seemed to be occupied by couples in passionate embraces. Lily and Joe finally found some privacy in what used to be the housekeeper's room.

'Oh Lily, you're just so gorgeous you drive me mad,' Joe said, wrapping his arms round her.

Lily closed her eyes and let his lips find hers. She liked him kissing her. He was a good kisser, not all teeth like some, and he made her feel all hot and fizzy inside. She held him tight and kissed him back, feeling her power over him as his breathing got thicker and more urgent. His hand found her breast, caressing with a gentle insistence that had her purring with pleasure.

Joe backed her against the wall and leaned against her.

'Lily – darling – I think of you all the time. I can't get you out of my mind. I love you, Lily –'

'Oh Joe . . .'

This time when she kissed him she daringly used her tongue, and heard him groan in pleasure and frustration. She could feel how hard he was through the thick layers of both their service uniforms. He moved his hips against hers, and she could feel herself going weak and dreamy. Then his hand slipped down her leg and started pulling her skirt up. Abruptly, she closed her hand round his wrist.

'Stop it.'

'Lily – please, Lily, I want you so much I could die –'

'No, Joe. I'm not that sort of girl.'

'But I love you, Lily. I want to marry you.'

'You mean you want to do it with me.'

'No! Well – I do, but I want to marry you. You're the most wonderfullest girl I ever met. I mean it, Lily, honest. Look –'

In the darkness, she could feel him moving. He was kneeling, he was actually on his knees in front of her. He caught hold of her hands.

'Please Lily, will you marry me?'

'Oh Joe –' she didn't know whether to laugh or cry. For when it came to it, she knew just what the answer was.

'You're very sweet. I like you very much –'

'*Like?*'

'But it's just . . .' she stopped, not knowing what to say. He was not Jack, that was what it was. He was nice and good-looking and a good dancer, but he wasn't Jack, and nothing less than Jack would do.

'Just what?' Joe demanded.

'I – I don't love you.'

'I see.'

Joe stood up. His voice was tight with anger.

'You were hot enough a moment ago.'

'Don't talk filthy.'

'I'm talking the truth. Truth hurts, don't it? You know what you are, Lily Croft? You're just a tease. A cheap little tease!'

He stumbled to the door and slammed his way out. Lily slumped against the wall, her heart thumping, listening to his angry footsteps retreating. Tears ached in her throat, welled up in her eyes and ran down her cheeks, but she was crying not for Joe, but for Jack.

'. . . and that's us at Brighton in '29. That monkey nearly bit Jack. Nasty little creatures. I don't trust 'em, but Jack, he wanted to hold it. Probably covered in fleas and all . . .'

'You boring poor Rita with them photos again?' Mr Wilkinson asked.

'I'm not bored, honest,' Rita protested. Mrs Wilkinson could hardly have found a more willing audience for her family recollections.

It was tea-break time at the factory. Mr and Mrs Wilkinson, old Wally and Rita sat on a set of chairs ready to go out, and took a well-earned rest. Rita looked around her. After just three weeks, the place was home to her, and the Wilkinsons a second family. She would have loved the job even if she had no emotional connection with it. She had the office sorted out and even had time to spare, in which she was employed as a sort of honorary apprentice, sharing the unskilled work with Mrs Wilkinson. There were huge problems getting anything like the amount of timber that they needed, and both women spent a lot of time coping with potential customers desperate for furniture and possessing all the necessary dockets. Every piece they produced could have been sold six times over. Understanding the endless government regulations was frustrating work, but the reward of seeing the point of something or, better still, thinking of a way round it was tremendous. Balancing the books at the end of each week gave her headaches. She went to the library and borrowed a battered old textbook on the intricacies of double-entry bookkeeping, spending her evenings frowning over it and working the examples until she had got the hang of it. After that, the worst job was much less of a nightmare.

Mr Wilkinson was more than happy with her work.

'Good day for us, when you happened along,' he said.

'He's at his best when he's making. He's not a clerk,' Mrs Wilkinson said.

Only Wally kept up a wall of disapproval, but Rita had learnt that this was not anything personal. He just hated all change. The war had brought too many changes, all for the worse as far as Wally was concerned. The no-nonsense Utility furniture he was forced to make was bad enough, but employing women to do even the lowliest part of a skilled craftsman's job was beyond the pale.

'. . . that was a lovely holiday, that was,' Mrs Wilkinson was saying, smiling over the photograph.

Rita took it from her and studied the picture. Against the background of the promenade at Brighton, Mr Wilkinson grinned fixedly at the camera, while Mrs Wilkinson looked anxiously down at her son. But they could only hold her attention for a moment. It was the eleven-year-old Jack who drew her eyes, a dark boy in shorts, jacket and school cap, smiling with delight at the monkey clinging to his arm.

'You all look so happy,' she said.

'Those were good days,' Mrs Wilkinson sighed.

'They're very precious, ain't they, these pictures?' Rita said. 'They keep people fresh in your mind when they're far away.'

Mrs Wilkinson looked sympathetic.

'You miss your hubby, do you?'

Rita flushed. These days, Ron hardly so much as brushed her thoughts.

'Oh – yeah – of course,' she lied. 'And my little boys.'

To cover her confusion, she opened her handbag and got out the latest snapshot of her sons and passed it to Mrs Wilkinson.

'See – that's Peter and that's Mikey. That was taken when my brother-in-law was on embarkation leave.'

'Ah – ain't they lovely? Fine-looking youngsters. You're so lucky, you know, having two. My Jack's the only one. For a long time, I thought we wasn't going to have any. Me and Bill, we was married eight years before I fell for Jack. In a right state, I was. I always wanted to have a big family, you see, and when it seemed like there wasn't going to be any babies at all it was like the end of the world. I was just so happy when I found I was expecting

Jack, I was laughing and crying all at the same time. I couldn't stop. There was a big smile all over my face the whole time I was carrying him.'

Rita was sad, thinking of how very differently she had felt when she discovered she was pregnant. Poor little Peter. She loved him so much now, but he had not been a wanted baby.

Mrs Wilkinson shook her head over the picture of the boys.

'Must break your heart to have them away.'

'It does. I hate it. But I'd never forgive myself if I fetched them home and then they was hurt in a raid.'

'I know what you mean. You dunno what to do for the best, do you?'

That was true enough, in more ways than Mrs Wilkinson dreamed of. When she was at the factory, Rita knew she was doing the right thing. But when she got home again she was never so sure. Her mother thoroughly disapproved, however many times Rita pointed out that Jack was away.

'But what'll happen when he comes home on leave?' Florrie asked.

'I won't go in, if it worries you that much,' Rita said, though she knew she did not mean it.

Her mother was not convinced.

Worse still was Lily's reaction. There had been one short note stating that she was never going to speak to her again, then nothing. Rita continued to write once a week, but Lily did not reply. When she wrote home, it was to her parents, and Rita was not so much as mentioned in passing. Florrie found it very hurtful.

'The family's falling apart. There's poor Joan out there in Dagenham with a new baby and me miles away not able to help her out, and poor little Lily wearing a uniform, and none of my grandchildren around at all, and now you go and make Lily fall out with you. It's wicked, that's what it is. Times like this, we should all be closer. Families need each other. But us, we're getting further and further apart. It breaks my heart, it does.'

It gave Rita many a sleepless night to know she was the cause of all this trouble. By the time Christmas week came, she was seriously considering giving up the job. She was just being selfish, keeping it on. For the sake of family unity and her mother's peace of mind, she ought to find something else. On Christmas Eve she travelled in on the bus, silently rehearsing ways of telling the Wilkinsons. On and off during the day, she tried to open the subject, but somehow always got sidetracked. As they closed up early at four o'clock, she knew she must say it before she left.

It was just Wally and Mr Wilkinson in the building. Mrs Wilkinson had been busy standing in queues for most of the day. Rita took a deep breath.

'Look, there's something I –'

But just at that moment, Mrs Wilkinson came hurrying in.

'Oh, I'm glad I caught you. I told Bill to make you wait –'

'Rita wants to get on home, Elena.'

'I know, I know, but not before she sees what we got.'

Now that she looked at them, Rita could see they were both bursting with some pleasurable secret.

'I know we said no presents, seeing as everything's so scarce, but this is different, and you're not to be offended or nothing,' Mrs Wilkinson said. 'Go on, Bill, fetch it here.'

Mr Wilkinson reached behind a pile of timber in the far corner of the factory. When she saw what he was holding, Rita gasped.

'A tricyle!'

'For your little 'uns,' Mr Wilkinson said, placing it in front of her.

Rita gazed at it through a blur of tears. It was a big sturdy machine with proper spoked wheels and solid tyres, painted maroon. It was exactly what she had been searching for unsuccessfully for three months. Peter and Michael would go wild with excitement over it. It would make their Christmas. It would make their year.

'It ain't new, of course. It was our Jack's. But Bill's cleaned it and oiled it and that. It's come up a treat, ain't it?'

'It's – it's just lovely,' Rita managed to stammer. 'But – but I can't – I mean –'

'Well, it don't look like we're going to have no grandchildren yet a while,' Mrs Wilkinson said sadly. 'And it's a waste to have it standing there doing nothing when there's kiddies could be having fun with it. Besides, me and Bill are very fond of you, y'know. I never had no daughter, more's the pity, and it's been lovely having you around. Livened the place up no end, it has. So we want you to have it, for your boys.'

Rita could not speak. She threw her arms round Mrs Wilkinson and burst into tears. Resignation was out of the question.

The fourth Christmas of the war was an uneasy one in the Croft household. George and Queenie had refused an invitation to come to Trinidad Street. They were going to Queenie's sister's. Florrie was hurt, even though she had expected it and didn't get on with Queenie. George was still her son, and their children her grandchildren. Lily had not got leave: she would be extra busy helping prepare Christmas dinner for the entire aerodrome. Another black mark against Rita, as far as her mother was concerned. Joan turned up, of course, tired from all the broken nights and a hellish journey on a packed train with four children and a baby. The occasion was saved by the presence of the newest member of the family. While the four older children rampaged around the house or rode up and down the street on the wonderful tricycle, Florrie nursed little Teddy in her arms. Joan and Rita insisted that she sit down and looked after the baby while they got on with the dinner, and then Rita insisted on making Joan take a break while she coped with everything. Though she tried to cover it up, Joan was suffering from baby blues. She could think of nothing but Ted spending Christmas in the Burmese jungle.

'I know I got to be brave and carry on, for him and for the kids. But sometimes it's very hard,' she said to Rita, with massive understatement.

Rita put an arm round her.

'You're doing wonderful, Joanie. It's people like you what are the real heroes of this war.'

'I don't feel like a hero. I just wish Ted could see his son. That's all I ask for.'

Over the dinner of roast pork, when glasses of beer were raised to toast absent friends, none of the three women dared catch each other's eyes, for fear of crying.

157

*

All in all, Rita was guiltily relieved to get back to work.

'Did you have a nice time?' Mrs Wilkinson wanted to know.

Rita was hard put to know what to say. She certainly couldn't admit to all the family tensions.

'Yeah, lovely,' she said.

'Made the best of it, eh?' Mrs Wilkinson said. 'You got to keep cheerful, ain't you, but it's hard when your menfolk are away.'

'Yeah,' Rita agreed, thinking how having Ron away was one of the few unmixed blessings of the family celebrations that year. 'But it was wonderful to see the boys, and they just went wild about that trike. You should of seen their little faces! I had it covered up with a sheet in the corner, and they opened their other presents, and Peter said, "Where's your present, Mum?" I told them to look for it, and they found it, and at first they couldn't believe it was for them. They just stood and stared at it. And when I told them it really was theirs they took it out on the street then and there, no coats on nor nothing, and Peter pedalled and Mikey stood on the back and hung on and away they went. I couldn't hardly get them to come in for dinner.'

Mrs Wilkinson smiled.

'Ah – that's nice. I'm really glad to hear it. I wrote and told Jack we was giving it to you, and he was pleased.'

Rita felt suddenly breathless. She had assumed that Jack did know she was working at the factory, but this was the first time she knew for sure. What did he think about it? Was he pleased? Did he think she was shamelessly chasing him? Or that she was playing some cruel game, when she had told him that they must not meet again? There was so much she wanted to know, and so much she could not ask.

'Oh – er – he don't mind, then?' she managed to say.

'Of course not, dear. He said he was glad it was going to be used, and to wish you a happy Christmas.'

A glow of pure happiness spread through Rita. He must still think well of her if he said that. She wanted to hug herself for sheer joy, to run and skip like a five-year-old. The dusty factory with its boarded-up windows was at once the most beautiful place in the world. She had to suck her cheeks in to stop a big grin from spreading over her face. It took a huge effort to control her voice, and make it sound normal.

'That's nice of him. P'raps you'd – er – thank him for me, when you write? And – and – wish him a happy New Year.'

To her relief, Mrs Wilkinson did not appear to notice anything odd about her.

'You'll be able to tell him yourself, dear. He's got a leave coming up in a fortnight's time.'

'Oh –'

This time, she really did not know how to keep a calm exterior. She could only be grateful to Mr Wilkinson, who came to interrupt them.

'Come on, now, Elena, stop boring the poor girl with all our family news. Some of us have work to do, you know. Here we are with an order book as long as your arm and all you do is talk.'

Mrs Wilkinson sniffed.

'Thinks he's running a blooming sweatshop,' she muttered, and went off to the house in a huff.

Rita retreated to her office. She opened the day's post and sat looking at it, but did not read a word. Jack was coming home on leave. For a long time, her thoughts got no further than that. In a fortnight's time, he would be here. She would see him again. The prospect filled her with such a mixture of delight and fear that it hurt.

Mr Wilkinson's voice startled her back to the present.

'Can you lay your hands on the invoice for that rotten load of pine they sent us?'

'Oh, er – yeah –'

Invoices, invoices. It was difficult to make her brain respond even to a simple request like that. She could feel her cheeks burning and her hands shaking as she turned over pieces of paper.

'What's the matter, girl? Been overdoing it over Christmas?' Mr Wilkinson asked.

'Yeah – er, not used to it,' she stammered.

More through luck than judgement, she found what he wanted.

'Here.'

'Thanks. Huh, yeah, just as I thought. I'm going to give them a piece of my mind. Useless stuff. Only fit for orange crates. Can't make decent furniture with timber like that.'

'Yeah – er, no –' Rita said.

Fortunately, Mr Wilkinson was not listening.

She tried to deal with the letters, but her concentration was all to pieces. Soon, Jack would be there. How was she going to be able to keep up a pretence of being a remote acquaintance in front of his parents? Perhaps it was only a forty-eight-hour pass. She could cope with that. She would only see him on the Saturday. But even as she thought it, she felt disappointed, and knew that what she really wanted was a chance to get to know him properly. It would be dangerous, with his parents looking on, but to have him around for a whole week would be wonderful. He would be sure to come and help his father, and she would have lots of opportunities to speak to him.

If he wanted to speak to her, that was. Doubt clawed at her. Maybe he was just being polite when he sent that Christmas greeting. After all, strangers wished each other a happy Christmas. It didn't mean anything. He might have found somebody else. He might be in love with some girl from the camp, or from the village.

At dinner time, she waited for Mrs Wilkinson to open the subject again. She did not have to wait long. After a complaint about the length of the queue at the butcher's, Mrs Wilkinson started talking about her son.

'It's always the worst time, when you know they're coming on leave. Don't you think so, Rita?'

'How do you mean?' Rita asked. She certainly didn't look forward to Ron's leaves, but she didn't think that that was what Mrs Wilkinson meant.

'Well, if anything was to – you know – happen to him, it'd be worse if it was just before you was going to see him. When you been looking forward to it, like. Not that it's like it was when he was on ops, but I still worry.'

'Yeah – yeah, you're right.'

She did follow the reasoning.

'How long is he coming for, then?' She managed to get it out. Her voice sounded a bit high and unnatural, but she had asked it.

'A week. A whole week,' Mrs Wilkinson said.

Rita could have hugged her.

Somehow, she got through the day without managing to make too much of a fool of herself. But as she stood waiting for the bus back to the Isle of Dogs other thoughts started to creep in. One thing was very clear – she must not let on at home about Jack's leave. Which brought the guilt back. She ought not to be in a state like this over his coming home. She was not a free agent; she was a married woman. But however much she told herself this, still she could not help counting the hours till she would see him again.

# 21

1943

Rita was not sure which was worse – living with the Wilkinsons' eager anticipation of Jack's leave at work or covering up when at home. Either way she did not know how she was going to go on acting like this. Mrs Wilkinson spent hours discussing what her son would like when he came home, and queuing to try to get whatever it was she had decided upon. Mr Wilkinson endured this with growing irritation.

'For God's sake, woman, it ain't the end of the world!' he burst out, when his wife came home disappointed at not getting the tin of ham she had waited two hours for. 'It's always the same when he comes on leave. Panic, panic, panic. He don't give two hoots if there's ham for tea. He's just glad to be out of it for a few days. You know how it'll be – he'll sleep a lot and go out every evening. And that's how it should be. He don't want you fussing around all the time.'

'Fussing? You call it fussing? When he could be put back on ops again? Even now he's in danger. They're always bombing the aerodromes.'

Mr Wilkinson's voice took on a bleak tone.

'You think I don't know that, girl?'

Rita glanced at him. She had been trying to keep out of the argument, but something in the way he spoke drew her eyes. The lines in his face seemed deeper, as if etched in acid. All at once she realised just how much he loved his son, how, beneath the cheerful exterior, he was worrying every minute.

Mrs Wilkinson hardly heard him. She was still letting loose her own feelings.

'– could I live with myself if I didn't do everything I could? You think I should just sit by and do nothing? Act like he's just walked in from a day at the seaside? What sort of a mother d'you think I am?' She turned to Rita. 'You know what I mean, don't you?'

Rita nodded, avoiding Mr Wilkinson's eyes.

'Most of the time you can't do nothing about it. You just wait, and hope for the best. But when they come home, you want to do something,' she said.

'Yeah, yeah that's just it. You said it, in a nutshell. You see –' she turned to her husband. 'Rita knows how it is.'

Rita went and tidied the office for the umpteenth time. Mrs Wilkinson could express her love by chasing after delicacies and erupting into rows and all the hundred and one other little things that helped ease the anxiety if only for a moment. She did not know how lucky she was. The only thing Rita could do was to see that her part of the family business was running perfectly. As she filed away some invoices, she found that her hands were shaking, and wondered once again just how she was going to keep up the appearance of being just a friend when Jack did arrive back.

The evening he was due, she left work in a state of almost unbearable tension. She fidgeted around the house, trying not to look at the clock, and failing. Now, his train was due in. Now, he would be arriving at Prittlestone Road. Now, he would be telling his parents all his news, toning it down maybe, so as not to worry them too much. Would they mention her at all? Would he ask after her? Just what would he say?

That night she could not sleep. She ran desperate measures round in her head. She could tell the Wilkinsons she was ill, or that there had been a family emergency and she could not come in, and tell her family that she had been given the week off. And then she would resign. She could find another job easily enough, and the Wilkinsons had got along without her before she arrived, so they would manage again.

But as half-past six and the time to get up crept slowly nearer, she knew that she could not keep away. Whatever the consequences, she had to see him again. She got out of bed to another freezing morning and pulled on her work clothes. She could not face breakfast, and by the time the stale-smelling bus had got to Whitchapel, she was feeling distinctly queasy. She stood on the pavement, her legs wobbly beneath her, and took several deep breaths. This was it. She set off for the factory.

As usual, Wally was there before her. Mr Wilkinson was just unlocking the doors as she arrived; she could hear his whistling as she crossed the street.

' 'Morning Rita, Wally. Ain't it a beautiful one? Sort of day that makes you happy to be alive.'

Wally just grunted. Rita found herself grinning back at Mr Wilkinson.

'Yeah,' she agreed. 'It's lovely.'

She picked up the post in her gloved hands and looked at the fronts of the letters, but none of them made any sense at all. Mr Wilkinson told her all about Jack's arrival. His train had been held up, of course, and Mrs Wilkinson had started to think something had happened, but then there he was at last, only an hour late and looking very well considering.

'The wife's creeping round the house on tiptoe, letting him lie in. She likes to take him up breakfast in bed when he's home.'

Rita's heart twisted painfully. She felt so envious of Mrs Wilkinson she could hardly breathe. After a while, even Mr Wilkinson noticed that she was not saying very much.

'You're a bit quiet this morning,' he remarked. 'What's up?'

'Oh, er – bit of a funny tummy. Nothing really,' Rita stammered. 'I – I'll get on now, shall I?'

She bolted for the safety of her office cubbyhole. There she forced herself to at least look busy, but she could not concentrate on anything. How soon would she see him? After going through every combination of events and timings, she decided that it could not possibly be before eleven o'clock. When he did make an appearance she must look calm, relaxed and efficient. It was essential that she give no hint of her feelings. Having got all that clear in her head, she made a huge effort to deal with the day's post.

She was in the middle of a daydream when a voice startled her back into the real world.

'Hullo, Rita.'

She jumped and twisted round, her cheeks burning. She had just been thinking about him and here he was, in the flesh, right beside her.

'H-hello,' she managed to say.

His sheer physical presence in the small space was over-whelming. She ached to fall into his arms and hold him so tight that she would never let go, but a movement just beyond his shoulder caught her eye. His mother was hovering behind him, watching and listening. Jack held out his hand and Rita automatically clasped it. His grip was firm and warm, and lingered just a bit longer than necessary.

'It's n-nice to see you again,' she found herself saying. 'How are you? You're looking well.'

'Thanks, yes, I'm fine. Plenty of canteen food, you know. Mum and Dad have been telling me all about what a little treasure you are. It certainly looks a lot more organised in here.'

Rita flushed again, this time with pleasure. Her hand was still tingling.

'Yes, well, thanks – I'm doing my best. And your mum and dad are such lovely people to work for, it's hardly like doing a job.'

'I'm glad they got someone in to help. They need it, with all the men called up.'

'Well, I'm not much use as a chippie, but I'm learning. I know which tools are which now, and I'm quite handy with a bit of sandpaper –' She chattered on, conscious that she was talking a lot of nonsense, but wanting to hold his attention as long as possible. All too soon, though, his father dragged him away to see the latest pieces of furniture and complain about the quality and quantity of timber available.

'– now you wouldn't think it'd hurt the war effort to let us have a nice bit of beech, would you? Or oak? It's not like they're building warships out of the stuff these days, after all –'

Rita sat back in her chair and unashamedly eavesdropped. She had got through the first meeting without making a complete fool of herself, and now she gave herself up to the pleasure of listening to his voice. Father and son wrangled for a while over whether or not Jack should help in the factory right there and then, and in the end Jack won, insisting that he found woodworking relaxing, and anyway there wasn't much to do by himself of a morning in London at this time of year. Rita kept

165

looking at him covertly as he sawed up lengths of timber for chair legs, storing up memories for when he was away again.

At dinner time, Mrs Wilkinson insisted that they all eat together as usual. 'We're all one big family here,' she said. 'Don't make no difference now Jack's here, so don't you go sloping off by yourself, Rita.'

As Rita chewed her way through cold sausage sandwiches and a hunk of her mother's eggless Madeira cake, the talk turned to bombing raids. There had been a successful attack on the Krupp's armaments works in Essen.

'That's the stuff. Stop the supply of arms and you'll cripple them.' Mr Wilkinson approved. 'I reckon you boys got the upper hand now. The so-and-so's don't dare come over here half so often now.'

Jack shook his head.

'I'd like to think so, Dad, but it's got a lot to do with the Russians. The Nazis are knocking hell out of them instead.'

'We can't relax yet. They still get through,' Rita said, shuddering as she remembered the noise and the fear.

Mrs Wilkinson patted her hand.

'Rita was bombed out of her last job. She was in it when it come down.'

'You weren't?' Jack's voice was sharp.

Rita looked at him. His face was tight with shock. Just for a moment, she was sure that he still felt the same way about her. Then he realised his parents were listening and assumed a tone of ordinary concern.

'That must of been nasty. Were you trapped?'

Rita nodded. 'Nearly four hours,' she said, in a matter-of-fact voice.

Mrs Wilkinson chimed in.

'Poor love, she don't go on about it, but it was terrible. Very lucky to be alive, she is.'

'It's an ill wind, though,' Mr Wilkinson said. 'If that hadn't happened, she wouldn't of been out of a job, and we wouldn't of had her here. I dunno how we ever managed without her.'

'That's true,' Jack agreed.

The afternoon was the liveliest Rita had ever known in the

factory. Jack insisted on staying and helping, and Mrs Wilkinson came back immediately she had cleared up from the meal. The Wilkinsons gossiped about family members and Jack told tales of happenings at the airfield. In the happy atmosphere even Rita relaxed enough to chip in with remarks and anecdotes. But at no time did Jack make any attempt to speak to her on her own. She was just part of the team, someone to be included in the general chat. The time flashed by and Mrs Wilkinson went off to get the tea, and as the end of the working day drew near Rita began to wonder whether she had imagined Jack's reaction to the news of her having been bombed out. Maybe there hadn't been anything in it. Maybe it was just the concern that anyone would show on hearing of another's close escape from death.

As she got her coat and made ready to go home, she could hear Jack and his father discussing the evening ahead.

'You going to the dance at the church, then?'

'Yeah, I might. We could go for a pint first, though, if you like. See the regulars again.'

'That'd be nice, son. They always ask after you, y'know.'

Rita was seized with a sense of hopelessness. Jack had his own life to get on with. At the airfield he had his work and his mates, and now when he was home there was family and old friends to look up. She really did not fit in at all. Her throat tight, she called a husky goodnight to anyone who might be listening and hurried out without waiting for a reply.

All the way home on the bus she lectured herself on her stupidity. She had been an idiot to expect anything else. She had been mad to take the job in the first place. She was probably an embarrassment to Jack. There she was, the married sister of an ex-girlfriend, whom he had once fancied a bit. He was most likely regretting all those things he'd said to her. The last thing he wanted was to be reminded of it by her being there all the time.

That evening, she went to the pictures to try and take her mind off things. But for once the magic did not work. Instead of the lovers on the screen, she kept seeing herself and Jack, and knew that she was acting like some silly kid, yearning after the impossible.

The next morning she went into work determined to be what

167

she really was – just an employee. Mr Wilkinson let her in as usual.

'Don't reckon we'll see Jack till midday,' he said. 'It's always the same when he comes home. First day, he can't keep still, in here doing things and out in the evening seeing people. Then he calms down a bit, like, and sleeps like the dead. Catching up, you see.'

'Yeah, I expect he needs it,' Rita said, at once relieved and disappointed that Jack was not likely to appear any minute. She wondered once again how she would get through the day.

The one person who seemed unaffected by the excitement was Wally. He was his usual taciturn self, rarely volunteering a remark, and answering direct questions with monosyllables.

'And what do you think of all this fuss over Jack coming home?' Rita asked him, as they heaved a piece of timber from the diminishing pile at the back of the factory.

The old man ran a practised eye over the grain of the wood.

'He's all right, is the lad. Knows good craftsmanship when he sees it.'

From Wally, this was an accolade.

Just as Mr Wilkinson predicted, Jack turned up in time for the dinner break. Mrs Wilkinson teased him about his late night and tried to find out who he had been dancing with and whether he had walked anyone home. Rita listened in painful suspense, but learned nothing. Jack refused to be drawn, throwing out hints and giving meaningful looks but not admitting to anything.

As they drank the last cups of tea that could be squeezed from the pot, he addressed her directly for the first time that day.

'D'you mind showing me what you done in the office, Rita? I like to keep up with everything that's going on here.'

'Yeah – no – I mean, of course,' Rita stammered.

She took a deep breath, trying to stop making an idiot of herself. 'I hope you'll like what you find,' she said.

'Oh, I'm sure I will.'

'She's real natural with the paperwork,' Mr Wilkinson said.

There was only just room for two people to get into the office corner. Rita sat down quickly, acutely conscious of Jack's closeness. Every nerve seemed to be on end in anticipation of a chance touch, an accidental brush of the hand or leg. She raced into an explanation of what she had done, where she had put everything, how she organised things, gabbling until it felt as if she was making no sense at all.

'It's all very impressive,' Jack said, when she allowed him space to speak. 'You've done wonders.'

Rita shrugged.

'I done my best.'

'I'm really grateful. Dad's not a businessman. My grandfather was. He built the firm up and he kept it going all through the Depression. If we can just keep it running till this war is over, then afterwards there'll be tremendous opportunities. We could really go somewhere with it.'

'Yes,' Rita said, thrilled that he should let her into his confidence like this.

'It was a lucky day when you chanced by like that.'

Rita felt breathless. He had seen through her.

'Yes,' she said again.

'Quite a coincidence, really.'

Rita could feel her heart thudding.

'I – I had the address of a place round the corner. Ridgewell's. You know it?'

'I know where you mean.'

There was a pause. Both of them knew that she had not actually needed to walk down Prittlestone Road to get to Ridgewell's. Jack perched on the edge of the desk. Rita did not dare look up at him; she stared at his leg, just an inch away from hers.

'I didn't know quite what to think when I heard you'd come to work here.'

'I really didn't know Ridgewell's was near here till I got here. And then when I saw this road, I just had to come down it, and then your mum and dad were out in the street fixing the damage and I just sort of got talking to them,' Rita said. It was the truth, but even as she said it, it sounded totally unbelievable.

'I see.'

'And when your dad said he needed someone to help in the office, well, it seemed like a really nice job. Much nicer than assembly-line work.'

169

'Yes.'

'So I – I said I'd give it a go.'

'And the fact that it was my dad's place had nothing to do with it?'

'No.'

'I see.' Jack stood up. 'Well, thanks for all you're doing.'

He went out into the main part of the factory.

'I think I'll go for a walk, Dad. I'll see you later.'

Rita was left gazing at the empty desk.

## 22

The pressure of the complicated web of lies was growing more and more difficult for Rita to bear as the week progressed. It was hard enough trying to be her normal self in front of Mr and Mrs Wilkinson. Much worse was coping with Jack. He was very good at being cheerful and friendly, but every now and then she would catch his eye, and the accusation there would chill her to the core. He obviously did not believe a word she had said to him about her motives and reasons. He thought she was playing some game of her own.

On the last day of his leave, they were talking during dinner hour about the company's future.

'Once this war's over, people are going to be desperate for something new. They'll of put up with second-hand and this Utility stuff you're turning out now, and they'll want something a bit individual. We got to be ready to give it to them.'

'That's easy enough. We got plenty of lovely designs we can turn out once we're allowed,' his father said. 'All we need is a decent supply of timber, and the men back to work it.'

'I think we need more than that. That'd just take us back to where we was before the war. We ought to be thinking beyond that. We ought to expand, move out to the suburbs somewhere, to one of them new industrial estates.'

Mrs Wilkinson looked alarmed.

'I dunno about that, Jack. We've always lived round here. We're established. Your dad's got all the contacts and that. And what about when the men come back? Their homes are round here and all.'

'Not all of them. Some of them of been bombed out. A lot of their wives and kids of been evacuated. It won't be the same, there are going to be changes. People are going to want something better,' Jack said.

'They said that after the last lot. "Land fit for heroes" and all that, and look what happened – not a lot for the ordinary bloke and his family,' Mr Wilkinson said.

'Yeah, but it'll be different this time. Everyone's been in it. Not just us lot in the Services. All the people on the Home Front as well. All the women and kids. They won't stand for going back to how things were after what they been through, and quite right too. They'll want decent homes for a start, and nice furniture. Not just the ones with money, but ordinary working people as well.'

Mr Wilkinson looked sceptical.

'That's all very well, son, but where's the money coming from? People can want nice furniture as much as they like, but we can't give it away.'

'For a start, look at all the rebuilding that's going to have to be done, Dad. There's work enough there for years, and that means people'll have jobs and a bit of cash in their pockets. And like I said, they're not going to stand for being put on the rubbish dump after this war. The government's going to have to do something to make sure we all get a decent standard of living.'

'It'd be nice to think you're right, dear,' his mother said.

'I think he is right. People go on taking this austerity, and being directed away from their homes to jobs they never done before, and conscription and all that, and they don't grumble, 'cause there's a war on, but they won't take it afterwards,' Rita said.

Wally sniffed.

'Blooming Bolshies, if you ask me.'

'There's a lot of them around. You should of heard them where I used to work. All for the Russians, they were. But they was the ones what got production up. They weren't skivers. It was all this "Workers of the world unite" business. It's the same at other places and all,' Rita said.

Mrs Wilkinson shook her head.

'I don't know. Sounds like we're going to be taken over by a lot of commies.'

'That'd be the end for us. Wilkinsons'd be collectivised, or whatever it is they do to family firms,' Mr Wilkinson said.

'It won't be like that. What I'm saying is, people won't take being downtrodden no more. They'll expect something better, and the government'll have to see they get it,' Jack said.

Rita jumped in without thinking.

'Quite right, too. They'll have to do something about the docks for a start. All my life I seen men going down every morning hoping they'll be called on, and their wives not knowing if they got money coming in that day or not. I've had to wait to see Ron weren't coming home before I could go out and buy food for the kids. That ain't right for a start. All the people down on Dog Island, we get the worst of the bombs every time. When the men come back, they won't want to go back to the calling-on system again.'

'Hark at her. You better watch out, Dad, I think we got a little trade union leader amongst us,' Jack said.

Rita flushed.

'I'm just agreeing with you, that's all.'

'Really?'

Rita could almost hear him thinking, *That makes a change.*

Mrs Wilkinson sighed and stood up.

'I don't know what it's all coming to, that I don't. I'm going to see if I can get some fish for tea. You fancy fish, Jack?'

'That'd be lovely, Mum.'

Rita went back into the office, wishing she could just go home and never come back. It had all gone wrong. Whatever she had expected from Jack's being home, it wasn't this silent warfare. It was her own fault: she should never have walked down Prittlestone Road that day. She had upset her mum and Lily, angered Jack and made herself miserable, and at this rate it wouldn't be long before either she or Jack said something that aroused the Wilkinsons' suspicions. It was a total disaster.

There was a sound of footsteps behind her. Someone else came into the office. Rita sat very still, not daring to look round. She knew who it was.

Jack's voice was tight with the effort of keeping it low enough not to be overheard.

'Just what the hell are you playing at, Rita?'

Rita fiddled with a pile of government directives.

'Nothing.'

'Like hell. What are you doing here, for Christ's sake? And don't give me all that bull about just happening to walk down this street.'

Something inside her snapped, jolting her into admitting the truth.

'What do you think? I'm here because of you. Because I'd find out how you was through your family. Because I'd get to see you again. Because I couldn't bear not to know whether you was alive or dead. There. Now you know. Satisfied?'

There was immediate relief at having admitted to the truth at last, then a terrible feeling of nakedness. She had thrown all her defences away, handed complete power to him. She waited for the world to fall in.

'No I'm not.'

Out of the corner of her eye, she could see his fist clenched on the top of the filing cabinet.

'It's so stupid, fooling around like this. All this time wasted, Rita. If you felt like this all along, why wait till the last minute? Why ever didn't you tell me before?'

She could see clearly now from his point of view. Time was the one thing he didn't have. Tomorrow he was going back. All the time she had been pretending, they might have been happy. She put her hands to her head, her fingernails digging into her scalp, welcoming the prick of pain.

'I wanted to, but I couldn't. Don't you see? Nothing's changed. I'm still married.'

She could feel the anger and frustration emanating from him. It must look as if she was simply playing hard to get.

'Then we're back to where we was, ain't we? If nothing's changed and you're still married, why are you here?'

It was a nightmare. She didn't really know herself, so how could she explain?

'I told you. Because I couldn't help it.'

There was silence for what felt like an age. Then he spoke, and the accusation was gone from his voice, leaving only sadness.

'Rita, you're an idiot. You're too loyal for your own good, you are.'

'I know.'

'Come out with me tonight.'

He laid a hand on her shoulder, and her whole body flooded with longing. Tomorrow he was going back. Tonight was her last chance. She looked up at him, and everything suddenly became very simple. There was only one thing to do, and that was to follow her heart.

'All right.'

He gave her shoulder a squeeze, and she tilted her head to touch his hand. All the misgivings evaporated. She knew this was right.

They met up at Piccadilly Circus underground, amidst a swirl of men and women from all over the world. GIs in their tailored uniforms, Australians with turned-up hats, romantic-looking Poles, Free French, Dutch, Canadians, Gurkhas, all washed up for a while in this place before being swept on by the tides of war. The carefree atmosphere of so many people far away from the constraints of home was catching. When Rita spotted Jack in his air-force blue and bomber jacket, she ran to fling herself into his arms.

Jack laughed with surprise and delight.

'Is this the same girl who's been playing just-good-friends all week? What's happened?'

Rita held on to him tight and smiled up into his eyes. For once, she felt young and free again.

'I've escaped, that's what.'

'Wonderful!' He held her close and kissed her with slow thoroughness. 'That's for starters. Now, what do you want to do – go to the pictures? Dancing?'

'I'm always going to the pictures.'

The thought of going dancing with him was so tempting. She just ached to say yes. It would so wonderful. But it was too public, even here, in the West End. People she knew were always coming up this way now for a good night out at one of the big dance halls. The joy of the meeting clouded a little. She was not really free.

'Let's just go for a drink, and talk. We never really get the chance to talk. There's always people around, or about to come in or something.'

175

'We'll do better than that. We'll have a meal, go to a restaurant.'

'But I've had my tea.'

Jack laughed.

'Live a little! Just for once, have too much to eat instead of too little. A real posh evening dinner.'

Rita sighed with pleasure and rubbed her face against his.

'Sounds lovely.'

They found a small place off the Haymarket that was coping gallantly with the food shortages. The leek soup was really tasty, the lamb casserole had proper chunks of tender meat in it and the apple pie had plenty of filling. Jack asked to see the wine list, but shook his head over the choice of two that the place had to offer.

'Too sweet,' he said.

The elderly waiter gave a wry smile.

'I know, sir, but it's all we have left. Liberate France for us, and we'll buy something drinkable.'

Rita looked at him in amazement.

'What's all this, then? Ain't beer good enough for you no more?'

'The rubbish they palm off on us as beer these days ain't, that's for sure. You have to drink enough to sink a battleship before you get any effect at all,' Jack said. 'No, beer's fine for a night down the pub, but I tell you, I've learnt more than how to read a map and stay alive these last three years. We got this bloke in my hut, Billy Robbins. His old man is a butler in some huge stately home. Now his boss, Lord What's–it, he was a pilot with the Royal Flying Corps in the last war and he likes our Billy and always wants to know exactly how he's been doing. So every time Billy goes home, he has a long jaw with the old boy and gets given half a dozen bottles of the best in the cellars to bring back to us lot. Now, Billy don't let us just swill it down and get blotto. We all have to sit round and smell it and taste it and generally get to tell one from another. It's amazing. I never knew there was so much to a drink. When this war is over, I'm going to really learn about wine. I'm going to go to France and travel around drinking the stuff.'

Rita felt a stab of pain. After the war he could do whatever he liked. But she would not be part of his plans. She would have Ron back home again.

'Sounds wonderful,' she said, with difficulty. 'Who else have you got in your hut?'

Jack told her all about the men he was working with, then Rita spoke about her parents and the boys and Joan and the new baby, which led on to the subject of childhood, and they compared their experiences and memories.

'We used to go down Island Gardens of a Sunday. Or for a real treat, it was Victoria Park,' Rita said.

'Itchy Park!'

'Yeah, that's what we used to call it and all. I wonder why? It was the lake I loved best. Them boats. I loved them rowing boats. My brother George, he always used to have the oars because he was the eldest and he was the boy. It used to make me so mad! He was useless at it, and I knew I could do better. Then one day, he like went to row but his oars never went in the water and he fell right over on his back. I did laugh. And then I saw my chance, and I hopped over and grabbed them while he was still trying to sit up. And I was right, I could do it, and I was better than him. He never forgave me for that. I can still see his face, all red and hot, and me rowing around the lake, captain of the boat.'

'I liked the boats and all. I used to go there in the school holidays with my mates, and if we had enough money, we'd get two boats out between us and have races and bump into all the other people and annoy them, till the bloke in charge used to blow his whistle and bellow at us and tell us we'd never get to go on them again. Of course, that only made us worse.'

'Jack, you little so-and-so. I thought you was better brought up than that.'

'Me? Oh, you don't want to listen to what my mum says about me. She thinks I'm wonderful, but I used to play her up something dreadful.'

'I'm sure you didn't really.'

The evening passed in a happy flow of memories and opinions. They found they thought alike on any number of things, from which flavour ice-cream was best to whether going to church really mattered.

The waiter brought brandies with their coffee.

'Compliments of the management, sir, madam. A small tribute to the bravery of the RAF.'

Neither of them noticed the passing of time, until the waiter coughed meaningfully beside their table and they realised that the restaurant was empty. Regretfully, they went out of the cosy light into the winter blackout.

They walked with arms round each other, slowly, scarcely noticing the black shapes of other people in the darkness. Rita sighed and laid her head on Jack's shoulder.

'I think that was the nicest evening I ever had in my whole life.'

'Glad you came now?'

'Oh yes.'

Jack drew her into a doorway, and Rita moved into his arms. Their lips met in a long kiss that grew deeper and more passionate as the seconds passed, lips and tongues longing for each other. When at last they drew apart, it was to rest forehead to forehead, panting in the friendly night, their breath mingling.

'I love you, Rita. You're everything I ever wanted.'

'Oh Jack, don't say that –'

It was the same for her. She knew that he was the right one.

'Why not? It's the truth.'

'I know, I know. Oh, what are we going to do?'

'That's for you to say.'

She knew what she wanted to answer. Instead she began kissing him again, until there was nothing left of the world but the two of them.

'Oh Jack, I do love you so much, b——'

He silenced her with another kiss.

'Don't spoil it. Just say it again, without the "but".'

She looked up at him: she could just make out the outline of his head, and the faint glimmer of the whites of his eyes. She put her hand up and ran her fingers over his face, feeling the contours of his nose and cheeks, the start of stubble on his jawline, imprinting it on her memory. Tomorrow her arms would be empty, and memory would be all she had.

'I love you, Jack.'

She put everything into her kiss this time, all the tenderness and need that had been building up for so long, all that she had been holding in check.

The journey home passed in a happy daze. Jack insisted on taking her right to the door and Rita did not bother to argue. She no longer cared if they were seen. It did not matter. By the boarded-up front of the shop, she held him for the last time.

'Promise me something, Rita.'

'What is it?'

'It's my parents. They're really fond of you. I think they almost look on you as a daughter. You'll look after my mum and dad for me, won't you?'

Fear tore at her. She clung to him with desperate strength.

'Don't say that.'

'But will you?'

'Yes, yes of course, but –'

*But don't talk as if you're not coming back.*

'Thank you.'

He kissed her one more time, then held her arms and took a step away. The space between them was already cold and empty.

'I hate goodbyes. I'm not going to drag it out. I'm going to go, now. Take care, my darling Rita.'

And he was gone, swallowed up almost at once in the darkness. Rita tried to call out to him, but the words cracked in her throat.

'I love you, Jack. Stay safe.'

# 23

Rita could not shake off the sense of foreboding. Every morning as she woke up it slid its queasy fingers round her consciousness, making her feel physically sick. Wherever she was, whatever she might be doing, Jack's words kept echoing through her mind: *Look after my mum and dad for me.* He had brushed with death twice now. The third time, his luck might not hold. She told herself that he was not in mortal danger now, but still the feeling clung.

The days piled up and grew into weeks, then months. Ron still did not come home, for which she was hugely grateful, but Lily made a weekend appearance. In front of the family, she made much of the fun she was having, but when she got Rita to herself, she made it quite clear what she thought of a sister who deliberately got a job with the parents of the love of her life. Rita was no longer so upset by it all. She was sorry to have hurt Lily, but the feeling that Jack's days were numbered was so strong that she could not in the least regret what she had done.

Her weeks revolved round visiting the boys and the arrival of Jack's letters. She had two sources of news from him now. Mrs Wilkinson always read out bits of his letters to her, particularly if he sent his regards or made some reference to her. But he also wrote to her direct, typing the company address on a brown envelope and trusting to his father's leaving all the opening of correspondence to her. She read these precious letters until she knew them by heart, then hid them beneath the loose floorboard under her bed. On bus journeys, or evenings in, or during the many nights when she couldn't sleep, she composed replies on her head. Once a week she wrote it all down, but somehow it never came out the same when she acually put it on to paper.

One day in April, the warning went. Rita looked up from her typing, listening with disbelief. Then she looked across at Mr Wilkinson and Wally, who had stopped in the act of fixing the top on a sideboard.

'So-and-so's are coming in daytime again.'

Wally gave a snort of disgust.

'Wouldn't put nothing past them.'

Mrs Wilkinson came running into the factory from the house.

'The siren's going. It's a raid.'

'All right, all right. I know.'

'We got to get down the shelter.'

'I dunno. It won't be a big one. Not in daylight.'

All four of them went to the door and looked out into the street. Other people were doing the same. Some were gazing up at the sky. It was a beautiful clear spring day. It seemed odd that death should come out of such a cloudless blue.

'What d'you think?' someone called across from the upholsterer's.

'Can't hear no planes.'

'Can't hear nothing above that bloody siren.'

'D'you reckon it's false alarm?'

'Might be south of the river.'

'Yeah – they won't get this far. Not in daylight.'

There was a definite warmth to the sunshine, a promise of summer. Mr Wilkinson shrugged.

'I got work to do. You girls can go down the shelter if you like.'

Mrs Wilkinson refused to go without him. Rita had no desire to go and stand in a smelly street shelter because of something that wasn't going to happen. They all went back to work.

She had almost forgotten the incident by the time she was heading for home that evening. Like every other Londoner, bomb raids were part of her everyday life. If they didn't affect you directly, you dismissed them. There were plenty of more important things to think about. It was only as she got on the bus heading for the West Ferry Road that she suddenly realised that the alarm had been for real.

'You live on Dog Island?' the conductress asked.

'Yeah. Trinidad Street, near the West Indies.'

'You know they caught it from that raid?'

'No! where?'

'Dunno exactly, dear. I only come on duty half an hour ago.'

The feeling of dread hit her so hard she almost groaned out

181

loud. She knew her mum. She would have refused to leave the shop. Perhaps her dad had made her. He was an air-raid warden, after all: he had to make the family set a good example. The journey, always long and frustrating, seemed to be taking for ever. The bus ground along with such agonising slowness that Rita wanted to get out and run. She tried to remember what the tides were doing. If there was a ship going into the docks and the swing bridge was open, she could be sitting waiting on the Poplar side for half an hour.

The woman sitting next to her couldn't help but notice the state she was in.

'You new in town, dearie?' she asked.

'No. Lived here all my life.'

'You been evacuated, then?'

'No!'

The woman couldn't understand it.

'You got to calm down, dearie. No good getting y'self all stewed up like this. If it's got your name on it, that's it, but otherwise, why worry? How did you get through the Blitz if this is what it does to you? It's a wonder you didn't crack up.'

Rita couldn't explain it.

'I'm not like this usually. It's just – I don't know. This time –'

A beefy hand gave her knee a comforting stroke. Her travelling companion knew intuition when she met it.

'The hospitals do wonderful things these days, dearie.'

Rita nodded, unable to speak.

There was no hold-up at the bridge. The bus shuddered along the West Ferry Road, past the rows of boarded-up shops and flattened bomb sites. As it got to her stop, she leapt off before it even came to a halt and began running along the road and round the corner into Trinidad Street.

She stopped, her chest heaving. At first she thought it was all right. No more buildings had gone down. There were no craters. Then she realised that the shop was cordoned off. Her weary legs and aching lungs forgotten, she raced down the street, not seeing the people who came out to stop her, not hearing their voices. The front of the shop looked as if a giant fist had smashed into it. Splintered boarding and shards of glass lay all over the pavement, mixed with flour, sugar, lentils, tea, pearl barley, dried peas and lurid splashes of plum jam and puddles of treacle.

'Mum! Dad!'

Unthinking, she made to push through the cordon and plunge inside, but found herself caught between two sets of strong arms.

'It's all right, Rita. Get a grip, girl. They're all right. Your mum's up the Royal London and your dad's with her –'

'Hospital!'

She looked wildly from one face to the other, vaguely registering familiar features.

'Bring her in here,' a female voice said. 'I got a cuppa tea made.'

Rita found herself ushered into a neighbour's house and sat down in the back room. A thick cup of sweet tea was put into her hands.

'I can't stay. I got to get to the hospital –'

'No, no. Won't do you no good going up there. Your dad's with her, and it ain't bad. She weren't crushed nor nothing. She was under the counter when the blast got the place, and she was cut and bruised with all the flying glass and tins and that. She'll be all right, Rita, I promise you. Now drink that tea up. I got some brandy in the cupboard, I'll put a drop of that in it. Good for shock.'

Reluctantly, Rita sipped at the laced tea. The people round her gradually came into focus and she recognised one of her father's colleagues from the ARP and Mr and Mrs Dodds from over the road. The bomb had landed in Alpha Road, they told her, but the blast had caught the shop. Her dad, who was off duty, had been down at the Mudchute allotments bartering his rabbits for vegetables, and just as Rita had feared, her mother had refused to go to the shelter, instead just ducking beneath the counter at the last minute.

They couldn't persuade her to stay put, though. The moment she had finished the tea, she stood up to go to the hospital and get some news. She had just reached the door when her father walked in.

'Dad!' She fell into his arms. 'Dad, how is she? Is she –'

'She's all right, girl. Concussion and some nasty cuts and bruises. They're keeping her in overnight.'

'Keeping her in! Why?'

'Observation. Just routine, they said. I got to telephone 'em in the morning and find out when to go and fetch her.'

'Oh thank God –' and to her own distress, she burst into tears. All the worry of the last few months together with the shock surfaced in a storm of weeping.

'I'm sorry,' she kept sobbing, trying to stop and finding that she couldn't.

The men, embarrassed, melted away. Mrs Dodds put her arms round her and let her cry on her shoulder.

'That's right, lovey, you let it all out. Do you good.'

It was a long time before, with puffy eyes and aching throat, she subsided into the occasional racking sob.

'I'm s-so sorry,' she said. 'I feel such a fool.'

She felt strangely hollow inside.

'That's all right, lovey. Gets us all at times. Can't always be brave, can we?'

It was arranged that Rita and Jim should stay with the Dodds for the night. Rita slept better than she had done for weeks.

In the morning she was able to face things again. Yesterday had been a lapse. Now she had to get back to being strong. There was the heartbreaking job of clearing up to be done. It wasn't certain yet that the building would be safe even if it was shored up, but in the mean time Rita did not want her mother to come back to find her precious stock scattered amongst the dirt of the street. She went to the phone box to let the Wilkinsons know what had happened. Mr Wilkinson's voice crackled over the bad line, full of concern.

'Any carpentering work needing doing, girl?'

'Well – lots, but it's rough work, not cabinetmaking.' She knew enough by now to tell the difference.

'Don't matter. Wally and me'll be down there.'

Neighbours came to help, exclaiming over the terrible waste as they scraped up the sludge of food, wood, dirt and glass. The overworked building inspector looked briefly at the shop and agreed with Jim's decision that it just needed some posts and buttresses to hold it together. Mr Wilkinson and Wally arrived with their tools, and they and Jim immediately took to each other, setting to work to make things safe. Rita went to fetch her mother from the hospital.

Florrie looked white and frail, and older than her fifty-odd years. There were bandages on her head and her left hand, and livid bruises all down the left side of her face. But she was unbowed.

'What's the shop like?' she wanted to know. 'Is it all right?'

'It's taken a bashing, but it's going to be habitable,' Rita assured her.

'Good. That's all I want to know.'

'But what about you, Mum? You don't look too good. I don't think they ought to of let you out yet.'

Florrie would not hear a word against the hospital.

'They was wonderful in that place, wonderful,' she said. 'Them nurses, run off of their feet they was, but always cheerful and always time to see if you was all right.'

'But your head must hurt something terrible.'

Florrie would not admit it.

'It ain't nothing. I got all my faculties. I ain't got nothing broken, I ain't got nothing terrible happened to my insides. Not like some of them in there. What some of them poor women are suffering, Rita, it breaks your heart, it does. No, I'll be right as rain in a few days. Back behind the counter again.'

This was just what Rita had feared. She almost wished the shop had been condemned. Then there would be no argument: her mother would have to move out. As it was, there was now going to be a major battle, and she was not at all certain she would win. She pretended astonishment.

'Oh come on, Mum, you're not going to carry on, surely? Not even you would do that now.'

'And why not, might I ask?'

'But – but – it's plain as the nose on your face, Mum. It's dangerous. If that bomb'd been a few feet nearer, you'd of been killed.'

'But it weren't, was it?'

'But it might of been. You got to move somewhere safe, Mum –'

'Rubbish. It is safe. We've had our bomb now.'

'It ain't. It weren't your bomb, it was someone else's. Next time it might be yours.'

'I ain't moving.'

All the way home in the bus they argued, till Florrie lost her temper.

'For Gawd's sake, girl, leave off! I ain't a baby. I'm staying, so shut your bleeding mouth.'

Rita was shocked into silence. Her mother hardly ever swore, and certainly not on a public bus. Then she saw Florrie's hands shaking, and was filled with remorse. Her mother was still shocked. Now was not the time to cross her.

'I'm sorry, Mum,' she said, to make amends. 'I didn't mean to upset you. It's just that we don't want to lose you.'

Florrie took a shuddering breath.

'That's all right, pet. You mean well. Just don't go on at me, that's all.'

Rita bided her time. She managed to get her brother George on the telephone at Ford's and told him what had happened. The next day he arrived together with Joan, who had taken the unprecedented step of leaving all the children with Queenie except the baby, whom she was still breastfeeding. While the men finished the job of making the building safe, Florrie, Joan and Rita swept and beat and cleaned through the house and the shop, routing out the dirt and plaster dust that had showered everywhere. And while they worked, Rita and Joan brought up all the arguments they could think of to persuade Florrie to move out.

'You can say what you like, but I ain't going,' Florrie told them. 'That Hitler's not going to move me. He can throw what he likes at me, but I'm staying put. I'm not giving in to the likes of him, nasty little man.'

'Hitler won't know, Mum. It won't make no difference.'

' 'Course it will. If everyone gave in, we'd lose the war, wouldn't we? And besides, the people round here need me. What with the ones what of gone and the ones what been bombed out, there ain't half the shops round here there used to be. I got twice the people registered with me that I had at the beginning of the war. Where'd they all go if I closed?'

'They'd find somewhere, Mum.'

'Not open the hours I do. What about all them poor working mums? When'd they get their shopping done if I wasn't open up to seven every night?'

They tried another tack. Joan had the trump card in baby Teddy.

'We need you, Mum, and so do your grandchildren. If you was killed, the kids wouldn't have no gran. Teddy wouldn't even remember you. He's too young. He wouldn't ever know what it was to have a gran.'

But even that did not persuade Florrie.

'What about your dad? He can't go, he's got his responsibilities as a warden. And I can't leave him. He needs home comforts, not some digs somewhere.'

Nothing they could say had any effect. Joan, Rita and George gave up. Florrie and Jim were to stay, and Rita with them.

As she lay down in her own bed again that night, Rita expected to fall asleep straight away. She was dog tired. Over the last three days she had come to believe that this must be the disaster that had given her the feeling of doom, and after all they had survived it. But as she pulled the covers up, the sick dread was back, gnawing at her heart. Jack. She was sure Jack was in danger.

The next morning when she got into work, she was greeted by faces that echoed her fears.

'A letter come from Jack yesterday while we was round at your place, girl,' Mr Wilkinson said. 'He's been posted to a place in Norfolk. Fenny Howe.'

'Oh?' Rita said. She could hardly breathe. She knew what he was going to say.

'Yeah. They put him back on ops again.'

## 24

'There was more about our boys on the news last night, did you hear it?' Mr Wilkinson asked. 'They been hitting the Ruhr again. More than seven hundred planes went over. Just think – seven hundred!'

But how many didn't come back? Rita wondered. She hung on to the thought that they would have heard by now if Jack had failed to return from that particular raid.

Mr Wilkinson was chattering on about how the Allies had really got them on the run now, what with the Eighth Army winning in the desert and the Yanks blazing away in the Pacific.

'It ain't all good,' Rita said. 'Look at Burma.'

Mr Wilkinson looked at her as if what she'd said was treason.

'That's just a tactical retreat. And anyway, it's only a sideshow.'

'Not for the men in it,' Rita said, thinking of Joan waiting for news of Ted.

But Mr Wilkinson was not listening.

'That's the stuff to hit them with. Thousands of tons of high explosive. Of course, the Dambusters did a grand job, but it's the boys like Jack and his mates what do the real stuff.'

This time Rita could wholeheartedly agree.

There had been nothing in the first post for her today. She had not heard from Jack for a week and neither had his parents. She glanced up at the clock: nearly time for the second post. Perhaps today she would hear. She wouldn't be terribly disappointed if it was a letter for his mum and dad, just as long as she knew he was all right.

The doors to the factory stood open, letting in the May sunshine. Dust danced in the golden shafts of light. Mr Wilkinson went on about how everything was looking up, and even Wally seemed a degree less morose as they had had the good fortune to buy up a load of well-seasoned beech.

'Lovely stuff – look at that grain,' he said to Rita. 'Come up beautiful, that will. Pity we got to make this blooming Utility rubbish with it. Crying shame, if you ask me.'

A figure stood silhouetted in the bright doorway. Rita, squinting towards the light, recognised the outline of the postgirl. With difficulty, she stopped herself from running and snatching the letters out of the girl's hand. She sorted through the pile. There, amongst the bills and invoices, was the plain envelope with the typed address and the Norfolk postmark. She scuttled into the office and tore it open. As she scanned the letter, her breathing steadied. He was fit and well, they had been on some big raids but got back all right, he was missing her terribly –

'Anything special there?' Mr Wilkinson called across.

'No! No – usual old stuff.'

'I thought we might get something from Jack.'

'Yeah.'

'But it might of gone to the house.'

'No – I mean yes.'

There was going to be a big dance at the airfield for midsummer. They were going to clear the largest hangar and they had booked the Powers Girls to play. Jack wanted her to come, if she could possibly make it.

Rita gazed at the letter. More than anything else in the world, she wanted to go. The thought of dancing all night with Jack was unbearably wonderful. Last time, in the West End, she had been afraid of being seen, but up there in Norfolk they would be safe. They could be a proper couple, and Jack could introduce her as his girlfriend. The Powers Girls' playing was a bonus. She could get to talk to Poppy Powers, who was a legend in Trinidad Street: she was so busy playing to the troops that she had only once been back on a flying visit to her old home since she returned from the States.

'Rita?'

She realised with a jolt that Mr Wilkinson was talking to her. Flushing, she hid Jack's letter under the day's pile.

'What? Er, sorry, I was miles away.'

'I said, have you got that invoice for the beech?'

'Er, yeah – hold on.'

Somehow, she got through the rest of the morning. At dinner time she said it was much too nice to stay in, and went for a walk.

The sun blazed down on her pale, indoor face and heat bounced back from roads and brick buildings. Sweat began to break out all over her body. The beautiful weather only served to highlight the ugliness of her surroundings. When it was grey and cold you didn't notice it, it was just part of life, but when the sun shone from such an unbroken blue sky it seemed a sin not to be amongst green fields and trees, or by the sea. Rita came upon a bomb site. It was one of the early ones, roughly flattened and already sprouting willowherb, evening primrose and young buddleias. Amongst the factories and tenements, it was almost a wild garden.

Rita scrambled in and sat with her back against a heap of grass-grown rubble. Insects scuttled around the weeds. Sparrows flew down and hopped about hopefully, waiting for crumbs. She opened her packet of sandwiches, decided she wasn't hungry, and watched as the sparrows went wild fighting over the feast. How easy life was for them: all they worried about was the next beakful of food. She gazed at the small feathered bodies, black, beady eyes and stick-like legs, at the furious fluttering of wings as a victorious bird attempted to take off with a crust, only to be forced into dropping it by a rival.

What was she going to do about this dance? She had to go, that was for certain. She could ask Mr Wilkinson for the Saturday afternoon off. That was easy enough: she could make up some reason for needing the time and he was generous enough to give it her without questioning. But how could she explain a night away from home to her parents? And, even worse, to the boys? She would never get back on a Sunday in time to go and see them. It was no good saying a girlfriend had invited her, since they knew all her friends and their families and she was sure to be found out.

The hot sun beat down on her head. There was a rank smell of weeds in the air and the persistent hum of machinery from a nearby workshop. Too many nights' broken sleep crept up on her. Despite the pressing problem of the dance, her eyelids began to feel heavy. Drowsiness settled over her like a comforting blanket. For a while she fought it. She only had half her dinner hour left. There was stacks of work waiting for her at the factory. She had to think of a way to get to Norfolk. But the sun was stronger than she was and she drifted into a doze.

The clatter of a consignment of metal boxes being delivered nearby woke her with a start. Her head was muzzy, her limbs heavy, her eyelids glued together. It took a few moments for her to remember where she was. Then she looked at her watch and gave a squeak of horror. Gone half-past one – she had been asleep for over an hour. She jumped up, grabbed her bag and began hurrying back along the grimy streets. Her back and bottom ached where she had been lying on lumpy bricks. Her head was beginning to thump. And she had still not thought of how she was going to get to see Jack.

'I'm ever so sorry, I fell asleep – I didn't notice the time –' she gasped as she rushed into the factory.

Wally gave her a look that said just what he thought of her, but Mr Wilkinson was his usual cheerful self.

'Don't matter, girl. Like you said, it's too nice to be cooped up. Me and Elena of decided to go down the cottage on Saturday if the weather holds, so we'll pack up dinner time.'

The cottage was the Wilkinsons' new toy. Mr Wilkinson had bought it for a song from someone who was selling up and moving out of the East End and down to the West Country.

'It ain't exactly thatched roof and roses round the door. More like a garden shed in a nettle patch,' Mr Wilkinson had said when he had first been to see it. 'But it's got potential. Nice lot of outbuildings and plenty of land round it. Nothing like land, you know. Must be an investment.'

Mrs Wilkinson, who came from peasant stock, agreed with him, though she was bothered about there being no shops nearby.

Now, Mr Wilkinson was chatting on about what they were planning to do the coming weekend. The place needed plenty of repairing and cleaning out, and the garden had to have a scythe taken to it. He and Mrs Wilkinson were going to enjoy themselves. Rita listened with half an ear, nodding and agreeing. Then it came to her, in a flash of inspiration. The weekend of the dance, she could tell her family she was going to the Wilkinsons' cottage to help them out. It was perfect. She was hard put not to fling her arms round Mr Wilkinson and hug him.

The next two weeks passed with agonising slowness. Her parents took the story all right, saying it would be nice for her to have a break, but the boys were very disappointed when she told them she would not be seeing them the next Sunday. Peter sulked and kicked out at everything within range, and Mikey cried and clung to her. Rita felt dreadful. It broke her heart to hurt them like this, but she would see them the week after, whereas Jack – Jack could be shot down at any time. She lived in even worse fear of the fateful letter arriving now. It would be unbearable if he was to die just before she was due to see him again. In desperation, she promised the boys a holiday in the cottage later on, when it was fixed up, which mollified them a bit. She just prayed that she would be able to come up with the goods. Worrying about them missing her added to the strain, making the sleepless nights even longer.

At last, just when it seemed the day would never come, it was Saturday. Rita packed a bag with one of Lily's dance dresses and the navy and white outfit she had bought on the Oxford Street shopping trip. Both of them made her feel even more guilty but she wanted to look nice for him. She would have bought something new if she could, but she had used up all her coupons getting things for the children.

She hardly took in a word anyone said all morning, but as Mr Wilkinson was full of his trip to the cottage, it hardly mattered. Mrs Wilkinson bustled in and out distracting everyone with lists and questions, and Wally was the only one who really got any work done. At midday they gave up pretending. The Wilkinsons set off for Fenchurch Street with a handcart full of tools and household goods, and Rita made for Liverpool Street with her overnight bag.

Once on her way, the worries evaporated. She was going to meet the man she loved. Excitement bubbled and fizzed inside her. She wanted to skip along the pavements, sing on the bus, tapdance up the station steps. She hardly had to queue at all for a ticket, and as she handed over the money she blessed all those hours of night shift she had worked. She could pay for this without worrying, and there was still plenty in her savings account. Diving into the Ladies, she changed into the navy dress. She had lost a bit of weight so it was slightly too big, but when she pulled in the belt it still looked good on her. It was a pity she didn't have navy shoes to match, but her black courts were still in good condition. She brushed her hair and pinned it up at the sides, put on some precious powder and lipstick, and placed the little straw hat at a jaunty angle on her blonde head. She smiled at her reflection in the mirror. Her face was glowing, her eyes sparkling. She looked beautiful.

'Hubby coming home, dear?' a passing woman asked.

'Yeah,' Rita lied. With a jolt of guilt, she looked down at her wedding ring. When the woman had gone into a toilet she hastily pulled it off and dropped it into the bottom of her handbag. Then she took a last look at herself. Reassured, she picked up her bag and went to wait for the train, pitying everyone else on the platform. Surely nobody was as lucky as she was.

It was one of those miraculous journeys that happen once in a blue moon. The train was on time, and she not only got a seat, but a window one. Her fellow passengers were a cheerful bunch of Americans who flirted outrageously with her the entire way, offering a non-stop supply of cigarettes, gum and sweets, which they called candy. Feeling young, carefree and admired, Rita responded in kind, though she made it quite clear she was not serious by telling them she was going to meet her boyfriend. They pretended utter heartbreak, but carried on teasing her just the same.

'You don't have none of them nylons, I suppose?' Rita asked. She had heard about these wonderful things, but never actually seen any.

'Honey, I got some right here in my pocket. You give me just one kiss, and they're yours,' one of them said.

Laughing, Rita shook her head.

'I'm saving my kisses. They're worth more than nylons.'

The GI groaned.

'You British girls. So beautiful and so hard to get.'

The train steamed into Norwich only ten minutes late. As she

193

stepped down from the carriage, helped by her new friends, the GI who had offered the nylons reached into his jacket pocket and pulled out a slim cellophane-wrapped envelope.

'Here, honey, you take 'em anyways. You got such cute legs you just gotta wear them.'

Rita was so touched she put her arms round his neck and gave him a smacking kiss on the lips, then with the Americans' laughter ringing in her ears, she set off down the platform to find out about her connection.

She had just twenty minutes until the local train went out. After all the sweets she had eaten, she was dying for a drink, but thought there would be no hope of getting one in that time. But her luck held. There were only a handful of people in the buffet queue, and the tea was lovely, not at all stewed. She even had time to go to the Ladies again.

The little branch line train was crowded with stout ladies carrying shopping bags and the usual selection of service personnel, but still she managed to squeeze a seat. Standing in the space between the seats was a group of aircraftsmen, eagerly discussing the evening ahead. Poppy Powers's name was mentioned.

'I knew Poppy Powers,' she said, before she could stop herself.

'You did?' the men said, looking at her with expressions ranging from envy to disbelief.

'Yeah. Her gran used to live round the corner from us on Dog Island. Poppy moved out when I was only a kid, but I remember her coming back for her gran's funeral. It was a slap-up do. Half the street was out of work at the time and some of the people hadn't eaten anything decent for months, and she puts on this huge funeral breakfast and invites the whole street. Me, I'd never seen nothing like it. There was kids running about with pork pie in one hand and cake in the other, not knowing what to eat first.'

'She's all right, is Poppy Powers. She could've stayed over in the States, but she came back the minute war was declared, and she's been to all the hot spots,' one of the men said.

'Yeah, and she doesn't just do the big places. She's been down air-raid shelters and on troopships and to places right out in the sticks. Cheered up a lot of people, she has.'

'And her music's good and all. Better than Tommy Dorsey any day.'

'Nobody's better than Tommy Dorsey.'

'Glenn Miller is.'

They discussed bands and bandleaders for the rest of the journey. Now that she was nearly there, Rita began to get nervous. She was hot and sweaty, and the navy dress had got creased.

'Is it far to Fenny Howe?' she asked.

'Two stations.'

Her stomach churned with a mixture of excitement, love and nerves. Two stations, and she would be there. She took out her powder compact and peeked in the little round mirror. What would Jack think? Would he like what he saw? She was terribly shiny about the nose. She dabbed on some powder and touched up her lipstick. What with her shaking hands and the rattling of the train, it was a wonder she did not spread it halfway across her face.

The little engine stood and panted for what seemed like an hour at the next station, taking on water.

'I could do with taking on water,' one of the airmen said.

'I could do with taking on beer.'

Rita just wanted to get there. At last the train moved off, rumbling through cornfields bright with scarlet poppies and dotted with trees. A plane lumbered overhead.

'Wellington,' the airmen said, without even having to look.

Rita felt as if she was going to burst.

The train was juddering and squealing to a halt. As one of the airmen opened the door, a waft of sweet air flooded in.

'Fenny Howe!' called a thick Norfolk voice outside.

Rita stood up, her knees turning to string. One of the men lifted her bag down. She staggered on to the platform.

The late afternoon sun dazzled her. For a moment she could see nothing but light and steam. There were lots of people getting off, nearly all in RAF and WAAF uniforms. She panicked. He wasn't there. She was stranded in the middle of nowhere.

'Rita!'

On a great wave of joy, she turned round. There he was, tall and handsome, striding towards her.

'Jack! Jack darling!'

She dropped her bag and ran into his arms.

# 25

Oblivous of the people swirling round them, they kissed with fierce hunger, trying to make up for all the long weeks of waiting. By the time their lips parted, the station had cleared and the platform was empty. Dizzy with happiness, Rita clung to Jack, revelling in the feel of his strong body close to hers at last.

'I thought this day would never come.'

'Me too. It's so good to hold you again. You can't imagine.'

'I can. I do. Oh Jack, I've missed you so much.'

They kissed again, less frantically this time, rediscovering each other.

Rita sighed with pleasure and looked up at him. His olive skin had acquired a deep tan, against which his brown eyes glowed as he gazed at her, but the lines of strain were deeper than ever.

'How are you? You got a lovely colour. You look like you been on a foreign holiday.'

'No such luck. But we get to sunbathe behind the huts – it's a perfect little suntrap. What about you? You look more beautiful than ever, but you've lost weight.'

'Yeah, well, I been worrying about you, ain't I?' She tried to make a joke of it, but didn't quite succeed.

Jack hugged her, stroking her head.

'My poor darling. You don't want to lose any sleep over me. I've survived so long I must be indestructible. I'm the crew's lucky mascot, I am. They know if I'm with them they'll be all right.'

Rita shivered. Despite the warm sunshine she felt a chill in her heart.

'Don't.'

She must not let the feeling of doom spoil the short time they had together.

'I think of you all the time.'

Jack took her face in his hands.

'I'm so glad you made it. I been looking forward to this so much it hurt.'

She looked into his eyes, and saw her own love mirrored there.

'Me too. I was so afraid something'd go wrong at the last minute and I wouldn't be able to make it. But now I'm really here it's like a dream come true.'

Jack kept one arm around her waist and picked up her bag.

'Come on, let's make the most use of the time we got.'

The airfield was on the far side of Fenny Howe from the station. As they strolled up the lane towards the village, Jack explained that he had booked her a room at the pub for the night. He had to be back at the airfield by six, but a transport was coming down to the village at half-past seven to pick up the local girls who were invited to the dance, so Rita could catch that. Rita felt a slight sinking of disappointment.

'It'll only be for an hour or so. Give you time to wash and change and that,' Jack pointed out.

'Yeah, you're right. It's just that I wanted to spend every moment with you.'

Jack gave a laugh and pulled her round to kiss her again.

'Just wait till later, then I'll see what we can do about that.'

Rita shivered in anticipation.

'I want to meet this crew of yours,' she said. 'Are they going to be there this evening?'

'You bet – just try and keep them away.'

'And I want to see all over the airfield. I want to know all about where you live and who you're with, and then when you write to me I'll be able to picture it all in my head. It'll make it all real for me.'

'Then that's what we'll do. A grand tour.'

It was a perfect summer's afternoon, late golden light slanting across fields of green corn and the air full of the humming of insects. The fields were bright with scarlet poppies and the hedgerows with wild roses; the warm scent of grass, leaves and flowers hung over the land. Rita sighed with pleasure. It was heaven. All this peace and beauty, and the man she loved. She could hardly hold so much happiness.

The village was a collection of pretty flint cottages with red pantiled roofs, roses and hollyhocks brightening their 'Dig for Victory' gardens. The pub, the Dun Cow, was totally different from the city establishments Rita was used to. It was so low she practically had to bend her head to get in the door, and the beamed ceiling in the one bar was black with three hundred years of smoke. Benches like church pews were set round the walls and there was a fireplace big enough to sit inside. The only modern touch was a bent aircraft propeller attached to the chimney breast.

'Off a Dornier what crashed on the cricket pitch,' the landlady proudly explained.

Rita was so fascinated with the place that she almost did not mind Jack having to leave. The room to which the landlady showed her was right up under the eaves of the pub, with sloping ceilings and an uneven floor. A brass bed covered with a faded pink taffeta bedspread stood in the middle of the room, a bright red rug beside it. An old-fashioned washstand stood in the corner.

'I'll bring you up some hot water,' the landlady offered. 'And there's tea, if you want it.'

Rita remembered that she had not eaten properly all day. She had been too nervous at breakfast, and in too much of a hurry to catch the train at midday. The prospect of tea and a sandwich was very welcome.

She opened the little dormer window and looked out over neat gardens and spreading fruit trees to where the fields marched off to the far horizon. A drowsy late afternoon peace hung over the village. A dog lay asleep in the back yard. Chickens clucked and scratched in the next garden. In the distance the square grey tower of the church in the next village could be seen rising from a fringe of yews. From here, you would not even guess there was a war on.

So this was what the country was like. She began to see why people went on about it. If she could live in a place like this, with Jack, she would be perfectly happy.

Jack. She must get ready for the dance. She turned away from the window and waltzed about the little room, hugging herself. Tonight they would dance together. Singing, she began to undress.

The journey to the airfield was in a lorry, crammed in with a gaggle of highly excited girls. Jack was there to meet her amongst the crowd of men.

'You look lovely,' he said, taking in the pretty white dress splashed with red flowers. 'It's so nice to see a girl who ain't in uniform.'

Rita smiled in delight. She knew she looked good. Lily's dress fitted to perfection and on her legs she wore the American nylons, their slippery sophistication making her feel like a film star.

'You look really handsome,' she replied. 'All them girls on the lorry will be dead jealous of me, coming here and snatching the best man from under their noses.'

True to his promise, Jack took her all over the camp. The canteen, the Nissen huts, the control tower, the hangars – Rita stored it all up in her mind. This was his world, and she wanted to share in it.

Music floated on the warm evening air. From all over the field, people were making their way towards the open doors of the largest hangar. Rita could hardly keep her feet from dancing.

'Come on,' she said, 'it's starting.'

Inside the hangar the air was already crackling with excitement. This was one dance that did not need warming up. Tickets had been sold out from the moment they were released, and everyone was out to wring the last ounce of fun from the evening. The entertainments committee had done their best to dress the place up, hanging up faded Christmas decorations and a string of flags, but these were eclipsed by the splendour of the Powers Girls. The thirty-piece line-up of women had brought their own lighting, which glinted on polished instruments and sparkly music stands, and they were dressed in the height of fashion in clinging satin evening gowns. Eyes starved of colour and glamour drank them in, amazed that such exotic creatures should be here in rural Norfolk.

The band was playing 'Chattanooga Choo-Choo', and already some couples were quickstepping. One pair was doing a stylish jitterbug, feet flashing, arms weaving and the girl's skirt flying, their energy clearing a space round them on the floor.

Rita gazed about her at the lofty space of the hangar, the crowd of people, mostly in uniform, and the brilliant band. It was so long since she had been to a dance that she had almost forgotten just how much she enjoyed them. And this was no ordinary dance: this was very obviously going to be a first-rate one.

'Oh – it's just wonderful,' she breathed, her face glowing.

Jack smiled down at her.

'You're so beautiful, specially when you're happy.'

A group of young men bore down on them, all younger than Jack; a couple of them looked no more than eighteen.

'So this is the mystery girlfriend. No wonder you kept her out of our way.'

'Blimey, Wilko, what a smasher.'

'Come on, Wilko, you going to introduce us?'

Keeping a possessive hand on Rita's shoulder, Jack introduced the members of his crew. Now the names she had come to know gained faces. Ray the captain, fair-haired and serious. Flash the co-pilot, as handsome and insolent as his nickname, Bonzo the top gunner, Taffy the rear gunner, Rozzer the bomb aimer. Laughing at their enthusiasm, Rita shook hands with them all. So these were the men on whom Jack's life depended, and who trusted him to get them safely to the target and home again through the night skies.

Flash ran lazy blue eyes over her from head to toe, obviously liking what he saw.

'Never knew you had such good taste, Wilko. Care for a dance, Miss Johnson?'

Rita hesitated, thrown by the 'Miss'. Jack had simply named her as Rita Johnson. She was glad she had taken the wedding ring off.

Jack's grip on her shoulder tightened.

'Not until I've danced with her, you old lounge lizard.'

And before Rita had a chance to say anything more, he swung her on to the dance floor. As they moved faultlessly into a foxtrot, Rita smiled up at Jack.

'You ain't jealous of him asking, are you?'

'Who, that slimy gigolo? No – you're not the sort of girl who'd fall for his type.'

'You wasn't going to let me say yes or no, though, was you?'

'Not likely. I want you all to myself.'

Smiling, feeling totally wanted and loved, Rita gave herself up to the pleasure of dancing with him. Jack led with assurance, steering her round the crowded floor, backing and turning with style. Rita found it blissfully easy to follow, her feet knowing just where to go, so that they flowed together, their bodies in harmony, as if they had been dancing with each other for years. With Jack's arm round her back, her hand in his, she was floating on air, and when the band started to play 'I'm in Heaven When We're Dancing Cheek to Cheek', she could only agree with every word of the song.

By the time the band took their first break it was getting unbearably hot in the hangar, even with the doors open, with the heat of the dancers added to the stored heat of the day. Along with dozens of others, Jack and Rita escaped outside and sat down on grass crisped by the sun. Jack drew her to him and kissed her.

'Enjoying it?'

'Mmm. It's the best time I ever had in my life.'

'Me and all. Everything's just right, ain't it?'

Everything except the fact that tomorrow she must go home and soon he would be up over Germany again. Rita pulled his head down and kissed him fiercely, wanting to blot out the future, to leave only the here and now. Jack responded, pushing her down to lie on the grass and running a hand sensuously over her breasts. She purred with pleasure, letting the delicious sensations run over her in waves. Jack's hand slid inside her dress, his fingers caressing her bare flesh, his thumb teasing her nipple. Rita gasped and pulled him closer, twining her legs with his.

'Rita, Rita, you're so lovely –'

His lips were hot on her skin, rousing her, while his hand travelled across her stomach, over her hip, down her leg.

'Mm, what's this?'

'Nylons.' She had almost forgotten them.

'Nice – all smooth and silky. Like you.'

His hand ran up and down the slippery surface.

Someone passed within inches of them, making them jump. Rita became aware of movement around them: couples necking, couples walking back to the hangar. Through the still air came the sound of the band playing 'Let's Face the Music.'

'We're too close to everyone here. Shall we go for a walk?' Jack asked.

Rita hesitated. She wanted to go with him, to follow through what they had started. But she also wanted to dance some more.

'Let's go back in for a bit. There's always later. And I want to meet Poppy Powers.'

Jack groaned.

'I see. I'm less important than a bandleader, and woman bandleader and all.'

'It's not that – it's just – I want to do everything this evening. Dance, and kiss you, and – well, it was so wonderful dancing with you, and I looked forward to it so much and for so long, and I just want to do it a bit longer, that's all.'

Jack smoothed a hand up her leg again, reaching the bare flesh of her thighs.

'You sure?'

She wanted him to go on. The music faded from her ears. His fingers tantalised her, making her ache with need. Involuntarily, she opened out to him.

'No – yes – oh please –'

Jack gave one last lingering caress, then sat up.

'Come on, we're going dancing.'

'But –'

'It ain't every day you get to hear the Powers Girls play. You don't want to miss nothing, do you?'

'Jack –'

He stood up, then caught hold of her hands and pulled her to her feet.

'I love you, Rita.'

Something made her look away, beyond the hangar. There, with the lowering sun behind them, stood a line of Lancasters, stark and sinister. She shuddered.

He followed her gaze, then caught her chin and turned her face to his, and kissed her.

'Forget it, sweetheart. Live for now. Tonight, everything's perfect.'

## 26

The sweaty heat of the hangar enveloped them like a blanket. The mood was electric, the big floor crowded with dancing couples, a moving sea of grey-blue enlivened by flashes of gold and the bright summer dresses of the civilian women. The music lifted and transformed them, turning ordinary young people with heavy burdens into the stuff of dreams. When the band played, they were no longer land girls or mechanics or cooks or gunners, coping with shortages, uncertainty and loss. For the space of a magical evening they were Fred Astaire and Ginger Rogers, and they lived in a fantasy world of glamour and romance.

Rita was swept up in the mood. The uniforms, the line of planes outside, only served to intensify it. Live for now. That was all that mattered. She held on to Jack, moved with him to the music and sang along with the words, every one of which seemed to have a special significance. Around her, other love affairs were blossoming, other special moments were being created, but she knew nothing of them. She was wrapped up in her own intense cloak of happiness.

Up on the makeshift stage of packing cases and planks, the Powers Girls were playing 'That Lovely Weekend'.

'Says it all, don't it?' Jack said.

'Mmm. Just right.'

'D'you want to make a request? They play requests.'

So many songs, all good in their own way. For the moment, Rita couldn't think of one that hadn't already been played that evening. Then a picture floated into her mind of summer evenings before the war, before she married Ron, of children dancing round a gramophone that someone had taken out into the street, and the record that was played over and over again, one of Poppy Powers's own compositions.

'I like that one of theirs. You know, that old one – "I Still Remember You".'

'Yeah, that's nice. We'll go up when this one's finished.'

They stood at the edge of the stage as the number ended, and Poppy Powers came over in answer to Jack's wave. The famous wide smile and dancing green eyes were devastating close to, so that you didn't notice the fact that she was no longer young.

'Wotcher. Enjoying y'selves?'

Everyone said how friendly she was, how fame hadn't spoilt her, but still it came as a surprise to have someone so well known greet you like a neighbour in the street.

'Oh, it's just wonderful. I never had so much fun in my life,' Rita said.

'We been talking about nothing else for weeks,' Jack told her.

Poppy Powers looked genuinely delighted.

'You two must be from my neck fo the woods,' she guessed.

Rita nodded.

'Trinidad Street,' she said.

'You never! Blimey, you never know who you're going to run into nowadays, do you? So who are you? No – let me guess. You must be a Turner. That hair of yours is natural, ain't it? Only Turners got that colouring, and not all of them.'

'Right! I'm Florrie's girl,' Rita laughed.

'Well stone me – how's things down on Dog Island? Place has taken a right pasting, ain't it? Nothing left of Cinnamon Alley when I went back last.'

'We're surviving. My mum, she got hurt a while back, but she won't leave the shop. Says people need her.'

'That's the spirit. And you –' Poppy turned her attention to Jack – 'you're never from Trinidad Street and all?'

'Whitechapel.'

'Near enough.' Her eyes went to the N-and-wing badge on Jack's uniform. 'And you're a navigator.'

'Yeah.'

'And you're both in love, I can see that.' Poppy looked at Rita again, and to her amazement she saw that the bandleader's eyes were filled with tears. 'I know what it's like, y'know. Bloody tough. My old man fought in the last lot. Look – I'd really like to talk some more, but I got to keep the show on the road. Can I play you something?'

206

'Oh yes, please – "I Still Remember You",' Rita said.

Poppy smiled.

'You couldn't of chosen better. I wrote that for my Scott, when we was apart.'

She bent forward, and kissed first Rita, then Jack.

'You look after her, Sunshine,' she said. 'Us Trinidad Street girls are something special.'

'I know. I will,' Jack promised.

'Enjoy the rest of the evening.'

Poppy went to the microphone to announce the number. Jack smiled after her.

'Ain't she wonderful?'

'Ain't she just,' Rita agreed.

They drifted round the floor to the strains of the romantic song.

The evening went through a rowdy stage, with a Paul Jones and couple of spot prize numbers, then settled into the last, slow phase, with couples wrapped round each other. Rita leaned against Jack, dancing in a dream, conscious only of the lilting music and the closeness of his body, hot against hers. Their arms moved out of a ballroom hold and into a clinch. Rita nestled her head into his neck and closed her eyes. She hardly noticed when the number ended.

'Come outside?' Jack asked.

Dreamily, Rita opened her eyes and looked up at him. Around them, people were finding partners for the next dance. She was aware of a burning need to kiss him.

'Yes,' she agreed.

Outside the light was fading. The cool air caressed their hot cheeks as they fell into each other's arms and kissed long and hungrily. Jack ran his fingers through Rita's hair.

'I love you.'

'I love you too.'

There were gigglings and scufflings and exclamations around them from other couples seeking the privacy of the twilight. Jack gave her another short kiss, then pulled away.

'Too many people round here. Come on.'

He kept one arm firmly round her waist and headed off across the airfield.

'It's got its uses, this double summertime,' Jack said. 'At least we're not stumbling around in the dark.'

'Where are we going?' Rita asked.

'Trust me.' She did.

They went away from the collection of huts and hangars, the music fading to a gentle background as they walked. The colours were fading too, into greys, against which the white daisies and cow parsley shone with a final intensity. Long grass swished beneath their feet, and Rita could hear the small noises of unseen night creatures.

'I think I'd like to live in the country. It's so quiet,' she said.

'It's nice in summer,' Jack agreed.

'Where are we now?'

'Near the perimeter fence – see?'

Rita did see: the chain-link and barbed wire that cut the field off from the rest of the countryside making it a kingdom all of its own.

Jack stopped, and spread his jacket on the ground.

'It's nice and comfortable here. And dry.'

He pulled her gently down to sit beside him on the jacket, then drew her into his arms and kissed her.

'Do you know, this is the first time we been together without something interrupting us, bombs or family or whatever?' he said.

Rita realised that he was right. At last, they were really alone. Home, family and responsibilities seemed so far away as to have ceased to exist. There was just the two of them, in the soft summer night.

'Lovely, ain't it?' she said.

They kissed, slowly, for there was all the time in the world. Jack ran his hands over her and she pressed closer to him, holding him tight, feeling the muscles of his back beneath the fabric of his shirt. Together, they lay down on the soft grass and breathed in the scent of hay. Rita's head spun as he caressed her, his fingers moving seductively over her body, lingering just long enough to arouse.

'Oh, that's so nice –' she breathed.

Jack's hand worked on her breast, sending waves of pleasure through her.

'I've dreamed of doing this so often. Having you here. Having some time. Always before there was somewhere one of us had to go and –' there was a hint of laughter in his voice – 'you had too many things on.'

He undid the buttons of her dress and slid his hand inside. Rita caught her breath at the feel of his fingers on her warm flesh and any last lingering reserve dissolved in the sensuous pleasure. Instinctively she reached to undress him, pulling at his shirt, undoing the buttons. Jack sat up and pulled it off over his head and got out of his trousers. Then he peeled off her dress and unhooked her bra.

'There –'

For a moment he stared at the glimmer of her pale body, while a breeze wafted across her and she ached for his touch. She gazed at him, lean and hairy and muscled, drinking him in.

'Jack –'

He lay down, and Rita felt the heat of his skin on hers and the scent of him and the weight of his body; it felt so right that she twined her arms and legs round him and kissed him deeply, revelling in their nearness.

'Rita, Rita, I never knew how beautiful you were. All this, wasted for so long . . .'

He ran his hand slowly over her buttocks and down her leg.

'I been keeping it for you.'

'Darling,' his voice was blurred with excitement. 'God – I do like these nylons. I can see why the Yanks give 'em out.'

He slid over the shiny surface and up inside her thighs until she was writhing with need.

'Nice?'

'Oh, yes, yes –'

His fingers slipped between her legs. She cried out loud and strained against him, pulling his head down to kiss him with passion.

'God, Rita, you're wonderful – you feel so good . . .'

As his fingers teased and explored, she could feel him hard against her thigh, and a great aching void opening inside her, a need that made her groan aloud and arch towards him. Just as she thought she would die if she waited any longer, he rolled on

209

top of her and thrust into her. She gasped at the fiery pleasure, all
the pressure of the long months of waiting driving her on. She rose
to meet him, wanting him deeper and deeper inside her, straining to
take every bit of him, to reach the peak that was building between
them. They rolled over and over in the grass, until she lost all sense
of who or where she was, till there was nothing but the love and
passion she had suppressed for so long flaring into a raging fire.
They came together in a shattering flood.

Rita drifted up into warm waters. Jack's weight was solid and
reassuring on top of her. Her body felt sleek and light with well-
being, but a great lump of emotion was lodged somewhere in her
chest, pressing on her until it erupted in great gasping sobs.

'Darling, darling, what is it? Did I hurt you?' Jack held her and
stroked her head and shaking shoulders.

'No, no, it was wonderful –'

'What is it? What's wrong?'

'I don't know – nothing – nothing's wrong . . .'

She could hardly explain it herself.

'It's just – I'm so happy – I never knew it was like that.'

'It's not been like that for you before?'

'No, never – it was – amazing . . .'

'I'm glad.'

Safe within his arms, she wept until the lump had dissolved
and she was left weak and spent and utterly happy.

Jack kissed her wet face.

'Better now?'

'Yes, I'm sorry. I dunno what come over me.'

'I love you.'

'I love you. I love you so much I can't bear it. Oh Jack, what
are we going to do?'

In answer, he made a trail of kisses down her body, lingering
on her breasts, circling her belly.

'We're going to do it all over again.

And to her astonishment, she found that she was ready, and
the delicious need was beginning to build once more.

'Oh yes –' she breathed. 'Oh yes please –'

It was four in the morning before she crept into her little room
under the eaves of the pub.

## 27

'I don't know how I'm going to bear it,' Rita said.

On the station platform the sun was still warm and the air still sweet. The birds still sang, but now they were mocking her. She was on the edge of a black abyss. When the train came in and she had to say goodbye to Jack, it was going to swallow her up.

'There'll be other times,' Jack said.

'Yes.'

But other times weren't now, and now was when she wanted to be here, to stay, to keep him with her and never let him near one of those evil aeroplanes again.

'I'm so glad you came. It's been wonderful.'

'That's why – it's been so wonderful I just can't bear it to end . . .'

She tried to hold back the great aching river of tears, but it throbbed in her throat and turned her voice into a squeak.

Jack held her in his arms. She clung to him with fierce strength, trying to imprint the feel of him on her body's memory, making the most of the last few precious moments.

At the end of the platform, the signal arm moved. Around them, other passengers stirred and looked expectantly up the line. There was a singing along the rails. Then, inevitable as death, Rita could hear the puffing of the engine, growing louder as it drew ever nearer.

Jack took her face between his hands and kissed her, long and slow and deep, leaving her breathless and trembling. The train was at the platform.

'I love you, Rita.'

'I love you.'

He opened the door, handed in her bag. She climbed inside and hung out of the open window. Jack held her hand.

'Look after Mum and Dad for me.'

'I will. Oh Jack, take care – stay safe –'

The guard's whistle shrilled. The engine tooted, and began to move. Rita leaned right out and planted a last swift kiss on his lips. And then the train was off, carrying her away, and he was already becoming part of the past. She waved and waved, shouting above the snorting and clanking of the engine.

'I love you, Jack —'

A bend took him out of sight. She sank back on to a seat, not knowing whether the carriage was empty or full. There was nothing now, nothing but a terrible bleak emptiness, and the dread that she might never see him again. The tears she had damned with such difficulty came bursting through. She dropped her head into her hands and wept in great tearing sobs.

The journey was a nightmare. For the first part of it Rita hardly noticed where she was or whether the train was going or not. It was only when she got to Norwich and had to pull herself together and find the right platform for the London train that she realised they had been over an hour late getting in and she had missed her connection. She stared up at the departures board, not really taking it in. It hardly mattered. Compared with the terrible hurt inside, nothing mattered. But she did have to get back to London somehow. With a great effort, she tried to make sense of the letters and numbers. They danced in front of her aching, swollen eyes, making no connection with her brain.

'Something wrong, dear?' a motherly voice asked. A beefy lady porter had paused by her, leaning on her trolley.

'The — the next London train,' she managed to say. Her throat was raw.

'Five past four. See? Platform Three.'

'Thanks,' Rita said automatically.

Five past four. Slowly, her dulled mind worked out that it would be late evening before she got home. She went to queue for the Ladies. After waiting for ages, she finally got in and looked at herself in the mirror. A blotched and puffy face with red-rimmed eyes stared hopelessly back at her. She splashed water on and felt just a tiny bit better, then looked for a towel. There were none. She tried to dab herself dry with a handkerchief sodden with tears, and ended up crying again.

The buffet was closed. The station was gradually filling up

with people, and all the benches were taken. Rita sank down on her bag and rested her head on her knees. She no longer cared what she looked like or what people might think. She sat huddled in misery, just waiting for time to pass.

She did not realise at first that the London train was being announced. When she did, she panicked. Scrambling to her feet, she looked wildly about. There seemed to be hundreds of people, mostly in uniform, all streaming on to Platform Three. She grabbed her bag and started scrabbling for her ticket. It wasn't there! Desperately, she turned out the entire contents of her handbag. Just as she thought she really had lost it, there it was, just where she had put it in the first place. Weak with relief, she cluched it in her hand and started to run towards the gate. The flood of people had thinned to a trickle. Doors were slamming. The collector waved her through.

'Hurry up, love. It's just about to go.'

She stumbled past the guard, his green flat raised, and wrenched open the first door she got to. She climbed up into a solid wall of bodies.

The train was packed to bursting. All the seats, all the spaces between the seats, all the standing room in the corridors was taken. Rita eased her shoulders between a thin soldier and a bearded sailor and put her bag by her feet. The carriage jerked, everyone was thrown against each other, Rita got an elbow in her ribs and a heavy boot on her toes.

For half an hour or so they trundled on, all packed together with a pall of cigarette smoke slowly filling the very little unused space. The train stopped. Then it went on very slowly for about five minutes before stopping again, this time in a station. Nobody got off, but several more tried to get on. Rita did not even have a partition to lean against or something to hold on to. She was standing in the centre of a mass of bodies, braced against the motion of the train. At least it did start moving; for that she was grateful. Everyone around her had huge kitbags. All were dressed in rough uniforms with protruding buckles and buttons that stuck into her, and all were sweating in the close heat.

Gradually the misery of her body began to match that of her heart. Her legs ached, her feet and ankles were swollen, she was bruised and jolted and her head was throbbing, and the air was so choked that she thought she was going to suffocate. The journey seemed to go on for ever, while ahead of her, in the future, she could see nothing to cheer her, just the terrible black pit of no more Jack.

Just when she thought she would collapse if she had to carry on much longer, she saw that they had entered the outer suburbs of London. Nearly home. But the prospect did not bring the comfort she needed. Home meant having to make out she had had a busy time helping out the Wilkinsons, followed by a short journey back. It meant having to act, and to lie. It meant having to hide her aching heart and chat to her mum as if nothing was wrong in the world, when all she wanted to do was to crawl into bed and stay there for ever. She was not sure whether she could do it.

The train pulled into Liverpool Street. She could hardly believe she had left it only the day before. It seemed like another lifetime. Wearily, she negotiated the buses; at least she could do that without thinking.

The London streets seemed dirtier than ever, in tune with her mood. Only twenty-four hours ago she had been dancing with Jack. Only twenty-four hours ago she had been on a peak of happiness. She got off at the West Ferry Road and plodded round the corner and into the battered remains of Trinidad Street. Children were whooping and yelling on the bomb sites. People were sitting out on their steps in the last of the evening sun. She hardly heard them as they called out to her. There was the shop. She couldn't face talking. She would tell her mum she was ill and go straight to bed.

Someone stepped out of the door. Someone in army uniform. Rita stopped short, staring. The blood seemed to drain from her. It couldn't be. But it was. Ron.

She was stunned, unable to speak, to move. Ron, here? She couldn't take it in. Then panic set in. She couldn't face him. She had to get away. She was just about to turn around and run when he saw her. He marched forward and caught her arm.

'Where the hell have you been?'

'I – I –'

He was glaring at her.

'I said, where the *hell* have you been?' he demanded.

Rita swallowed.

'Ron – I – what are you doing here?'

'My leave, ain't it? My leave. I come home, and what happens? My wife ain't here. She's gone off God knows where for the night.'

'I – I didn't know you was coming.'

'Too true you didn't. Thought you could just bugger off for the weekend. Some homecoming. Where you been, all dolled up like that?'

Rita realised she was wearing the navy and white outfit. It was creased and dirty from the dreadful journey, but still it had some of its former elegance. She wouldn't have worn it to go to the Wilkinsons' cottage. But she had no other cover story.

'I been down to Essex. Laindon. Been helping my boss and his wife.'

'No you ain't. I went to meet you at Fenchurch Street. Thought I'd give you a nice surprise, like. But you weren't there.'

Rita tried to think, but her brain was sluggish with misery.

'No, well, I only just got back.'

Ron stepped even closer to her. He glared into her face. As he spoke, he poked at her chest with a hard finger, emphasising each word.

'*You* only just got back, but *they* got back over an hour ago. I know. I saw them. And they said you ain't been near the place.'

Fear churned in her belly. He mustn't find out. He mustn't know about Jack. If he knew, he would turn it all into something squalid and sordid; it would ruin the love that she and Jack had.

With a sudden swift movement, Ron snatched her bag and marched back into the shop.

'Stop it!' Rita cried. 'You give me that back.'

But Ron took no notice. He slammed the door behind him and turned the bag upside-down. Rita tried to snatch it from him.

'Give it back. You got no right.'

Ron dodged her clutching fingers and shook the contents of the bag on to the floor. Out came her sponge bag, her underwear, the pretty dress, the American nylons. Ron pounced on these.

'Where d'you get them things from?'

'A Yank gave 'em to me.'

'Oh yeah? And what did you give him in return, eh? What?'

For a split second she almost went along with his suspicions, just to put him off the truth. But so outrageous a lie did not come easily to her.

'No! He just gave them. They're like that, the Yanks. Generous.'

'Huh. Show-off bastards, coming over here pinching all our women.' He stooped and picked up the dress, brandishing it under her nose.

'What's this, then? Dance dress? You been dancing, ain't you? Where you been, eh? Just where was you last night?'

Anger came to her aid, hot and swift. How dare he question her like this?

'All right,' she said, 'All right – if you must know.'

She paused, then out of the blue, inspiration came to her.

'I went down to Lily's airfield. They had a dance on there, and she asked me along.'

She held her breath. Her heart was thudding in her chest. She looked at him as he stared back at her, at the twist of his thin mouth, at his pale malicious eyes, at his undershot chin. God, she hated him. She had never known up to now just how much she hated him and everything about him. He had ruined her life.

'Bitch!' His hand lashed out, slapping her so hard across the face that her head rung. 'At your bleeding sister's, eh? Well, we'll see about that. We'll see what she has to say.'

He flung out of the shop, banging the door behind him.

'Bastard!' Rita yelled. She picked up a tin of peaches from the shop counter and flung it at the door. It hit with a splintering crack and dented. Rita slid down to the floor, sobbing, and began to gather up her possessions. This really was the end of the world.

'Rita, lovey –'

There was a sympathetic arm around her shoulders, gentle words in her ear. The smell and feel of her mother.

'Oh Mum –'

She twisted round and gave herself up to the offered comfort, crying in great sobs. But the magic was gone. She wasn't a little girl any more. She wasn't suffering from a cut knee or the taunts of a classmate. Nothing her mother could do or say was going to change the situation. She couldn't even tell her why so was so distraught. Her mother would be shocked if she knew.

'What is it, lovey? It's not like you to give way.'

Where to start? What to say? She could only think of all the things she mustn't say.

'It's Ron.'

That was true enough. But even so, a slight note of astringency crept into her mother's voice.

'Well, dear, no one's old man's perfect. That's life.'

You made your bed, you lie on it. The words didn't have to be spoken, they just hung on the air between them.

'I know but – but –' the words burst out before she could stop them. 'I had such a lovely weekend, so lovely, and then I come back and there's him . . .'

'Well, he was here on leave, dear. You really didn't ought to have gone off when he was coming home. Very cut up, he was. And then when you wasn't on the train I'm not surprised he was angry. Any man would of been.' Florrie was really serious now. 'Where was you, Rita? You wasn't with the Wilkinsons, was you?'

'I – I –' Then it hit her. *Lily*. Ron was on his way to see Lily. She had to speak to her before he did. She scrambled up, panic churning in her guts.

'I got to phone Lily. I got to talk to her. Her number –what's the number of the airfield?'

'But why – ?' Florrie asked, unable to follow the chain of events.

A scream of impatience erupted out of Rita's throat.

'Mum! Just tell me the number. Now!'

Florrie did not know. Phoning was only for emergencies. She had not spoken into a telephone more than twice in her whole life. It took nearly ten minutes for her to find the paper with the number on it. Rita snatched it up and with the last reserves of her energy, raced down the street to the box in the West Ferry Road. Fifteen frustrating minutes later, she was left staring at a dead receiver. First the operator had not been able to get through.

Then when the call was finally connected, the girl at the airfield had refused to have Lily found. Rita screamed at her, saying it was a matter of life or death. After a long time, and a lot of muttering and crackling on the line, the irritating voice came back. ACW Croft was not on duty at the present.

'Hell, hell, hell!'

Rita slammed the receiver down. She had to speak to Lily. Her hands shaking, she picked the thing up again, stuffed some money into the slot, and asked for the number of Lily's billet. The was a great deal of clicking and buzzing. Then the operator's measured tones.

'I'm sorry, caller, I am unable to connect you. Press button B to get your money back.'

'But I got to get through!' Rita shouted. 'Try again.'

The voice on the other end was icy.

'I'm sorry, caller, there are no lines available to Hampshire at present. Please try again later. Press button B and get your money back.'

Her head throbbing, her knees shaking, Rita sagged against the door, defeated. There was nothing for it but to try again in the morning. And hope that Ron would not manage to get down to Hampshire tonight.

## 28

'Lil! Lil, hurry up. You're late. There'll be hell to pay.'

'Go away –'

Lily groaned. Her head was hammering. Her stomach was fluttering. Her mouth felt like the proverbial bottom of a birdcage. She couldn't think why. She hadn't drunk that much, and anyway the beer was so weak it wouldn't have affected a baby. It must have been off. Come to think of it, it had tasted odd.

'Li*lee*, come on. You'll be put on a charge for sure if you're late again!'

'I don't care.'

'Well, I do. Get up.'

Betty whipped back the covers. Lily tried to claw them back, but her friend held on tight.

'It's for your own good,' she insisted.

Lily didn't have the strength to argue any further. Groaning, she lowered her feet to the floor and sat up. Then she put her head in her hands.

'I feel like death.'

'You shouldn't've gone drinking last night.'

'I know, I know. Don't nag, for Gawd's sake.'

By degrees, she allowed Betty to get her to the bathroom and into her uniform. Together, they hurried downstairs and out to the stable where they kept their bikes. It was half-past five of a perfect summer's morning. The birds were singing, the sun was shining, and as they set out down the driveway, the lime trees gave off a heady scent.

'Ain't it just lovely?' Betty sighed. 'Makes you want to sing.'

Lily grunted. The sunlight hurt her eyes and the lime blossom made her feel queasy.

'All right for some,' she said.

Well might Betty sing. She had just got engaged to a fitter from the machine shop called Wilf. Not that Lily envied her. She wouldn't have agreed to dance with him, let alone marry him. He was tall and gangly with a prominent Adam's apple and hands ingrained with black grease. But Betty loved him and he loved her. It was all beautifully simple. That much Lily did envy.

'Your turn'll come, Lily.'

'Thanks for nothing.'

They scrunched to a halt at the end of the driveway and opened the high iron gates. Once upon a time, a lodgekeeper would have run to let visitors in or out.

'Amazing, en't it, us living in a place like this? I'm glad they never took these gates away to make tanks or whatever.'

'Mmm,' Lily said.

Feeling as she did today, she couldn't care less about the gates or the house or anything else. She tried not to think about the day ahead: the greasy breakfast smell in the kitchens, the piles of dirty dishes, the cabbages waiting to be washed.

'I still don't understand why you gave that nice Neville the elbow,' Betty said. 'He was a right smasher, he was. Lovely eyes, lovely dancer, and mad about you. You're daft, you are. You don't know when you're well off. You ought to've hung on tight to him. I would've, if I was you.'

'But you ain't me,' Lily pointed out.

She didn't really know why she had told Neville to sling his hook. He'd been the most dashing boyfriend she'd had in ages. Good-looking, and fun to be with and, what was more, quite posh. His dad was a lawyer or something and Neville drove a natty red sports car, when he could wangle the petrol.

'Half the girls on the camp are crazy about him,' Betty said.

'More fool them.'

That had been half the attraction. They'd all been dead jealous when the MG had pulled up at the door and she had run down and jumped into the passenger seat. Their tongues had been hanging out. But when it came down to it, you couldn't keep on going out with someone just because everyone else wanted to. When it came down to it, Neville wasn't Jack. So she chucked him.

'Warren was more fun. And richer,' she said.

'Money ain't everything,' Betty said.

'Don't half help, though,' Lily said. 'And he had nylons, and doughnuts, and gum.'

'All Yanks've got them. But you had to pick him. I don't know what you saw in him.'

Warren showed her a good time. He told her stories about life in Texas that sounded like something out of the pictures. And with his dark hair and dark skin, he sometimes reminded her a little of Jack.

'You wouldn't understand.'

'No, I don't. Anyone could see he was only out for one thing.'

'Ain't all men?'

'My Wilf en't.'

Lily could believe that. He didn't look like he had enough lead in his pencil.

'Anyway, I can deal with that.'

'Yeah, so he goes and chucks you. And you go and get pie-eyed and now you've got a hangover. All because of him.'

'Oh, stop going on. You're worse'n my mum.'

'I'm only doing what a friend ought to.'

'I can do without friends like you.'

'Oh well, if that's the way you feel –'

Highly offended, Betty put all her sturdy strength into pushing the pedals on her bike. Lily watched her as she powered off up the lane, her back clearly speaking what she thought of friends who did not appreciate the effort she spent on them.

'Good riddance,' she muttered out loud.

She did not really mean it, but she needed some defence against the day. She felt ill, she was in for a bollocking when she arrived, and half the girls on the airfield would be crowing over her being given the push by Warren. She could kill him. As if it wasn't bad enough being the one who was chucked rather than the other way round, he had gone and stood her up outside the cinema in Alton High Street. He could hardly have picked a more public place. She hated all men.

Just as she expected, it was a bloody awful day. She was given all the worst jobs to do, and twice had to make a dash for the latrines and throw up. After the second time she felt rather

221

better, but it did not cure the sourness in her heart. When everyone else was taking a brief break for elevenses, she went out for a breath of fresh air. She leaned against the warm wall of a hut and lit a cigarette, drawing the soothing smoke deep into her lungs. That was better. She closed her eyes, letting the warmth of the sun play on her face.

'Oh – Lily – Lily Croft. It is Lily Croft, isn't it?'

Reluctantly, she opened her eyes. It was one of the telephonists. Lily disliked the telephonists. They thought themselves a cut above the kitchen crew.

'Might be. What's it to you?'

The girl looked po-faced.

'Oh, nothing. It's just that my oppo said there had been someone trying to contact you. Your sister, I think she said. Last night. But of course you were off duty then. I do hope it wasn't bad news?'

'No.'

Nosy bitch, just trying to get hold of some gossip. As if they didn't know enough, listening to everyone's calls. But curiosity stirred, closely followed by a twinge of fear. Why on earth had Rita been trying to phone her up, and at night? Perhaps it was bad news. Something happened to Mum, or Dad. Disturbed, she went to ring the billet. Yes, there had been a call for her there. Her sister. But she had not said what it was, just that everyone was all right.

Puzzled now, Lily went back to work. If it wasn't bad news, then why had Rita tried twice to contact her? She bent over the carrots, cutting them up with deft ease. Rita had never tried to phone her before. None of the family had. It was all very strange.

The last rush up to dinner time began. The kitchens became a boiling inferno of steam and short tempers.

'Lily! There's bleeding brown job asking for you.'

Lily put down her knife, grateful for any distraction.

'What's one of them doing here?' someone asked.

'Who is it, Lil?'

'Search me.'

She never went out with army men. Not with all these airmen to choose from, plus the Yanks down the road. A sailor she might

222

be tempted by, but never a soldier. Waiting till the corporal's back was turned, she went to the back door of the kitchen. It was Ron.

'Well blow me,' she said. 'What the hell are you doing here?'

He was clearly in a foul mood. He did not even give her one of his leers.

'What d'you think I'm doing here? D'you think I come all this way for my bleeding health?'

Lily shrugged.

'I dunno.'

She didn't much care, except that she might now get an answer to the mystery of Rita's calls. If it wasn't for that, she might well have gone straight back in the kitchen and got someone to chuck him out. She was sure he wasn't supposed to be here.

'Was Rita here Saturday night?'

The question so surprised her that she could only gape at him.

'What?'

Ron gritted his teeth with impatience.

'Rita. Your sister, you stupid bitch. Was she here Saturday night?'

The anger and resentment that had been boiling in her all morning surfaced.

'Don't you come here calling me names. I'll get the MPs on to you.'

He backed off a bit at that. She guessed he had got in through the fence somewhere.

'You don't have to do that,' he said. Then, rather less aggressively than before, 'Well, was she?'

Lily played for time. There was something funny going on here.

'Was she what?'

'Here. Was Rita here Saturday night?'

Lily looked at him. She always had loathed him. Nasty little creep. She was not going to tell him what he wanted straight away, if at all.

'So what if she was?'

'So I want to know, that's what.'

Lily smiled. She was beginning to enjoy this.

'Why?'

'Because she said she was. For a dance.'

Suddenly, it all fell into place. Rita knew he was on his way to see her. She had been trying to get through to her to make sure the cover story was in place. But a cover story for what?

'Maybe she was –'

'Bitch!' Spit flew from Ron's mouth. 'The bitch, coming down here for a dance. All night. That's where she met the Yank, I suppose. I'll get her for this –'

What Yank? Lily couldn't think what he was getting at.

'– but then maybe she weren't,' she said, cutting in on his invective.

'What?'

'I didn't say she was, did I?'

Where had Rita been that she needed to say she had come down to Hampshire? Not just out for the evening in London, that was for sure. She must have been away all weekend, which was not like Rita. She always went to see the kiddies on Sunday, regular as clockwork. Then with sickening certainty, she knew. There was only one place Rita would go, and that was Fenny Howe. To see Jack.

'For Christ's sake, Lily!' Ron was beetroot red in an attempt to hold on to his temper.

She had never forgiven Rita for taking Jack off her. If Rita hadn't done the dirty on her, she might have been engaged to him by now. She might even have been married to him. Mrs Jack Wilkinson. She would have been a happily married woman, instead of a kitchen hand with a hangover who'd been stood up in the High Street where everyone could see. She looked Ron straight in the eyes.

'She weren't here. I ain't seen hide nor hair of her since last time I went home. Weren't no dance here this Saturday, neither.'

'Then where the bloody hell was she?'

Lily shrugged.

'P'raps you better ask her that.'

'You bet I will.'

Ron marched off, leaving Lily with the satisfaction of revenge.

That would teach Rita, she told herself. Let her get out of that one. If she thought she was going to lie to cover up for her going to see Jack, she had another think coming. Ron was her husband, and she had better remember that, not go pinching other people's boyfriends.

But somehow, it was poor compensation for losing Jack.

## 29

'That was a funny old do yesterday evening, weren't it?' Mrs Wilkinson said, first thing Monday morning. 'Your hubby turning up at the station like that. What made him think you was with us? Got in a right state, he did, when you wasn't there.'

Rita tried to think. She had forgotten that the Wilkinsons were involved with it as well.

'Oh – er – it was all a mix-up. Got his lines crossed,' she mumbled.

Mrs Wilkinson gave her a suspicious look.

'But you always go and visit your kiddies of a Sunday, don't you?'

'Well that's him all over. Don't never listen to nothing. Don't tell me nothing neither. I never knew he was coming home on leave,' Rita said. She prayed that Mrs Wilkinson would not ask any more questions. She did not know if she could take it. It must have shown in her face.

'You feeling all right, Rita?' Mrs Wilkinson asked.

All right was so very far from what she was feeling that it was almost funny. Rita could feel the hysterical laughter lurking somewhere in the churning of fear and misery inside. She nodded, hardly trusting herself to speak. If she did, the laughter or tears might come bursting out.

Mrs Wilkinson was full of concern.

'You don't look well at all. P'raps you need a break. Do you no end of good, that would. You should of come with us this weekend.'

If only she had. She wouldn't now be waiting for Ron to come back. But then – she would not have missed seeing Jack for the world. Whatever happened, however bad she felt now, she still had that memory, shining and perfect.

'Yes, that's what you need,' Mrs Wilkinson carried on, 'a nice couple of days in the country. Me and Bill, we feel like new people. It's so quiet down there, you wouldn't never believe it. You wouldn't know there's war on. Birds singing and all that. Not that we sat around. Dear me no! Worked like slaves, we did. Look at my arms – see, all covered wtih scratches. Brambles, that was. Brambles all over the garden. But we got a lot of it cleared. Bill, he's going to plant vegetables. Just think – nice fresh cabbages and spuds and that. Be lovely. And the little cottage, you ought to see the state of it. Wicked, really, the way it's been let go, specially when there's people bombed out of their houses. You must come and see it. Bring them kiddies of yours. They'd like to play in the garden. Do 'em good, it would.'

Rita went through the motions of listening and agreeing and thanking, but she hardly heard one word in ten. Where was Ron now? Had he managed to speak to Lily? Would Lily support her story, or would she not realise and drop her in it? She could cope with Ron thinking she had been dancing with Lily. He could make as much of that as he liked, she didn't care. If he thought she was playing around with someone down in Hampshire, then let him. But she couldn't bear it if he found out about Jack. What she and Jack had was beautiful and precious. If Ron said so much as a word about it, it would become tarnished. Ron soiled everything he touched.

And it was not just him. Their marriage was a disaster, but at least it was a marriage, on the surface. If Ron were to divorce her, her mother would be devastated. And the boys would suffer. The other children at their school would find out and call them names; call her names in front of them. She couldn't bear that. It wasn't their fault that they had her and Ron as parents. She had to keep up at least an appearance of normality, for their sakes.

'. . . me make you a nice cup of tea, dear. Time of the month, is it? You didn't ought to of come in today.'

She hadn't wanted to come in, but then she couldn't have stood staying at home, waiting. Of the two, going to work seemed preferable. There was more to distract her. When it came to it, though, nothing was riveting enough to stop the thoughts and the worries from chasing round her head in demented circles.

'I had to,' she said.

'Rubbish. These men, they don't understand what we women

go through. If you're having a bad time, you ought to stay in bed with a hot-water bottle on your stomach.'

Rita's eyes filled with tears. Mrs Wilkinson was so kind, but it would take far more than a comforting hot-water bottle to cure what she was feeling. She accepted the tea with thanks and tried to concentrate on what she was doing, but found she was staring at the same piece of paper for ten minutes at a time without it making any sense at all. She glanced up at the clock. Yesterday, just yesterday, at this time, she was standing on the platform with Jack. She had him in her arms. She kissed him. Just twenty-four hours ago. It seemed like a year.

The day dragged on. How long did it take to get to Hampshire and back? Maybe Ron had not managed to get a train last night. But it wasn't that far. Even with the trains as bad as they were, he was sure to be waiting for her when she got home. Supposing she didn't go home. Supposing she just walked out of here and disappeared. The idea curled seductively round her brain. She even worked out a few practical moves. Go to a station. Take a train. Find lodgings. Find work. But she knew she was only pretending. To do that would be to walk out on everyone she loved. The boys. Her parents. It would be like destroying part of herself. No, she just had to face whatever was coming.

The sunshine was still bright as she came out of work at six o'clock, but whereas in the country it had been clear and glorious, here it only showed up the dirt and devastation. Sultry heat breathed back from the brick buildings. Rita felt sick and physically weak. She had not eaten anything all day, not had a decent meal since breakfast yesterday at the Dun Cow. The sun chased her over the street to where black shadows invited.

A figure stepped out of a doorway. A man in khaki. Ron. Rita gasped, just swallowing down a cry.

'Surprised? You didn't ought to be. You never thought you'd get away with it, did you? Bitch.'

He caught hold of her arm, his fingers digging into the soft flesh above the elbow. He was sweating copiously inside his heavy uniform. Rita swallowed.

'I dunno what you're talking about,' she said.

'Don't give me that.'

Other people were coming out of the factories and workshops, calling out to each other, remarking on the weather, heading for home. Just as normal. Rita felt apart from it all, as if there was a sheet of glass separating her from real life. For her situation wasn't normal, and neither was the expression on Ron's face. It was fanatical with hatred. Hatred, and something else: something sinister, almost a sort of twisted enjoyment.

'Let me go.'

She tried to twist out of his grip. His fingers tightened like a tourniquet and he gave a wrenching tug at her arm.

'Oh no. You're coming with me. We got things to talk about.'

For a fleeting moment she considered calling out for help. But the eyes of the homegoing workers avoided hers. Just a soldier meeting his woman from work. It was none of their business what happened between man and wife. If they knew the truth, they would probably be on Ron's side. He had a right to be angry. She had done the dirty on him.

'Get moving.'

He started walking along the street, pushing her in front of him, propelling her with vicious pressure on her arm.

'Stop it,' Rita said. 'You don't have to –'

'Oh yes I do. It's the only thing whores like you understand. Move!'

The toe of his army boot met her leg. She winced and gasped.

'You heard me.'

They reached a building abandoned by its owners, an old workshop with its windows boarded up but a door sagging partly open on one hinge. Ron put his boot to it and dragged her inside. She tried again to get away from him as he attempted to kick the door shut, but he fetched her a punch to the ear that left her head ringing and momentarily stunned her.

Real fear flooded her. She had to get out of this. She had to get away. Now. Now. She looked around at a dusty space half the size of the Wilkinson factory lit by glass skylights, miraculously unbroken. The windows were boarded up. Behind Ron was the door, the only way out, but he would get her before she could drag it open. Her breath was coming in gasps. She looked down. Various pieces of debris were scattered about the floor. She stooped to grab a length of wood, but he was too quick for her. His boot crashed down on it, trapping her fingers underneath. She yelped with pain, then cried out as his fist struck her head again. Dull red lights floated in front of her eyes. She staggered and fell.

He was looming over her, wielding a length of timber: two by two, her brain automatically registered. She tried to scramble away, but each move she made, he blocked, laying about her body and legs with the club. She found herself backed against the wall. Trapped. A cold sweat broke out all over her and trickled down her body. She crouched, her eyes flickering between his face and the crude weapon in his hand.

He looked down at her, a mirthless smile stretching his thin lips.

'Now – talk.'

Rita swallowed.

'Come on, out with it. You given me the runaround all right, ain't you? All the way down to bleeding Hampshire.'

A last foolish defiance forced her to talk back.

'No one asked you to.'

Crack. The wood smashed into the side of her knee, wringing a gasp of pain from her.

'Where was you? And don't give me none of that crap about going to some dance with your bleeding sister. Your sister ain't seen hide nor hair of you, and there weren't no dance, either.'

So Lily had let her down. She deserved that. Lily had loved Jack.

'Where was you?'

The timber swung again, this time coming for her head. Terrified, she ducked, putting up her arms as a shield. She had to escape. There was no escape. The length of wood hit her forearms with a force that made her cry out.

'Tell.'

'I – I –' Her mind was a terrifying blank. She needed a lie, a good lie, but none came.

'It was that Yank, weren't it? That bastard Yank what gave you them bleeding nylons. What else did he give you, eh? Eh?'

'Yes!' She snatched at his unknowing gift, desperation losing her tongue. 'Yes, yes, yes. I been seeing a Yank. And I'm glad. Glad! Because he's everything you're not. He's kind, and clever, and brave, and he treats me like I'm something special. When I'm with him, I feel like I'm a proper woman. And you know why, because he's a proper man. Not like you –'

With a howl of anger, Ron threw the timber across the floor and launched himself at her, his hands reaching for her throat.

'Bitch! Whore! I'll teach you –'

Rita tried to fight back, kicking, biting, scratching, but nothing she could do made any difference. She hurt all over: the pain where the timber had thudded into her was excruciating, and her bruised arms and legs would not obey her. Ron was much stronger than she remembered. Army life had toughened him up. He forced her on to her back, kneeled on her, his hands pinning her wrists on the ground above her head. His face was inches away from hers, red, triumphant, dripping sweat.

'Now,' he panted. 'Now, we'll see who's the real man.'

For a moment, Rita did not realise what he meant. Then he let go of one of her arms and began to undo the buttons of his trousers.

'No –' she moaned.

She knew she had no strength left. She couldn't get away now if she tried.

'Yes. You filthy whore. By the time I finished with you, you ain't going to want no other man up you never again.'

Rita gathered up the saliva in her mouth and spat in his face.

'Bitch!'

The flat of his heavy hand smashed into each side of her face, once, twice, three times. She braced herself.

'No –'

She looked at him covertly. He was sitting back on his heels, surveying the dusty workshop. She could see the angry purple of his erection.

'No, that's too good for you. Something else, something you'll hate – yes.'

He got to his feet and pulled her up. Every bone and muscle of her body protested.

'Over here –'

He dragged to where a broken-backed chair stood abandoned.

'Yeah, yeah, perfect,' he gloated.

He gave her a violent push that sent her staggering, then forced her down beside the chair.

'Kneel. That's right, kneel. Lean over. Right. Yeah –'

She bit her lips, trying not to whimper, trying not to let him have the satisfaction of knowing her terror and her humiliation. Her skirt was dragged up, her knickers wrenched down, and then there was a slicing pain, driving into her, tearing her apart. It went on and on, punctuated by his grunts and his swearing.

'You hate that, don't you? You bitch, you filthy whore. You hate it –'

Tearing and jabbing, until she was nothing but a burning pulp inside. And then he turned her over, and entered her from the front. There was a last cry, and it was over.

She stayed perfectly still, gasping for breath, trying not to sob. She heard him get up.

'You listening?' he aimed a kick at her. 'You better be. You tell that fancy man of yours there ain't going to be no divorce. You're my wife, mine. Nobody else has a bit of what's mine. If I find you been playing away again, you know what you'll get. And next time I'll make sure no man will ever want to look at you again.'

She heard the clump of his boots on the floor, the dragging of the door as he opened it. And then he was gone. She slid down to the floor. Every cell of her body felt violated. She lay and wept. Not until it was dark did she attempt to get up and make her painful way home.

## 30

It was not until she woke that Rita realised she had actually managed to sleep. With the blackout curtains over the window, it was difficult to make out what time of day it was, but from the light filtering under the door and the sounds in the street and from downstairs she thought it must be mid-morning. She did not want to face this day, or any other. She turned over and buried her head in the pillow.

Moving was agony. Her whole body ached, with points of worse pain where the bruises were, but it was nothing to what she felt in her heart. The events of the previous day reeled before her again. There was nothing she could do to stop it. Ron's face, his words, his actions, battered against her brain and reverberated through her body, until she groaned out loud. She was not safe even here, in her own room under her parents' roof, for he was inside her head, tormenting her. She curled up, squeezed her eyes shut, put her hands over her ears, but she could not shut him out: *bitch . . . filthy whore . . . bastard Yank . . .*

An instinct for self-preservation made her snatch at the phrase. One thing she had saved from the wreckage. He did not know about Jack, or he would have used it against her. As long as he thought it was some unknown American, the worst had not happened. She hung on to the thought like a life-raft. Through everything that had happened, she still had those precious hours with Jack, walking down the lane, dancing in the hangar, making love under the stars. They were still complete and safe, protected from Ron's touch. She blessed the cheerful generosity of the GI on the train. Little did he know just how important his gift had proved to be. She even found it in her heart to be grateful to her sister, for even though Lily had not backed up her cover story, at least she had not let on about who she might have been seeing, despite the fact that she must have suspected the truth.

*. . . my wife . . . no divorce . . .*

There was no way out. With Ron refusing to let her go, she was tied for ever. What court would give her a divorce if she tried? Who was going to believe she had been raped? He was her husband. He was only taking his marital rights. The bruises to her body would fade, and nobody could see the ones to her heart and mind.

The doorhandle turned. Rita lay still, pretending to be asleep. She did not want to talk to anyone, not even her mother. Especially not her mother. Florrie didn't understand.

Footsteps creaked softly over to her bed. She could hear her mother's breathing. Then fingers touched her head, loving, soothing.

'My poor baby,' Florrie whispered.

Rita was so surprised that her eyes flicked open.

Florrie was remorseful.

'Oh pet, I didn't mean to wake you –'

'I wasn't asleep,' Rita admitted. Her throat was cracked and dry. Even talking hurt.

Florrie sat down heavily on the bed. She stroked Rita's hair.

'What happened, lovey? You can tell your old mum. You was in such a state last night I didn't like to ask.'

Rita licked her lips.

'No.'

'I been and telephoned them Wilkinsons. Told them you was poorly.'

Through the blur of pain, Rita felt a mild astonishment. Her mother went and used a phone.

'Thanks,' she whispered.

'I knew something was up when he came home in such a paddy. Real nasty look there was on his face. Didn't say a word to us, he didn't. Just marched straight through the parlour and up the stairs into here. We could hear him banging around and swearing. Then down he came, with his kit. Still not a word. Stalks through, knocking the teapot off of the table with his kitbag, and out of the door. Just like that.'

A small tendril of relief curled through Rita's churning emotions. Ron had packed up and gone. She might not have to face him again, at least not this leave.

'Good,' she said.

'And now I seen what he done to you, he better not show his face round here again, neither. I don't care what you done, that ain't no excuse for beating you up like that. That's wicked and cowardly, that is, wherever it was you been last weekend. Not that I'm saying I approve, mind, but a man's got no right to hit his wife like that. If ever he lays a finger on you again, I'll kill him, so help me.'

Wincing, Rita turned over to stare at her mother. She had to. There was such a force of venom in her voice that she needed to see her expression. Florrie's thin face was set, her eyes burning with ferocity.

'I mean it,' she said. 'I done it before and I'll do it again.'

Rita could feel the force of her will.

'You *what?*' she gasped.

'I said, I done it before. Killed a man what was murdering his wife.'

'*Mum!*'

Florrie's mouth clamped shut in a tight line.

Rita reached out to put a hand on her arm. Such an extraordinary statement could not be left hanging in the air, unexplained.

'Mum, what do you mean?'

'I can't tell you. I said too much already. I didn't ought to of opened my mouth.'

'But Mum –'

'I was just so cross. I can't bear it, seeing a woman beaten like that. And my own daughter and all. It brung it all back.'

'What? Brung what back?'

In the pressure of the moment, even her own situation was pushed aside.

Florrie was obstinately silent.

'I'll ask Dad,' Rita threatened.

'He knows. Your aunties and uncles know and all. But they won't tell, so don't bother asking.'

'But –'

'How are you feeling this morning, anyhow?'

Rita sighed. There was no getting round her mother when she made up her mind.

'Dreadful,' she said.

'Poor pet. I'll bring you some tea and toast.'

Rita could not take it all in. Sympathy was the last thing she had expected.

'Mum, why – ? I mean, you always said he was my husband whatever and I had to stick with it.'

The hard anger crept into Florrie's voice again.

'Not if he lays about you like that. I can't bear it, that sort of violence. I seen too much of it when I was a kid. My dad –'

She stopped abruptly. When she spoke again it was quietly and almost matter of fact, avoiding Rita's eyes.

'It was him what I killed. He was beating up my mum and she was crouching there, whimpering, and suddenly I snapped. I couldn't take it no more. I picked up a broken chair leg and I hit him. He fell against the range and stove his head in. Your Uncle Harry carried him down the river and dropped him in. The police thought he'd been in a drunken brawl.'

She looked at Rita.

'So now you know. So keep your mouth shut. I don't never want to talk about it again. I'm going to get you some tea, and some witch-hazel for them bruises.'

She was gone, and Rita was left staring at the ceiling, reeling with the shock.

The revelation did nothing to lessen her own troubles. She was still torn and humiliated, still burning with hatred for Ron, still fearful of his returning some time, still legally tied to him. On top of this she now had to contend with the knowledge that her mother had been instrumental in killing her grandfather. It was all too much to take in. The only thing she could rest her mind on was Jack, but even that was no real comfort, for though she had the beautiful memories, she could not depend upon anything in the future. When she looked ahead there was nothing but darkness, blocked by the shadows of Ron and the Lancaster bombers. Looking at that, she hardly felt the sting of the witch-hazel on her wounds.

By the next morning, she decided she must go into work. It still hurt to walk, to sit, to stand, but staying at home did nothing to distract her from the mental distress.

'You sure you'll be able to cope?' her mother asked.

'I don't know. But I got to try. I'll go mad, sitting round here.'

She limped to the bus stop. The same people were waiting. The same route was taken. The usual things were said by the passengers. Outwardly, nothing had changed. But only this time last week she had boarded the bus so full of hope and feverish excitement, looking forward to her weekend away, worrying only about what to say to the children and how to keep from letting the Wilkinsons guess the state of her feelings.

'Cheer up, ducky,' the conductress said. 'It might never happen.'

'It already has,' Rita told her.

But even as she said it she knew it was not true. The very worst had not happened. The Wilkinsons had not got a letter from Jack's commander. She tried to hold on to that.

She reached the stop in Whitechapel and walked to Prittlestone Road, but when she reached the corner she was seized with such a sick terror that she nearly threw up in the street. For just twenty yards away was the building into which Ron had dragged her. She stood rooted to the spot. She could not pass it again. She just could not. She turned back, only to stop on the next corner. If she did not go in to work she was letting Ron get the better of her. But she could not go past the place again. She would go round the block and approach the Wilkinson factory from the other end of the road. It was longer, and in her present weakened state she could do without the extra distance, but it was preferable to passing that broken door. Trembling, she started walking.

She was so taken up with her inner turmoil, and with breaking Ron's hold over her actions, that there was no room for the usual dread she felt when approaching the factory, not knowing if bad news awaited her there. Instead it was a beacon, a goal to be reached. She fixed her eyes on it, not letting herself look beyond to where the deserted workshop stood. There was Wally waiting outside as always, looking as if he carried all the cares of the world on his shoulders. But then gloom was just part of Wally; she would have been surprised to see him anything other than glum. They nodded at each other as she reached the entrance, equally wordless. Rita leaned against the wall. Her legs felt like rubber.

There was a rattling inside as the bolts were drawn. Rita wondered just how she was going to get through the day. Perhaps she should not have come. Staying in bed for another day suddenly seemed the better choice. The door opened, to reveal Mr Wilkinson.

Rita cried out in shock. He looked terrible. He seemed to have aged ten years since last she saw him. His normally cheerful face was grey and drawn, his eyes hollow. All the foreboding of the past months came back and hit her with a terrible certainty. She stepped forward, gripping his arms, staring into his face, willing him to deny what she feared.

'It's not – ?' her voice cracked with the strain.

Mr Wilkinson said nothing, but his face trembled.

Rita swallowed.

'Jack?' she managed to whisper.

He nodded.

The world spun around her, a dark void. No, it couldn't be true. She didn't believe it. She wouldn't believe it. A merciful numbness stole over her, protecting her. She was vaguely aware of Wally shuffling off into the factory. She and Mr Wilkinson were left facing each other in the doorway.

'When – How – ?' the questions would come out only as disjointed words. 'He ain't – tell me he ain't –'

'Monday night, over Berlin.'

Mr Wilkinson's voice was a feeble trace of his normal one. She would hardly have known that it came from the same man.

'But is he – ? Did they see – ?'

She couldn't form the words, couldn't ask if anyone had seen him die. She stared into Mr Wilkinson's face, willing him to give her some shred of hope to hold on to.

He shook his head, just a shadow of a motion. Speaking seemed to be an effort for him.

'They saw three parachutes. They don't know who it was.'

Oh God, please, please let one of them be him.

Mr Wilkinson was speaking again.

'The wife – terrible state –'

Rita became vaguely aware that she was not reacting right, not playing the part of a mere employee. She was not saying what

238

people usually said. She tried to come out with the correct words.

'I'm so sorry – if there's anything –'

'It's the wife,' Mr Wilkinson repeated. 'I can't – our only son . . .'

Rita knew she did not have the strength to support anyone else in their grief. She could hardly cope with her own. But she had promised. It was the very last thing Jack had asked of her. *Look after Mum and Dad for me.*

'I'll go to her,' she said.

The front door of the house was open. Rita went in. She had no idea what she was going to say. What was there to say that could be of any comfort? No words could take away the fact of the plane being shot down, of only three of the crew getting out.

Mrs Wilkinson was sitting at the kitchen table. She looked up as Rita came in. The flesh of her face seemed to have retreated, leaving harsh bones pushing against the skin. Spread out before her on the green chenille cloth were all the photographs she had so proudly shown to Rita in the past, the pictures of Jack as a baby, as a schoolboy, as a young man.

There didn't have to be words. Rita sank to her knees beside Mrs Wilkinson. The two women clasped each other and wept.

# 31

'You stuck-up cow!'

Joan's fingers closed round the nearest thing – a pot of jam. Months of bottled-up emotions surged to the surface, like a pressure cooker about to blow. Looking after all the children, Ted's going away, the new baby and now, grinding into her day and night, the news of Ted's capture. And through it all, there had been Queenie's snide remarks, which had grown steadily worse since George had at last been called up. All through the long months she had coped with it all. Good old Joan. Reliable Joan. Sensible Joan. But there were limits, even to her control.

The pot was cool in her hot hand. Queenie was glaring at her with that loathsome pursed-mouth expression on her face.

'How dare you speak to me like that in my own house, you common little slut?'

The pressure cooker burst. Joan lifted the jam and threw. With a glorious sense of release she watched as it hurtled across the kitchen, narrowly missed Queenie's head and smashed against the kitchen wall, the glass shattering into lethal shards while the jam splattered like thick blood. There was a split second of shocked silence. Then Queenie gave a shriek of outrage.

'Just look what you've done! My kitchen! The mess! Jam everywhere!'

It was everywhere. It speckled the window, the dresser, the sink, the floor. Where it had hit the wall it trickled down in a sticky river. It was the most spectacular thing Joan had ever done in her life. She felt a welling up inside her and hardly knew whether it was a scream of rage or a river of tears. It erupted as laughter, wrenching out of her in furious gasps. She had no control over it. Her stomach heaved with laughter, her lungs ached, her face creased up and tears rolled down her cheeks. Through a blur, she saw Queenie's expression of disbelief and horror, and laughed all the more. Faintly she realised that this was the very best thing she could have done, that Queenie could have reacted to anger or tears, but that she just did not know what to do about laughter. Enjoying herself, revelling in the release from all constraint, she picked up the milk jug and threw the contents over Queenie.

'That's what I think of you and your kitchen and the mess!' she cried, hardly able to get the words out for laughing.

The milk plastered Queenie's colourless hair to her head. It dripped down her face and off the end of her sharp nose. Queenie just stood there, her mouth opening and shutting, spluttering with rage. Enchanted, Joan picked up the sugar bowl. This was wonderful. She was outside of herself. The rules no longer applied. She could do whatever she liked.

'No!' Queenie screamed.

Joan hefted the bowl in her hand, taunting her.

'Put it down, put it down, you – you –'

Joan tipped the bowl, letting the precious sugar run out over the floor. It crunched satisfyingly under her feet.

Queenie pounced, her face sharp and vicious as a weasel. She snatched the bowl out of Joan's hand and slapped her hard across the face. Joan gasped.

'You guttersnipe! Get out of my house! I never want to set eyes on you again.'

The laughter died. Joan's cheek stung. She looked back at Queenie and at the hatred in her eyes. With something close to surprise, she saw the red-spattered kitchen. Through the window she could see the old black pram under the apple tree with little Teddy asleep inside.

'Don't worry,' she said. 'I'm going.'

She turned and walked into the hall and up the stairs. A scuttering sound caught her attention. She looked round the door of the back bedroom. There were the children, hers and Rita's, huddled together on one of the beds, looking silently back at her with frightened eyes. With a jolt of guilt, she realised that she had not given them a thought while the row had been going on. They might well have not existed. Now the enormity of what she had done began to come home to her. In her rage she had taken a decision that would change their lives as well as hers. She took a deep breath, stepping back once more into the role of protector.

'It's all right, my lovies. Just a silly argument. Nothing to be scared of.'

She tried to keep her voice light and reassuring, but it came out with a tremble in it. She could see that the children were not fooled. Doreen's little face was white and set. Bobby's mouth began to wobble and a wail escaped. Peter sat with his little brother Michael gripped tightly in his arms, his eyes fierce with apprehension.

'It's all right,' she repeated. 'Now, how would you like to go and see Granny Croft?'

The effect was magical.

'Oh yeah!'

'What, now?'

'Honest? Granny Croft?'

'That's right, now, right away. Come on, get your things together. All your clothes and toys. You help, Doreen, and you, Peter. Put them all in piles and I'll find bags. That's it. I'm going to get little Teddy's stuff.'

She went into the cramped boxroom that she and the baby shared. As she started to open drawers and heap her meagre possessions on to the bed she found her hands were shaking. It spread to her legs, until she had to sit down. She was still angry, but all the strength seemed to have drained out of her.

Somehow, it was achieved. None of them had much in the way of worldly goods. In less time than Joan would have thought possible, it was all packed into two cardboard suitcases and a number of string bags and haversacks. Most of it was loaded on to the pram. Peter and Michael stood by their tricycle, looking defiant. Joan opened her mouth to say they couldn't take it, only to close it again. She was blowed if she was going to leave it here for Queenie's kids to play with.

'Yeah, that can come too,' she said to their unspoken question. Their faces broke into smiles. Peter hung bags from the handlebars.

Queenie's offspring crept round the side of the house to watch them go, but of Queenie there was no sign. The two groups of children made faces at each other, which for once Joan did nothing to stop. Then the gypsy procession set off down the street. Joan felt curiously light. It was such a relief to think that she would never have to put up with Queenie again that she did not consider the consequences.

The feeling carried her through the difficulties of the journey. She had only just enough money in her purse to buy their tickets. Getting four children, one baby, a pram, a tricycle and all their luggage on the tube was difficult, but at least the line was above ground at Dagenham. Getting off at the other end was a nightmare, eased by the helpfulness of passers-by. After that, they had to walk. Joan's euphoria began to wear thin. The children soon tired, and started demanding rides on the pram, but that was already overloaded with bags and suitcases. Then they began squabbling over the tricycle. The suitcases slid down on top of the pram and as she was going down a kerb one fell off and burst open. Michael rammed the trike into an old lady and caused a row. Teddy, normally the most placid of babies, was long overdue for a feed and kept up a fretful wail. Then it started to rain.

Joan could have sat down and cried. Instead, she tried to rally her small party.

'Come on, darlings, it ain't much longer. It's only a bit of rain. Worse things happen at sea. Soon we'll see Granny Croft.'

The thought of getting to her mum's kept her going. She only had to reach Trinidad Street and everything would be all right.

The swing bridge was open when they reached the Island, so they had to wait for twenty minutes while a ship went through, drab in its camouflage. When they finally got over, the West Ferry Road seemed to go on for ever. The children whined about hunger and thirst and blisters. Joan snapped at them and Bobby began to snivel.

At last, there was the corner into Trinidad Street. Joan felt a great flood of relief. Nearly there. People she knew called out to her. Kids ran up. The poor old street had a forlorn look, with the rain drizzling down on the bombsites, but still it was home. There was the place where her house used to be. There on the far

243

corner was the shop. The children suddenly found a spurt of energy and ran ahead to push open the door. Joan could hear the familiar jangle of the bell. She backed in, manoeuvring the pram over the step.

Five minutes later, she was sitting in the back parlour with Teddy snorting greedily at her breast and the children wolfing doorsteps of bread and jam. Florrie put a cup of tea beside her and sat down across the table from her.

'Now then,' she said. 'What's all this about?'

Joan told her, and as she did so her mother's face grew more and more grave. When Joan had finished, she gave a gusty sigh.

'Really Joan, whatever got into you? I thought as I could count on you.'

It was not the reaction Joan had been hoping for.

'I couldn't stand it no longer,' she said.

'But to walk out like that!' Florrie paused and looked at the children. 'You lot finished? No? Well, you can take them slices and go out in the yard. Go and see your grandad's rabbits. But don't go giving them all your food, mind. They got enough of their own.'

Quiet of a sort descended upon the parlour. From the shop came the voices of Jim and the customers, from the yard the high-pitched squeals of the children. Joan changed Teddy from one breast to the other, comforted by the round weight of him snuggled against her. She looked down at his rosy little face, fiercely concentrating on what he was doing.

'I thought you'd of understood,' she said. Tears pricked at the back of her eyes.

'Understood what? That my family's falling apart?' Florrie's voice was hard.

'But Mum, you didn't never like Queenie —'

'I know, but she's your brother's wife. She's family. And what with George and Ted both away, you ought to stick together all the more.'

The fear that lurked forever in her heart surfaced.

'Ted ain't just away, Mum. He's been captured by them Japanese.'

'Oh Joanie —' Florrie leaned across the table and put a hand on her arm. 'Oh pet, I never knew. You never said —'

'I only heard a few days ago.'

'But at least he'll be safe now, lovey. Out of the fighting and that. Once you know where he is you'll be able to send letters. The POWs in Germany, they're all right. It ain't easy, but they're safe.'

'But it's such a long way away, Mum. Germany's bad enough, but the Far East, it's like the other side of the earth. Weeks and weeks it takes to get there, and it's like, really foreign. Not just a bit different, like what Germany is.'

Florrie's hand tightened.

'Don't you see, lovey? That's why we all got to stick together. All us women. Family's all we got. We ain't got no money, and the government never done nothing for us. We just got each other. I know Queenie's a stuck-up madam who thinks she's a cut above what we are, but George went and married her, and her kids are my grandchildren, same as what yours are. You can't go falling out like this.'

'I know, Mum, but –'

'But nothing. I was counting on you, Joan. There's Lily gone off just like the men and living in some billet somewhere, and God knows what Rita's up to. She looks like the world's fallen in, she does.'

'Rita?' Joan had little sympathy for her sister. Rita had not had to keep explaining to Peter and Michael why their mum had not come to see them as usual. 'It's all right for her. She can go gallivanting off to Laindon any time she wants. She's got this job she likes so much. Not like me.'

Florrie's lips tightened.

'Yeah, well, she didn't go to Laindon, did she? God knows where she did go.'

Joan listened as her mother told her what she had seen and heard last weekend. She laid the now full and happy Teddy against her shoulder and patted his back, and remembered Rita's confession of being in love, and her own suspicions of Rita's motives in taking the job with the Wilkinsons. It didn't take a lot of thinking to guess where Rita might have been. Joan was indignant.

'She ain't got no right. Dumping her kids on me and acting like what she's single.'

'Yeah, well, I agree with you, lovey. But that Ron, he's a nasty bit of work, he is.'

'Still don't mean she can play away like that,' Joan maintained. 'It ain't right.'

Her mother sighed. Joan looked at her. She had aged a lot these last few months. The injuries she had received had taken more out of her than she ever admitted. Her face was thin and lined and her hair was now nearly all grey. Her mother was getting old.

Florrie was holding her with her eyes.

'You see what I mean, then, lovey? You're the one I trust. You're the one what thinks the same as what I do. It's up to you and me to hold the family together.'

Joan felt the burden of responsibility settle ever more heavily on her shoulders. It was no use thinking she could shift it on to her mother, not any more. She was a grown-up woman now. It was up to her to look out for her mum, not the other way round. But she just could not face the thought of trailing all the way back to Dagenham and making it up with Queenie.

'I know what you mean, Mum. But I can't go back right now, really I can't. I'd have to do all the apologising. She wouldn't never admit she's the littlest bit in the wrong. As far as she sees it, she's perfect. So don't ask me to go crawling back to her, not yet, 'cause the words'd just stick in my throat and choke me, honest they would.'

Florrie got up and collected the cups.

'I ain't going to go turning you out of the house. It'll be lovely to have you and the kiddies here for a bit. But after that, something's got to be done. There's Lily coming home on a week's leave in ten days. I love you all, you know that, but I don't see that we got the room.'

So that was that, Joan realised. Lily could go and have a whale of a time being a WAAF, Rita could have weekends away with her boyfriend and get away with it, but good old Joan had to take four kids and a baby and go back to flaming Queenie. She was not in the best of moods when Rita came in that evening.

246

## 32

Something had to be done, Rita could see that, even through the fog of pain that hung around her. The tiny house was full to bursting with all the children. Joan, usually so good-natured, kept making remarks about it being 'all right for some', and Lily was due home on leave. With Lily cooped up in the house as well, things were going to explode, and she knew who would get the blame – wicked Rita, the unfaithful wife, stealer of boyfriends and deserter of children.

Most of the time, she didn't care. Let them all hate her, what did it matter? Nothing mattered now that Jack was missing. The only consolation she had was the children. It was a real comfort to have the boys snuggled into bed with her each night, one on either side. It was only when she saw her mother's haggard face that her conscience nagged at her, and a chance remark of Peter's sparked the very obvious solution in her sluggish brain. She spoke to the Wilkinsons.

Four days before Lily was due to arrive, Rita came in from work and waited for everyone to sit down for their tea before forcing a smile on to her face and into her voice.

'Well now, is everybody ready for a nice surprise?'

Joan gave her a hard look.

'We could all do with one, that's for sure.'

Her tone indicated that she didn't hold out much hope of Rita coming up with anything worth listening to. Rita took a breath and carried on.

'How'd you all like a week's holiday in the country?'

All four children looked at her in amazement, then burst out in a chorus of delight.

'Honest? A holiday?'

'Yeah, smashing!'

'The country? Will there be cows, real cows?'

'Can we take the trike?'

Joan looked unconvinced.

'How come you got holidays to give away all of a sudden?'

'It ain't mine, it's the Wilkinsons'. They said we could have the cottage any time we like,' Rita explained.

Joan raised her eyebrows.

'Oh, so there really is a cottage, is there?'

Before Rita could bite back at her, the children started in with questions about what it was like. They had no reservations about the holiday; it was the best news they had heard for a long time. The adults were less easy to win over. Florrie said she couldn't leave the shop, Jim had to be at his warden's post, Joan had no money left for train fares. Rita gradually won them over. The money was easy, it was to be her treat. Jim must be due some time off, and some of the part-timers would be sure to cover for him. Only Florrie was adamant.

'Come on, Mum, there must be someone who could take over for a few days. It'd do you good. You need a break more than any of us do. It's lovely out at Laindon. Mr and Mrs Wilkinson of told me all about it. A pretty cottage and a big garden, all peaceful and quiet. You wouldn't know there was a war on. Just what you need. You got to come along with the rest of us.'

It was Joan who found the solution. Seeing that the children were set on going, she suggested a couple of stand-ins for the shop, women whom even Florrie could trust to keep it ticking over until she came back. Jim chimed in, saying that he wouldn't enjoy a break if he didn't have his old lady with him, and in the end Florrie gave in.

The mood in the house miraculously changed. Instead of snapping at each other and trying in vain to keep at a distance, they all set to plan the holiday. What they should take, how they should get there, how they should carry everything, was endlessly discussed. Rita came back from work with information about what was and wasn't at the cottage. The food had to be thought out, sleeping arrangements sorted. The children raced around in a high state of excitement. The adults wrote lists and packed bags.

Lily arrived home, tight-lipped. She looked more pretty than ever, and her uniform the height of elegance beside the others' rationed clothing, but she was not ready to forgive Rita, and neither was she very pleased to find the house invaded by hordes of children and her bedroom taken over. But even she was ready to unbend a little at the thought of a real holiday.

'Seaside would of been better, but I suppose beggars can't be choosers, and at least the weather looks like being good,' she conceded.

It was such a treat to be out of London. Even Florrie had to admit it.

'It's so clean,' she kept saying, as the train rumbled its way slowly down the line.

The sun that in London only served to highlight the dirt and destruction here shone on green pastures and trees and fields of swelling corn. The children ran from one window to the other, pointing things out. Joan sat happily taking it in, with Teddy sitting on her knee watching the others, wide-eyed. Lily slouched in a corner, smoking.

'It's so pretty, ain't it?' Joan said to her.

Lily shrugged. 'All right if you like that sort of thing. Hampshire's nicer, if you ask me.'

Rita saw it all with an ache in her heart. Last time she had been on a train like this, she had been on her way to meet Jack. But anything was better than all being crowded into the shop.

The first afternoon and evening were taken up with settling in. It was a long haul from the station up the road – hardly more than a lane – to the Langdon Hills, and then along a dirt track to Oak Cottage. The place itself was a bit of a surprise. They had all been imagining something close to the picturebook sort of cottage, with thick white walls and a thatched roof and roses round the door. It turned out to be a wooden structure, tarred against the weather, and with reddish tiles.

'Call that a cottage? More like a blooming shed,' Lily said scornfully.

They all stopped at the gate, and regarded it with various degrees of disappointment. Rita felt dreadful. All the weight of responsibility for this holiday rested on her shoulders, and already it was not going right. Then Peter spotted the little pathways running through the overgrown garden, and dragged the others off with him to explore. Florrie put on her cheerful voice.

'It's quite pretty in a way, ain't it? Just look at them roses!'

They looked, and she was right: there were roses, beautiful creamy yellow ones, and round the door, too.

'A shed with roses. Wonderful,' Lily muttered, with heavy sarcasm.

Her father rounded on her.

'Look, it's a holiday, ain't it, girl? We ain't had a whole week's holiday since you was a nipper, so shut up moaning and help get all this stuff inside.'

There was plenty to do that first evening – beds to be made up, water to draw and the kitchen fire to be lit. Supper was bread and scrape and a cup of tea, but only Lily complained, and Florrie shut her up, much to Rita's surprise. She was even more surprised when she woke up the following morning and found that she had actually slept all night, for the first time in many months. She lay on her camp-bed, listening to Joan and Lily's steady breathing and the sound of birdsong. No traffic, no factories, no shouting, no sirens. Best of all, no blackout curtains. They had had to undress and wash downstairs last night and feel their way into the bedroom, but it was well worth it, for now she could lie and watch the sunlight dancing on the rough plastered wall. As yet, it brought no peace to her shattered heart, but it was a thousand times better than waking to another day in London.

The weather was kind to them. High summer hung over the land. Wild flowers bloomed in the fields and hedgerows, bees and butterflies fluttered about, birds took food to growing fledglings. The children spent all their time outdoors, often wearing nothing but their vests and knickers. They made mud pies in the earth and dens in the undergrowth. Jim fixed them up a swing with some rope and a plank he found in an outhouse. The trike became a tank or a jeep or an armoured car, forging a way through enemy territory. Rita decided to take over the cooking. Lily was fed up with it from being in the kitchens all the time, and Joan and Florrie from having to cater for their families on rations. To Rita, it was something of a change.

In the drowsy heat, the adults gradually adjusted to a holiday pace. None of them was accustomed to doing nothing, but with the sun hot on their heads and the drone of insects threading hypnotically through the air, they all slowed down. Florrie sat in an ancient deckchair, knitting or minding Teddy or any of the others who needed attention. Jim dozed with a newspaper over his head, or pottered about fixing things and fetching wood for the kitchen fire, which needed continual feeding. On the very first morning, Lily stripped down to her bra and petticoat and sunbathed, much to her parents' disapproval.

'What's it matter? It's only us here,' she said, and turned over to do her back.

By the afternoon, Joan had rolled up her sleeves and tucked her skirt into her knickers and joined her. Rita, finishing the drying up, looked out of the kitchen window at her sisters. She longed to go and join them, but was not sure of her reception. Lily had not yet spoken a word to her beyond what was strictly necessary, and even Joan was distinctly cool. Were they right? And was she, therefore, in the wrong? She knew she was. They had every cause to disapprove of her, and she didn't blame Lily a bit for hating her. She would hate anyone who had taken Jack away from her. But she did wish that they could see it just a bit from her point of view.

Mikey came trotting round the corner of the cottage, intent on some errand. Rita leaned out of the window.

'Hello, darling.'

He stopped short, and his face broke into a big smile.

'Mum! I forgot you was here.'

The words tore at her heart. Her own son, and he was surprised that she was with him.

'Yes, lovey, I'm here all the time. Every minute. What do you want to do, eh? How about a walk? We could go and explore through the woods.'

'Yeah!' Mikey's eyes lit up. 'Like an adventure. Just you and me.'

Rita took off her apron and went outside. Mikey put his grubby little paw into hers and looked up at her with his engaging grin. Rita bent down and hugged him tight, hiding her

251

tears. At least she still had her boys. They were all hers, to love. Thank God they still loved her, despite everything. She resolved to try harder to deserve that love.

It was on the third morning that she found Joan leaning against one of the outhouses, sobbing. She put her arms round her.

'Oh Joanie – what is it? You worried about Ted?'

Joan nodded.

'I'm sorry, it's silly . . .'

'It ain't silly. You must be worried sick.'

She held her sister until the sobs began to subside.

'There – feel a bit better now?'

Joan nodded, and blew her nose.

Carefully, Rita said, 'It is sure, ain't it? I mean, he was taken prisoner, definite, not just missing?'

'Yeah – definite.'

'You know he's alive, then. That's something, y'know. Where there's life, there's hope.'

More hope than she had. More than just the desperate wish that one of those three parachutes had been carrying Jack, that he had not been shot on the way down or on landing . . .

'I'd be so happy if I just knew he was a prisoner,' she said, without fully realising she had voiced it out loud.

There was a heavy silence. Rita bit her lip. She hadn't meant to let that slip.

'You mean Jack? Jack Wilkinson?' Joan said.

No point in denying it. Ron certainly wasn't anywhere near enemy territory.

'Yeah. His plane was shot down. Over Berlin. Three of them got out, but they don't know who.'

There was another silence while Joan digested this. When she spoke, it was slowly, as if thinking it out as she went along.

'You love him, don't you?'

'I can't help it, Joanie.'

'I know. It's just – but it must be terrible for you, not knowing.'

Rita looked into her sister's face and saw the dawning of sympathy. She tried to explain.

'I never meant to, you know. I mean, I never thought to

myself, "I fancy that boyfriend of Lily's. I'll get him off of her." It just sort of happened.'

'It didn't ought to of happened,' Joan said. 'But – I can see how it did, if he's as wonderful as what you and Lily seem to think he is.'

Rita sighed.

'He is to me.'

Joan could almost feel her fixed view of things changing, as if the world was slipping slightly around her. She didn't want it to change. Holding on to the ways she knew meant keeping a grip on the life she had always known, and shared with Ted, and hoped to share again. But, as everybody said at every possible moment, there was a war on. Everything was changing. Women were taking decisions without their husbands. Women were leaving their homes and doing their bit for the war effort. Women were putting on uniforms and joining the Forces. Part of her, the old part, said that that meant there was all the more reason for sticking to what was right. But the newer, more flexible part saw that Rita might be forgiven. The problem revolved in her mind as she sat in the garden or went to fetch the bread and milk and vegetables, giving her a much-needed break from worrying about Ted and wondering whether she could stick going back to Queenie and eating humble pie. It was still bothering her the next day as she walked across to where Lily was laid out in the sun.

'You're getting burnt, you are,' she said. 'You'll go all red and get blisters if you're not careful. Come into the shade.'

Lily made a groan of protest, but got up. They sat down under a tree burdened with baby apples.

'Be a smashing crop of these in the autumn. I wonder if Rita'll come out here and help pick them,' she said.

'Huh. Rita. She can go take a long walk off of a short pier.'

'Lily! She is your sister, you know.'

'She ought to of thought of that when she took my Jack.'

'Lil –' Joan tried to think back to how it had all happened. 'Now be honest. What happened first, him writing you the Dear John letter or her falling for him?'

'I dunno,' Lily snapped. 'What does it matter? And why are you taking her part all of a sudden?'

Joan frowned, trying to decide whether to tell her. Would it set her against Rita even more? But she ought to know.

'You – er – you don't know then, about Jack?'

'What about him?' Lily's voice was sharp with suspicion, as if she expected Joan to tell her that Rita was about to run away with him.

'He's been shot down. They don't know whether he's alive or dead.'

The colour drained out of Lily's face.

'No!' she whispered.

'It's true.'

Surely Lily could find it in her heart to be a bit sorry for Rita? Her sister was sitting with her fists clenched, staring very hard at a nearby patch of nettles.

'Lil –'

'I don't want to talk about it!' Lily said.

Joan could hear the tears and the anger. She got up.

'I'm going to walk down the village. You want to come?'

'No. Just leave me alone.'

Joan sighed. Perhaps it was best to leave her to it for a bit, to take it in. It was a shock for her, after all. This terrible war, was there no end to what it was going to do to people? Homes smashed, men sent away, loved ones killed. And it all seemed to have been going on for so long now. How much more would they have to take? Then she thought once more of Ted, in prison somewhere steamy and hot, at the mercy of those Japanese, and knew that whatever she had to bear, she would do it, just so long as he came home again.

When she got back from her walk she went to join Rita, who was sitting on the back doorstep, shelling peas.

'Dad got 'em from up the farm,' she explained. 'They're lovely – you try, you can eat 'em raw, they're really sweet. I thought I'd mix 'em up with that mash left over from dinner and fry the lot for tea in that bit of bacon fat left in the pan. Sort of like bubble and squeak.'

They sat popping the pods and running the peas into the pan, where they landed with a satisfying tinging noise. Rita was right: they were nice raw.

'Must be because they're fresh picked,' Joan remarked.

The children came in from the cow field beyond, laughing and panting, and drank water straight from the pump, splashing it over themselves and each other. Joan and Rita watched them indulgently. 'They're having the time of their lives here,' she said.

'Yeah. Look at 'em, bunch of hooligans.'

'It was a smashing idea of yours, coming here. It's done us all a world of good.'

Rita gave her a look of gratitude.

'Thanks. Only trouble is, we all got to go back soon, ain't we? Have you thought what you're going to do? About Queenie and that?'

'I dunno –' Joan sighed. There was so much to think about. 'Mum'll be upset if I don't go and make it up with her, but honestly, Reet, I don't know if I can. I mean, she'll be even worse after all this do.'

'It ain't so bad in London now. Not like during the Blitz,' Rita pointed out.

'I know –'

'And Mum'd love having you and the kids around again.'

Joan looked at her sister. Rita was up to something. She knew her too well.

'What are you trying to say, Reet?'

'Oh – it's just that after having the boys back like this, it's so hard to say goodbye again.'

Joan waited. They both watched the four children dancing about squealing and flicking water.

'The thing is, I don't know whether I could bear being parted from them again. I was thinking how lovely it'd be if we could all stay here for the duration.'

The thought had crossed Joan's mind as well, but only as an impossible dream. She could not see any way that all of them could stay.

'Mum'd never come, and Dad's got his warden's job.'

'I know.'

They both looked at the happy children and at the peaceful countryside beyond, baking beneath the hot sun. But Joan's practical brain had to see the other side of it.

'What about money? You wouldn't get a job like yours out here. And you can't hardly live on army pay.'

'I know that and all,' Rita said.

'And it'd be knee deep in mud here in the winter. And it's miles down to the shops and the school. And there's no gas or electric. And that pump wouldn't be much fun when it's cold.'

'You're a flaming killjoy, you are,' Rita complained.

Boring, sensible Joan. Well, someone had to keep their feet on the ground. Look at the troubles Rita and Lily had brought on themselves by not thinking. Look at the problems she had made the one time she flew off the handle. She didn't know where she was going to stay once this holiday was over.

'It's true, though,' she insisted.

'I know,' Rita had to agree. 'We're not really country people, are we? I suppose I'd miss having the neighbours around and all.'

'Mmm . . .' It had been nice to get back to Trinidad Street and see the old faces. Some of them, anyway. The ones who hadn't been killed or bombed out or evacuated.

'Like you said, it ain't as bad as it was, is it?' she asked. 'Lots of people in the street have got their kids back from the country.'

'Lots,' Rita agreed.

'And I can't face going to Queenie's, whatever Mum says –'

'Let Queenie stew in it, I say. Snobby cow. She'll miss you, Joan. Now you're gone, she'll see how much you done for her in that house.'

'Yeah –' Joan chewed at her lip. It was such a difficult decision. It wasn't just her, after all, it was the kids.

Rita cut through her thoughts.

'The thing is, whatever you decide, I think I'll keep mine home now. I won't see a lot of them, what with having to work and all, and it's a lot to ask of Mum, minding them after school and that, but at least we'll be together. Mum's right, you know, families ought to stick together. We're all we got, when it comes down to it.'

Like a fog lifting, the way became clear for Joan.

'You're right. And Mum and Dad are more family than flaming Queenie. I'll stay and all, and then I can take some of the load off of Mum's back.'

She looked at her sister, at the way her strained face had relaxed into a big happy smile, and put her arms around her.

'Oh Reet, you are a fool. You know what your problem is, don't you? You want everything, and we can't never have everything?'

'I know. But I can't help wanting it.'

Joan laid her cheek against Rita's. Poor old Reet. As if there wasn't enough heartache, with the war on, without her yearning for what she couldn't have. But then, that was the way she was made. Nobody could change that.

On the last afternoon, the whole family walked into Laindon and queued for fish and chips, holding the newspaper in which to wrap it. Lily ran her eye automatically over the line of people: women, kids, old men, a couple of soldiers on leave, but one was with his wife and the other wasn't worth a second glance. Roll on tomorrow. She had enjoyed being away from the hours and the rules, but just lying around doing nothing all day was pretty boring. She really missed the girls at the billet and the men at the aerodrome, and even the noise and clatter of the kitchen. Most of all she missed the gossip and the flirting and the dances and the Americans down the road. Her gaze came round to her sisters, waiting patiently like the rest of the married women, their arms folded across their stomachs. They didn't have a lot to look forward to. Not like she did. During the course of the week this truth had been creeping up on her, and she had been trying to ignore it, locked as she was into hating Rita. Even now she only let it into her conscious thinking with reluctance. But there it was – she didn't have Jack, but now Rita didn't have him either, and Rita was still stuck with that slimy bastard Ron, whereas she had an RAF aerodrome and an American base to choose from. On impulse, she sidled up to Rita.

'I heard about Jack,' she said.

A closed expression came over Rita's face.

'Yeah?'

'What – what happened, exactly?'

It was important that she should know.

'They were on an op over Berlin, and they got shot up. Fighters. Three men got out, they know that 'cause they saw the parachutes. That's all I know. You know how it is, they never tell you details. It's just all official words. And I only know that much 'cause Mrs Wilkinson showed me the letter.'

Not for nothing did Lily work at an aerodrome. She knew what the chances were.

'So if it was him – what got out, I mean – it might be weeks before you know?'

'Yeah. Just got to wait. And hope. And pray.'

Rita sounded so bleak that Lily found her hard wall of jealousy cracking a little.

'I – I'm sorry,' she found herself saying, without even knowing exactly what she was sorry for.

Tears stood in Rita's eyes.

'Oh Lil – I never set out to take him away from you. You got to believe that.'

'I dunno . . .'

'It was after he, you know, finished with you. And I – well, I just couldn't help it.'

Lily could understand that. Any girl with eyes in her head would fall for Jack. But still – her own sister, her married sister. That was what was so hard to take.

Joan cut into the conversation.

'It's the war. It drives you to it, makes us all do things what we wouldn't never do normally.'

'Even you,' Rita said.

'Yeah, even me.'

Lily looked at Joan, good old Joan with her head done up in a scarf and Teddy settled on her hip, every inch the mum, and was distracted into imagining the row between her and Queenie.

'You never really threw a jar of jam at Queenie, did you?'

'I did and all. It missed, mind you, but I did throw it. It was lovely. It went everywhere. All over her precious kitchen.'

Lily felt a laugh building up in the pit of her stomach.

'I wish I could of seen it.'

'And then – then I threw the milk at her. That got her. It went right over her head, and soaked her hair, and ran all down her face. Dripping, it was, all down her.'

The laugh bubbled up, reaching Lily's face. She looked at the other two. They both had the same expressions of malicious glee. 'Oh Joan,' she squealed. 'You are a one! All down her!'

Then they were all laughing uncontrollably, gasping and crying and holding on to each other. Every time one of them stopped, she only had to look at the others to set off all over again. They giggled until they felt weak and had to sit down on the pavement.

Florrie, watching them, felt a peace creeping over her. It was going to be all right. Her family was pulling together again.

## 33

As usual, it was crowded on the train. So crowded that at first it looked as if there wasn't even standing room. But Lily was a seasoned traveller now, a very different person from the girl who had first made her way to training camp, not knowing where she was going or what she was taking on, fuelled only by a burning resentment. She shouldered her way on, and using her eyes and her smile, easily got a space made for her in the corridor. Nearly everyone seemed to be service personnel. Nearest to her were a group of Canadian soldiers, some naval ratings and a couple of ATS girls, while over their shoulders she could see green berets and grey-blue caps. She set down her bag and leaned against the partition, acknowledging the nods and smiles. Only this morning she had woken up in the cottage, and just an hour or so ago she had said goodbye to the family at the door of the shop in Trinidad Street, but already it seemed like another world. She belonged here, with this mixed bunch of people.

She had to admit, she had Rita to thank. If it hadn't been for her, she would never have had the courage to join up. When the time came for her to be called up she would most likely have gone into munitions. As it was, here she was in the WAAFs, having the time of her life.

One of the Canadians produced a packet of cigarettes and offered it to her. Lily accepted one gratefully. She was right out.

'You going far?' he asked.

'Whiley Green. You?'

The usual exchange of basic information. He was rather nice. Lovely blue eyes, cheerful smile. More than all right for passing the journey. His pals weren't going to let him have it all his own way, though. Lily could see that they all liked what they saw. The week at the cottage had made her colouring more striking than ever, bleaching her hair even fairer and giving her a tan. Even if there had been lots of competition she would have got plenty of attention. As it was, there was only herself, the two ATS girls and all these men. She settled in for an enjoyable ride.

The Canadians competed for her favour.

'What's it like at this Whiley Green? Bit slow, is it?'

'I'll bet it's a one-horse kind of place. We're just outside of Bournemouth. You know Bournemouth? Plenty to do there.'

'Yeah, a whole lot going on. Dances, concerts, movies. Just right for a pretty girl like you. How about you coming over to see it? I'll show you around any time you please.'

'Don't you listen to him, sweetheart. He's a hick, he knows nothing. Now me, I can show a girl a really good time.'

They introduced themselves to her – Joey, Jimmy, Sam, Gray, Cliff and Bob, Bob Marriot, the one who had given her the cigarette. They asked all about her, flirted and entertained her with tales of their exploits, so that the long miles sped by and she hardly noticed how much her legs were aching. They kept her supplied with cigarettes and at one wonderful station managed to get her a cup of almost fresh tea. When she finally reached the station nearest to Whiley Green they all hung out of the windows and waved her goodbye.

Lily was still smiling to herself as she hefted her bag and walked out to the forecourt to see if she could get herself a lift. It had been fun. But no more than that. However nice he might be, and however good-looking or glamorous or rich, she was not going to fall in love with any man ever again. Oh no, she'd done that once and it was nothing but a mug's game. Lily Croft was young and pretty and free, and that was the way she was going to stay.

Within twenty-four hours of being back, it was as if she had never been away. The life of the billet and the aerodrome took her over. Friends asked about her leave, and she chatted on about it, exaggerating to make more of an effect, but it hardly seemed real. This was what life was really about: her mates and the goings-on here at Whiley Green.

She was surprised when at the end of her first day back there was a telephone call for her at the billet.

'Sounds nice,' whispered the girl who handed her the receiver. 'American?'

Lily shrugged.

'Hi there,' a transatlantic voice boomed down the line at her. 'Great to hear you again, Lily. Remember me? I said I'd call you.'

'No,' Lily said.

'Hey, c'mon, don't break my heart. Only yesterday and you've forgotten me already? I've thought of nothing but you from the moment we waved goodbye. It's Bob Marriot, honey. From the train. Remember now?'

'Oh – yeah.'

Deliberately, Lily killed all enthusiasm in her voice. But despite herself, her heart beat a little faster. Bob Marriot. He was a bit of all right.

Not at all put off by her hard-to-get tactics, Bob asked after the rest of her journey and how things were at the aerodrome as if he had known her for months. Two girls wanting to make outgoing phone calls made impatient gestures.

'I got to go, there's people waiting,' Lily said.

'Not before you promise to come and see me. There's a big dance here on Saturday night. Can you get away for it?'

'Oh – I dunno. I think I'm going out Saturday,' Lily said.

'Yeah, you are, you're coming here,' Bob insisted.

'I'll think about it. Got to go now. See you!' Lily said, and put the receiver down.

'All yours,' she said to the next girl, and scampered upstairs, trying without success to suppress the big smile that spread across her face. A dance in Bournemouth. That would be good. And with Bob Marriot. Yes, that would be good too. For a bit. That was all, just for a bit of fun.

Bob rang every evening for the next four days. On Friday, Lily capitulated and agreed to meet him for the dance, just as she had planned to all along. She bounced into the dormitory and flopped on to her bed.

'Was that the Canadian again?' Betty asked.

'Yup.'

'You agreed yet?'

'Yup. Meeting him at the main station at Bournemouth.'

'Thought you would. You coming down the pub, then? It's the semifinal of the darts tournament, remember.'

'I dunno –' Lily gave it some consideration. 'I think I'll stay in and do my hair.'

Betty feigned amazement.

'Stay in on a Friday? You? This Bob Marriot bloke must be quite something.'

Lily shrugged.

'He's all right.'

Betty gave her a thoughtful look.

'You're not still carrying a torch for that Jack, are you?'

Lily lay back on the bed with her hands clasped beneath her head and stared up at the ornate ceiling. A fortnight ago she would have said yes without hesitation. Now – now she realised that she wasn't sure.

'He's been shot down,' she said. 'My sister told me. Over Berlin. He might of bailed out safely, but they don't know.'

Betty immediately sat on the bed and gave her a hug.

'Oh Lil, how awful. You poor thing –'

But she didn't feel it like Rita was obviously feeling it. It had been a shock, yes, but it wasn't like it was the end of the world.

'What a terrible thing to find out when you're on leave. Must've ruined your holiday for you.'

'Yeah,' Lily agreed. But to herself she had to admit that it had not ruined her holiday. The fact was, the great aching hole left inside her when Jack gave her the elbow had healed without her even noticing it.

'Still,' she said. 'Life goes on, don't it? Can I have a borrow of your shampoo? I gave mine to Joan for the kids.'

Rita still had the gnawing worry of wondering whether Jack was dead or alive, but she was free to do what she liked.

Each day as Rita got to work, she looked at Mr Wilkinson's face. 'Any news?' she asked, though she knew from the moment she saw him what the answer was going to be.

They reassured each other, saying the same things about information about POWs being slow to get through and there being hope yet.

It was comforting, having the Wilkinsons to talk to. But Jack's safety was not her only worry, and the other one she bore alone.

For with every day that passed, it seemed more likely that she was pregnant. If she could just be sure that it was Jack's, she wouldn't mind. In fact, she would be delighted. To have a little bit of him to care for would help if the worst came to the worst and he was dead. But it could be Ron's, and the thought of bearing a child conceived in such pain and brutality filled her with horror. Perhaps she was just late. With all that had happened, it was quite likely. After all, they did say that shock and that sort of thing put your system all out. She hurried to the toilet a dozen times a day, hoping to see a trace of red, but every time she was disappointed.

July dragged into August. The children were all home from school, playing on the bomb sites and racing up and down the street on the tricycle. Coming home from a hard day at work, Rita would see them leaping out ambushing each other or tearing around shrieking and making shooting noises, pointing at each other with two fingers made into a gun. Sometimes they would stop and wave to her as she passed, sometimes they were too engrossed in what they were doing, but always it lifted her heart to see them there.

Joan was not so happy.

'Running wild, they are,' she complained one evening. 'Dad gives 'em all what-for, but it ain't the same. They need a father's hand, not their grandad's. Your two in particular, Reet.'

Rita was tired. It had been a long week and she had spent the last half-hour before she left work trying to reassure Mrs Wilkinson that they could still hear about Jack. She did not want to have to sort out anything at home.

'They're all right. They're good kids really. Anyway, we can't do nothing about it. Ted's in the Far East and Ron might just as well be, for all the good he is as a father.'

She did not care how wild the boys got, so long as Ron stayed away. She never wanted to see him again. The very thought of him made her feel sick inside. And what if she was pregnant, and it was Ron's? She found her attention wandering. Joan was speaking again.

'. . . be keeping an eye on them all the time. There's so much to do in the house, and the queuing. I queued for two hours yesterday for oranges, and I got just one. One orange! You don't know what it's like.'

'You don't have to keep an eye on them all the time. They're not babies. It's natural for them to go out and play in a gang. All boys do that.'

She knew that what Joan was really saying was that Peter was getting them all into trouble. She began to realise just what a difficult time Joan had had at Queenie's, keeping them all under control. Seeing them once a week was very different from living with them all the time, and in the time since she had last had them with her they had grown from being hardly more than toddlers into tough little schoolboys. Peter, always the one with the strongest personality, had Bobby and Michael hanging on to his every word.

'I suppose so,' Joan said. She looked no happier.

'You're not regretting coming back here to Trinidad Street, are you?' Rita asked.

'No, no – it's lovely being with everyone again. It's just –well, seeing where we used to live all flattened like that. The kids play in it, you know. Their old house, and they play soldiers all over it. Sometimes I feel like there's nothing left of what we used to be. Ted's away, and the house is gone – nothing's ever going to be the same again.'

'You still got the kids,' Rita pointed out. 'And Ted will come back, some time. You'll all be together again, you'll see. Just think what Ted's face'll be like when he sees little Teddy.'

Joan sighed.

'I know. You're right really. It's just – I wish I knew where he was. If I could only write to him, know he's all right, that he's not ill or injured or anything. Send him things. It ain't like the POWs in Germany. No Red Cross, no letters, no parcels. And for all I know he might not even be in Burma no more. It's the not knowing.'

'Yeah,' Rita said. 'I do know what you mean.'

How long before the not knowing about Jack turned into a creeping certainty that he had not made it? Every day brought it nearer.

'Yeah, well, I suppose you do,' Joan conceded.

They were interrupted by Doreen coming wailing into the kitchen.

'It ain't fair, they won't let me play –'

Joan listened to her complaints and found her a hanky.

'Never mind. Dry your eyes. We got spam fritters for tea.'

Rita, who had been hungry up till then, felt suddenly queasy. The very suggestion of spam fritters turned her stomach.

'I'll just have bread and marge, thanks,' she said, and made a dash for the lavatory. But she knew what she hoped for was not going to happen.

The next day, Saturday, was rainy. The house seemed to be bursting with noisy children. Peter was teasing Doreen, and Teddy was teething.

'I can't have all them kids around my feet, it's my busy day today,' Florrie complained.

Rita fetched her purse. 'You can all go up the Saturday morning pictures,' she said to the children.

There were cheers and yells. Rita handed out change and fixed them all with as hard a look as she could muster.

'Stick together, mind. *All* of you, Doreen as well. And if I hear you been naughty, there won't be no next time. Got it?'

She could see that Peter wasn't really taking it in, but they all nodded and agreed, and rushed to get their coats.

'That'll keep 'em out of mischief,' she said. 'And I'll help you with the coupons and that this afternoon, Mum.'

She shivered as she waited at the bus stop. Her umbrella had broken and there was no getting another one. After the lovely weather they had had at the cottage, it seemed cold and dismal. She looked at the faces around her. Everyone was pinched and miserable. Sometimes she harboured the unpatriotic thought that the war might go on for ever. Of course, it would never do to say something like that out loud, but next month it would be four years since war was declared, and still there was no end in sight. The rain soaked through her headscarf and trickled down her neck.

A woman walking past stopped and stared at her.

'Well, if it ain't Rita. Thought you must of gone away somewhere and never told us, but here you are, large as life and twice as natural.'

Rita found herself confronted by one of her sisters-in-law.

'Oh, hello, Dot,' she said, trying not to sound too unenthusiastic. She never had got on with any of Ron's family.

'Ain't seen hide nor hair of you since I don't know when,' Dot complained.

'I'm working,' Rita said.

'You got Sundays off, ain't you? And Maisie ain't seen them kids for months. They're her grandsons, you know, just as much as they're your mum's. You ought to bring 'em round.'

Rita knew that very well. It was just that she had been putting it off. Seeing Maisie meant having to face the fact that she was still very much married to Ron and connected to all his side of the family.

'Nothing stopping her from coming round ours,' she objected.

'She can't walk far, and well you know it. Takes her all her strength to get to the end of the road and back,' Dot said. 'Forgetting your duty, that's what you're doing. Disgraceful, I call it. Neglecting a sick old woman and keeping her grandchildren from her.'

Rita had never been more glad to see the bus come crawling along the road.

'I'll come,' she promised.

'You better. And bring them boys. I know you got them home again,' Dot shouted after her as she climbed on to the platform.

Rita sat down next to a fat woman who seemed to take up nearly all the seat. The bus smelt of wet clothes and stale cigarette smoke. She ought to go and visit Maisie, but she did not want to. She tried to think of something nice, but there was nothing to rest her mind on. Jack . . . her missed period . . . Ron . . . Maisie – it went round and round.

At Whitechapel she got down and hurried through the rain to the factory. She had just about conquered her fear of going past the building where Ron had attacked her, but she still felt sick as she trotted past, head down, trying not to look at it.

Wally was at the door before her, as usual. His collar was up and his flat cap pulled down. His lugubrious face was more deeply seamed than ever. 'Blooming awful, ain't it?' he remarked by way of a greeting.

Rita felt in complete accord with him.

The door rattled and opened. Mr Wilkinson appeared. A transformed Mr Wilkinson, wreathed in smiles, glowing with happiness. Rita felt breathless; her heart thudded in her throat. She stared at him, hardly daring to believe what she saw, willing it to be true.

'You – you've heard?' she croaked.

Mr Wilkinson nodded. If possible, his smile grew even wider.

'We heard. We got a letter. The best possible news, girl. He's in prison camp.'

'Oh, that's wonderful!' Rita cried.

She flung herself into his arms and burst into tears.

She did not see Mrs Wilkinson come up behind her husband, nor the knowing glances that husband and wife exchanged over her head.

## 34

'What a good thing I kept that smock of mine. I nearly cut it up to make a dress for Doreen,' Joan said.

'Yes,' Rita agreed.

'And you'll be looked after good. The government gives you all sorts of things. Not like before the war. Vitamins, orange juice, all that sort of stuff. It's no wonder my Teddy was two pounds bigger than either of the others. And your green ration book, of course. You'll get extra milk and eggs and meat –'

Joan was full of enthusiasm over her sister's pregnancy. Rita supposed she might have expected that. Joan adored babies. What Rita couldn't understand was her mother's attitude, after Florrie's reaction to Ron's treatment of her. For of course both of them, and everybody else, assumed it was Ron's baby.

Only her father was less than happy.

'Can't move in here for women and kids, and now there's going to be another,' he complained.

He spent a good deal of his spare time tending his rabbits, and went off to his warden's post each day with a look of real relief on his face.

'Crusty old so-and-so,' Florrie said fondly. 'He loves 'em really.'

What would they all say, Rita wondered, if she told them it might be Jack's baby? The pressure to confess was boiling constantly within her, but she always managed to hold her tongue just in time. In the enclosed space of north Millwall, cut off from the rest of the East End by the great bend of the Thames and the West India docks, everyone's chief entertainment had always been minding anyone else's business. It was this stranglehold of what the neighbours might think that had forced her to marry Ron in the first place. Things had changed since the outbreak of war, of course. People had fled or been bombed out or killed, and those that were left had more pressing concerns.

Waiting for news of absent menfolk or searching for a replacement for a broken cup occupied their thoughts. But still on the doorsteps or in the interminable queues, the women chewed over the local gossip. The ins and outs of births, marriages and deaths kept them going through bomb raids and shortages. A good family crisis took their thoughts off the dangers facing sons and hsubands in the desert or the North Atlantic. Like Florrie, they felt that with children evacuated, menfolk and now daughters away doing their bit, it was even more important for families to stick together. Wives who cheated on absent husbands came in for especially virulent criticism. Didn't they know there was a war on? The fact that it was the loneliness and enforced separation of the war that caused these lapses was not taken into consideration. The women knew right from wrong, and they insisted that everyone else see it their way.

For her own part, Rita did not care, but she knew that her mother would be deeply hurt, and her father hardly less so, if it got about that the Crofts' daughter was expecting a baby by another man. So she kept her mouth shut, and nobody knew that what she really feared was that the baby was Ron's.

Sometimes she felt an outsider in her own family. In the evenings, when the blackout was up and children had finally been packed off to bed, the three women would sit in the parlour, knitting or mending or sorting the coupons, and listening to the wireless. Florrie and Joan would chat about the children and how to stretch the meat ration and who most needed the next lot of clothes coupons. Rita joined in, but her heart was not in it, and when she made a remark about work, or the Wilkinsons, she could see that they were only answering out of politeness. A whole large area of her life meant nothing to them. As for Jack, she hardly mentioned him. It had been hardest the day she heard he was safe.

She came home bursting with the news. Happiness surged and bubbled inside her, spilling over into irrepressible laughter and childlike skips of joy. She wanted to hug everyone she saw, to share her happiness with them, to see the same light in their faces. It was wonderful, a miracle – Jack was still alive. She hurried down Trinidad Street at the end of the day, calling out to neighbours, stopping to speak to the boys, sweeping Michael off his feet and swinging him round till he screamed.

'Oh Mikey,' she gasped. 'Ain't it lovely?'

'What?' he asked, hopefully.

'Everything,' she said.

Michael stared at her, mystified by the ways of grown-ups.

'I thought you got me some sweeties,' he said.

'Oh darling, you and Peter can have my ration as soon as it comes up next week, you know that,' she promised.

Rita breezed into the shop, and there was her mother, serving the usual after-work queue of weary women. Her mood subsided just a little. She must not let on in front of them; her mum would never forgive her. Swallowing down her elation, she said hello to everyone and asked after their families. Then she escaped into the house. Joan was in the kitchen, peeling potatoes.

'Oh Joan,' she began. Then she noticed the droop to Joan's shoulders, and remembered that she had still had no news about Ted, let alone from him. Nothing beyond the bare facts that he had been taken prisoner by the Japanese.

Joan looked around.

'Wotcher, Reet. All right?'

All right was so feeble a term that Rita had to laugh. All right? She felt on top of the world. Everything was wonderful.

'Yeah,' she said.

Joan studied her, knife in hand.

'What's up? The war ended and nobody told me?'

Rita could hold back the news no longer, but with a great effort she rephrased the way she broke it.

'The Wilkinsons got a letter today.'

'Well, it's got to be good, or you'd be in floods,' Joan guessed. 'He's safe, then, is he?'

'Yeah, he's a POW.'

The smile Rita had been trying to rein back spread over her face. Joan looked bleak.

'Well, that's nice, ain't it? He's out of the fighting and you'll get to hear from him and you'll be able to send him stuff. Couldn't be better, really.'

There was a bitterness in her voice that Rita had never heard

271

before. It stopped her from going and putting her arms round her sister.

'Oh Joanie, if I could do anything to get Ted back from the East, I would. You know that.'

Joan nodded. With a palpable effort, she pulled her face into something resembling a smile.

'Yeah, I know that, Reet. It just ain't fair, that's all.'

Rita knew just what she meant. She got to go out to work, meet new people, have love affairs, and still fate was kind to her. Joan stayed at home, did all the right things and had her house destroyed and her man snatched away. It certainly wasn't fair.

'It's the war. War ain't fair,' Rita pointed out. But it did nothing to mollify Joan.

After that, she stopped herself from mentioning Jack at home.

At work, it was different. The Wilkinsons' favourite topic of conversation was their son. Any little luxury they could get hold of in the way of cigarettes or chocolate or soap was hoarded up to put in a Red Cross parcel for him. Letters were read and reread both for their actual content – usually very bland because of censorship – and for clues as to Jack's real state of health and mind. In the first, most important letter, they learnt that he had been slightly injured and suffered from burns on bailing out of the plane, but that he was mending fast. The prison camp was described as 'not so bad', with huts like big garden sheds surrounded by barbed wire and guards. The food 'kept body and soul together' and the beds were like shelves.

Rita thought long and hard over the letter she wrote back. Should she mention the baby? She longed to tell him, to bind him more closely to her, to let him know that their love had borne fruit. But the uncertainty stopped her. Sometimes, in the middle of the night, she was seized with panic. Supposing the baby looked like her? Then she would never truly know, and neither would the poor child. It might go through all of its life thinking the wrong man was its father. Chewing the end of her pen, she restricted the letter to reminding him of their weekend together and assuring him that she still loved and missed him more than she could say. Then she couldn't make her mind up whether to ask him to write to her. There would be no disguising who the letter came from now, no borrowing of typewriters and office envelopes. If the Wilkinsons found that he was writing to her they were sure to start guessing. The neighbours' disapproval she could live with, but she wanted to keep the Wilkinsons' good opinion. On the other hand, she desperately wanted to hear from him, to know that he still loved her. Once again, it was the baby that stopped her. How could she demand love letters from one man when she might be carrying another one's baby? She could see no way out.

Summer turned into autumn and then winter set in, bringing dreary days of grey skies and endless rain. The Allies advanced northwards through Italy, the Russians slowly regained control of their own soil, the Americans fought from island to island in the Pacific, while in Britain it was announced that some conscripts would be sent not into the forces, but down the mines.

At the factory, thoughts were still with Jack.

'I do hope he's all right,' Mrs Wilkinson kept repeating. 'He says there's a stove in his hut, but is there any fuel? And has he got enough blankets? It's much colder in Germany than in England, they say. They have snow there every year, and for much longer than what we do here.'

'He's young and tough,' Mr Wilkinson said. 'He don't feel the cold like what we do at our age.'

Mrs Wilkinson looked unconvinced.

'But they're not feeding them proper. You need decent food to keep warm.'

'He don't say that,' Mr Wilkinson pointed out.

'No, but it stands to reason, don't it? They ain't going to give prisoners much, not if they're on short rations themselves.'

Jack's letters told them about his companions, a mixed bunch from all three services and several of the Allied nations, and about the work they were forced to do mending the railways that Jack's RAF colleagues had damaged. Always there was a carefully worded message at the end of each letter: 'Give my regards to Rita and tell her I hope she's keeping A1', or, 'All the best to Rita, I hope everything's all right with her.'

Rita hoarded up the brief sentences in her heart, to be brooded over at night. What did he really mean by them? How did he feel towards her? She ached to know.

By November it was obvious to all and sundry that she was pregnant.

'Why didn't you tell us before?' Mrs Wilkinson asked.

'I didn't want no fuss,' Rita said.

Mrs Wilkinson was not mollified.

'You didn't ought to be lifting heavy weights and that. You ought to be sitting as much as possible.'

'I'm all right, honest. I'm feeling fine,' Rita assured her.

It was true. Physically, she was very well. Thanks to the rationing system that gave extra protein to expectant mothers, and the fact that vegetables, especially carrots and potatoes, were among the few things that were in good supply, she was eating better than she ever had in her life. The baby was the easiest she had carried yet. If she could have been sure that Jack was its father she would have been on top of the world.

The usual questions followed: when was it due? Did she want a boy or a girl? Easily answered.

'What does your hubby say about it? Is he pleased?'

Rita felt suffocated. She had not told Ron. She had not written to him or heard from him since the night he had assaulted her. She supposed she was going to have to tell him once it was born, but she was putting it off as long as possible.

'He – er – he don't say a lot. He don't like kids much,' she managed to say.

Mrs Wilkinson looked shocked.

'That's wicked, that is. Children are a blessing. I wanted a big family, lots of strong sons and beautiful daughters, lots of noise and laughter in the house. But it weren't to be. It was just the one. My Jack.'

Sadness shadowed her strong-featured face. Both of them thought of Jack under armed guard in enemy territory. Then Mrs Wilkinson made an effort and pulled herself back to the subject in hand. She reached out and patted Rita's swelling stomach.

'You take great care of that little baby. It's a precious gift.'

Rita had to turn away to stop herself from blurting out the secret, that it might be the Wilkinsons' grandchild that she was carrying. With every day that passed, it was more difficult to stop the words from spilling from her.

Lily came home on a forty-eight-hour pass. Life was just wonderful for her, it seemed. Everything was fun, everyone was her friend, except for a few for whom she cherished a violent hatred. Their station was the most important in the whole war effort and she was an integral part of it. Her accounts of what she had been doing were littered with references to Bob Marriot. She had been dancing with Bob, cycling with Bob, to a fancy restaurant with Bob. In contrast with Rita's life, Lily's seemed totally carefree.

As if to hammer this home, the Monday after Lily went back, a letter arrived for Rita. The moment she saw it, she felt sick. Ron. Why was he writing, after all this time? Slowly, reluctantly, she bent down to pick it up. She wanted to burn it, to pretend it had never existed, but somehow she was unable to do it. A letter had to be opened, however bad it might be. She turned the envelope over and over in her hands, trying to guess its contents. Was he coming on leave? Was he going abroad? Had he – a sudden hope leapt within her – had he found someone else? Fuelled by this wonderful fantasy, she ripped it open. The contents were brief: a single sheet written on one side in Ron's unmistakable scrawly hand and bad spelling.

So you thourt youd get away with it did you. You thourt you wouldnt tell me you was in the club but my mum wrote me so I know. That must cramp your style. Nobody going to look at you when you got a belly on you are they. You just woch your Yank wont want you now. And you just remember your married to me and now you got this kid and all and there aint going to be no getting out of it for you so just you think about that.

Ron.

Hatred churned within her, hot and bitter. Heavy chains were hung about her, weighing her down, restricting her movements, imprisoning her. 'Bastard!' she spat, ripping the letter into halves, and quarters, and tiny pieces. 'Bastard! You just do it out of spite, don't you?'

She could hear Joan moving about in the kitchen. At any

moment she was going to call out and ask if there was any post. She had to get rid of the hateful thing. She stuffed the pieces into her pocket. The parlour fire was dead, not due to be relit till the evening. She could not burn it on the stove, as Joan was in the kitchen. She went out and shoved the evidence in the dustbin, shaking it so the pieces got mixed up with the old tealeaves, marge papers and ashes. She was shaking with anger and loathing, and a horrible sense of impotence. If Ron insisted on carrying on with the marriage, there was nothing she could do.

Somehow, she bluffed her way through the usual morning chaos with the family and got herself on to the bus for work. The Wilkinson factory sat in her mind like a haven of peace. There she could get away from family problems and immerse herself in supplies and dockets, receipts and government directives. To her relief, Mrs Wilkinson was not around. Mr Wilkinson had a cold and was too concerned about his streaming nose and muzzy head to notice that Rita was unusually pale and quiet. Wally, thank goodness, could always be relied upon to mind his own business. The first post was already on the desk. She sorted through it, her boiling emotions gradually subsiding into a growling simmer. The ordered routine of the day claimed her. She went through the usual round of jobs, concentrating on keeping her mind on the task in hand, not always with success. At times, words from the letter rose to the top of her mind, making her grind her teeth in rage. If Ron had appeared in the doorway, she would have snatched a chisel or a bradawl and attacked him without a moment's hesitation.

The second post arrived. A couple of business letters and – Rita stopped dead, staring at the third envelope, not able to take it in. This could not be happening. Not today, after this morning's shock. But there was no mistaking it. A letter from Germany. From Jack. Addressed to her. Her knees felt suddenly weak, her head light. With a rush of fear and possessiveness she glanced up, clasping the precious letter to her chest. Mr Wilkinson and Wally were busy on the far side of the factory. She was safe. She scuttled into her office cubbyhole and for the second time that morning ripped open an envelope with trembling fingers and beating heart.

The letter was written in pencil on rough brownish paper. At the first line, she gasped aloud.

How can you do this to me, Rita? What are you playing at? I don't understand you. It was bad enough to have you tell me not to write. You know how I hate all this pretence and cover up. I lie in bed writing all these letters in my head to you and you won't let me send them. What does it matter what people think for God's sake?

But now I find out that you're pregnant. What am I supposed to think? You write and tell me you love me and miss me, and yet you don't tell me you're expecting our child. What sort of love is that? It seems to me that everything you write is one big lie. I'm stuck in this godawful hole and you carry on as if I don't exist. But I do exist, Rita. If you can remember it, I did have something to do with the baby you're carrying, and I think I have a right to be told about it. How long are you going to go on pretending like this? Are you going to tell the child who its father is, or have you just cut me out of your life altogether? I thought better of you than that. I thought you really cared for me, but it seems like I was wrong. All you want is a handy lie to protect you from what the neighbours will say. Perhaps it was all a lie from the start, and you just wanted a bit on the side. If that's it, then it's over, but I warn you, I'm not giving up my child.

There was no signature.

Rita sat gaping at the letter, scorched and shaken by the blast of raw emotion that leapt from every word, that manifested itself in underlinings that practically gouged through the flimsy paper. Jack's searing anger and frustration left her reeling. Hot tears sprang to her eyes and ran down her cheeks. She could not bear it that he should so misjudge her. She had to put it right, had to explain. Her first reaction was to reach for pen and paper, to write that minute, to tell him why – but then all the barriers rose up in front of her. How could she tell him that the baby could be Ron's? Would he believe that she had been raped by her own husband? Even if he did, there was the thought of all the eyes that

277

might read her words: private, intimate words that should only be spoken between lovers would be scanned by censors. She put the pen down again. She had ruined everything. She had done it all wrong. And now it was too late. Jack hated her. Ron would not let her go. She was bearing a baby who would never know who its father really was. Everything was falling apart, crumbling around her. And it was all her fault.

## 35

1944

Rita lay sleepless yet again, unresolved problems pressing in on her with the darkness. She listened to the boys' steady breathing, envying them their easy surrender to blissful unconsciousness. Once she had been like that, had gone to bed tired from the day, closed her eyes and known nothing but dreams till the morning then woken up refreshed and ready for the day ahead. Such a long time ago that had been, before she married Ron. Even recently, things had been better than they were now. Looking back, the time after Ron was called up and before Jack was shot down seemed easy and carefree.

The baby moved within her, fluttering its limbs against the walls of the womb, bringing on the familiar lurch of wonder mixed with apprehension. Rita put her hands on her swollen belly, feeling the ripples, and wondered when she would sink into the cow-like state she remembered before each of the boys were born, when all she cared about was the new life she carried. What a relief it would be just to disregard all the worry about Ron and Jack and simply think about the baby itself. But even that was not straightforward. She had a horrible nagging fear that she would not be able to love the baby if it turned out to be obviously Ron's. However often she told herself that she adored Peter and Michael despite their father, she felt that this one could be different. The way in which it had been conceived might colour the way she felt about it, even though she knew it was not the child's fault. She ached with pity for the poor little thing – unloved, unwanted, rejected – felt the burden of guilt drag at her. She was its mother. She was responsible. She stroked the bulge, trying to reassure it.

'I'll treat you just like the others,' she promised, but she feared it might be a terrible effort to do so.

But if it was Jack's . . . how different that would be. If only Jack would forgive her for not telling him. She still had not told him the full story, finding it impossible to admit to him that the child he claimed might not be his. Countless sheets of paper had been wasted, the letter started and torn up. She had never found writing easy, and writing about something so difficult, so intimate, to someone hostile and disappointed in her just did not work. Whatever she said sounded wrong. She knew that if he read it, it would only make matters worse. In the end, she resorted to half-truths, saying that she had intended telling him when it was born, but not before, since she did not want him to worry about her. In reply, he had told her that she had no right to keep it to herself. After that, it was back to the brief messages at the foot of his letters to his parents, only now she had to share them. 'Regards to Rita and Wally. I hope they're keeping well.' Rita and Wally. She could hardly believe how much a harmless-sounding phrase like that could hurt. Rather than risk saying something that would make him hate her for ever, she stopped writing to him.

She tried to turn her mind to something else. Lily was coming home next weekend. That would at least make a change.

Lily's visits always turned the house upside-down. Florrie made a big effort to welcome her baby home and spoil her as far as rationing would allow. Food was hoarded for days beforehand in order to put on something approaching a spread for Lily. All the sleeping arrangements had to be changed. Everyone was required to alter their usual weekend timetables to be around for Lily.

As usual, Lily bounded in full of life and strength, praising the virtues of service life to the skies and totally dominating the conversation. She made the occasional pretence of being interested in what her family and old friends and neighbours had been up to, but in fact she was totally bound up in herself and life at Whiley Green. Just like last time, her accounts were heavily sprinkled with references to Bob Marriot.

'You been going out with him for a long time now, ain't you?' Joan remarked.

'Yeah, ever since we went on holiday.'

'Must be the longest you ever been out with anyone,' Rita said.

'Nearly,' Lily said, with a loaded look.

Florrie wanted to know more about him. What was he like, what did his parents do?

'Oh, he's very nice. Canadian. He's a driver. You know –goes off on these long night convoys. It's a wonder they haven't sent him abroad. He keeps expecting it, but still he's here. His parents? I think his dad's in haulage. Lorries. Got their own business, anyway.'

'That's nice,' Florrie approved.

'Could mean anything. Might just be one rusty old truck,' Jim said.

Lily tossed her glossy head.

'I ain't thinking of marrying him, if that's what you think. Blimey, no! I ain't that stupid!'

On the Saturday evening, Rita, Joan and Lily went to the pictures, on Florrie's insistence. Once out of their mother's earshot, Lily became more open about her relationship with Bob.

'He's crazy about me. Writes every day he don't see me. The other girls all laugh at me, but really they're dead jealous. They all fancy him and all. I mean, he's smashing looking, and he never gives even a look at any other girls. It's like there's no one else in the world but me.'

'That's nice,' Rita said.

It was all for her benefit, to make her envious, Rita realised. The trouble was, it succeeded. To have that sort of love lavished on you was just so wonderful. And to be free to accept it, to revel in it the way that Lily could, was more than wonderful. By contrast, what little was left of her relationship with Jack seemed tarnished, threatened, horribly fragile. Lily could boast to her heart's content, enjoy the jealousy of her friends, decide whether she was going to see Bob at every opportunity or give him the runaround, or even ditch him. The only difficulty she experienced was the one they were all grappling with – the war. At any time, Bob could be snatched away and sent abroad. But even then Lily would be free to be true to him or not, as she chose. The contrast with her own complicated life was painful.

Joan sounded anxious for her little sister.

'What do you feel about him, Lil?'

'Oh, he's the top brick off of the chimney.'

'So this is serious, is it?'

'No it blooming well ain't. I ain't getting serious about no one. I mean, he wanted me to go away with him this weekend. Said he'd wangle a leave as well and we could go away together –'

'Lily! You never –'

'Course not, stupid. I'm here, ain't I? Look, you don't have to worry about me, you know. I ain't daft. I ain't going to get myself into trouble and I ain't going to get hurt. I mean, I ain't like some round here.' Lily looked pointedly at Rita.

Anger boiled inside Rita. She had had enough of Lily and her boasting.

'What are you getting at?' she demanded.

Lily shrugged.

'Plain as the nose on your face, ain't it? You only got to look at the mess you're in. You might of stolen my Jack off of me, but it ain't done you much good. You're still stuck with your Ron and now you're carrying his kid. You won't catch me making stupid mistakes like that. I ain't letting any man get the better of me.'

'At least I ain't a heartless little bitch like you,' Rita exploded.

Lily gasped and whirled round to face her.

'You bleeding well take that back!'

Joan tried to calm them down, but her words went unheeded. Rita could not stop now that she had started.

'It's true. All you got in your head is dancing, and flaunting your flaming conquests. I tell you who I feel sorry for – your Bob. He sounds like a decent bloke. He deserves better than a hard little teaser like you.'

'You cow!'

Lily's hand flashed out and she slapped Rita round the face. Rita bit back a squeal of pain and hit back.

'Stop it, stop it!' Joan flung herself between them and grabbed Lily's arms.

'Let me go!'

'No – not till you promise to stop.'

'She started it.'

'She's pregnant, in case you ain't noticed. And anyway, you can both flaming well stop it. What would Mum say? You'd cut her to the heart, you would, fighting in the street like this.'

Lily subsided, muttering. Rita felt ashamed. Joan was right: if Florrie got to hear of this she would be deeply hurt. But she still meant every word she had said.

'I think you better make it up before we get home. We don't want Mum suspecting nothing. You know what she's like about keeping the family together,' Joan insisted.

'You can talk,' Lily retorted. 'Look what you done to Queenie.'

'I wrote to her just before Christmas and apologised,' Joan said. 'I didn't want to, but I done it, for Mum's sake and for George's. He is our brother, after all. And we're sisters, and we didn't ought to be fighting.'

Rita took a steadying breath, then forced the words out.

'I'm sorry, I didn't ought to of said that. You just drove me to it. I don't need you to tell me I made a mess of things, that's all.'

It was all Lily needed. Her mood swung immediately.

'Poor Rita. It must be horrible for you stuck here and having a baby and all.'

Nothing, not even family unity, was going to drive Rita into admitting anything more. She shrugged.

'It ain't so bad. You wouldn't catch me dressing up in a uniform and marching.'

By the time they got home, they were able at least to put on a face of normality for Florrie, but never had Rita been more glad to see the back of her sister than that weekend.

Just to add to everyone's worries, the Luftwaffe decided to stage a rerun of the Blitz. The raids were not as heavy or as frequent as the dreadful winter of three years ago, but still Rita and Joan and their parents debated as to whether the children ought to be evacuated. As usual, Florrie refused to budge. Joan could not face the thought of going back to Queenie.

'There's other places,' she pointed out. 'We could rent a little cottage somewhere, like what we did on holiday. You ought to come this time and all, Reet, what with the baby and everything.'

Rita was torn. For the children's sake, she knew it made sense, yet she was loath to leave the Wilkinsons. They were her only link with Jack.

'I mightn't be able to get another job in the country. We'd be pushed to manage on just the army pay.'

Neither sister was really keen on going somewhere where they didn't know anyone, and now that the war seemed to be going the Allies' way, it seemed a bit cowardly to make a bolt for it.

'I reckon Jerry'll soon give up. He knows he can't crush us Londoners,' Jim said.

So it was decided that they should stay, but Jim insisted that they went back to sheltering each night. There were new deep shelters now, with rows of bunks, as well as lights and toilets and running water. The women groaned. They had had enough of sheltering.

'You got to, for them kiddies' sake. And what with me being a warden and all, you got to set an example to the others. I don't want to be digging no more bodies out of the rubble, specially yours,' Jim told them.

When she found out that Rita was going straight to the shelter after work and not going home for days at a time, Mrs Wilkinson was horrified.

'That's no way to live. You got that little baby to think of,' she protested. 'I'm going to speak to Bill about this. It's criminal, that's what it is.'

It only took a few minutes' forceful talking from Mrs Wilkinson to convince her husband that Rita ought to be working part time only. Gratefully, Rita agreed. Through January and February she worked from ten till three each day. Then at the beginning of March, she was told she must stay home and rest until the baby was born.

'But I don't need to rest,' Rita lied.

'Rubbish. You got to save your strength.'

'But the office – the paperwork –' The letters from Jack.

'We'll manage,' Mr W. insisted. 'If we get in a muddle, we do. Some things are more important.'

Both of them looked at Rita's stomach, and the baby, as if sensing the attention, drummed its hard little heels up under Rita's ribs.

'You come back when you feel up to it, after it's born. You don't have to have it minded. You can bring it in with you and I can take care of it,' Mrs Wilkinson said.

'That's so kind of you. There ain't many employers'd do that,' Rita said, overwhelmed.

'It'd be a pleasure. I love babies. And anyhow, you're more like family now, ain't you?' Mrs Wilkinson said.

Afterwards, Rita went over these words many times in her mind, trying to decide just what they meant. Was it just that she was part of a small family business, or did the Wilkinsons suspect more than she had thought?

It was really strange, not having to go to work. Rita had almost forgotten what it was like not to be bound by a timetable and felt cast adrift. The best thing was being able to take the odd nap during the day. The bunks in the shelter were narrow and hard, and with the baby taking up more and more room, stretching and kicking restlessly inside her, it made it even harder than usual for her to get to sleep. But otherwise, she felt very much the spare part at home. Everyone else had their role. Florrie worked in the shop, Joan looked after the house, Jim had his warden work and his rabbits, the children had school and their own world of friends and make-believe. Rita pottered around offering to help, but none of them really needed her. She did not even have to do much in the way of preparation for the baby. Little Teddy's things were there to be passed on; washed out, maybe, but still wearable. It was all very different from being at the factory, an essential part of the organisation. She found herself going over to see the Wilkinsons a couple of times a week, and sorting out anything that needed urgently seeing to.

It was while she was at the Wilkinsons' that she felt the first twinges of pain, low in her back and quite unmistakable. She caught her breath. Mrs Wilkinson looked at her sharply.

'You all right, dear?'

'Yeah – yeah, quite all right. I think I'll be getting home now,' Rita said.

The problems quieted. There was just one overriding purpose now – to find a safe place to give birth to the baby. Every jolt on the bus ride home made her clasp her belly protectively. The bus seemed to grind on for ever, making detours round recent bomb damage, and when it finally got to the Island the swing bridge was open and they were held up for a quarter of an hour. Rita kept telling herself that it would be ages yet before the baby was born, that Peter had taken twenty-four hours to come into the world and Michael ten, but it did nothing to quell her impatience. She had to get home. Just as a much stronger pain flowed through her, the gates opened and the traffic began to move.

Florrie only had to take one look at her as she came into the shop before snapping into action. Lifting the flap in the counter, she took Rita's arm and shepherded her through to the parlour, calling to Joan as she did so.

'Run down the phone and ring for an ambulance. Rita's started.'

Rita could hear the ripple of excitement running through the customers as the connecting door closed behind her. She would be the chief topic of speculation in the pubs and the shelters that night, but she did not care. Nothing mattered now. She was home, and everything was under control. Soon she would be at the hospital.

When the siren went three hours later, she heard it but took no notice. The pains were coming strongly now, running right round her body, while in the next bed of the crowded antenatal ward a woman several years older than her was insisting on telling her every detail of her seven confinements. Most of the time Rita managed to just say 'Yes', 'No', or 'Really?', but occasionally she found a question flung in her direction.

'. . . but my mum wants a girl and my Reggie's set on another boy. What do you want yours to be?'

'Oh – a girl,' Rita said.

'Girls are nice. I love little girls. But they're more of a worry, don't you think . . .'

Rita stopped listening. She really *did* want a girl. If it was a girl, it wouldn't matter so much whether it was Jack's or Ron's. It would be hers. They would face the world together, whatever happened. Another pain started, clamping her like a fiery band of iron, squeezing her in its fierce grip until she cried out.

A middle-aged nurse appeared at her bedside.

'Getting nasty, is it, dear?'

She whipped the curtains round the bed and made a brief examination. A disapproving tut-tut issued from the business end of the bed.

'Two fingers. Why didn't you tell me before, dear? We'd better get you downstairs.'

Rita felt like giving her two fingers.

'I can't see what's going on down there, can I? How – oh!' The pain came again, going on and on. On the edge of her consciousness Rita knew she was being lifted on to a trolley. By the time she could take stock of her surroundings again, she was out in one of the endless, dimly lit corridors. The raid could be clearly heard, the familiar sickening whine of high-explosive bombs and roar of falling buildings. A young face framed in a nurse's headdress loomed over her, white with fatigue but stretched into a professionally reassuring smile.

'Nasty one tonight, Mother. But we got a delivery room down in the basement. You and the baby'll be quite safe down there. Your first, is it?'

'Third,' Rita managed to say.

There was a ripping noise very close by, then a deafening explosion. The whole building seemed to shake and a blast of cold air whipped along the corridor. Never in her life had Rita felt so vulnerable. She could do nothing to protect herself or the baby from the death falling down on them.

'Run, for Christ's sake!' she screamed.

There was a jolting nightmare of green walls, dim lights and swing doors, the nurse's pale face swimming in and out of view. She was being carried downstairs. There were grunts of effort from the nurse and whoever else was holding the trolley. Another crash. Plaster flaked down from the ceiling and the lights went out. The nurse's voice quavered through to her, saying something about everything being all right.

'It ain't bloody all right, you stupid cow –' Rita yelled as another contraction grasped her, blotting out everything with its shattering pain.

Then there was a yellow light in the darkness, and more

movement, and she was inside a room. She sensed she was underground. Another face. An Irish voice, cheerful, unruffled. Competent hands on her racked body.

'Everything's coming along fine, dear, you're doing splendidly so you are. Got here just in time. Ready to push now, are we? That's it, come along now —'

The pain became focused, filled with urgent purpose. Rita heaved and pushed. Her bones were being forced apart, her body ripped open.

'That's it dear, that's grand, I can see the top of the head. Push again —'

A tearing, and a pause. Rita was panting, running with sweat.

'Nearly there now. Just one more effort, dear.'

Rita concentrated her whole being. There was a slithering and a release, and a cry of pleasure from the midwife: 'There it is! A beautiful little girl.'

A hiccup and then loud wail of protest. Her baby, her own new baby, alive and crying.

'Oh —' Rita struggled to raise her head and look between her upraised knees. The midwife was already bundling the protesting infant into a towel, wiping its face, clearing its nose. 'Is it all right?' Rita asked.

'All right? Why, it's a lovely bonny baby, so it is. Big, too.' The midwife's back was to her now, doing something on the other side of the room. 'Eight pounds three ounces! Lovely size, good and strong.'

'There now, little one, you come and see your mammy.' She tucked the baby into the crook of Rita's arm, and the crying ceased.

Rita gazed at her baby daughter. Two smoky blue eyes in a red creased little face stared back at her. On top of her pulsating skull, still smeared with blood, was a thick fluff of dark curly hair. Tears welled up in Rita's eyes in an overwhelming wave of love.

'You're so lovely,' she whispered.

The midwife was busy with the afterbirth.

'What are you calling her, then?'

There was only one name for this baby. Rita smiled as she said it, warm with the triumph of birth.

'Jacqueline.'

## 36

'And your husband's name, Mrs Johnson?'

The elderly registrar looked at her over the top of his half-moon glasses. It was the question that Rita had been dreading. She swallowed.

'He ain't – I mean, the baby's father's name's John William Wilkinson.'

Her voice came out loud and defiant.

The registrar pursed his lips in disapproval. 'Your husband is serving abroad, I take it, Mrs Johnson?'

'Er, no –' She had not been expecting this question.

'But you've not – ah – been together within the last nine or ten months?'

'No – I mean yes – I mean . . .'

She stopped, not sure whether lie or truth was the best way to what she wanted to achieve. Her brain was still in the befuddled state of the newly delivered mother. Her breasts ached. The tiny office with its putrid green walls seemed to close in on her.

The registrar fixed her with unsympathetic eyes.

'Mrs Johnson, as you are a married woman, then your husband is legally the father of your child.'

Rita was horrified.

'But – it can't be – she ain't. She don't look a bit like him.'

'Nevertheless, *Mrs* Johnson,' he laid an unpleasant emphasis on the Mrs, 'that is the position, unless you can prove otherwise. So – your husband's name, if you please?'

Nothing Rita could say would change his course of action. In the end she had to give Ron's name, rank and birthplace. She felt she had betrayed both Jack and baby Jacqueline.

With precise movements, the registrar blotted the certificate and handed it to Rita. She looked at it with distaste. A nasty legal lie.

'Thanks for nothing,' she said, and shoved it into her bag.

She was sick of the lies. She had hoped that after the baby was born there would be no more pretending, but if anything it was worse than when she was pregnant. Her family all went along with the fiction that Ron was baby Jacqueline's father, for appearances' sake. Worst than that, Maisie came to see her a couple of days after the baby was born, bringing a matinée jacket of a particularly nasty shade of yellow and exclaiming over her latest grandchild. If Florrie had not by chance been there at the same time, Rita would have told her just where she was wrong, but her mother's warning stare made her hold her tongue.

Now she was free to go home at last. Her ten days' lying-in was over, she felt remarkably well and strong and she was longing to be with the boys again. More than that, she wanted to show the baby to the Wilkinsons. With them, particularly with Mrs Wilkinson, lay the answer to little Jacqueline's parentage. If Mrs Wilkinson saw the likeness that Rita was sure was there, then it was certain. At least with them there would be no lies or pretences.

Florrie complained when she prepared to set off for White-chapel the morning after her arrival home.

'You think more of them Wilkinsons than you do your own family,' she accused.

'They got a right to see the baby,' Rita said.

Florrie rounded on her.

'Don't you let me hear you say nothing like that again, my girl. We've always been a respectable family, we have. It was bad enough when you had to marry Ron on the quick. Don't you go blackening our good name now with something you can't ever prove, d'you hear me?'

'I hope as I can prove it today,' Rita retorted.

She wrapped Jacqueline up in two shawls, then buttoned her inside her coat. It was a sharp March wind outside and she did not want the baby to catch cold. On the bus, women cooed over her and asked after names and weight and likenesses.

'She's just like her dad,' Rita said proudly.

She marvelled at the fact that it was less than a fortnight since she last travelled this way. It seemed a different age. Already, she could not imagine a life without Jacqueline.

When she got off the bus, there was the difficult part of passing the deserted workshop. Rita scuttled by, keeping her eyes firmly on Jacqueline's little head, but she could not prevent the old sick feeling of revulsion from gripping her. She held the baby tighter, as if someone might come and snatch her from her arms. When she reached the Wilkinsons' factory, she was out of breath. Panting, she banged on the door.

'Well, here's a sight for sore eyes!' Mr Wilkinson exclaimed, beaming. 'And what of you got here? The little stranger? Elena'll be that pleased. Been talking about you, she has, only this morning. Come on in, and we'll put the kettle on. Elena! Look who's here.'

Tears pricked Rita's eyes. He was such a nice man. She hoped he would not think any the less of her when he found out the truth about the baby.

Mrs Wilkinson came bustling over. She was wearing a floral apron and had her hair tied up in a scarf, and had obviously been taking over Rita's role as unofficial apprentice and tool-passer. When she saw Rita she burst into exclamations of welcome.

'Ah – and is this the baby? Let's have a look at her, then. Take some of them layers off of her. Ah – ain't she beautiful? Lovely hair! Oh, and look at them little hands. I love their fingernails, don't you? Like tiny shells, so perfect. Oh look, she's opening her eyes. She's going to have brown eyes, ain't she? They're turning already. What of you called her?'

Rita took a steadying breath. Her heart was knocking inside her chest. This was it.

'Jacqueline.'

'Oh –'

There was a brief, meaningful silence, then Mrs Wilkinson got up. 'Come with me,' she said, and bustled through the door leading into the house. Rita followed her into the crowded front parlour, and sat down on the armchair that Mrs Wilkinson indicated. A photograph was thrust into her hand.

'Look at this.'

Rita looked. It was a formal studio portrait, a family group, with Mr Wilkinson staring stiffly at the camera and his wife gazing down at the baby which she supported carefully upright on her knee. The infant Jack was about two months old, round-eyed with amazement at his strange surroundings. He looked exactly like Jacqueline.

Rita raised her eyes to meet Mrs Wilkinson's.

'It's true, ain't it?' Mrs Wilkinson stated. 'She's my Jack's.'

Rita nodded. She watched the conflicting emotions crossing Mrs Wilkinson's face. Disapproval, longing, distaste. She took the photograph back. Her expression hardened.

'Your hubby's been away a long time, ain't he?'

Hot anger raced through Rita. She was being judged without Mrs Wilkinson knowing anything of the real situation. It wasn't fair.

'It weren't like that, if that's what you're thinking. I'm not just a service wife missing out on . . . on a bit of the other.'

'No?'

'No.'

Still Mrs Wilkinson did not soften. She deliberately avoided looking at Jacqueline, lying bundled in Rita's arms.

'But you are a married woman. I thought better of you. And of my Jack.' The last was just an afterthought. After all, the rules were different for men, and Mrs Wilkinson's son was nothing less than perfect.

'Married? Yeah, in name. It weren't exactly made in heaven, Mrs Wilkinson –' Rita stopped short of saying how she came to be married. That would just confirm the fact that she was a tart. Perhaps she was. Out of her three children, only one had actually been conceived within wedlock.

'We ain't seen eye to eye for a long time, me and Ron. He ain't bothered to come back and see me and the kids for ages.' Except that once, nine and a bit months ago. 'The boys of almost forgotten what he looks like.'

'I see.'

But she didn't. Rita realised that. The Wilkinsons had a happy marriage. Mrs Wilkinson was thinking of how dreadful it would have been if she had been unfaithful to her Bill. She had no idea what it was like to be tied to someone like Ron.

'And me and Jack –' Rita stopped again. She and Jack had been in love. She still was in love with him, but she had no idea how he felt about her. 'We was in love,' she said.

She looked down at Jacqueline. The poor little thing. It wasn't her fault that her mum had messed her life up good and proper before she was even born. She deserved a better start than that. At least she deserved two sets of grandparents. The baby was snuffling restlessly, her mouth moving unerringly towards the source of food. Rita could tell that she was working herself up to a good yell. Her already rock-hard breasts began leaking in response. She felt like having a good yell herself. Mrs Wilkinson was saying something, but Rita did not catch it. She was watching the way Jacqueline was screwing up her little face. In just half a minute or so she was going to go red. Already she was waving her fists about. Sure enough, the first hiccuping cries started. Rita undid her layers of winter clothing and put the baby to her breast, wincing as the hard little gums clamped on her sore nipple. Jacqueline sucked with single-minded concentration, and Rita watched her, equally absorbed. It was only when she laid her on her shoulder to wind her that she realised that Mrs Wilkinson was watching the pair of them, and that the hostility had gone out of her face.

'She's a beautiful baby,' Mrs Wilkinson said, as Rita settled the infant on to the other side.

'Yes,' Rita agreed.

'Is she good?'

'She's hungry, but she don't cry a lot for no reason.'

'Jack was like that.'

'Yeah?'

'Greedy. And I suppose I spoilt him, him being the only one, and a boy.'

'Mmm.'

'Always did like his own way. Not that he was nasty about it. Oh no. But he got me round his little finger good and proper. Only got to look at me, really.'

'Yeah,' Rita said. 'I know what you mean.'

Mrs Wilkinson talked on, reminiscing. Jacqueline slowed up, and finally fell asleep from the effort of feeding, her little face soft and satiated. Mrs Wilkinson reached out her arms.

'Can I?'

Rita handed her over and began to button herself up.

Jacqueline stirred, burped, made a few-hearted sucking motions and went back to sleep. Mrs Wilkinson held her against her body and ran a gentle finger over her, tracing the outline of her face and limbs. Two tears welled up and ran down her cheeks as she bent to kiss the baby's head.

'Nine months ago must of been just before – ?'

'Yeah. Couple of days before,' Rita agreed. It seemed the time had come now to be open. 'I went up to Fenny Howe to meet him. There was a dance, and the Powers Girls was playing. He invited me.'

'He wrote me about the dance. It came after – after we heard. He never said nothing about you being there.'

'No, well, he wouldn't of, would he?' Rita said.

Mrs Wilkinson was still smiling at the baby, crooning to her between remarks to Rita.

'We did wonder, me and Bill. I said to him, if only you was single, like, I'd of been only too pleased, only of course you wouldn't never of been here if you was, 'cause you would of been called up. I mean, we're both very fond of you. Bill, he said, no you wouldn't never, you wasn't that sort, but then when we got the telegram, and again when we heard he was in POW camp, well, you acted like you was more than just a family friend.' She looked up, attempting to get something like the former fierceness into her voice. 'I'm not saying as I approve, mind. I don't. Wedding vows should be made to be kept, to my mind, but – well –' her gaze rested on the baby again. 'There is a war on, I suppose, and everything's all upside-down, and you say as you and your hubby don't get on –'

Rita carefully let out the breath she had not realised she was holding.

'I always felt like you and Mr Wilkinson were like a second family to me,' she said.

'And what does your mum say about all this?' Mrs Wilkinson asked.

'She don't approve, neither. I got plenty of stick from all of them, I can tell you. My mum, she just pretends the baby's Ron's.'

'But she ain't. That's clear as the nose on your face. She's Jack's, all right.' *And mine, her tone implied; my grandchild.*

'What's – what's Mr Wilkinson going to say to all this?' Rita wondered.

'Bill? Oh, you just leave him to me. I'll put him right,' Mrs Wilkinson said.

Rita felt a smile tugging at her lips. She could believe that.

Mrs Wilkinson stood up.

'Now then, young Jacqueline, you go back to your mum for a bit. I'm going to put the kettle on. No – better than that. I'm going to find a little something to wet the baby's head.'

She foraged around in the sideboard and produced a tray, four small glasses and a quarter-full bottle of brandy.

'Come along,' she said, and led the way back into the factory.

Mr Wilkinson and Wally were called over, and tots of brandy handed out.

'I reckon we got something to celebrate today,' Mrs Wilkinson said, with a meaningful look at her husband.

Mr Wilkinson took the hint, and raised his glass.

'Here's to little Jacqueline. A long life and a happy one,' he said.

'To Jacqueline,' everyone chorused.

*And*, Rita silently added, *to Jack*.

## 37

'Second Front NOW' the writing on the side of the barn demanded, in large grey letters. It had been there since January. Lily cycled past it every day on her way to work. Everyone had been expecting a second front for ages. Now, in Hampshire, it was becoming obvious that something was stirring. Huge numbers of men and a massive back-up of equipment was building up, passing along the country roads and massing in camps close to the coast. Everyone felt the suppressed excitement. At last, it was going to happen. The Allies were going to take the offensive.

Lily was annoyed. On Thursday she had arrived back to find that a message had been left for her. Of course, it had to be the girl she most disliked who delivered it to her, a redhead who competed with her for the unofficial title of Most Sought-After WAAF. She bounced up to Lily with her face pulled into an expression of extreme sympathy.

'Oh Croft, I'm so sorry, there was a phone call for you. Just now. You only missed it by five minutes. Got held up on the way home, did you?'

'I was just talking to that new flying officer. You know, the one with the Humphrey Bogart eyes,' Lily lied, just to stay ahead. She knew the other girl had her sights on him.

'What a good thing your boyfriend didn't know that.'

Lily's heart turned over, but she kept a casual face.

'Oh, it was him, was it? What did he have to say?'

'I'm so sorry to have to be the one to tell you this, Croft. It's such a shame. He said he can't make it for Saturday night. Isn't that dreadful of him? And at such short notice, too.'

With a piece of acting that would not have disgraced Lauren Bacall, Lily gave an unconcerned shrug.

'Plenty more fish in the sea. That flying officer'll be pleased, for one. And that gorgeous Yank what does the fantastic jitterbug.'

She went on in the same vein for a while before making off upstairs. Once there, she went and locked herself in the lavatory, the only place in the house where she could be guaranteed some privacy. She squeezed her eyes tight against the threatening tears. The real pain was unexpected. Bob was the one who was serious about the two of them, not her. She was the free agent, the one who kept the upper hand. She was not going to cry over him, she was not. She had vowed never to let a man get one over on her again. She thumped her clenched fists on her knees. How dare he? How dare he stand her up? And through that bitch, too. Well, he needn't think she was going to be here waiting for him when he chose to call again. Oh no. Nobody got a second chance with Lily Croft. Bob Marriot had had it. He was out.

She was still stinging from it the next day as she got to the 'Second Front NOW' notice.

'D'you think it really is going to happen?' her friend Betty asked, as they cycled past.

'What?' Lily's mind was on Saturday night. She had to get someone really smashing to be seen with.

Betty gave an exaggerated grin.

'The invasion, you goon.'

'How do I know? I ain't Churchill,' Lily retorted. She had far more pressing things to worry about. Like, just what was Bob playing at?

It wasn't until later that she realised that world events were ruining her weekend plans. All leave was cancelled. No un-authorised person was allowed inside a six-mile zone back from the coast. Lily spent Saturday evening at the local pub and got soaked going there and coming back. Even the weather was against her. It was cold, wet and stormy, echoing her own bad mood.

On Sunday morning she was on duty serving up the break-fasts, slopping tinned tomatoes on to thick slices of toast. One of the girls came up behind her.

'You're wanted on the phone, Lil. Says it's urgent. Cut along quick before you're seen.'

Lily handed over her ladle and scuttled off, dodging behind

sacks of potatoes to avoid the eye of the chief cook. She grabbed the greasy receiver of the wall phone.

'Yes?'

'Lily?'

The familiar voice sent a complex of emotions coursing through her. Immediately she went on the offensive.

'Oh, it's you. Hello, stranger.'

'Listen, darling –' His voice was low and intense. 'I'm real sorry about yesterday –'

'Oh, don't bother y'self. I got plenty of other offers,' Lily told him.

'I would have written and explained, but we're supposed to be incommunicado. They'll have my balls if they find out I've been phoning. Listen, I only got a couple of minutes. This is very important, Lily. I want to ask you something.'

Despite herself, Lily was intrigued.

'What?' she said.

'You know how much I love you, Lily –'

'You're always saying so. Not enough to get away to see me last night, though.'

'I wanted to, Lil, believe me, but I just couldn't. Look, I been wanting to ask you for ages, but, well anyway it's kinda urgent now. Will you marry me, Lily?'

'*What?*'

For once, Lily was caught off guard. She had not been expecting this. Not like this, anyway. Not out of the blue on a Sunday morning.

'I want us to get married. You're the only girl for me, Lily. The only one I ever felt like this about. What do you say, darling? Will you?'

Somebody came clumping up behind her.

'What's up, Croft? Been stood up again?'

Lily flushed.

'Sod off!'

'Lily!' came Bob's shocked voice down the line.

'I don't mean you,' Lily told him. All the same, he had made her look stupid in front of everyone.

'What's it to be, darling?'

'I don't know,' Lily snapped.

Someone was calling her name above the clatter of the kitchens. Bob was insisting on an answer.

'Look, stop nagging me, will you? This ain't what I call a proposal. First you let me down, then you call me up when I'm working.'

'But it's real important, honey. I got to know now.'

'Why?'

'I can't tell you. Just give me an answer, please. Say you'll marry me.'

'No.'

'Lily –'

'I said no. Nobody treats me like this.'

'But Lily, I can explain.'

'Go on, then.'

'But not now. Look, Lily, I got to go. Say you'll wait for me, darling. Promise me that.'

'Give me one good reason why I should.'

'Croft! Where the hell are you?'

The shout drowned what Bob was saying.

'What?' she said.

But the line was dead. Lily slammed the receiver down.

'Damn, damn, damn!'

She stumped back to her post, fuming with frustration, and just escaped being put on a charge. She spent the rest of the day dropping things, not listening, and misunderstanding orders. Everyone shouted at her, and she yelled back.

By the next morning, everyone at the aerodrome was sure that the invasion was about to get under way. The bombers were flying short missions, just across the Channel. Lily was still cursing herself. How could she have been so stupid? Bob must be part of the invasion force. That was why he hadn't been able to come on Saturday. That was why he couldn't explain. Why hadn't she realised this? But it was too late now. All she could do was wait for news.

The wireless broadcasts were so frustrating. They told of heavy fighting, of beachheads, of bravery, of losses on both sides, but not of what Lily wanted to know, namely, was Corporal R.

Marriot all right? New words burst into common usage – Omaha, Juno, Sword, Overlord, D-Day; and new place names became familiar – Caen, Port-en-Bessin, Creuilly. At the aerodrome, the RAF told of their mastery of the skies. They were shot at from the ground, but the resistance in the air was peanuts. Lily took some comfort from that. It must be a good sign.

At the end of the week a letter arrived from home, from Joan, but containing everyone's news. Lily scanned through it. All the usual stuff. Mum had managed to get hold of a consignment of tinned peaches, and there had been a queue right down the street and a good deal of bad feeling amongst those at the end who missed out. Little Teddy was getting into everything. Baby Jackie had had a cold but was better now.

Lily paused over this, puzzled at something, till she realised that it was the fact that she was equally bored by accounts of both children. The fact that Jackie's father was her ex-boyfriend meant nothing. It was Bob who filled her thoughts.

Then the tone of the letter changed. They had had a note from Queenie: their brother George was part of the invasion force. Mum was dead worried. Lily gave a mental shrug. George would be all right. He always was. He wouldn't have been part of the first landings, he would be following up, doing some cushy number somewhere repairing vehicles. Not like Bob. She carried with her a sick certainty that Bob was in the thick of it.

As usual, it was Betty whom she turned to.

'What am I going to do? I was a right cow to him. I never even said goodbye. He was cut off halfway through saying something.'

'You've had rows before. He's always come back,' Betty pointed out.

'But he can't come back if he's in Normandy somewhere. He ain't even wrote to me. He always writes to me when he's away, always. But this time I ain't heard nothing.'

'Well, like you said, he's in Normandy. It ain't like a convoy to Scotland or something.'

'No, I know, it's about a million times more dangerous. That's why I'm worried sick. Supposing he's been injured? How will I know?'

'You tried writing?'

For once, Lily was silenced. That simple idea had not occurred to her.

'No,' she admitted.

'Well there you are, then. Send it to his unit, Normandy, France. They'll know where to send it.'

'Oh Betty, you're so clever! What'd I do without you?'

'That's what I wonder,' Betty commented. 'You love him, don't you?'

Lily gave a wry smile.

'Yeah, I do. I never knew it till now, but I do.'

In Whitechapel the Wilkinsons, Rita and Wally were discussing the progress of the Allies.

'You heard anything about your brother?' Mrs Wilkinson asked.

'Not yet. We asked Queenie to let us know the moment she got any news,' Rita said.

'What's that?' Mr Wilkinson interrupted.

They listened. It was a loud chugging, like a motorbike, but it seemed to be in the air. They all went outside and stared up into the sky. What looked like a small plane was passing overhead.

'Never seen nothing like that before,' Mr Wilkinson said.

Other occupants of the street were gazing at it as well.

'Don't look like one of ours,' someone said.

'What the hell's it doing over here in broad daylight? Why ain't the RAF and the ack-ack after it?'

Then the noise stopped.

'Engine's cut out,' someone commented, unnecessarily.

There was a brief silence, then a huge explosion. The glass in the factory opposite, replaced only the week before, shattered. Rita screamed and ran inside to where Jackie was wailing in her pram.

Shaken, the Wilkinsons and Wally followed her. 'What on earth was that?' they all asked each other.

They were soon to find out.

'Flying bombs. V1s,' Jim said, grim-faced, when Rita got home that night. 'Hitler's latest little present to us.'

People preferred to call them doodlebugs. It made them sound comic, even cosy, but there was nothing funny about them. They came over from France in a steady stream, day and night. Nobody knew where they were going to drop next. Rita cornered Joan in her bedroom, out of their parents' earshot.

'We got to do something about these dreadful things. It ain't like air raids. There ain't no warning, you can't get to no shelter. Them kids could have one drop right on them at school.'

'Yeah, I know, but what we going to do?' Joan said. 'Evacuate? I know I made it up with Queenie, but I really couldn't face going back there again, Reet, not with six of 'em now –'

'I weren't thinking of Queenie, and anyway, I ain't sending the kids away without me no more. I lost too much of their childhood last time. And I can't part with Jackie, I'm still feeding her, and I just couldn't bear it. No, I was thinking of something else.'

She had lain awake planning it the last couple of nights, turning it over and over until she had the whole thing worked out.

'We could go to the cottage. All of us – you, me, all the kids, Mum and Dad and the Wilkinsons and Wally and his wife. There's room, if we convert some of them outbuildings. It's summer now, we could have it all snug by the autumn, and the Wilkinsons could carry on with their business. And if there ain't enough work for all of us to join in, there's sure to be some war work going at some factory somewhere nearby. What do you think?'

She was so convinced of the absolute rightness of the plan that she was surprised to see Joan looking doubtful.

'Well, I don't know – Mum and Dad won't like it for a start –'

'If we both insist, and tell her we're both going, and taking all the kids, I bet she'd come too.'

'She won't leave Dad, and he won't leave his job, not if he's going to be needed again, digging people out after these doodlebugs.'

'We'll work on them. But what about you, Joanie? Will you come? Course I'm going, definite, even if it means just me and my kids. I'll take yours and all, if you like. I don't mind looking

302

after all six of 'em, if it means they're safe. I tell you, these flying bombs scare the pants off of me. I've lived all through the Blitz and I've done firewatching and I've put out incendiaries and I been buried under a building, but I'm not staying here for one of them things to fall on me out of the blue.'

Joan was frowning, still working it all through.

'Yeah, I'll come,' she decided. 'But what about the Wilkinsons? Do they know about all this?'

'Not yet. I'll put it to them tomorrow. Then we'll have a go at Mum and Dad.'

It took her three days to persuade the Wilkinsons. At first they refused point blank, then they said it would be impossible to move the whole business out to the country. Rita kept at it. She had promised Jack that she would look after them, and even though Jack's letters were still very cool, she was determined to stand by that promise. Then came the news that an old friend of theirs had been killed by flying glass from a V1 blast. Mrs Wilkinson decided that Rita was right, and carried her husband along with her. Once Mr Wilkinson was convinced, he even admitted that he knew someone with a lorry who could move all the equipment for them. A date was set; they started packing up and informing all their clients and suppliers of their new address.

Triumphant, Rita went home to tackle her parents. Together, she and Joan put all the arguments to them that they could, but all to no avail.

'You go, and take the kiddies. I'll miss you all something dreadful, but you're right, you ought to get them out of it,' Florrie said. 'But I ain't coming. What'd people round here do without me?'

'They'd just have to go to another shop. You're not the only one open on Dog Island,' Rita said.

'I'm the only decent one. And anyhow, I ain't leaving your dad.'

'I can't run out on my job,' Jim insisted.

Rita and Joan pointed out that he had done five years of faithful service and his back was getting worse by the day, but he was adamant. He had come this far; he was going to see it through.

'I lived all my life on this street. I ain't running out on it now.'

Rita lost her temper and called them a pair of stubborn old idiots. Florrie told her to curb her tongue.

Moving day came, the children were wild with excitement at the thought of going to live out in the country, the pram and two handcarts were loaded up with clothes and bedding and personal possessions, but Florrie and Jim stayed behind. With tears in her eyes, Rita hugged them both.

'Promise you'll get in that Morrison the moment you hear one come over,' she begged.

'Yeah, yeah. Don't you worry about me. They ain't got me yet and they won't now. You just look after all them little 'uns,' Florrie told her.

'You'll come out and see us all as soon as we got straight?'

' 'Course. Now off you go. You'll miss the train.'

A week later, just as they were beginning to get everything sorted out and the business started up again, the Wilkinsons received news from a neighbour in Prittlestone Road. A doodle-bug had hit the workshop next door but one. The fire had spread down the row and the Wilkinsons' factory had been burnt out.

## 38

'Another blooming winter coming up, and still it's not over,' one of the WAAFs grumbled as she and Lily cycled back to the billet through the early autumn wind and rain. 'I thought once we had D-Day it'd be over in a few weeks. Now it looks like it's going to go on for ages still.'

'Yeah,' Lily agreed.

Six months ago she would have been happy for the war to go on for ever, just as long as nobody she loved got killed. Now she wasn't so sure. She still had a string of admirers, still went out to dances and pubs and the pictures with them, but her heart wasn't in it any more. Since Bob had gone off to Normandy, the game had lost its fun. There was only one man she really wanted to see, and he was in France.

'You'd think old Hitler'd give in, now he can see we're winning. We got nearly all of France back now.'

'Yeah, the Canadians got Calais,' Lily said. She did not take much notice of how the war was progressing, but she did follow what Bob's lot were doing. Within the last week or so, they had liberated Cap Gris Nez and now Calais. Perhaps that would mean that Bob would get some leave.

'You heard from what's-his-name recently?' her companion asked, as if reading her mind.

'Oh yeah. He writes all the time,' Lily lied.

That was the worrying thing. She had not heard from him for over a fortnight. It was not like Bob. Even though she had turned down his marriage proposal, he still wrote passionate letters to her. And she often wrote back, sometimes even admitting that she was missing him.

It wouldn't have been quite so bad if she had still had Betty to confide in, but her friend had been posted up to Yorkshire and none of the other girls filled that gap in her life. Betty had understood her, had laughed at her flaunting of her sex appeal rather than feeling threatened or annoyed by it. The others were not so charitable. She had a reputation for grabbing anything decent in trousers that came within five miles, and they resented it, especially if it meant that they didn't get a look in. The trouble was, it had grown to be a habit. She could no more leave a good-looking man alone than an alcoholic could resist a drink. She just had to give him the eye, to prove that she was as attractive as ever. Of late, she had found that she was rather lonely.

They arrived back at the house and parked their bikes in the old stables. The smell of boiled cabbage hung in the air as they went in through the back way and hung up their heavy rain-capes. Lily's feet were soaking and felt like blocks of ice. The shoes she had recently been issued were really poor quality and let in the rain however much blacking she rubbed into them. In the tiled hall they both looked in the pigeonholes for post. There was just one letter for Lily. Not the standard service issue envelope, she noted, with a sinking feeling of disappointment, but one addressed in an unfamiliar hand and postmarked Kent. She squelched upstairs and took off the crippling shoes before opening it.

The contents were brief and to the point. The letter was from a hospital in Canterbury.

Dear Miss Croft,

I have been requested by Corporal Bob Marriot to write this to you on his behalf.

He wishes to tell you that he loves and misses you very much and wants to see you again.

You might like to know that he has a chest injury, sustained at Gris Nez, and that he is as comfortable as can be expected. Visiting hours are from two till three and seven till eight each day.

Yours truly,
Agnes Goodhew (Nurse)

For several minutes, Lily sat staring at the letter as the full impact of it sank in. Bob was injured. Bob was hurt so badly that he had to ask some nurse to write for him. This couldn't be happening. It couldn't be true. But there it was, in a neat hand on brownish recycled paper. *He loves and misses you very much.* Bob needed her. Her whole existence focused on this single fact. With a cry, she jumped up. She had to go and see him straight away. In her stockinged feet, she rushed downstairs to demand to see her commanding officer.

There were times when the powers that be wore a remarkably human face. Within thirty-six hours, Lily was on the train heading for London. She only had a twenty-four-hour pass, but it was enough to get to Kent and back. Enough to let Bob know what she now realised herself – that she loved him and only him. It was nearly half-past one by the time she got to Canterbury. Lily was frantic. She had to get to the hospital by two. She must not waste a moment of the precious hour they would be allowed together. The next bus, she was told, was in forty minutes' time.

'Sod that,' Lily growled.

She found out in which direction the hospital lay and jerked her thumb at a passing army lorry. It squealed to a halt and a fresh-faced boy younger than herself leaned over and looked out of the window.

'Where you heading for, darling?'

It took just two minutes for her to persuade him to drive her right to the door.

She arrived just in time to join a bunch of anxious relatives waiting outside the door of the ward, all bearing whatever small gifts could be found amongst all the wartime shortages. At 14.00 hours precisely, they were allowed in. Lily scanned the long line of iron-framed beds. Some of the men were sitting up ready for their visitors, others had hidden themselves behind newspapers or books. None of them looked like Bob. She walked the length of the ward, for once hardly noticing the hopeful expression that lit the eyes of many of the men she passed. In the very last bed a man lay pale and unmoving, his eyes closed. There was a frame over his chest to keep the weight of the blankets off his body. With a shock, Lily realised that the gaunt face was Bob's.

'Oh my God,' she breathed.

She had known that it must be serious but it was not until this moment that she fully comprehended just how ill he was. She ran forward and clasped the hand that lay on top of the cover, holding it between both of hers and lifting it to her lips.

'Bob? Bob, it's me, Lily. Oh please say something. Tell me you're going to be all right.'

The dark eyelids flickered in the white face. For a long moment he looked at her, uncomprehending. Then recognition dawned.

'Lily?'

His voice was faint and cracked.

'Oh Bob – I come as soon as I could.'

'That really you?'

Tears rose in her eyes and trickled down her face. Her big, cheerful Bob, full of strength and confidence, was reduced to this fragile invalid.

'It's really me, Bob. Your Lily. I got your letter and I went straight down and asked for a pass and they give it me. But what of they done to you, darling? You look terrible.'

The faintest of smiles tugged at the corners of his mouth.

'Thanks.'

'Oh I didn't mean it like that – I meant, well, you look ill.'

'Copped it in the chest. Nasty big hole. Missed my heart, though.'

'Thank God for that. When I got your letter, I was so worried. I thought – if anything was to happen to you, well, I'd just die. You are going to get better, ain't you?'

The fingers laced with hers tightened just a little.

'I am now you're here.'

'I got to get back tonight. We only got an hour now and another one this evening.'

'Make the best of it, then. Tell me what you've been up to.'

Lily chattered on about Whiley Green and the billet and the other girls and the people she worked with. Bob said very little. Several times his eyes closed and he fell into a doze for a few minutes. Lily nearly cried aloud with frustration. How could he go to sleep on her when they had so little time together?

'Sorry – can't help it.'

'I'm boring you, is that it?'

'No, no. Just got no stamina. Weak as a bloody kitten. You never bore me, darling, never.'

'Neither do you. All the others get boring, but you don't.'

It was true, she realised. She always looked forward to every meeting, every letter. She never got fed up with his company.

'I'm not very exciting to be with at the moment. Can't exactly take you dancing.'

'I'd rather be here than anywhere else in the world,' Lily told him, and she was totally sincere.

'Love you, Lil.'

'I love you, Bob.'

'Honest?'

'Honest.'

At the end of the ward, a bell rang. Visiting hour was at an end. 'I'll be back this evening,' Lily promised, as a sergeant-major of a ward sister came bustling in her direction.

She was not going to let the woman intimidate her. As they reached the door, she asked if she could have a word with her.

'Just for a moment. I do have a ward to run,' the sister said.

'I want to know how bad he is. Corporal Marriot. The truth, mind. None of this "well as can be expected" rubbish.'

The sister's face took on a stonewall look.

'I'm afraid I can only give that sort of information to relations. You are not related, I take it?'

Lily considered lying, but rejected it. The woman probably had it worked out who she was. She would have been told about the letter.

' 'Course not. He's Canadian, ain't he? All his family's over there. I'm all he's got here. I'm his fiancée.'

A slight stretching of the truth, but the old cow wouldn't know that.

'In that case – I suppose it would be in order, Miss – er – Croft, wasn't it?'

So she did know.

'Yeah.'

'Corporal Marriot has sustained extensive wounds to the chest. One lung has collapsed and there is major infection.'

Lily went cold. It sounded dreadful.

'But he is being treated with penicillin –'

'What's that when it's at home?'

'A new drug, Miss Croft. What the uninitiated are pleased to call a wonder drug. I would not go that far, but we have found that deaths from infection are now almost a thing of the past. Your fiancé is a fit young man. It will take a while, but he has a very good chance of recovery.'

Lily could have hugged that boot-faced old trout.

'Oh thanks a million, Sister. You're a love, you really are.'

The woman's expression cracked slightly.

'We try to do our very best for all our patients, Miss Croft.'

The worst of her worries soothed, Lily hitched a lift back into town and killed the waiting time by going to see a film she had seen already and trying to find something nice to take to Bob. Grapes were out of the question, of course, but there were plenty of apples around. She bought a couple of pounds of nice red ones, queued for sticky buns at a bread shop, and found the latest edition of *Picturegoer*. Seven o'clock found her back at the hospital again.

This time she knew just where to go. Bob was looking out for her, and she was sure he looked better than he had done that afternoon. He gave her a real smile as she walked up the ward towards him.

'Back again,' she said. 'I got you these.'

Bob hardly glanced at the gifts she was holding out. He was looking at her face.

'It's great to see my fiancée again.'

'Oh –'

Why had she said that? She should have kept her big mouth shut.

'I had to tell her that. She wouldn't never of told me nothing otherwise,' she said.

'How about making it the truth?'

Lily looked at him. He wasn't really any better, it was just that instead of being pale he was flushed. His eyes had the glittery look of someone with a high temperature. Someone ought to give him more of that penny-whatsit.

'I dunno,' she said. She sat down and put her presents on the bedside locker. 'Something to remember me by when I've gone.'

'I never forget you for a minute, Lily. What do you say, eh? You going to marry me when I get better?'

310

· Lily chewed her lip. She did love him. Just looking at him lying there so sick and helpless made her go all hot and weak inside. But marriage was such a big step. It meant giving up all the fun and being a grown-up and doing responsible things like paying rent and having kids. She was not sure whether she was ready for all that.

'Let's get you better first, then we'll talk about it,' she said, and changed the subject, telling him about the film she had seen.

The hour seemed to fly by. Once again the bell sounded. Lily groaned.

'Why can't they give us longer? Look, I got a forty-eight-hour leave coming up in three weeks. I'll come then. I'll book a night at a boarding-house and come in every visiting time. And I'll write to you and all.'

It was the biggest commitment she had ever made to him.

Bob's fingers closed on hers with something near to their old strength.

'Say you'll marry me.'

Lily looked at his thin face, at the fever-bright eyes, and her hard little heart gave way.

'All right,' she agreed.

He gave a great sigh.

'That's all I wanted to hear.'

Lily leaned over and kissed him on the lips.

'Only if you get better, though.'

'I will now. You're the best medicine there is.'

The sister was rounding up the stragglers. Defiantly, Lily gave him one more kiss.

'Take care, my darling.'

She walked out of the hospital an engaged woman.

It was a long and tiring journey home. Lily did not get to London until gone eleven, and by then it was too late to catch a train to Whiley Green. She called in on her surprised and delighted mother to cadge a bed for the night, and set off on the paper train first thing in the morning, arriving back on duty with just twenty minutes to spare.

Everyone wanted to know where she had been and why. Lily told them the outline of the tale, but something stopped her from

311

boasting about her engagement. It was not until she got into bed at the end of the day that she had time and peace to really think about it. When she did, she found she was wondering whether she had done the right thing. Without the sight of Bob lying helpless and sick in front of her, it was not so easy to remember just why she had agreed to marry him. Did she really want to give up her freedom, and stick to him and only him for the rest of her life?

She wished she had someone to talk to. If only Betty was still here, she could tell her all about it, and ask her advice. But there was nobody amongst the other girls whom she felt she could confide in. Her thoughts turned to home. What about her mum? But she would be against it, because she would not want her daughter moving hundreds of miles away across the Atlantic. Or Joan? She would be for it, because she thought every girl ought to get married and settle down and have lots of babies just like she did. Rita. Lily turned it over in her mind. At first she rejected the idea. She still did not totally trust Rita, but at least she had been through it as far as men and marriage was concerned. She knew all the joys and pitfalls and would give good advice. She would write and ask Rita to phone her.

She could hear the surprise in Rita's voice as she took hold of the receiver three days later.

'Are you all right, Lil? You said it was terrible important. And what's all this about not letting on to Mum when I see her?'

'Yeah, I'm all right. It's just – well, you know Mum.'

It was a bad line, crackling and humming. Lily marshalled her thoughts.

'Look, Reet, I wanted to see what you thought about something. Well, about getting married –'

The voice at the other end went up several tones with excitement.

'What's that? You're getting married? To that nice Bob? Ain't he in France?'

That was reassuring for a start. At least she seemed pleased about it.

'No, he's in Kent. Canterbury. He's been wounded –'

There was a crescendo of crackles, then Rita came through again.

'. . . bad? You been to see him?'

'What? Well, yeah, he is bad, but they say he'll pull through.'

'Hang on, Lil, I got to see to Jackie. It's raining stair-rods here and I got her parked outside the phone box.'

There was a lot of banging and the distant sound of Rita being bright and loving. Lily gritted her teeth with impatience. Why couldn't Rita listen? This was the most important decision of her life.

'Sorry about that, Lily. She's all right now. So he's in hospital?'

'Yeah, and oh, Rita, he looked terrible. So ill. I went and saw him twice, and he asked me to marry him and I said yes –'

'That's wonderful, Lil! I'm really pleased for you, truly I am. That's lovely news.'

All the anguish of indecision swelled inside Lily and burst into a howl of despair.

'I don't know, Reet. I just don't know whether I done the right thing. I said yes, and now I can't be sure. It's terrible, I don't know what way to turn. What do you think?'

There was silence on the other end of the line, punctuated by buzzing and roaring sounds.

'Rita!' she yelled. 'Rita, are you still there?'

The line cleared, and her sister's voice came through as plain as if she were in the next room: 'I'm here. Look, Lily, do you love him?'

'Yes, but – I don't know if I love him enough to settle down.'

'Do you like him? I mean, as a person, a friend?'

Lily was able to answer that one without hesitation.

'Yes.'

'Can you bear to think of life without him?'

Lily thought, and it was frightening.

'No,' she said, with conviction.

'Well, then –' Rita said.

The fog lifted. It all became very clear. The future stretched out before her, defined.

'Oh Rita, thanks a million. You're a real brick,' she said.

A wry laugh vibrated down the line.

'Glad to hear it.'

'I mean it, Reet, honest. I was in a real tizz. Now I know it's all going to be all right.'

'I've run out of money, Lil. Can I tell the others about it?'

'Yes, yes, tell everyone. Give 'em all my love.'

'Ours to you, sis. Take –'

The pips went and the line went dead. Lily put the receiver down, feeling exhausted and exhilarated all at the same time. She danced round the panelled hall, and grabbed the first person who happened along.

'I'm getting married, I'm getting married!' she cried, and whirled round laughing and crying.

'I'm getting married to the loveliest man in the world.'

# 39

Rita missed her dad's news bulletins. If she could not be around to listen to the six o'clock or nine o'clock news on the wireless, then her dad would always have the latest to pass on to her. When she had been living at home, it had often irritated her. After all, for years it had been nothing but bad news. But since D-Day there had been steady advances across Europe, and now the Americans had crossed the Rhine. There was no electricity at the cottage and batteries were unobtainable, so they were without a wireless. Whoever went down to the village to do the shopping each day always bought a paper, but somehow it was not the same thing reading about it as hearing Alvar Lidell or John Snagge telling you.

There was so much now that they personally needed to know. Joan was desperate for news of the war in the Far East. The Americans had bombed Tokyo, but the Japanese did not seem any nearer to surrender. Rita and the Wilkinsons watched the slow advance towards Jack's camp, and were worried by rumours that prisoners were being force-marched away from the liberating forces. George's unit was following the fighting, not in the front line, but still in danger. Then there were the V2 launch sites. As soon as one was bombed or captured, another seemed to come into use. Every so often, either Rita or Joan would try to persuade their parents to come and join them at the cottage, but to no effect. Florrie and Jim were staying put.

'It would be crowded if they did come,' Joan pointed out.

'I know, but it just sickens me to think that they could still be killed when the war must be nearly over,' Rita said. 'We could squash them in somewhere. And spring's around the corner now.'

It had been a tough winter. February had been bitterly cold.

They were all city-dwellers, used to pavements and buses and corner shops. Living in the country was very different from the East End. They had to walk long distances along muddy tracks to get to the shop, the pub, the school or the telephone. The nearest neighbours were half a mile away instead of next door. Water had to be pumped up. But they all grew tougher and fitter, and the children thrived. Gradually the local community came to accept them. They began to see that country life could have its advantages. It showed in the many 'after the war' discussions that they were now having.

'I think I should of been a farmer's wife. My grandfather's family was all fishermen and farmers,' Mrs Wilkinson said.

'Anyone in particular you was thinking of marrying?' her husband asked.

Mrs Wilkinson laughed and dug him in the ribs.

'Wouldn't you like to know? But seriously, I think we ought to stay out here after it's all over. I like it here, mud and all.'

'We can't run a proper business from this shack. We ain't even got a telephone,' Mr Wilkinson objected. 'I mean, now we're only just ticking over anyway, what with restrictions and that. But after the war, it'll be different. All them poor homeless people'll want new places and furniture to go in them. We'll need a proper factory close to where people live.'

'You don't have to have a factory next to the house. You could rent a place down by the Southend–London Road, where they got electric and everything. People'd cycle in to work each day,' Rita said.

'I dunno about moving back to London,' Joan said, following her own line of thought. 'The kids love it here, and our street ain't the place it used to be. But then there's Mum and Dad to think about. They won't never move. It all depends on Ted, really. It's what he wants.'

'Well, don't you forget, lovey, he can always have a job with us,' Mrs Wilkinson said.

Mr Wilkinson was still thinking about what Rita had suggested.

'I dunno about setting up a whole new place out here,' he said. 'Seems a bit drastic. We always worked from the East End. We got all our suppliers and contacts there.'

'Jack was always saying as how we ought to move. He said so before the war. Don't you remember, Bill? Go out to the new estates, expand ourselves, that's what he always said.'

'Yeah, and I always said what was good enough for my dad and his before him was good enough for me,' Mr Wilkinson argued.

'Things are going to be different after the war,' Rita said.

Everyone was saying that. Things had to be different. They hadn't gone through more than six years of suffering and shortages, grief and homelessness for nothing. There had to be work, for a start. No more unemployment. And there had to be decent houses, and proper schooling for the kids. Rita agreed with all this. Things had to get better for the ordinary people. But for herself, she found it impossible to look ahead. She wrote regularly to Jack, telling him about their daughter, about the family and all that was going on at the cottage. He wrote brief, matter-of-fact letters back, the letters of an acquaintance rather than a lover. She did not know what to make of it. He was obviously still angry with her, and it was impossible to explain it all in writing. On top of that, she didn't really know what he was going through over there in Germany, being forced to work for the enemy. She needed to see him face to face for them to sort it all out. And of course, there was still Ron. She had not heard from him since he had been posted to Coventry three months ago.

So it was painful discussing the future of the Wilkinsons' business. She had lots of good ideas about what they should do after the war, ideas that she was sure Jack would agree with, but if Jack no longer loved her or trusted her, then there would be no place for her. Ted would be welcomed in, Joan would be a family friend, but Rita would be out on her own somewhere or, worse still, with Ron.

On a rainy morning in the middle of March she looked out of the parlour window to see the postgirl plodding up the track pushing her bike. She felt the usual lift of hope. Was there a letter for her? One from her mum would be nice. Better still, one from Jack, though they were always more hurtful than pleasing. Not that she was due one from him. On impulse, she pulled on a raincoat, took a pair of boots from the selection lined up in the porch, and set off to meet the postgirl.

' 'Morning, Glad! Nice weather for ducks,' she called, as she got near.

'Don't blooming talk to me about it. I got a blooming cold,' the girl said. 'Here, three for your lot.'

Rita snatched them up with breathless thanks, and fanned them out. Two business letters, and one for her and Joan, in Lily's handwriting. Although she had not really expected one from Jack, she couldn't help the sinking feeling of disappointment. But she swallowed it down. It was nice to hear from Lily, and unusual too. Her sister wasn't much of a one for writing. She splashed back to the cottage and called for Joan. Together they read the short note.

> Dear All,
>     This is to tell you that Bob has got his discharge and we are getting married on the 5th April. Mum wants it to be from home so you're all invited and we'll have a real knees-up.
>     Kisses to all the kids,
>     Lots of love,
>     Lily xxxx

'Well! Ain't that lovely? Our Lily getting married at last. Oh, I am pleased,' Joan exclaimed.

'Yeah,' Rita agreed.

Joan looked at her with disapproval.

'Now come on, Reet, you ought to be happy for her.'

'I am,' Rita said. 'Honest. He sounds a nice bloke. It's just –'

It was just that Lily sorting her life out made her own future look all the more foggy. She made an effort to join in with Joan's pleasure in the event. Joan was full of it for the rest of the day and into the evening, coming up with new aspects and demanding Rita's opinion. How were they going to get anything like a wedding do together, and would they have to make do with a cardboard wedding cake with plaster icing? Would George be able to get leave and come home for such an important family occasion? How on earth were they going to find anything worth

318

having in the way of a present? Rita shoved her own problems to one side and tried think of some solutions. After all, it was going to be Lily's big day. They must do all they could for her.

The next day's paper brought news of the latest advances. The Wilkinsons looked up the place names on the map of Germany in Jack's school prize atlas they had brought with them.

'Won't be long before they get to him, and then they fly them home in no time at all,' Mr Wilkinson said.

Tears welled up in Mrs Wilkinson's eyes.

'I just can't wait to see him again. My poor boy. He won't look the same as what he used to, that's for sure. We got to be ready for that.'

Rita didn't care what he looked like. Jack could be fed and washed and clothed. He would recover physically. But what was he like inside? How did he feel about her, and Jackie? One thing she knew for sure: if he came back to find she was still married to Ron, he was not going to like it. Something had to be done.

She stood in the middle of the kitchen, frowning. It was no use writing to Ron. She had to go and see him, and soon. She had to do something before Jack came home. Tomorrow. She would start out first thing tomorrow. The decision made, she was suddenly full of energy. There were things to be done. She had to ask Joan if she would mind the kids, and she had to get some money out of her dwindling savings. She snapped into action.

The longest trip Rita had ever made in her life before had been to see Jack at Fenny Howe. Then, she had been full of love and expectation. This time it was different. The Midlands were unknown territory to her. She had heard of Coventry, of course. Everyone had. It had been so terribly bombed during the blitz. She told herself that women younger than herself, girls of eighteen, made journeys like this every day now. Lily thought nothing of trekking halfway across the country.

It was not the journey itself that daunted her, but the task at the end of it. She went over and over possible scenes in her mind, but her knowledge of Ron and his bloody-mindedness always led her to the depressing conclusion that if he had made his mind up that he was not going to divorce her, then he wouldn't. That would mean that if Jack still loved and wanted her, they would simply have to pretend to be man and wife. It was all right by her. She didn't care, as long as she had Jack. But Jack might not like it, and her parents and the Wilkinsons would be horrified. More important still, she was not sure how she stood where the boys were concerned. Could they be taken away from a mother who was living in sin? Could Ron insist that they went to live with him and his mother? She could not risk that. It would be unbearable. There had to be a way to persuade Ron. So she rehearsed all the arguments she could think of, Ron's possible replies, and her answers to them. The row went on and on, round her brain, while the grey countryside slid by outside the grubby windows.

She began to wonder whether she was doing the right thing. Perhaps she should just get off at the next stop and take the return train to London. She should give up this stupid dream of happiness and be grateful for what she had got. After all, she had a husband. Plenty of women were widows. Come to that, plenty of women had not made it through the war. She thought of all her mates at the factory, the ones who had died beneath the building, of the laughs they had had, and the jealousies, and the friendship. Did she owe it to them to carry on her life in a way they would have approved of? And as for her mum – but then she remembered the morning after Ron raped her, and her mother's revelations. She had found it very difficult to believe at the time that Florrie, the respectable upholder of family standards, was responsible for her own father's death. Her mother had never referred to it again, and Rita had almost come to think that she had imagined it. Almost, but not quite. For Ron was her cousin, and also related to the man who had beaten his wife so savagely and so repeatedly that at last his children had been driven to retaliate in kind, and Ron showed every sign of being just the same sort of man. Rita did not want her children to see her knocked about, did not want them to be terrified by the blows and the anger, or be forced to stand up for her against him. No, whatever the consequences, she had to get away from Ron. No marriage at all was better than staying with him. With new strength, she tried to prepare herself for the coming confrontation.

It was late afternoon before she arrived at Coventry. She had no idea where Ron's billet was, apart from the bare address. A burly female porter gave her directions and told her which buses to catch. Rita found the right bus stop and waited. Her stomach rumbled with hunger and trepidation. How long was it all going to take? She had counted on seeing him and getting back to London in the same day, but supposing he was out, or refused even to see her?

When the bus finally came, she felt better. At last she was really on her way. There were notices in the front windows of many of the houses leading to the station, offering bed and breakfast. If the worst came to the worst, she could always stay at one of them. It would all cost a packet, but it would be worth it, if she could persuade Ron to let her go. A germ of anger started inside. Why did it have to be her? Ron didn't love her. He certainly didn't like her. He hadn't wanted to marry her in the first place, but his family and hers had made him. So why was he hanging on now? Just to prove he could. Just to stop her from having something she wanted. The more she thought about it, the angrier she became. He had no right to treat her like this.

A change of buses, a walk, and she was there, weary but buoyed up with fury, knocking on the door of a terraced house very similar to her old home in Trinidad Street.

She was put off her stroke a bit by the woman who answered the door. She had been expecting a middle-aged or elderly person. Instead, a girl of her own age stood there, her hair fashionably rolled around her chubbily pretty face.

'Yes?' she said.

'I've come to see Ron,' Rita stated.

'Oh –' The woman looked surprised, then pleased. 'Well, here's a turn-up and no mistake. You must be his sister. Come on in. He's out, but he'll be back shortly for his tea.'

Rita was about to correct her, but stopped, driven by some instinct of self-preservation. She was ushered into a kitchen where two small children were squabbling over a battered toy car.

'Give over, you two. Make y'self at home, dear. Like a cup of tea? It's a long journey up from London. I'm Josie – but of course you know that, don't you? He's written and told you all about

321

me, hasn't he? Well, it's really nice to meet someone from Ron's family at last. Which one are you, then?'

'I'm Rita,' she said, giving nothing away.

''Rita? I don't remember him mentioning a Rita. But you're a big family, ain't you?'

'Yeah, lots of us,' Rita said truthfully.

So Ron had never talked of her. Did that mean that this Josie did not even know he was married?

'He – er – he all right, then?' she said, wondering how to get to the truth.

'Oh yes, dear. Blooming, you might say. He has his little grumbles, but then, don't they all, eh? Men? Always going on about his sergeant and the weather and the hours and that. He don't like this rain. Gets in his bones, he says, and of course sometimes I ain't got the coal for a decent fire when he comes off duty, but he don't mean it really. He just likes to go on a bit –'

Josie liked to go on a bit, but cheerfully. She was a sturdy young woman, shorter than Rita and with generous curves swelling under a tight jumper. She held forth about Ron at length. Sometimes Rita could recognise the man she was talking about, but at others he sounded like a completely different person. Josie certainly seemed to be a very accommodating landlady, making him meals at all hours of the day and night, drying off his clothes, darning his socks.

'Sounds a lot better than what he got in barracks,' Rita remarked.

'Oh yes dear. There was talk of him being sent up there, but then they got a new lot of recruits in and he stayed on here. I was glad, I can tell you.'

'Yeah,' Rita agreed.

She noticed a photograph of a young man in a desert uniform on the mantelpiece.

'That your husband?' she asked.

'Yes –' Josie sent a fond smile in his direction. 'Poor old Jimmy. He copped it at El Alamein. I was real cut up, I was. Didn't stop crying for a week, I was that upset –'

Rita only half heard her. So Josie was a widow. It was all beginning to fall into place.

'– and then Ron came along and it all changed,' Josie was saying.

Rita began to pay close attention.

'Well, I missed poor Jimmy something dreadful, I did. I mean, I loved him. But it wasn't just him, like. I mean, I missed – you know – a bit of the old slap and tickle. But you mustn't get me wrong. I mean, I don't want you to think I'm just a tart. I never went out looking for it. I never thought like that when I said I'd billet soldiers. Oh no. I mean, Ron, he was different. From the moment he set foot in here, well, I just fell for him. I never thought it'd be like that again. Like I was a kid. I mean, I'm a mam, and a widow. You don't expect it to be like that, do you? But it was. And he fell for me and all. That was the lovely thing. I mean, there's all those young girls, free as birds, and me with two kids, and he falls for me. It was like a dream come true. I never thought there'd be anyone else after poor Jimmy died, but there is, and now he says, once this war is over, he'll move in permanent and marry me –'

Rita felt the ground shift under her feet. She stared at Josie, hardly able to believe her ears. This chatty, ordinary woman was the answer to her prayers. As Josie rambled on, she began to feel sorry for her. It was going to be a very nasty shock when she found out that Ron had been leading her up the garden path all this time. She waited for a pause in the flow of words.

'Josie,' she said carefully. 'You got any brandy or anything in the house? Because there's something I think you ought to know –'

## 40

Josie's face went white and slack. There was bewilderment in her wide eyes.

'His wife? But you said –'

'You thought I was his sister. I never said nothing.'

'But . . . but . . . so he's married. But I thought – he never said. Not a thing –' her voice was shaking with a sense of betrayal.

Rita looked at the other woman's shocked expression. If it had been anyone else's husband she would have told her that he was not worth it, that he was a bastard who had taken advantage of her, that she ought to kick him out of her life and try to forget all about him. But this was different. Josie was her passport to freedom.

'You thought he was single, did you?' she said.

'Yes – he never said nothing,' Josie repeated. 'I mean, I wouldn't never have – you know –' She blushed and waved a hand vaguely. 'He promised me. He begged me, and I wouldn't, I mean, I'm not that sort of girl. And then he promised me. As soon as the war was over, he said, we'll get married and he's going to move in here permanent. But now –'

She stared at Rita, blushing again as a new aspect of it hit her.

'What must you think of me? You must think I'm a real scrubber –'

'You wasn't to know,' Rita said. 'It ain't your fault.'

Josie burst into tears.

'What am I going to do? I love him. I can't go on without him. Not now, not when I got used to having a man about the place again. I'm no good on my own, I need a man –'

The two children, upset at seeing their mother crying, began to wail as well. Josie gathered them to her and the three of them howled. Rita took a breath, ready to shout above the noise, to tell Josie that she did not need to get used to being on her own again. But Josie beat her to it. She glared at Rita, her eyes red and hot.

'You're not having him back. He's mine, he loves me. I'm keeping him here if I have to fight you for him. He's mine, you hear me?'

Rita let her talk on, working up a boiling anger, while the children clung and sobbed with fear.

'— I looked after him, I got a right. He said he loved me. He don't love you no more, you don't mean nothing to him. I'm the one he wants, I'm the one he's living with and I'm not letting you walk in here and take him away from me —'

Her voice rose and cracked. Rita jumped into the brief pause.

'It's all right, Josie,' she said. 'I ain't come here to take him away from you.'

'I don't care, I'm not going to let him — what? What did you say?' Josie stopped short. The expression of disbelief on her face was so comical that Rita nearly laughed out loud.

'I said, I ain't come here to take him away from you,' she repeated. She nearly added that she had come here to do the opposite and that Josie was welcome to him, but she stopped herself just in time. She had to go carefully here.

'The truth is, Ron and me ain't been getting on for a long time. We was very young when we got married, and you know how it is, with the war and being apart and everything. I mean, Ron, he knew that and all. I expect that's why he fell for you. You're, like, different from me. And once he met you, I suppose he didn't want to lose you by telling you he was married.'

Part of her stood apart from herself, marvelling that she should be making excuses for him. But it had to be done. The last thing she wanted was for Josie's volatile mood to change again, and for her to direct her anger against Ron.

'Oh — Oh —' Josie gaped at her, nodding. 'Well . . . I —'

The two children were still crying, not knowing what to make of all the adult emotions surging round them. Josie got up, scrabbled behind some jars in a cupboard and produced two boiled sweets.

'Here,' she said, popping one into each mouth, 'special treats. Now hush up, do.'

There was a sudden slobbering silence. Josie and Rita looked at each other over the tops of the children's heads.

'You don't want him back?' Josie, said, as if she did not quite believe this.

'No.' She could see the dawning of suspicion in Josie's face. More explanation was needed. 'The thing is, well, I met somebody else. I come here to see if I could sort things out with Ron. Come to some arrangement, like.'

'Ah –'

'This war's done for a lot of marriages. Ain't nobody's fault. Lot of people got married in a hurry, and then we all got uprooted and sent off to places. Nobody's perfect, after all.'

'No. We're only human, aren't we?' Josie said.

A tentative agreement quivered between them as Josie seemed to realise that they were on the same side.

'I dunno about you, but I could do with another drop of brandy, if you can spare it,' Rita said.

For several seconds Josie stared at her, unsure which way to jump. Then she capitulated.

'Me too,' she said, and slopped a generous slug into the glasses. Rita raised hers.

'Here's to – to – future happiness,' she said.

'Future happiness,' Josie agreed.

They settled down to wait for Ron.

It wasn't long before the front door rattled and swung open. Josie hurriedly shoved her children out into the garden and told them to stay out there and play. Despite the new situation, Rita's stomach churned. She might have the upper hand now, but this was the first time they had met since the night he had raped her. Revulsion, fear and anger raced through her. She laced her fingers together to stop them from shaking. He was going to get the shock of his life when he saw her sitting here.

'Josie! I'm back.'

Josie swallowed.

'I'm in the kitchen.'

Ron stopped short in the kitchen doorway, an expression of sheer disbelief on his face.

'Rita? What the hell – ?'

Sweet revenge brought a smile to Rita's lips.

'Hello Ron. Remember me? We got married, didn't we?'

For fully half a minute Ron spluttered in articulate amazement. Then he took his usual path and resorted to anger.

'You bitch! What d'you think you're doing, walking in here like this?'

But Josie brought him up short. Tears of reproach swam in her big brown eyes.

'Oh Ron, how could you? I trusted you. You let me think you was free, and all the while you was married, and with kiddies too.'

'Married? To her? That's no marriage. Like a bleeding iceberg, she is.'

'But you still wanted us to stay married, didn't you, Ron? Insisted on it, didn't you? Wouldn't hear of nothing else. Made sure I got in the family way and all.'

'Oh Ron,' Josie repeated. 'And you said you loved me –'

'But I do love you, doll –' Ron said awkwardly.

*Doll!*

'You got a funny way of showing her,' Rita said. 'Stringing her along like that. Or did you just want to get into her bed?'

Josie's round face crumpled up.

'You said you'd marry me after the war was over. I believed every word you said, I did. And all the time you was having me on, and cheating on your wife as well. You just about broke my heart, you have –'

'I never told you I wasn't married,' Ron blustered.

'You never told me you was, neither.'

'And you said you wouldn't ever divorce me,' Rita threw in, beginning to enjoy herself.

Ron looked from one woman to the other.

'Stop bloody nagging! I never done nothing you didn't want, Jose –'

'Oh, that's not true! I'm not a tart. You begged me, you did.'

'I think you wanted to have your cake and eat it,' Rita said. 'Keep me in my place and have all your home comforts with her.'

Ron rounded on her.

'You're the one to blame. You're the one who went with a Yank –'

'There never was no Yank. I dunno where you got that from.

327

It's just one of your ideas, that's all. I don't even know any Yanks. And even if there was, it don't change nothing with you and her. You still been stringing her along, telling her fairy stories. And what about the kids? What am I going to tell them?'

'How the hell do I know? You're their mother. I never asked you to come here, you done it off of your own bat. We was all right here, Josie and me. We was getting along fine. Now look what's happened. You have to come and muck it all up. Why couldn't you stay where you was, you nosy cow?'

It was the same old Ron. Nothing changed. Always trying to shuffle the blame on to someone else. Nothing was ever his responsibility, or his fault. She went for him.

'Oh, so you was just going to stay here, was you? Is that it? You was going to stay here and just never come home? And then what was you going to do? Marry her without saying nothing? That's bigamy, that is. That's against the law.'

She could see that Ron knew he was cornered, and that he was just going to try to shout his way out of it. When he found that that didn't work, he would simply refuse to talk about it any more, and go off down the pub.

'Oh Ron,' Josie wailed, 'you wasn't, was you? You wouldn't do a thing like that to me? You said you loved me –'

'For Christ's sake, woman!' Ron yelled. 'What's all the bleeding fuss about? I said I'd marry you, didn't I?'

'But you can't marry me. You're married to her.'

'I'll get a divorce. There. That all right?'

For a long, sweet moment, Rita savoured the taste of triumph. Then she smiled, and said gently, 'But supposing I don't want a divorce?'

Josie and Ron glared at her, thunderstruck.

'But –'

'You said –'

'P'raps I changed my mind.'

She watched Ron squirming. How was he going to get out of this one?

'I've had enough of this,' he growled. 'I'm going to have a drink.'

He turned and made for the front door. Josie cried out and flung herself at him. Rita had to shout to make herself heard.

'In that case, I'll go and have a word with your commanding officer. I don't think he'll be very pleased to hear about what's been going on here. Not very happy about having to clear up domestic messes, that sort,' she yelled.

Ron stopped. Josie hung on to his arm. Rita looked at him. He was stiff with anger. This was one tight corner he would not be able to run out on.

'What's it to be, Ron?' she said.

'You promised,' Josie put in.

Ron sucked in a breath through gritted teeth.

'I want a divorce, Rita.'

'What's that? I didn't quite catch it. I never heard you say "please".'

There was a long pause. Then the word came out, as if it hurt him to say it.

'Please.'

Rita picked up her bag. She had to freeze her cheeks and lips to keep herself fron grinning.

'All right, Ron. Seeing as you asked so nicely. I'll start seeing about it first thing tomorrow.'

She edged round the pair of them in the narrow hall and made for the door.

'Good luck, mate,' she said to Josie. 'You'll need it.'

Then she was out of the door and on the street. She had done it.

## 41

Rita was exhausted and exhilarated all at the same time. Of all the ways she had thought that this confrontation might go, she had never imagined it would all work out as well as this.

She moved in a daze, hardly knowing what she was doing. The star of good fortune that had smiled on her still seemed to be working, for she got to the right bus stops, arrived at the station just five minutes before the London train was due, and it was not only more or less on time, but had a few seats left.

She sank down on one, tired out but still fizzing with amazement at her new status. She was free, or as good as. For the first time since she was seventeen, she had Ron off her back. It felt as if a great cloud had moved back from her sky. The sensible part of her knew that it was not all going to be sunlight and roses from now on. She still did not know how Jack felt. She had three children and could well be faced with bringing them up and supporting them alone. She had no home of her own, and if Jack wanted no more to do with her, then she would not be able to carry on with her job. But none of this could touch her. She felt strong and capable. She would cope, whatever happened. She had her family, she was fit and had a brain in her head. Now that Ron was to become part of the past, she could do anything. She could make her own decisions, choose her own path, without him holding her back. It was only now that she fully realised just how restricted she had been. The war had been much to her advantage, making it patriotic to work, conscripting Ron into the forces, but still he had been there, a dead hand on everything she strove for. Now she could look forward like everyone else, to the new world to be built after the war was over.

People round her talked and smoked, offered sandwiches and swapped life stories. Rita joined in, but gave nothing away. It was all too new to tell to strangers. She held it inside her, a glowing ball of excitement. The woman next to her had been to visit her injured son. The new squaddies were expecting to be posted to Germany. The young woman with the two toddlers had been staying with her mother-in-law ever since her husband had been killed, but was now going back to her own mum.

'Are you a Londoner, dear?' the older woman asked. 'You saw a bit of action in the Blitz, I expect?'

'Just a bit, yeah,' Rita said.

She chattered on about fighting incendiaries on the roof, and being buried alive, and having her house fall down round her, but all the while she was floating in a warm sense of being extraordinarily lucky. The war had given her lots of opportunities she would never have had. Nobody she loved had been killed. She had met Jack. If, God forbid, it didn't work out, she had still known that love, and she still had little Jackie. And even Ron had given her the two boys.

It was gone eleven by the time the train drew into Euston. Rita got herself to the station entrance and gathered her thoughts. She was not going to get back to Laindon tonight, that was for sure. She would go and stay the night with her parents. She would have to knock them up, but they wouldn't mind; they'd be glad to see her. In the morning she would have a good heart-to-heart with her mum and start getting her used to the idea of a divorce in the family. And then she supposed she had to see about getting a lawyer or something. Still buoyed up with optimism for the future, she shared a taxi across London. Blow the expense. It was worth it.

Her fellow travellers got off in ones and twos until she was the only one left in the cab. The driver insisted on chatting to her, mostly about the V1s and V2s.

'. . . now these buggers – beg your pardon – dropping on you any time of the day or night. Now my old lady, she can't stand these 2s. She says, at least with the doodles you heard them coming, but these 2s, first thing you know is, you're dead, but me, I'd rather . . .

Rita stopped listening. She was trying to make out where they were.

'Here!' she cried. 'This is it. Trinidad Street.'

'All right, darling. Keep your hair on. I do know where I'm going,' the cabbie grumbled.

331

It was dark in the street. Everyone had gone to bed. But at least now that it was dim-out rather than blackout, the cab was allowed to use its headlamps. Rita could make out the houses of friends, the gaps where hers and Joan's houses used to be. She looked ahead, and the first awful fear hit her in the stomach. There was something wrong. A new gap. A black nothing on the corner. It couldn't be. It was mistake. She was seeing things.

The cab driver was slowing to a halt.

'Aye aye, something up here.'

The headlamps picked the scene out with a bleary yellow light. A crater in the road, roughly cordoned off. Heaps of bricks, splintered timbers, broken glass, fractured pipes.

Rita flung open the door and stumbled out into the damp night. Willing it not to be true, she stared at the destruction. This wasn't happening to her. It was all a bad dream. The corner shop was no longer there. Not there. Gone. Bombed.

'Mum!' she screamed. 'Mum! Dad!'

She scrambled over the cordon, slipped and fell on the rubble. Where was everyone? Why weren't they here? They had to help her. She had to get to her parents. They were there, somewhere, under the wreckage. Frantically, she began picking up bricks and flinging them aside. There was a movement beside her. Someone was pulling at her arm. The cabbie.

'Come on, girl, come away. You can't do nothing. It's dangerous —'

She shook him off.

'My mum and dad — I got to get to them —'

There were tears running down her face, her breath was coming in great tearing sobs. She wrenched at a long jagged timber and started an avalanche of choking dirt and rubble. Her hands were torn with splinters, her arms and legs cut and bruised, but she hardly felt them in her frantic struggle to dig through the collapsed building. She did not hear the cab driver walk off, muttering to himself, to knock on the nearest door. All she knew was that she had to get beneath this obscene heap that had once been her parents' home.

. Then there were people all around her, restraining arms, kind voices.

'Rita, come away, it's too late –'

'They didn't feel nothing, love. It was instant.'

'It's all right, Rita love, I'm here –'

'Joanie?'

Her sister's voice pulled her out of her shocked obsession. She grabbed Joan by the arms.

'Joanie, what happened? Where are they?'

Joan's face was white and haggard.

'They dug them out this morning, love. There wasn't nothing anyone could do. They must of gone the moment it fell.'

She had known it all along really, known it from the moment she saw that horrible hole. She had just been trying to keep from acknowledging it.

'Dead?'

Her mouth was dry and choked with brick dust. The word would hardly come out.

'Yes.'

There was a strange keening noise howling in her head. She let herself be led away.

Warmth and concerned voices were surrounding her. She vaguely comprehended that she was in a neighbour's kitchen and that she and Joan were being given tea and brandy. A terrible pain was tearing at her. Kindly hands helped her to undress, tucked her into bed, but she couldn't sleep. Joan appeared beside her. They clung together, weeping.

'Why, Joanie? Why did it have to be them? Why now?'

'I don't know, love. I just don't know.'

The long night dragged past and dissolved into a grey morning. Both women slept a little, and woke again feeling worse. Now that the first shock had worn off, Rita was able to ask questions.

'It was early morning,' Joan told her. 'Mum was just opening up the shop, Dad must of been out the back seeing to the rabbits. There was a warning, but no one took much notice, not even Dad. They said it just dropped out of nowhere.'

'And I was setting out for Coventry,' Rita said.

All day, she had been totally wrapped up in her own concerns, and all the while her parents had been lying dead and Joan left to cope.

333

'They sent a telegram. I got here about midday,' Joan explained. 'I never thought you'd come back here. The Wilkinsons said they'd break it to you.'

'Is Mrs Wilkinson looking after the kids?'

'Yeah, all of them. They'll be all right. Mrs Wilkinson's lovely with them. Like an extra nan.'

'I know.'

She could not worry about that now, not even about Jackie.

'What happened in Coventry, Reet? Did you see Ron?'

'Yeah.' It all seemed a long time ago now, and unimportant. 'Yeah. He's got someone else. His landlady. He wants a divorce.'

'Oh Rita –'

'So I got what I wanted,' she said, and broke down in tears again, for she would have given all her new-found freedom to have her parents back again.

It was a long and stressful day. There were officials to see, forms to fill in, the funeral to arrange. George and Lily and all the relatives had to be informed. The neighbours were very helpful. All of them had been through this before, either themselves or through supporting others. The news travelled fast. People called in to tell Joan and Rita how much their parents would be missed, what an excellent warden Jim had been, always looking out for the people in his care, what a fair shopkeeper Florrie had been, making sure that everyone got their share of what little there was, what good people they were, always there when they were needed, always ready to lend a helping hand. Joan and Rita were touched. It helped, to know that Florrie and Jim were appreciated.

Lily arrived back the next day, in a distressed state. A telegram arrived from George in France to say that he would be back as soon as possible. Another came from the Wilkinsons assuring them that the children were fine and they were to stay in London as long as they wanted.

The funeral was held the day after. The whole street turned out, what was left of it. All the relatives who were not away in the forces came. Everyone said what a loss it was and how dreadful that it had happened now that the war was nearly over. Joan, Rita and Lily were ashamed of the poverty of the arrangements.

334

There was tea and sandwiches, and that was it. Everyone understood. It was the same old story – there is a war on, you know. But all the same, they felt they were not doing right by their parents.

'Not like when old Mrs Todd went,' Rita said.

'Mrs Todd?' Lily said, not remembering.

'Poppy Powers' gran.'

Joan recalled that funeral clearly. It had been one of the high spots of her childhood. They had never seen food like it.

'Oh, but that was different. Poppy was famous by then, she was rich. She could afford to feed all the street.

'That was a proper funeral, though. That's what Mum and Dad should of had,' Rita insisted.

'Nobody has do's like that now. Not even rich people. Not with rationing,' Joan pointed out.

'I know, but they still should of had it,' Rita said.

They sat in the parlour of an aunt and uncle's house, just down the road from the crater where the shop used to be. The blast from the V2 had blown out all the windows yet again. They went over everything that everyone had said, all the kind words. One thing had been repeated by almost every person – it won't be the same without them.

'It's like the heart's gone out of the street,' one woman had said. 'They kept that shop going all through the Blitz and everything. Your mum, she opened up after they caught the last lot. Houses went down and people was killed, but as long as the shop and the pub was there, we knew it was all right. But now, I don't know, it ain't going to be the same.'

'She was right. The poor old street looks so sad now,' Joan said.

'It ain't the place it used to be,' Rita agreed. What should have been obvious suddenly struck her. 'We none of us got a home here no more. They've all gone: your place, Joanie, then mine, and now the shop. We only got the cottage at Laindon, and that ain't ours. We none of us got a home at all.'

It was a chilling thought. The tears that were constantly below the surface welled up again.

'I got to go back tomorrow,' Lily said.

It was all right for her, Rita thought. She was going to get married and go off to Canada. She was going to a new home, a new life with a new husband. It didn't touch Lily the way it did Joan and herself.

'Rita and me'll see to things,' Joan said.

Later, when Rita and Joan lay sleepless in the bed they were sharing, they dulled the pain a little by discussing the practicalities of the next few days. There were still things to be done, people to write to, yet more officials to see and forms to fill in. And George was on his way. Somebody had to be there for when he arrived. But then there were the children to think of: they couldn't leave Mrs Wilkinson with all six of them for too long. They argued over who should go and who should stay. In the end, they hardly knew how, they came to an agreement. They would both spend tomorrow seeing to whatever needed doing, then Rita would go back to Laindon and Joan would stay on to clear up anything still outstanding and wait for George.

'We ought to tell the Wilkinsons what's happening. If only we had a phone. If they just had one, that'd do, we could ring from a call box,' Rita said.

In the darkness, Joan gave a shadow of a smile.

'Phones. Hark at you. I never even used one till Ted went away.'

'Mum hated them.'

They talked about Florrie for a while. Then Joan came up with a brainwave: 'You could phone the pub. They'd give a message to the Wilkinsons.'

Rita felt for her sister's hand and squeezed it.

'That's it. Clever old you. At least we still got each other.'

'Yeah.' Joan sighed. 'We got to stick together, Reet, even more than ever. You and me, we're in charge of the family now.'

# 42

It took Rita three attempts the next evening to get through to the pub. When she did, it was a terrible line.

'Bill Wilkinson? No, he ain't in, love. They're all —'

'It's Rita here, Rita Johnson —'

'No, she ain't in neither. She's up in London, at a funeral.'

'This is Rita here. It's me speaking.'

'Oh. Sorry love. Couldn't hear you. What's up?'

'Can you give Bill a message for me?'

The line buzzed and crackled. The landlord was still talking through it. Rita caught the odd tantalising word.

'. . . shock . . . telegram . . . home . . .'

She assumed he was talking about her.

'Yeah, yeah, I know, it's been horrible. Look, can you hear me? Can you tell Bill I'll be back tomorrow. You got that? Tomorrow. Mid-morning.'

The line was still crackling. She wasn't sure whether or not he had heard her.

'You still there?'

'I'm here, girl. I'll tell him. He's sure to be in later . . . drinks . . .'

Rita thought she caught the word 'celebrate' but decided she couldn't have heard right. 'Thanks, mate,' she shouted down the deteriorating line.

She came out of the phone box with her ears ringing and the frustrating feeling that there was something she had not quite caught on to. Still, it didn't really matter, just as long as the landlord managed to tell the Wilkinsons that she was coming back. She walked back along the West Ferry Road and into Trinidad Street to join Joan. Her head ached and her limbs felt like lead from fatigue and emotional strain. The weather was as bleak as her thoughts, grey and wet, emphasising the drab streets, the shabby people, the destruction. She found herself wishing she could just crawl into a hole somewhere and forget it all. Somewhere warm and dry, where nobody would make any demands on her, and she could just eat and sleep and nurse the pain of grief.

'I know what you mean,' Joan said, when she explained this to her. 'But we can't, can we? We got to go on, there's the kids and everything. And Mum wouldn't of wanted us to break down, would she?'

Rita knew she was right. She couldn't give up, and that was all there was to it.

The next morning she kissed Joan goodbye and told her to give her love to George and to come back to Laindon as soon as possible. She shivered uncontrollably as she waited on the platform at Fenchurch Street. She had hardly eaten for the last three days and the raw March wind seemed to get right into her bones. The train was crowded as far as Upminster, but then the people thinned out and those left chatted hopefully about how soon the war might end, and what they were going to do once it was over. On one thing everyone agreed: it would not be like last time, with poverty and unemployment and ex-servicemen begging in the streets. There were going to have to be changes, big changes. Ordinary people were not going to be pushed around any more.

Rita sat listening without joining in. It was all so out-of-step with her own feelings. She could hardly believe that it was only five days since she had sat in another train, on her way to Coventry. It felt as if her whole life had been turned upside-down since then. The Rita of five days ago was a different person in a different age.

A young woman in a bright orange headscarf was holding forth.

'Now, my Billy, he's in the building trade. Brickie, he is. Says he's going to get together with his cousin and a couple of their mates and go into business. That's where the money's going to be, building. Any amount of it. Stands to reason – all them houses bombed. People are desperate for somewhere to live.'

'You seen them pre-fabs?' someone else asked. 'Got bathrooms and everything, they have. They just put 'em down on any bit of land and they're ready for you to move in.'

338

'Tin sheds, if you ask me. Not fit for human beings to live in.' an elderly man said.

Rita had seen them. Nice little homes they seemed to her. A clever answer to the terrible shortage of housing. She certainly wouldn't mind one. But right now she could not work up any feeling about them at all. She felt dead inside. All these people, busily looking forward, just as she had been so short a time ago. She tried to recall that wonderful feeling of optimism she had had travelling back from Coventry, how everything had seemed possible in the new world ahead. But that had been a fool's paradise. While she had been sitting there feeling warm and happy, her parents were lying dead. It seemed wicked that she should have been so cheerful at such a time. The fact that she could not possibly have known what had happened made no difference.

'Mind you, even when we've got Hitler, we still got to stop them Japs,' someone was saying. 'It ain't over out East. I should know. My boy's out in Burma. Forgotten army, they call themselves.'

Rita was pulled out of her introspection to think about her sister. Poor Joan had heard nothing from Ted since he had been captured. It was getting on for two years now. For all they knew, he too might be dead. At least she knew where Jack was, and could send parcels to him, and letters.

Jack. How was it going to be between them when he arrived home? At the moment, in her depressed state, she could only expect the worst. He would be changed by his experiences, without a doubt. He had been behind barbed wire all this time, under guard, often cold and hungry and made to work for the enemy. He had probably been in danger from the very bombers he used to fly in. It stood to reason that all this would affect how he felt. That was why he had reacted so violently when he found out that she was pregnant. But would he come to see things differently once he was home? Once they could talk things out face to face, would she be able to convince him that she had not set out to deceive him or to shut him out, that she was not playing a double game with him and Ron, that she had loved him all along but had her hands tied? On the way back from Coventry, she had been sure that it would all work out. Now, she almost felt he was justified in mistrusting her. He would be better off without her, after all. What man would want to come home to a divorced woman with two children from her previous marriage and a third who was registered as her ex-husband's? To make Jackie legally his own daughter, he would have to adopt her. If Jack had any sense, he would want to put the past behind him – the POW camp, the disastrous love affair, everything – and start anew with the family business and a nice girl with no complications in her life.

'. . . on, lovey, you don't want to cry now. It's almost over.'

It took a while for Rita to wake up to the fact that someone was talking to her. She had not realised that she was weeping. She tried to pull herself together.

'I know – yeah – sorry – it's personal –'

The woman patted her hand.

'That's all right, dear. We all got our troubles, ain't we? My boy . . .' She launched into a long and complicated family story while the rest of the carriage commented and sympathised. Nothing more was expected of Rita, to her great relief. The last thing she wanted at the moment was to explain her tears to all these people. She found herself longing for the days before the war, when nobody would have dreamed of striking up conversations with strangers in trains, let alone spilling all the intimate details of their lives. There was no getting away from people anywhere.

The train stopped at every station, dragging the short journey out, until at last Rita recognised the approach to Laindon. She did up her coat and lifted her bag down from the luggage rack, then from sheer habit got her little hand mirror out of her handbag and looked at herself. A hag looked back at her. At first she dismissed it. What did it matter what she looked like? But then it occurred to her that the children just might be there to meet her, and she mustn't let them see her like this. She combed her hair, scrubbed away the traces of tears, put on a lick of lipstick and wished for some powder. She still looked pretty dreadful, but better than before.

A quick glance up the platform told her that no children were waiting. Someone she knew emerged from the next carriage and they exchanged greetings as they walked along to the exit. She hardly noticed the other people on the platform.

'Rita!'

She stopped dead. She felt cold, then hot. Blood pounded in her ears. She stared, disbelieving. She must be imagining things. A tall man in stiff new RAF uniform was standing in front of her. A thin man with a gaunt face and warm brown eyes, unmistakably real, unmistakably –

'Jack!'

For a long moment she just stood there, taking in the fact that it really was him, in person, there before her. First shock held her paralysed, then when instinct prompted her to throw herself at him, she was held back by the thought that had haunted her journey. *Does he still love me?* Then Jack smiled, deep lines cutting his cheeks, and held out his arms. The spell was broken. She ran the last few steps, flung her arms around him, and held him as if she would never let him go.

'Jack – Jack – I can't believe it – it's too good to be true!' Words bubbled out of her totally uncontrolled, and all the while she felt the dear familiar contours of his body on hers, felt the strength of his arms, squeezing the breath out of her as they rocked together.

Then they both loosened their grip a little and looked at each other, gazing at each feature, relearning every line. He looked older than his years, unwell and heart-rendingly thin. It made her love him more than ever.

'You look dreadful,' she said, tears swimming in her eyes.

'Thank you. You look beautiful.'

'I don't.'

'You do to me.'

Their lips met in a long deep kiss that swept away all the loss and painful uncertainty. Rita's senses dissolved into it, till there was nothing on earth but the two of them.

'My darling girl,' he said at last, his lips close to her ear. 'Do you know how long it is since we last kissed?'

'Too long.'

That had been on a station too, on a hot summer's morning.

'Five hundred and eighty-nine days.'

341

Rita's heart sang. He had kept count. It must mean something. And the kiss must mean something, and the fact that he had come to meet her.

'I've missed you for every one of them,' she said.

Jack drew back a little and held her face between his hands, searching her eyes.

'Really?'

She held his gaze, willing him to believe her.

'Really. It was only ever you I loved, Jack.'

Seconds ticked by, measured by her beating heart. Then he bent and picked up the bag she had dropped.

'Come on,' he said. 'Let's go home.'

They walked with arms round each other, keeping in step. Rita tried to keep at bay the horrible nagging knowledge that there was still an awful lot of explaining to do, and that everything might yet go wrong. To delay it, she asked about how and when he had got back.

'We'd heard rumours for several days. The food had practically run out and the guards were very jumpy, then one morning we woke up and found they had all disappeared. The lot of them – gone. We were only just taking that in when this jeep drove up to the front gates and we realised the Yanks had arrived. That was quite something, I can tell you. Blokes laughing and shouting. Then after that it all happened very fast. We were airlifted back to Blighty, debriefed, deloused, given the once-over by the quacks, handed a nice new uniform and a travel warrant and told to go on leave. I sent the folks a telegram and got here the day before yesterday. Difficult to keep up with really. I'm still not quite sure whether I'm coming or going.'

'I'm not surprised,' Rita said. She was trying to see things through his eyes. She had to take it slowly, to give him time. 'It must be really strange, being back here again.'

'Yeah. Especially being out here at the cottage. I knew you were all here, of course, but it's not like being home.'

'Yeah,' Rita said, and despite her efforts to control it, her voice broke. 'We're all homeless now.'

'Oh Rita –' Jack stopped and held her close again. 'I been leading on about myself. I was so sorry to hear about your mum

342

and dad. They were good people. I always liked them. It's awful for you to lose both of them, and now too, when it's all nearly over.'

So many people had said the same sort of thing, but from him it meant so much more.

'Yeah, I think that's what hurts most of all. I ain't really got used to it yet. It was such a shock, coming home and finding a big hole where the shop used to be.'

She talked about it for a while and about the funeral, which led to news about Joan and Lily, and then the move out to Laindon and his parents, until it seemed that the only people they had not caught up with were themselves.

They reached the end of the track to the cottage. Rita was horribly aware of the great gap that still yawned between them. Something had to be done about it, and now. Once they got back, they would be swallowed up in the noise of family life.

'Can we sit down a minute?' she said, and led the way to a tree stump just inside the wood. They squeezed together on to it.

'You – er – you seen Jackie, then?' Rita asked.

She could not look at him. She stared at her hands as she laced them together in her lap, so tightly that it hurt.

'Yes. She's a smashing little kid. A real cracker. But why the hell didn't you tell me, Rita? Why did I have to hear about it from my mother?'

'I couldn't tell you.'

'But *why*, for God's sake?'

'Because –' she had to force the words out, each one wrenched from her throat – 'because I wasn't sure whether it was yours.'

'*What?*'

Jack jumped up as if he had been stung and stood staring down at her. Rita kept her eyes on her hands, but was horribly aware of him looming over her.

'When – when I got back from seeing you in Norfolk – Ron was there,' she halted. 'We had a row, and then he went off. I thought that was it, and he had gone, but when – when I got out of work the next day he was lying in wait for me in one of the empty workshops along the street from the factory, and he dragged me inside –'

She told the tale, sparing no details.

Jack paced up and down, then thumped his fist against a tree trunk.

'Christ, if I ever get my hands on that little bastard I'll have his balls off!'

Abruptly, he sat down beside Rita again.

'And I never knew a thing. You should of told me, Rita.'

'But I couldn't!' Rita cried. 'I couldn't explain it all to you. If I'd of seen you again, I would of, but you was shot down. It meant putting it in a letter. And would you of understood? He was my husband, after all, you might of thought I – I wanted to – with him –'

'Not like that. That was rape.'

'But I couldn't of explained. I'm no good at writing things down. I just thought, I'll wait until I'm sure, and then I'll tell you. I prayed that it was your baby, Jack. You don't know how hard I did. And then when she was born, and she had your chin and that lovely dark hair, I was so happy.'

'I see.'

She could feel the anger in him. She laid a hand on his knee. and the muscles jumped.

'She was all I had of you, Jack. I called her after you, because of that and because I sort of thought that if I did it would bring you back.'

'But you never tried to get rid of him. Ron.'

'I wanted to. God knows, I wanted to. I never wanted to marry him in the first place. But he wouldn't have it. He was hanging on to me, just to spite me.'

'After what happened –'

'But who would of believed me? He was my husband. He had rights –'

She stole a look at him. His face was dark and unreadable.

'You got to believe me, Jack. It wasn't that I wanted to keep things from you, or that I wanted to stay married to Ron. All I ever wanted, ever since I met you, was to be with you. I love you.'

Jack sighed.

'I love you. That's the thing, ain't it? None of this would matter if I didn't love you.'

344

Rita felt a lift of hope.

'And you do see why I couldn't tell you?'

'Yeah, I suppose so. There was plenty I never wrote about.'

'So –' Rita spoke slowly, feeling her way. She knew she still had not won him over. 'So, it's going to be all right, then?'

'Christ, Rita, I don't know. I don't understand you at all. You're thick as thieves with my parents, you say you love me, and yet you're still seeing him. You just come back from visiting him in Coventry.'

'Oh –'

With a lightning flash of understanding, she realised how it looked to him.

'It ain't like that at all. God, what must you think of me? That was the first time I seen him since – that day. I went up there to have it out with him, to get him to agree to a divorce. And d'you know what I found? He's been carrying on with a young widow. Promised to marry her and everything. So he's agreed. We made him, between us. Now it's just got to go through the courts.'

A slow smile spread over Jack's face.

'You really got shot of him?'

'Yeah. At last.'

Something of the triumph she had felt as she came home from Coventry began to glow again. It was darkened and over-shadowed by the rawness of her grief, but still there.

'I can't tell you what a relief it is. Like – like a great weight lifting off of my shoulders.'

'So you're going to be a free woman?'

'Yes.'

Jack drew her into his arms.

'Come here,' he said, and settled her on his knee. 'Now I can really enjoy being home again.'

For a timeless space, they gave themselves up to the joy of being together again. When the sharp March wind finally got through to them, they walked hand in hand up the track to the cottage, and into the new tomorrow.

# OTHER SAGAS AVAILABLE IN ARROW